Eye of Time
By Adrian Cousins

Copyright © 2021 Adrian Cousins

All rights reserved. This book or any portion thereof may not be reproduced or used in any manner whatsoever without the author's express written permission except for the use of brief quotations in a book review.

This book is a work of fiction. Names, characters, businesses, schools, places, locales, and incidents are either products of the author's imagination or used in a fictitious manner. Any resemblance to actual persons, living or dead, or actual events is purely coincidental.

...

Adriancousins.co.uk

Also by Adrian Cousins

The Jason Apsley Series
Jason Apsley's Second Chance
Ahead of his Time
Force of Time
Beyond his Time
Calling Time
Borrowed Time

Deana Demon or Diva Series
It's Payback Time
Death Becomes Them
Dead Goode
Deana – Demon or Diva Series Boxset

The Frank Stone Series
Eye of Time
Blink of her Eye

Part 1

1

Late Summer 1995

Play Bunnies

Douglas folded his umbrella after shaking off the excess raindrops. Then, two at a time bolted up the stone steps into the foyer of the Barrington Club. A prestigious gentlemen's club in an offensively opulent part of Knightsbridge.

This particular slice of Central London real estate, which afforded a mere ninety feet of pavement space, claimed to be one of the most expensive in the world.

The Club celebrated its bicentenary last year. However, it was a measured, imperturbable affair that mirrored the demeanour of many of the older and more established exclusive club members.

"Good afternoon, Mr Hartland," offered John Percival, the club's enduring doorman, as he doffed his top hat and extended his arm for Douglas to deposit his Burberry Mackintosh and Aston Martin complimentary umbrella.

"John," replied Douglas, as he returned a tight smile and deposited his outer-ware on the arm of the human clothes rack on offer.

"Will you be requiring rooms tonight, sir?" John asked, as he turned to place Douglas's drenched items in the cloakroom.

"No, thank you, John. I take it Lord Mayhorn is in?"

"Yes, sir, he's in the lounge." John offered a slight nod of his head as Douglas turned and strode purposefully across the ornate marble floor.

Douglas scraped his hand over his now thinning black hair and pushed open the heavy oak door into the William Lounge. The Morning Bar, as it was sometimes referred to, acquired its official name from William Pitt the Younger, the Prime Minister at the time of the Club's inception.

Scanning around the dark oak-panelled room, which lay heavily infused with cigar smoke, Douglas spotted his man gently puffing on a Havana whilst nestled into his favourite leather wing-backed chair. Douglas snaked his way through the chairs and side tables with their layers of patina formed over decades of use, providing a lustre from the graceful ageing process akin to the majority of the William Lounge's occupants.

Offering slight nods to the usual crowd, Douglas made a bee-line for Lord Mayhorn, who appeared slumped in his chair, probably recovering from another frantic day in the House of Lords. However, Douglas knew his close friend and ally only attended the House for gossiping purposes.

Douglas slapped his hand on the back of the wing-backed leather chair, thus startling Lord Kenneth Mayhorn, who then grinned at his long-time friend from right back to the days at Eton College and Oxford University. A time in post-war Britain when, according to Harold Macmillan, they'd never had it so good.

"Dougy old boy, bloody good to see you!"

"Kenny. Good of you to see me at short notice." Douglas swung into the chair opposite and raised two fingers – Churchill victory style – in the direction of the steward, indicating two large single malts were required.

"So, what you been up to in the House this week? Hopefully bashing back some of those absurd Tory bills which Major and his cronies seem intent on ramming through."

"Well, Dougy old boy, he and his cabinet have come up with some odd stuff recently. Although, it's not so difficult to rebuke now as it was when Margaret was in power." He chuckled, then shuddered at the memory of the Iron Lady who'd ripped him apart on many occasions. "Frightening woman, and hopefully the bloody last! Neither got a proper education. I really can't understand how the general public can think anyone without an Eton education can effectively hold office!"

"No, quite. Well, I'm sure you'll keep reminding them of their lack of suitability for the role." Douglas smirked and nodded a thank you to the steward, who placed monogrammed napkins and the two generous whiskies on the mahogany side table nestled between the two chairs.

Douglas always knew how to stoke up his old friend who had a diminutive view of all Prime Ministers over the last twenty years, who'd all failed to secure such education that Kenneth believed a prerequisite for successful leadership.

"Anyway, Dougy, you have that glint in your eye. I'm assuming you're looking for an ear to whisper into?"

Douglas nodded. "I'll get straight to the point. Great Britain's Architecture Foundation Millennium Landmark

Competition." He raised his eyebrow, indicating to Kenneth that he wanted to know what he knew.

"Ah, bloody mouthful that. Odd thing for you to have your toe dipped in? I would have expected you to be more interested in the Y2K issue."

"Y2K?"

"Millennium Bug, my friend. There's a school of thought that the code used to write all computer programmes will crash and burn as we hit the double zero digit ... the year 2000. Some even suggest we'll be thrown back to the dark ages pre the '50s, thus lacking any usable computer."

"Ha, you listen to too many conspiracy theories, my friend. No, old chap, I want to know who the front runners are for securing the Architecture Foundation prize. With your links and ear to the ground on pretty much everything, I thought you'd have the inside track."

Kenneth tapped the side of his nose and then retrieved his whisky. "Without my contacts and the perpetual flow of information, you'd come to a grinding halt, old boy." He grinned and sunk the whisky, raising his finger to the attentive steward for a refill.

"Well, Kenny, old chap, what d'you know?"

Kenneth shifted forward in his seat and glanced left and right, then whispered. "It's a bit hush-hush at the moment, although I'm hearing the front runner is the Millennium Forrest ... bat-stupid idea if you ask me. Also, would you believe the ArtAcre flare on the landfill dump is getting some support! I've got to say," he glanced around the room, then continued, "I think the whole idea is a ruddy waste of time!"

"What about the cantilevered observation wheel idea from the Barfield Architects?"

"Ferris wheel on the South Bank submission?" Kenneth asked, as he slumped back in his chair.

Douglas nodded as he plucked up his whisky whilst the steward placed two more on the table.

Kenneth pursed his lips and nodded. "It's got a few supporters. Not the worst idea out there, I wager. What's your interest in that?"

Douglas shrugged and grinned. "Civic duty to the Capital."

"Ha! Poppycock, old boy. You've got some financial stake in that one then, eh?"

"No, not at all. But the right word in the right ear will be appreciated." He stared into his confrère's eyes, nodded, then downed the whisky.

"See what I can do for you, Dougy, old boy."

"Kenny, I'd appreciate it." Douglas placed his empty glass down, plucked up the second glass and swallowed the single malt in one swift action. "There could be a sizeable incentive falling your way for the right word. The Millennium Eye must, and I mean, *must*, win the competition."

Kenneth nodded. "Right, Dougy, are you dining? If you're interested, I'm led to believe old Horsley is setting up a game in the Lexington Suite at ten … minimum ten grand in. You up for that?"

"Not tonight, I'm afraid."

Striking a match, Kenneth puffed on his cigar before continuing. "Shame, we could've nipped along to Frannie's afterwards. I believe there will be some desirable play-bunnies to relax with." He winked and delivered his boyish, cheeky grin. Although portly and balding, he now appeared older than a man should in his mid-forties.

Kenneth came from old-money stock, offensively rich, and Lord of the Brackley Estate in Hampshire. However, unfortunately for Kenneth, the days of attracting desirable young ladies' attention without opening his wallet were now long departed.

"Lovely idea, but I'm afraid I'll have to pass. Unfortunately, Marjory will be expecting me back in Gloucestershire tonight. My dizzy daughter, Phillipa, is presenting her new boyfriend for the weekend; some brash, ghastly investment banker type, I suspect."

Douglas thumped his hands on the chair's leather arms and stood. "So, my good friend, I'm afraid I'll have to take a rain check this time and play the dutiful husband thing this weekend. What a bloody bore!"

"Pity, as I hear there's some lovely fillies up at Frannie's. Ha, but when the good wife calls, we have to obey, eh!"

"I'm afraid so. Don't do anything I wouldn't do up at Frannie's tonight." Douglas winked and slapped his good friend's shoulder before gripping hard and digging his fingers into his skin. Douglas glared into his eyes. "Cantilevered Observation Wheel, my friend ... I'm expecting results."

2

September 1979

Profumo

Clare raked through her handbag, searching in the dim light cast from the neon restaurant sign above. The deep, cavernous bag yielded everything but what she was desperately looking for. Frustrated, she considered upending the contents onto the pavement and lobbing the bag down the street.

"Ah, got ya!" From the bag's deep depths, she recovered her packet of ten Silk Cut cigarettes and a box of matches. Clare inhaled a long drag of her cigarette, flicked away the spent match and leant back against the restaurant window whilst savouring the hit of nicotine as it calmed those cravings which had started to ravage her brain.

"Oh, there you are! I thought you were going to wait inside for me," exclaimed Jemma. She'd stuck her head out of the restaurant door searching for Clare, her closest friend from way back when. They'd met at elementary school in the early '50s and had remained close ever since. "I thought you'd given them up?"

Clare took another long drag, returning a cheesy grin as the smoke wafted out through her teeth. "Tobias thinks I have! I'll have to crunch down a packet of extra-strong mints before I get home."

"Make sure you do. You know Tobias detests the smell of cigarettes."

"He won't notice."

Jemma doubted that; she knew Tobias well. In fact, she knew him far too well, which was the problem and the reason she'd suggested a girl's night out. Tonight, she'd planned to come clean with Clare about Tobias. However, as the evening wore on, she'd lost her nerve. Also, if she confided in Clare, Jemma knew their friendship would end, and she just couldn't face losing her.

Jemma joined Clare on the pavement, adjusting the belt on her A-line camel-coloured mac after once again tipping her head from side to side to run her fingers through her shoulder-length blonde hair. Although she now wore it a little shorter than she preferred, Jemma still tried to style it like Farrah Fawcett.

Since her unexpected election victory and becoming a Member of Parliament in May, Jemma had quickly learnt to alter her look to give a more grown-up, conservative with a small-c appearance to what she preferred.

Clare radiated beauty. She had a drop-dead gorgeous figure, which her off-the-shoulder blouse and skin-tight leather trousers accentuated perfectly. John Travolta would have considered Olivia Newton-John ordinary if he'd met Clare on West Palm Beach. Clare had always been the gorgeous one, although Jemma knew she wasn't too shabby herself.

However, now turned thirty, and with her maiden speech in the House fast approaching, the look needed to be more Mrs T than one of Charlie's Angels.

Jemma was one of three female MPs of the new seventy-seven elected that year. When she'd stood for the group photo on that sunny day in May, Mrs Thatcher had made a point of instructing her in no uncertain terms that skirts were to be worn below the knee. She didn't expect her MPs to dress like Christine Keeler – this was the Houses of Parliament – she'd said, as she shook Jemma's hand, congratulating her on her victory in the previously Labour strong-hold seat of Fairfield.

Already at odds with her leader over Europe, it was a poor start. Jemma had, over the preceding few months, made a point of realigning her wardrobe to ensure she didn't receive any more disapproving looks.

"Okay, honey, I'm ready," said Clare, as she twisted the sole of her red stiletto on the cigarette butt.

"No, you go. I've ordered a taxi; it'll be here in a couple of minutes."

"No, silly, I'll take you home. You don't need to get a taxi."

"You live on the other side of town. That's right out of your way. Honestly, the taxi will be here at any moment. You go; it's late. And as you said, you have an early start tomorrow."

"Oh, hell yes. I'm not looking forward to that either! Unlike you MPs, who don't start work until the evening!"

"Hey, cheeky! I'll be in the House until midnight on Monday. There's a three-line whip in place."

Clare kissed her friend on the cheek. "Only joking, honey." She stepped back, holding Jemma's hands. "Shall I wait until the taxi arrives?"

"No, you go ... honestly; it'll be here any second."

"Alright. I'll call you on Monday to wish you good luck with your maiden speech. You'll be brilliant. I just know it ... I'll be rooting for you."

"Oh God, I hope so. I'm told that Mrs Thatcher will be in the Chamber to hear it!"

Clare rubbed her arm before turning to go. "Honey, you'll knock 'em dead; I know you will. Right, speak later. Love you lots." She turned and headed around the side of the restaurant towards the car park.

Jemma wasn't so confident about Tuesday's speech. She'd practised it that many times in front of her husband, Frank, she thought he knew it better than she did. Also, Frank would probably do a better job at delivering it. The thought of Mrs Thatcher listening to her babble on was terrifying. An ankle-length skirt was required that day, for sure. Her performance would undoubtedly need to be more Barbara Castle than Barbara Cartland.

Jemma waved at Clare as she pulled out of the car park in her brand new TR7, which Tobias had bought her when he'd purchased his Lotus Esprit. Both owned flash cars and, as Clare and Tobias were now creaming it in since setting up their partnership last year, they could easily afford them.

Whilst waiting for her taxi, Jemma checked her watch as the last few stragglers left the restaurant and, the lights clicked off. The remaining few punters staggered out from the Whitehouse Tavern opposite, leaving the street eerily quiet.

Fairfield wasn't exactly buzzing at the best of times, but late on a chilly September evening the town now appeared deserted.

After ten minutes of waiting, her taxi hadn't arrived. Now unable to nip back into the restaurant and use their phone, she headed up to the High Street to locate a phone box. She'd ring the bloody taxi company again and give them a right mouthful for leaving her waiting. If they had let her down, she'd have no other option but to ring Frank. Although he said he was going out with his dickhead mate, Paul, so was probably in no fit state to drive.

Puffed out after stomping her way through town and relieved the first phone box she reached hadn't been vandalised, Jemma dialled the number.

"Sorry, Mrs Stone. Harry got a flat on his way to you. I don't have another car out in town tonight that can get to you. Really sorry."

"Well, that's not good enough! I'm your MP, and that should be enough to make you realise I shouldn't be left stranded like this!"

"I don't care who you are, love. I can't magic a car up out of thin air! I suggest you ring that Thatcher woman; get 'er to come and pick you up if you're that important!" With that, the tosser at the taxi desk slammed the phone down, and the line disconnected.

"Oh, great!" Jemma slammed the receiver down, regretting using the MP angle. That was just the sort of pretentious statement she hated.

Preparing to force in another coin, she dialled home, hoping Frank was there and praying he wasn't splayed out pissed on the sofa. Of course, he wouldn't be happy about turning out again, but what choice did she have? She knew Lawson's was the only taxi firm operating at this time of night so, if no Frank, it was going to be one hell of a long walk home.

"Come on, come on, for Christ's sake, pick up the bloody phone!"

Whilst waiting for her husband to answer, the plethora of cards wedged into the back of the phone casing drew her eye. All were showing numbers for women offering all sorts of services, some of which she was unsure what they meant. Young Curvy Mandy, as she called herself, was offering a 'raw blow' for a fiver. God knows what that was, although it didn't take a huge leap of imagination to guess.

"Oh, bloody hell, Frank!" Jemma slammed the receiver down after the call clicked through to the answering machine, and she'd listened to that ridiculous message Frank had recorded.

Furious he hadn't answered, Jemma pushed her way out of the box and away from the gallery of cards, which made her wonder how those girls ended up doing what they do.

For Jemma, the days of low-cut tops, four-inch heels, boob tubes and miniskirts were long gone. Thank God for sensible, yucky shoes as she now faced the long walk home. Although her shoes were smart, with a modest two-inch heel, they weren't the sexy, high-heeled shoes she preferred. However, even on a night out in town, as she now represented the community, Jemma knew she must always purvey a conservative appearance.

Yanking up the collar on her coat, Jemma stomped her way home. The length of her strides increased as she bolted up the

High Street, now spurred on by the bubbling anger as she seethed about the prat at Lawson's taxis and Frank, who probably lay pissed on the sofa.

~

Those sensible shoes, although suitable for marching in, were the one item of clothing never discovered. Jemma's body lay buried in a shallow grave in Fairfield Woods, but too shallow to hide her scent from a Jack Russell called Pip that had furiously dug at her final resting place when out for a walk with his master ten days later.

Harold Clarke, a retired bus driver whose faithful companion had discovered Jemma, had puked up all over her body, suffered a heart attack and died the next day. He'd fought at the Battle of the Somme and witnessed some gut-curdling sights at the tender age of nineteen, but the vision of Jemma's body had been enough to finally split his heart.

The investigation into the local MP's murder held a prominent place on the national news for many months. After the anniversary of her death in 1980, the senior investigating officer took early retirement and the operation was scaled back due to resources being required elsewhere.

No one was ever convicted of her murder.

3

October 2015

Brillo

Father Collins waited a few feet away as Graham squatted and chatted to the two rough sleepers huddled up under the overhanging canopy of Waterloo tube station. He settled the old blue cool box on the ground and rubbed his hands together before checking the time. As it had just passed eleven, he knew they'd have to hurry to get back to St Mary's Chapel Mission to support his team with the overnighters they expected in for tonight.

He turned and glanced at Mr Kirk who, huddled in his long Crombie overcoat with the collar pulled up around his ears, didn't look out of place standing outside the station at this time of night, as if he was heading for the underground after sampling the delights of the local nightlife. However, Mr Kirk wasn't strolling along the South Bank after enjoying the local wine bars and restaurants' hospitality.

"You know the vast majority won't give their names or may well tell us where to go in no uncertain terms ... if you know what I mean?" said the elderly clergyman, as he turned back to check Graham was okay.

Mr Kirk, although normally referred to as Agent Kirk, nodded but didn't reply. This was the fourth night out with Father Collins and his volunteers, and as each night passed the outside temperature seemed to drop a degree or two.

However, Kirk was committed to his mission. So, come rain or shine, he had a job to do, and as always, he'd complete it to the required brief. Next week, he would move to the homeless support centre near the Barbican, where the process would start again. After that he knew he'd be reassigned, and then a new agent would take over to continue the search which had now proved fruitless for four months.

The intelligence received suggested their search area of roughly ten square miles of Central London was the correct location. However, the difficulty they faced and why they had been thus far unsuccessful was that over four thousand rough sleepers resided in their search area.

Graham stood, stretched his back, then shook his head as he glanced over to Mr Kirk. "Sorry, no joy. I know these guys. They're regulars and not the man you're looking for."

"Will they come in for the night?" asked Father Collins.

Graham huffed and shook his head. "No, I'm afraid not. Not willing to blaspheme and repeat what one of them said to me, but he was pretty clear in his rebuttal of the offer."

"He took the food and water, though?"

"Yes, of course."

"Good, good."

Graham pointed away from the station entrance. "There's a few near the old public toilets on The Queen's Walk along the Embankment. Usual crowd, so it won't help you I'm afraid, Mr Kirk."

"Right, Graham, let's move up and see those poor souls. After that, I think it's time to call it a night," said Father Collins, as he grabbed the old blue cool-box.

"Yes, I agree," said Graham, as he re-adjusted the hood of his coat to fend off the bitterly cold wind, which had now increased a few knots and would feel like gale force as they neared the Thames.

Father Collins turned to Mr Kirk. "I'm sorry it's another pointless night for you, Mr Kirk. Although we do appreciate your support."

Graham slapped Mr Kirk on the shoulder. "Yes, we do. Of course, I know you're here to find your uncle, but we are always looking for volunteers in the future?"

Agent Kirk returned a sympathetic smile and gently shook his head. "Gentlemen, I do appreciate your help, although I have to say trudging the streets in this weather is not my idea of an entertaining evening. No offence intended."

"None taken. We do hope you find Mr Stone soon."

The three of them tucked their heads down as they trudged their way up to The Queen's Walk. As they neared the open area near Jubilee Park, the biting wind would whip off the Thames and sting their exposed faces. So, none of them spoke as they headed towards the disused toilet block, where they spotted two heaps of cardboard that two unfortunate souls had used to barricade themselves into the alcoves in front of the toilet doors. To the untrained eye, it appeared to be a heap of rubbish from one of the nearby shops now stacked up and ready for the morning refuse collection.

The Queen's Walk and Jubilee Park were regenerated areas. The '70s built toilet block, which no longer fitted into the lush feel of the tourist area, was now due for demolition. The difference at night from the bustling crowds at day who queued to visit the London Aquarium, riverboat cruises and the looming London Eye, could not be starker. Like cockroaches, the rough sleeping community disappeared at dawn as quickly as they appeared at dusk.

Graham retrieved the food package and bottled water from the cool box and approached the cardboard structures. He knelt to have a chat, offer them food, and check the two inhabitants were in reasonably good health. Well, as good as health could be expected for these serial rough sleepers. Both Father Collins and Mr Kirk accompanied him, although maintained a short distance to avoid overcrowding and appearing intimidating. Unfortunately, not all *clients* were pleased to see them. On a few occasions, Graham had had to retreat for fear of being assaulted. However, this didn't deter him from God's work.

Graham tapped on the cardboard sheet which doubled up as this particular rough sleeper's front door. In its previous life, based on the red writing across one panel, the makeshift cardboard door appeared to have been some sort of outer packaging originating from China.

"Hi there. It's Graham from St Mary's. I have some water and food for you."

The top of an elderly gent's head appeared in the light from the torch lantern, which Father Collins held up to illuminate the graffiti-covered concrete alcove. This particular street artist's tag, *Brillo,* presumably had no affiliation with the famous oven-cleaning brand of soap-filled steel wire-wool pads. Cocooned in a filthy blue sleeping bag, the tramp-like character didn't move as he kept himself tightly wrapped up against the chilly wind.

"Piss off," came the response from somewhere beneath the dirty grey beard.

"I'll leave this water and food here for you. You know we can provide a bed for the night up at the Mission … it's going to be extremely cold tonight."

"Oh, it's you. Sorry, Father. Didn't realise it was you."

"It's not Father. I'm Graham from the Mission."

The rough sleeper shook his head but took the food parcel.

"Okay … alright. I've not seen you for a while. If you change your mind, you know where we are. God be with you."

"Father Collins, although I've not seen him for quite a while, I think I might recognise this chap. I can't clearly see his face, but he's got a mop of grey hair, so could be the right age."

The tired clergyman raised his eyebrow at Mr Kirk, suggesting he should check the man out.

Agent Kirk nodded and stepped up to the mound of cardboard. This was not the first time this week they'd identified a potential candidate who could be the man his employers were searching for. However, he'd become tired of this assignment and suspected, like all the others, he wouldn't be their man.

Agent Kirk called out to the cardboard heap. "Frank Stone?"

"Piss off."

Not deterred from the usual response he'd received several times already this week, he lifted the cardboard to peek at the grey hair poking out of the sleeping bag. He placed his gloved hand across his mouth to avoid sucking in too much of the pungent waft of stale urine.

"Are you Frank Stone?"

"Piss off ... bloody hell, what's the matter with you do-good-bible-bashing-fuck-stupid-gits ... I said piss off!" The grey hair sprung up through the hole at the top of the sleeping bag, revealing a heavily lined, leathery-skinned face partially covered by a wild grey beard. His eyes squinted at the light cast by the lantern.

Agent Kirk smiled and nodded. This was him, Frank Stirling Stone. The only pictures in Frank's file were over thirty years old, when this man was clean-shaven and wearing a sharp business suit. However, as an experienced agent working for the CYA, he'd become highly skilled at recognising faces.

"Frank ... Frank, it's Michael. Your nephew," lied Agent Kirk.

Frank Stone coughed, hacked up and spat a considerably large lump of phlegm onto the wall beside him. "Well, Michael, that would be difficult, as I'm an only child. So, as I said, piss off."

Bingo ... That confirmed it; he'd found his man.

"Mr Kirk ... Mr Kirk?" called out Father Collins.

Agent Kirk stood and backed away from his quarry, relieved to get clear of the foul smell emanating from Frank Stone. "Thank you, gentlemen; this is my Uncle Frank. I'm so grateful to you both." He wiped his eye to remove an imaginary tear.

Father Collins frowned. "Are you certain? Odd that he said he doesn't have a nephew."

"Well, he does, as I'm standing here. But after years on the street, I'm not surprised he's saying that."

"Well, what will you do now? He doesn't appear to be too thrilled to see you."

"Father, I'll wait until the morning. I think it's best to leave him at this time of night, and I'll come back early tomorrow with some help. The important thing now is to show him he has a family who care and love him." He delivered the lie with confidence – he had accomplished acting skills, which were essential in his line of work.

Graham grabbed Mr Kirk's elbow. "This is such good news. I really can't tell you how pleased I am. This is, without doubt, divine intervention. Bless you, and I wish you both good fortune."

Agent Kirk grinned. Although delighted to have found Frank, which meant this particular mission was coming to a close, it was essential to maintain the pretence in front of Father Collins and his particularly annoying sidekick.

Now he had work to do. Like a well-oiled machine, the Extraction Team would swing into action and hoover up this smelly git. Then he could move on to a more savoury mission that didn't require walking around the streets of London with God-squad whilst searching for some stinky old tramp.

4

Honey Ryder

"Good morning, all; good morning. Can we settle down, please?" Douglas Hartland stood and addressed the committee as he fastened both buttons on his blue double-breasted suit jacket. He took a final puff of his cigarette before stubbing it out in the smoked-glass ashtray positioned in front of his document folder on the oval walnut table. The room fell silent as the nine pairs of eyes belonging to the members of the CYA Selection Committee peered at him.

"Thank you. You all have a document folder in front of you detailing the candidates for our discussion today. The *Correction Target,* as we know, is Jemma Stone. The tech guys, led by Keith, have narrowed our choice of suggested *Change Agents* down to eight. We must make our final selection today, so I'm in a position to update the Board at the weekend. Keith, can you take us through the candidates, please?"

Keith scraped his chair back and strode to the front of the wood-panelled room. "Jon, can you dim the lights and put up the first slide, please?"

Jon, head of the Intelligence Team, nodded, leaned over and snapped the lights off after he flicked on the power switch to the projector. The carousel of slides chugged around to display a picture of a smartly suited gent smiling back from the white wall above the wood panelling at the end of the room. The smoke from the ashtrays wafted up, mingling with the light from the projector, accentuating the blue haze which engulfed the room.

Keith cleared his throat and pointed to the projected picture. "Gentleman, this is our first candidate. As the data will demonstrate, and in both mine and Douglas's opinion, this chap is our best option. We're all fully aware we only have three *Correction Years* available to us. Incidentally, my team is working through some interesting data that suggests we may have discovered a fourth, 2029. However, that's fourteen years in the future, and at this stage we cannot confirm it will perform as expected. So, gents, that leaves us with 1939, 1959, and 1979. As the Correction required for the *European Fault* is in 2023, and Jemma Stone is our target, clearly, 1979 is our best option."

Douglas leant against the sidewall panelling and raised his hand to interject. "Gents, as a reminder, the chosen candidate has to be expendable, so please bear that in mind because seven of the eight do have relatives who will miss them. So that's one reason why I believe this chap is our best option." He waved his hand at the projected picture on the wall to his right. "Of course, we will discuss all eight. However, if we choose this chap and, God forbid, he doesn't make it, we will have to send one of the other seven. Keith, sorry, carry on."

Keith nodded. "No apology required, sir. Okay, all the slides are in your document packs." He turned and faced the projected picture. "This is Frank Stirling Stone. He's a vagrant – hobo type character, sleeping rough since approximately

2005. Most of this time spent in and around the Central London area. Jon and his team believe he's still there ... somewhere."

Jon, who'd been under considerable pressure for some time now, felt the need to interject. "Err ... yes. My team are confident that our information is spot on."

"Bloody well better be after the last cock-up!" scoffed Geoff, Head of Extraction.

Douglas coughed to bring the room back into order. "Gents, no backbiting, please. To be successful, we all have to operate as one team. Furthermore, we know none of this is an exact science."

Geoff huffed and rocked back on his chair. "Douglas, I understand. But it's my agents in the field who are at the sharp end. If Jon's team keep providing shite intel, my team suffer!"

"Steady, Geoff! My team have the hardest bloody job ... it's not easy, you know!" spat back Jon.

"Gentlemen! Focus, please." retorted Douglas. As their respected leader, all members of the committee knew when the line was drawn.

Keith raised his eyebrows at Douglas, who nodded for him to continue. Once again, the room fell silent.

"So, Frank Stone. Born on 30th March 1949. Because Frank dropped off the radar some years ago, this is the only picture we have of him. However, that also makes him a perfect candidate. If you turn to page two in your packs, you'll find the research details regarding Frank Stone."

Keith waited whilst the Correction Years Association Committee shuffled the pages in their packs and studied Frank Stone's fact sheet.

"Right, as you can see, in 1979, Frank was Jemma Stone's husband. He ran a small but successful building business. Frank was an architect, and his business partner led the building side of the operation. Frank and Jemma didn't have any children, both of them were an only child, and all but one of the four parents have passed. As Jemma Stone is our preferred *Correction Target,* this does provide Frank with a high percentage chance to succeed in our mission to change Jemma's timeline."

Keith waited for a second as he turned back and faced the committee. All eyes were upon him, so he continued. "Right, October 1979. Jemma Stone's body was discovered in a shallow grave in Fairfield Woods, two miles from her home, which she shared with her husband, Frank." Keith pointed to the projected picture again. "This is the point that my Data/Tech team have possibly identified as the *Time-divide,* which we believe could be a point to correct the *European Fault."* Keith nodded to James, who'd leant forward and raised his right index finger.

James removed the cigarette from his lips and scanned the room as all eyes swivelled to look at him. James, the youngest member of the committee and newly-appointed Head of Group Services, was always the first to offer an opinion. Many of his peers found him frustrating. However, Douglas knew James added a different dimension to the committee and always valued his input.

"Keith, it states on page six that Frank was a suspect for her murder and subsequently arrested. What's to suggest he didn't actually murder her? Because if he did, that would suggest he is quite unsuitable?"

Douglas nodded at Keith, indicating he should answer, then chuckled to himself as the rest of the committee, apart from Penelope, raked through their packs whilst frantically trying to find the information James had highlighted.

"Great spot, James. This is our only concern regarding Frank. However, until we can locate him, which is proving difficult, we can't interview him and form an opinion on this point." Keith nodded to Henry, who'd raised his hand.

Henry, the oldest and longest-serving committee member, leant forward and coughed. "Err ... Wh-wh-wh ..."

James threw his pen down on his notepad and rolled his eyes. "Hen-Hen ... wa-wa ... t-t-t-t." The committee all laughed as James, as usual, took the piss out of Henry because of his stutter.

Douglas clicked his fingers. That small act was enough to instantly stop the laughter as all nine members stared at him, clocking his stern demeanour. "Gents! Can I remind you of the gravity of our decision today! We've spent nine years attempting to find a suitable candidate to prevent the *European Fault*. Now, as we're dangerously close to that *Time-Fault*, we're coming perilously close to the point where we'll no longer be able to complete an effective correction."

The committee all bowed their heads, now feeling suitably chastised. Douglas nodded to Henry to continue, who took a moment to breathe deeply before attempting to speak.

"Err ... err ... wh-what evidence do we have to suggest Jemma wo-would have become a Government Minister as it states in the pack?"

"Henry, great question. Jemma was elected to Parliament in May 1979 and, at the age of thirty, she was the youngest in a generation of the new MPs. Although at odds with some of Mrs Thatcher's policies, data suggests she would've progressed to enjoy a long and successful career. Jemma was a strong supporter of the European Union, and although her views were, as I said, at odds with Mrs T, all the data suggests her views regarding Europe would have shaped British politics through the millennium and beyond. Douglas, anything to add?" Keith glanced at his boss, who leant against the wood panelling.

"Keith, thank you. Gents, the most startling piece of information we have, which the Data team have calculated ... Jemma Stone, if she'd lived, had a sixty-nine per cent chance of preventing the *European Fault!*"

A murmuring shot around the room as they all took in this new information.

James was the first to respond. "Douglas, that's a strong percentage. But what's the calculation for Frank Stone?"

"Gentleman ..." Douglas paused momentarily before delivering this vital piece of information that he knew would convince them. All eyes swivelled to look at Douglas, who smiled, then raised his head. "Gentleman, Frank Stone has a thirty-nine per cent rating!"

"Thirty-nine! Are we sure?" scoffed Geoff over the melee of chatter that had erupted at hearing this unbelievable information.

"Douglas, that's over twenty per cent higher than any other candidate we've sent so far! Have Keith's team calculated this correctly?" James offered up over the noise of the continued murmurings.

Douglas lit another cigarette, returned to his seat, and scanned their faces as they all turned to follow his movement. They were all fully aware if this calculation was correct, it was the best odds they'd ever had. Douglas dragged the ashtray closer before reclining in his well-worn leather Chesterfield chair.

"Gentleman, we have conducted the triple check required, and I can confirm the calculations the Tech and Data team have provided are accurate. Jemma Stone's correction prediction, combined with Frank Stone, is a whopping fifty-four per cent!" Douglas grinned before taking a long drag on his cigarette whilst flicking ash from his suit trousers.

The Committee were stunned, causing an unusual hush to descend.

Penelope, head of the Preparation and Transportation Team, and the only woman on the committee, broke the silence. "Couple of points to question … what's the status on locating Frank Stone? Also, as he's sixty-six years old, if we do find him, will he be too old and in poor health to send back? I only ask because prior to my appointment, we've never been very successful with the over-sixties."

Douglas leant forward, placed his forearms on the table and pursed his lips. "Gentleman, we have now attempted to send forty-two candidates over nine years to deal with the *European Fault*. As you know, the best data odds were eighteen per cent … plus nine candidates didn't survive the journey." Pointing at Penelope, Douglas continued. "Penelope is quite right with her observation because we've only been successful with a handful of the over-sixties. However, considering Jemma and Frank Stone's combined calculation of fifty-four per cent, sending

Frank Stone back even at the age of sixty-six ... is, in my opinion, a must."

Penelope interjected again. "Douglas, as you know, since I've taken over my department, we've improved the survival rate considerably. Also, my team have improved our over-sixties travelling success by over a thousand per cent. So as long as we're given the correct time and we don't proceed with his travel too quickly, I'm totally confident my team can prepare him."

No one challenged Penelope. The committee members were fully aware she oozed confidence, and her razor-sharp tongue was capable of shredding them, as a few had discovered in the past. Penelope was used to working in the male-dominated organisation and had no problem that Douglas always referred to the group as *Gentlemen*. However, times were changing – Douglas was from a previous era. What the board, led by Lady Maud Huston-Smythe, knew, and so did Penelope, it was only a matter of time before she would replace Douglas to take the organisation in a more modern direction.

Douglas stood, stepped over to the wood panelling where he folded his arms, and once again leant up against the wall whilst crossing his feet – all eyes followed his movement. "Unfortunately, we've not located Frank, but Geoff and his team have a number of top agents working on this. When we locate him, I fear his health could be a problem due to his domestic living situation. So, Penelope, you're quite right; we'll require at least six weeks to get him in an acceptable condition to travel. However, gentlemen, that puts us, as I said, perilously close to the summer of 2016, the point at which we believe Jemma Stone has a correction timeline opportunity."

Douglas's hooked eyelids narrowed, an unconscious technique he applied when he needed to make his point clear. "If we reach that point and have not been successful, the Board will not sanction a correction to the *European Fault* through Jemma. We'll then be forced to resume our search for a suitable *Correction Target*." Douglas nodded to Keith to continue.

"In light of what Douglas has said, we have the seven other candidates to review who could change Jemma's future. However, all seven have a *Correction Prediction* below twelve per cent, so clearly not in the league of what we believe Frank Stone can achieve. Jon, can you move the slides on, please?"

Jon leant up and flicked the button on the projector. All eyes swivelled to the wall, which displayed two pictures of the same man. The left-hand image showed an elderly gent dressed in a blue blazer, smiling back at them whilst holding a trophy. If the side-burns and wide flared collar were anything to go by, the right-hand photo was clearly taken during the '70s.

"So, here we have Cecil Causton, Jemma Stone's father. The first picture is of Mr Causton winning the Hertfordshire Lawn Bowls singles title in 1996. The second is his profile in the Draper's Record trade magazine when he was sales director for a Norwegian soft furnishings company in 1979. Cecil, born in 1928, now eighty-seven, suffers from poor health and resides in a nursing home. His wife, Helen, died of breast cancer in 1989. He has a correction percentage of nine per cent, but obviously his chances of successfully making the journey back are perilously low." Scanning the committee's faces, Keith could easily deduce there was no need to elaborate any further as they had rarely successfully sent back any candidates who were over eighty years old.

Keith nodded at Jon, who moved the slides on to display the next set of pictures. A slim, middle-aged lady holding a whip appeared. Dressed in what appeared to be horsey attire, it was safe to assume the whip wasn't for use in the bedroom. The second picture displayed a much younger version of the same lady, presumably when in her early twenties. Dressed in a white bikini, she held up a flamboyantly dressed cocktail whilst relaxing by the pool. Although beauty was always in the eye of the beholder, it was clear that this lady could only be described as a total stunner as she posed in her Honey Ryder styled bikini.

Keith pointed at the projected images. "Clare Heaton. Jemma's closest friend since junior school. They stayed close right up to Jemma's death and is believed to be the last person to have seen Jemma alive. Born 1949, so she's sixty-six, as would Jemma be if she'd lived. Clare has a percentage calculation of eight per cent. However, the biggest issue we have is she's married with two daughters and four grandchildren. So, clearly, sending her back will be a problem as presumably she'll be missed. She still operates, albeit part-time, as a solicitor in family law. Positives for Clare, she is in the best of health of all our candidates."

"She certainly looks fit in that bikini. I reckon she could wield that whip! Well, I would!" smarted James, as he cracked his air-whip, which caused a rumbling of male sniggers around the room.

Penelope glared at James for his immature, chauvinistic, and sexist comment.

Douglas raised his eyebrows, that tiny act enough to bring the group back to order. Keith nodded to Jon again, who complied with the non-verbal request to move the projector onto the next slide.

"Our next candidate, Tobias Heaton, Clare's husband."

As with all candidates, the two projected pictures were a recent shot and one from thirty-odd years in the past. Tobias Heaton in both images appeared clean-cut, almost James Bond in appearance without the gun. Even in middle age, both Clare and Tobias could've modelled clothing, life insurance policies, stair lifts, and cruises around the Med in those catalogues which always drop out of the Sunday newspaper supplements.

"Tobias also has an eight per cent calculation. Aged sixty-eight, and now also works part-time in his own law practice with his wife, Clare. As with Clare, he's not a good choice due to the obvious points. However, back in 1979, he was also close to Jemma and Frank and supported Frank vociferously when he was originally arrested for Jemma's murder."

Keith nodded to Jon, and the projector carousel spun around to display the next slide. A picture of an elderly bald man, who wore a dirty retro England football shirt tightly stretched over his beer gut, appeared on the wall. In the battle to clothe his large frame, the outdated replica top was failing, as it appeared the man's belly was grotesquely sagging down from the bottom of the shirt. The bloated man grinned back at the camera with a pint in his hand. He clearly hadn't aged well, and the seemingly regular event of pouring pints of lager down his throat had changed his appearance from an athletic, handsome guy in the '70s to a repulsive oaf. Comparing the earlier picture to the latter one, it was clear to see at some point someone had realigned his nose as it appeared to be on the skew.

"Paul Wilson, born 1948. He was Frank Stone's business partner. Paul started his own business in 1989 after the building firm that Frank and he started was declared bankrupt earlier that year. Paul is now living in a rented one-bedroom flat after his business failed and he divorced in 2004. Paul has few relatives and would be a good candidate for travel. However, he has only a six per cent calculation. That said, he would be, I suggest, our second-choice candidate because we have been successful in the past with a lower percentage."

Penelope interjected before Keith could show the next candidate. "Do we need to see the rest? Clearly, Frank's stats are all we need to know, so it seems a foregone conclusion."

"Penelope, once again, you're quite correct." Pitstop, as the rest of the committee called her behind her back, appeared smug at receiving Douglas's praise.

Douglas nodded at her, then continued. "I think we all can see how strong Frank's stats are. But unfortunately, we haven't had any success in locating him. So please bear with us as we review the candidates because we *will* need to identify a second choice. Jemma Stone presents a wonderful opportunity to reset the *European Fault*. However, time is against us, so we must identify another candidate to travel in the unlikely event that we're unable to locate Frank." Douglas nodded to Keith to continue.

Jon flipped the carousel to display the next slide.

"David Bolton. A close friend to Frank, although they drifted apart in the '80s. Born 1950 and still lives in Fairfield. He's a retired supermarket manager, married with two children, seven grandchildren, and a leading light in the town's Chamber of Commerce. David has a percentage of twelve, so a great number, but reasonably impossible to travel with all his connections."

Keith once again nodded at Jon to move the slides on. A picture appeared of a pretty, slim lady with long chestnut hair. Of all the candidates so far, the passage of time had been the kindest on her.

James interjected, as he always did when pictures of young ladies were projected. "She looks like Kate Bush. You remember her in those skin-tight outfits? Wouldn't mind, I can tell you."

"James, you're a pathetic boy who lacks maturity. Someday soon, some woman is going to cut you down to size," ripped Penelope.

Penelope held his stare and, as her words hung in the air, James shrank back knowing he'd met his match.

Douglas glanced at Keith and nodded. Keith shuffled awkwardly on the spot, then continued.

"This is Jayne Hart. Born 1950, and was also a friend of Jemma's. They shared rooms together at university and regularly kept in touch. At this stage, we're unable to assess how Jayne has a connection to change Jemma's future. That said, her correction percentage is ten, so again a substantial number. However, she's a retired teacher and a governor at the secondary school in Fairfield, where she taught for thirty years. She's a well-connected lady in her mid-sixties, so obviously not an ideal candidate for travel."

"She could spank me with the cane any day!" interjected James.

"Oh, for Christ's sake!" exclaimed Penelope.

The room hushed as Penelope and James glared at each other.

Keith cleared his throat and continued. "Lastly, we have Dennis Tranil. Born 1938, so he's seventy-seven years old. He was Frank and Jemma's neighbour. However, he has a percentage of only four, and age is obviously against him. So, the last page in your pack, as always, is the correction table."

As they always did, the Committee members had already thumbed to the back page. They all pored over the data, which displayed the data that screamed the obvious decision they had to make. Frank Stone was potentially going to be the most exciting *Correction Change Agent* they'd ever found.

Keith turned and nodded to Douglas, then retook his seat. Douglas moved back to the front of the room and stood at the end of the large oval table.

"Keith, thank you. Gentlemen, as stated, can we vote on the agreed action so I can update the Board at the weekend?"

Miss Fuller, an unassuming woman in her early forties, gingerly pushed open the heavy oak door to the committee room, poking her head through the tiny gap. Because of her mouse-like frame and timid demeanour, she had earned the nickname *Squeak*, although it was never said to her face. She gently waved her hand in front of her face, trying to grab Douglas's attention. Douglas nodded, knowing that she would never interrupt a committee meeting unless it was urgent or a direct order from the Board.

Douglas strode purposefully towards Miss Fuller, who appeared relieved she'd grabbed his attention without having to speak.

"Gents, give me a moment, please," Douglas threw back over his shoulder as he stepped out of the room but held the door ajar. Within a few seconds, he re-entered and strode back to the front whilst rubbing his hands and sporting a confident grin.

"Gents, Agent Kirk has located Frank Stone." Both Jon and Geoff sighed with relief, as it was their combined departments who had the tricky task of locating and extracting suitable candidates for travel.

Douglas thumped the table. "If we all agree, we can bring him in for conditioning later today."

All nine members raised their right arms. Frank Stone would be their two-hundredth traveller that the Correction Years Association had selected for time alteration. Of all the travellers who'd gone before, the committee was in no doubt that this was one of the most important ones.

Douglas prayed that Frank Stone would make the journey back to 1979 without vaporising, as twenty-four previous travellers had before.

5

Dif-tor heh smusma

Agent Kirk propped himself up against the railings overlooking the Thames. He'd already checked to see that Frank Stone was still hunkered down under the cardboard heap by the disused toilet block and now awaited the Extraction Team to arrive.

As Frank was homeless, he was a perfect fit for travel. Also, this made it much easier for the Extraction Team because taking him shouldn't cause any difficulties. However, caution was always the priority, so he'd planned the extraction for 6:00 a.m. to complete the operation with limited onlookers.

The Association's primary goal of ensuring they continuously operated incognito was always at the heart of every operation. Too many prying eyes when performing extractions could lead to complicated and messy clean-ups. Furthermore, liquidating innocent bystanders who'd witnessed an extraction was always disappointing and caused a mountain of paperwork that Kirk detested completing.

When the team arrived, they'd move the three other rough sleepers on. He'd already checked the area's CCTV coverage, only spotting two cameras. So, he wasn't too concerned because the extraction would be swift. Also, the intelligence gathered stated Frank Stone wouldn't be missed. He hoped today's operation would be painless and silently prayed the Intelligence Team had not cocked up, thus allowing them to return to HQ for a debriefing before breakfast.

A guy walking a Labrador strolled past and then leant up against the railings about sixty yards ahead. Kirk knew he'd be a problem, so he hoped he moved on of his own volition before they performed the extraction operation.

The black transit van he'd been waiting for, parked beside the toilet block, flashed its headlights and killed the engine. Agents Hall and Kosanovich alighted the van as Agent Kirk strode towards them. He pointed to the heap of cardboard, indicating their man was lying underneath.

"Captain," Hall called out to Kirk.

Kirk nodded, ignoring the greeting and the stupid nickname his team had given him. He rolled his eyes as Kosanovich offered him the Vulcan hand gesture, something Kirk couldn't do without parting his fingers with his other hand.

Kosanovich uttered the Vulcan greeting "dif-tor heh smusma," and smirked.

"He's under that heap. Old guy, who'll probably mouth off a bit. Apart from that, he shouldn't be a problem. There are three others that we need to move on before we take him," stated Agent Kirk, as he pointed to three heaps of bedding and cardboard, which covered the three rough sleepers who his team would need to move.

Agent Kosanovich nodded to the dog walker, and all three of them knew they'd have to wait a few moments for him to move on. They stood and waited as a jogger passed them, who cast a quizzical glance at the trio as he bounced on by.

The last extraction they'd performed a few weeks back had, at the time, seemed relatively straightforward, as did this one. However, Kirk never took it for granted because working in the field was always unpredictable. Collateral damage was a serious issue and, when it happened, it caused a shitstorm that he wished to avoid.

The three agents had removed an unemployed Polish man from the Kempston tower block in Hackney. As this should be, it was a straightforward extraction. Their target was a loner with no relatives in the UK and certainly had no known acquaintances. However, it had turned to shit when a neighbour overheard the commotion and intervened when their target had not been as willing to be extracted as the intelligence supplied suggested.

The ensuing fracas in the grim, damp two-bedroom shithole of a flat had alerted their target's nosy neighbour, a woman in her late sixties. Because of this, Agent Kosanovich had no choice but to extract her as well. Now, a few weeks on, the nosy neighbour was still incarcerated at HQ whilst the Relocation Team worked on a suitable solution. Unfortunately, the longer the woman stayed incarcerated, it hampered the Association's ability to secure a successful relocation for her. Therefore, liquidation was now looking the most likely outcome for the poor woman.

Later that day, there was a heated encounter between the Extraction and the Intelligence gathering teams regarding who was to blame for the monumental balls-up. Fortunately for Agent Kirk, the CYA committee had concluded the fault lay with the poor intelligence provided, which resulted in the *removal* of a few of the team responsible for supplying the poor intel. Kirk and his fellow agents were quite clear what *removal* meant, causing him to shudder at the thought of their demise.

Every member of the CYA was fully aware of and bought into the fact that their work was critical to ensuring the world continued to be a safe place and maintain the preferred world order. All agents knew and accepted mistakes could not be tolerated, and they could suffer the ultimate sacrifice if those cock-ups led to exposure.

The frustrating thing about that particular operation was that the Polish guy failed to survive the journey, so the whole operation was a total disaster. Agent Kirk and his team's next assignment was to extract a new candidate to deal with the *Polish Fault*. However, firstly, they had to secure Frank Stone because the *European Fault* was by far one of the most significant projects the CYA had undertaken in decades.

For over fifty years, the Preparation and Transportation department was under immense pressure to improve the travel percentage success rate. Unfortunately, although it was significantly better since the Millennium, there was still an unacceptably high loss of those extracted who failed to make the journey. What happened to those who didn't make it? Even after a century of travel, no one knew. Douglas Hartland, the Head of Operations, now headed up the Failure Committee in an attempt to improve performance. The Board had tasked the committee to establish where these failed travellers ended up and in how many pieces.

The dog walker took another drag on his cigarette before pinging the butt into the Thames. He patted the Labrador's head, and then they moved on without a second glance at the three agents standing near the toilet block – the coast was clear – time for the Extraction Team to do their job.

Hall and Kosanovich nodded to each other, each pointing to the particular vagrants they were going to move on. Then, they set to work whilst Kirk kept a watch on the damp cardboard heap which covered Frank Stone. Within a few minutes, they'd be on their way back to HQ with what the Association hoped would be the solution to the *European Fault*.

Kirk knew the buzz around the corridors and committee rooms directly linked to the news regarding Frank and Jemma Stone's combined percentage, which was the highest ever calculated. Although the various teams were prone to cock-ups, the Calculation Teams were always spot on – Frank Stone could be the most successful *traveller* they'd ever had.

6

B.A. Baracus

Although no part of the UK's capital was ever quiet at any time, day or night, usually I could be guaranteed some modicum of semblance of noise-free time that afforded some sleep before dawn hauled in a new day. I shifted my head to peek out the small gap between my cardboard walls to assess the situation.

Leaving a peephole in the cardboard was always a strategy I employed. Although the vast majority of the time no one ever bothered me, it was relatively commonplace for another to want my pitch when I'd secured a spot out of the rain and away from the vicious wind which would often zip along the Embankment.

The London Eye loomed dark and heavy in the sky. As daybreak approached, although unilluminated, its skeletal frame with its giant pods hanging like caterpillar cocoons was clearly visible. The Victorian-styled lamps illuminated the concourse, casting shadows of a lone dog walker who leant on the iron railings smoking a cigarette whilst the obedient dog sat waiting to move on.

A jogger decked out in a reflective top and orange flashes on their running shoes powered on past the toilet block after rounding three men who stood slightly further away than the dog walker. I glanced at the men positioned in a tight huddle, who appeared not to be talking. Instead, they repeatedly glanced up at the dog walker and then nodded to each other.

Street living provided an enormous amount of people-watching time. I would often entertain myself as I spied on an individual whilst guessing their next move – everyone was so predictable. What was apparent, even in this dim light, the three huddled men were not on an early morning stroll, and the dog walker was their target or perhaps in the way. Well, it had bugger all to do with me. So, whatever misdemeanour they were up to, I hoped they performed it quietly so I could grab another few minutes of sleep.

I kept my position so I could peer out through the hole if I needed to and pulled the sleeping bag around my neck – the moments before dawn were always the coldest.

No sleep was coming as the new day arrived, although my plans for today were similar to every day – bugger all. Apart from a trip to the Mission, where hot soup would be on offer, then a scavenge along the pavements for half-smoked cigarette butts, and squatting by the station entrance with my paper cup and cardboard *homeless, please help* notice, I had no plans for my day. Whiling away the hours, hoping to fill my cup with change from the rushing commuters would be the day's highlight.

The problem was today was Sunday, the least lucrative payday of the week. So, the young woman in her suit and pink Michael Kors trainers wouldn't be exiting the station today on her way to work. Every day, Michael-Kors-pink-trainer lady dropped two pounds in my cup. Unlike most commuters exiting the tube station, she would notice me, offering a sad smile that directly contrasted to the look of disdain from the vast majority. Five days a week, like clockwork, out of the station at 8:35 a.m., she deposited two pounds in my cup and offered that sad smile. Every day, I doffed my imaginary cap to her as a thank you. No, Sundays were a shite payday.

Resigning myself to the miserable fact that sleep wasn't coming again, I peered out through the spyhole. The London Eye loomed large in my sightline as the low, weak autumn sun glinted off the stationary pods. The Embankment lamps flickered, a routine they performed each morning when the timer presumably prepared them to turn off as it cleverly predicted the approaching daylight.

The dog walker and the three huddled men appeared to have moved on. Whatever they were up to, they'd completed said task and quietly disappeared, leaving an empty Embankment concourse that would become a throng of excited tourists in only a few hours.

Us street dwellers were fully aware we're not the ideal background for the tourist selfies and group shots before they took their turn on the large white Ferris wheel. We all moved on from our allotted 'bedrooms' well before that time came. Otherwise, we would be forcibly moved, and then trying to return later could be difficult. We all had an unwritten contract with the authorities – move on and stay out of sight, keep the area free of hobos, and we could return to our reserved bed spots later that night with no bother. Not that we had those little reserved plaques that sit on restaurant tables. However, for the majority of the time, as a community, we respected each other's pitches.

Alerted by a kerfuffle at the other end of the toilet block, I swivelled my head to assess this early morning noisy shenanigans. It appeared some of my fellow campers were being encouraged to move on. Although this manoeuvre wasn't unusual, it was for this time of the morning. The two guys performing the removals, wearing black jumpsuits, didn't look like the police or council officials.

I stuck my head out of the gap as one of the 'jumpsuits' men started to manhandle the guy sleeping up against the entrance door to the other disused toilet block.

"Oi, what's going on?" I called out in my gravelly voice. I don't remember when my voice changed to sound like a 1950 diesel tractor, but it had been like it for many years.

Occasionally, street wardens or the police persuaded us to move on earlier than usual if there was some special event happening along the Embankment or in Jubilee Park. However, at this time of day, I and my fellow campers were never usually bothered.

Unsurprisingly, I received no reply from the men in black jumpsuits. Then my view was blocked by a man who stepped towards me, and I recognised him as the bloke from last night who reckoned he was my nephew.

"Oi piss off. What d'you want?" I croaked. I wasn't good in the mornings. Well, the truth be known, I wasn't good anytime. Sleeping rough for ten years takes its toll on a man's wellbeing – as I'd discovered.

"Frank. Good morning," said the guy in the Crombie coat as he squatted down near me.

I spotted behind him one of the 'jumpsuit' guys hand over a wad of notes to my bedroom companion, presumably a sweetener to move on without fuss.

"Who are you ... what's going on? Ain't you the bloke who said you were my nephew? Well, my old mucker, I ain't got one! So, piss off," I croaked again.

Crombie-coat man held out a wad of notes rolled up and tied with an elastic band. My eyes widened at the sight of a serious amount of cash; there were hundreds of pounds inches from me – but no one held out a wad of money to a homeless man. The best I could get if I sat all day outside the station entrance with my empty paper MacDonald's coffee cup was about a fiver, and that included the two pounds deposited by the Michael-Kors-pink-trainer lady.

"Frank, this is for you, my friend. Come with us, and you can have a hot breakfast." He waved the roll of notes enticingly in front of my face. I could almost smell the money. "Do that, and this cash is yours." Crombie-coat man covered his mouth and nose with his gloved hand, winced and coughed.

I know I wasn't the cleanest, but washing facilities weren't that easy to come by, and my pavement room wasn't exactly ensuite.

"You lot at the Mission win the lottery? Normally it's a bottle of water and packet of biscuits on offer, not a roll of notes."

"Frank, we're not from the Mission. We're from an organisation that would like to offer you some help."

I'd noticed the two 'jumpsuit' men were now strategically positioned a few feet behind Crombie-coat man. On their toes, they appeared ready to pounce like a couple of SAS soldiers, primed, alert and ready to spring into action. Shifting my head free of my sleeping bag, I shuffled up my cardboard mattress as Crombie-coat man turned and nodded at the SAS men.

Coughing and clearing my throat of unwanted crap that had accumulated in my lungs through the night, I narrowed my eyes at this suspicious odd man waving around a serious amount of cash. "Who are you? If you're not from the Mission and sent by that do-good priest, you must be some medical company looking to experiment on people." I glanced at the cash on offer, salivating at the gorgeous vision in front of my eyes, then back at Crombie-coat man.

"Frank, none of that. We have a proposition for you that doesn't involve medical science, religious indoctrination or sexual favours. I'm not authorised to give you any more information. However, my friend, if you come with us now, I'll introduce you to my governor who'll explain everything."

With aching bones, screaming, tired and weak muscles, I squirmed up the cardboard to a seated position. Not that my life was anything worth living, but I now became concerned as to why a smartly dressed man who clearly wasn't too enamoured by my pungent smell was offering me cash. "Why d'you give those others a roll of cash and not want them to come with you? Just gimme the cash and piss off."

"Frank, come with us now, or my associates will help you … Sorry, Frank, you don't have a choice." Keeping his hand tightly clamped over his mouth and nose, he raised his eyebrows whilst still enticingly waving the roll of cash.

"Piss off. You can't make me go anywhere with you," I spat back, as I snatched the cash before it disappeared. But it appeared clearly evident, as the two SAS types confidently advanced, I was going somewhere, so I thought I might as well have the money.

"Alright, alright ... call off the dogs. I'll come with you," I growled back, as I cleared my lungs onto the pavement once again.

"Good man, Frank." Crombie-coat man stood as I clambered from my cardboard home. A sneer covered his face as he witnessed my ungainly extraction from my not-so-clean bedding.

I was used to this reaction and, over the years, I'd become sanitised to the way people looked at you. Although mostly the general public averted their eyes, wishing to be immune from the likes of us. What that general public didn't realise, was that nearly everyone is only a few days away from losing everything. A few bad decisions, coupled with a run of bad luck, and you find yourself on the streets. Once there, it becomes almost impossible to return to the life you once had – I knew this better than anyone.

"Leave everything, Frank ... you don't need it," Crombie-coat man stated, stepping back a few paces. The SAS types were scanning around, looking for any onlookers. A couple of early morning joggers panted past near the embankment wall but didn't give a second look, or, as with most people, didn't want to get involved.

"That's my stuff! I can't leave it ... I need it." I peered up at him as I secured my bedding into my four-wheeled trolley, similar to what my grandmother used when nipping up the shops – although mine wasn't in such good condition.

"Frank ... Frank?"

I glanced up at him as I rolled my sleeping bag. It was clear I wasn't coming back; I could just see it in his expression. I dropped the bag, surveyed my possessions, and took one last look at what I owned before turning to face him. "Am I going to die? Is this it ... the end?"

"No, Frank ... I promise you; your life is going to get a whole lot better."

"Right." I turned and looked at him as he held out his arm, beckoning me to walk with him, although I didn't actually believe he desired to be anywhere near me.

"Do I get to keep the cash?" I asked, as I clenched my fist around the roll of notes which I'd stuffed into the inside pocket of my heavily stained parka coat.

"Yes, Frank ... the cash is yours, but only if you come now."

I'd noticed the two SAS types now circling as the three men seemed to corral me forward. If I refused to go, I had the prospect of the rest of my life living each day in this pathetic existence. I knew my health was deteriorating, and I was aware I looked at least twenty years older than my long-lost birth certificate suggested. I suspected my time on Earth was limited. The other option, and I doubted I had much choice as the SAS types closed in on my position, was to go with this lot and risk it. Glancing back at my worldly possessions, which consisted of four sheets of damp cardboard and my tartan-covered trolly, I deduced it was a reasonably easy decision to make.

"Alright, I'll come ... but you tell me how you know my name."

"Frank, we know your name and everything about you ... in fact, my associates know you better than you know yourself."

I shuffled along as they corralled me in a three-point pincer movement towards a shiny black transit van. With its roof donned with an array of various-sized aerials swaying in the gentle breeze, it appeared a giant insect with a long antenna had landed like something out of War of the Worlds. Although it could also have been something The A-Team would cruise about in, and I thought the two SAS types in their black jumpsuits would fit in nicely as part of that squad. I wondered if Crombie-coat man was the Hannibal Smith character, and maybe they were going to help me and not use me as live target practice or for some hideous medical experiment. I half expected to see B.A. Baracus sitting behind the steering wheel, although even if he were, I wouldn't be able to see through the dark-tinted glass. What was for sure, if I stepped into that van, there was no turning back.

Concerned about what I was heading into, I halted my shuffling as we neared the back doors of the van. The three of them tightened their pincer movement, appearing to be on high alert and presumably concerned I was looking to make a dash for it. Although, to be honest, I hadn't made a dash for anything in the last ten years because, apart from the call of nature, I had nothing worth dashing to.

"Where you taking me?"

"Frank, trust us ... you're going to be one of the luckiest men ever born."

7

This Is Your life

"That's everything. You won't see me again ... and I wish you luck." Crombie-coat man stepped to the door.

I turned to look at him. "What's your name?"

Yanking open the door, he stepped through and glanced back. "Kirk."

"As in Captain?"

Kirk nodded and closed the door. I heard the lock engage.

Two hours ago, I was tucked up in my sleeping bag in one of my favourite spots along The Queen's Walk. Now, I was in what I can only assume was a luxury hotel suite in The Dorchester. Well, that's what I imagined it would look like. However, I couldn't be sure, as I'd never stayed there.

Kirk had forced a cloth bag over my head as he ushered me into the back of The A-Team's van, just like in a spy movie. So, I presumed I wasn't in The Dorchester or a similar hotel because I doubted many guests attended the reception wearing a cloth bag on their heads. I'm reasonably confident that I didn't appear to fit the description of a usual guest in a posh, high-end hotel – also, guests didn't get locked in.

Kirk had said they knew more about me than I knew myself. So, when he showed me my full English breakfast all laid out on a hot plate, but they'd not provided any cooked tomatoes as I didn't like them, I guess what he said was true. Whoever they were, they knew at least two things – my name and my dislike for warm, tinned tomatoes.

As I poured myself a coffee from a silver pot, I plucked up two sausages from the hot plate and shoved them in my mouth like having two cigars stuck in either corner. Studying the pot, I made a mental note that once empty to stash it safely. If I was later turfed out of here and returned to my tartan trolly, I thought I could get a few quid for it. I munched on the two sausages as I inspected my surroundings. The thick, squidgy wool carpet and expensive modern furniture appeared new and unused, affording the suite a palatial appearance fit for a queen and not a homeless ageing tramp.

The suite consisted of three rooms. The opulently furnished lounge area, with an ornate mahogany table and chairs, a three-piece Chesterfield-style suite in brown leather which circled a glass coffee table, appeared to offer all the home comforts a man could ever need. What was missing was a TV – all hotel rooms had a TV, didn't they? The archway from the lounge area led through to the bedroom. The centre of the room housed the super-king bed with its plethora of plump pillows and cushions, which appeared incredibly inviting. Like a naughty child, I bounced up and down on the mattress as I tested the springs and deduced it afforded better comfort than the four millimetres of damp cardboard I'd become used to.

Kirk had stated the wardrobe housed a complete set of new clothes for me, so I pulled open the double doors and ran my hand through the selection which were all neatly hung on posh-looking wooden coat hangers. A collection of suits, sports jackets, slacks and shirts drifted across my hand, all high-end quality stuff. As with the collection of shoes, all the clothes appeared to be my size.

The bathroom offered a selection of toiletries that appeared to own posh names. Monogrammed on the fluffy white towels were the letters CYA – not The Dorchester or The Ritz, then. I padded back to the lounge area and plucked up two doorstops of bread, which I slotted a handful of bacon in between. Then, plonking myself on the leather Chesterfield, I studied the one-page document Kirk had shown me just before departing.

Mr Frank Stone.

We appreciate the somewhat irregular approach we have made this morning, but please rest assured we have your best intentions at heart. All will become clear later today.

Enjoy the food and comforts on offer, and rest. Please remove all clothing, place it in the bags provided and leave them by your room door. This suite will be at your disposal for the duration of your stay, so as I said, please make yourself comfortable.

I appreciate you will be full of questions, but I urge patience on your part. You are not in any danger, but we do require your co-operation. A physician will visit you at 2 p.m. today to assess your general health and any medication necessary, plus assign a dietary plan.

I look forward to meeting with you later this afternoon.

Douglas Hartland

CYA Director of Operations.

Okay, not exactly a welcome letter detailing spa treatments and restaurants on offer. Also, Director of Operations, what the hell did that mean? They'd locked me in and, although I'd never stayed in a posh London hotel, I doubted any offered rooms which didn't have at least one window. It appeared they'd secured me in a palatial concrete box.

Was this some clandestine government agency or a weird group of wealthy nutters who planned some heinous event for me to serve as their entertainment? But hey, since losing everything and living on the South Bank, what had I got to lose? Over the last few years, life had become pointless. So, as long as I felt no pain in whatever they had planned, what did it matter?

For sure, no one would miss me. Well, maybe Michael-Kors-pink-trainer lady might be surprised I wasn't in my usual position on Monday morning. However, I doubted that would be anything more than a raised eyebrow and not a genuine concern for my welfare. And what was CYA – perhaps the last word was Association?

I laid my half-eaten bacon-butty on the leather seat next to me, then realised that it might mark the leather – it had been a long time since I had to worry about being house-trained. I snatched up the butty and brushed the crumbs off – ha, perhaps I could re-join the human race.

Shovelling the last of the bread into my beard-covered gob, I headed off to the palatial bathroom. The marble shower with gold fittings oozed luxury and was certainly preferable to the mould-covered facilities I'd last had the pleasure of using up at the Mission. Although, to be fair to Kirk, and why he'd covered his nose when extracting me, I believe it could have been a while since I'd used any washing facilities to perform my ablutions, only popping in the Mission to use the khazi when nature insisted.

After enjoying the delights of the multi-jet shower and wrapped in a fluffy CYA-monogrammed dressing gown, I slipped my hand in the pocket to once again check the roll of cash hadn't disappeared. Then, safe in the knowledge that my new fortune was secure, I slipped under the quilt. As my head hit the squidgy pillow, I disappeared into a deep sleep.

The other odd thing, well let's face it, there were many, was there appeared to be a lack of clocks in any of the rooms. So, when I awoke, I had no idea of the time or how long I'd been asleep. If that's what it was, the welcome letter stated 2:00 p.m. for the physician's assessment. As that person hadn't arrived, I could only assume it was earlier than that.

Shaved and dressed in my new clothes, I ventured back to the lounge area. Whilst I'd slept, it appeared someone had replaced the breakfast offer with a platter of cheese and biscuits, dates and grapes, a bottle of sparkling water and various yoghurts arranged in a dish full of ice cubes. A leather file with a business card on top lay on the coffee table. Typed on the card were two words – *'Read This.'*

Laying a heavy linen napkin across my lap to protect my new slacks, I tucked into my lunch. I glanced down at the crumbs that landed on the napkin as I took my first bite of a cracker with a slice of extra mature cheddar on top – ha, I chuckled. In a few short hours, I'd become re-domesticated.

I settled into reviewing the file. Perhaps this was the spa treatments and gym facilities menu. Maybe I could grab a facial and pedicure. I flipped over the cover of the leather-bound file to discover there were no massage treatments on offer. Instead, the first page displayed a picture of myself, albeit from forty years ago, and I had no recollection of when it was taken. The young Frank appeared happy as he smiled back at me. With his chiselled jaw, blond, almost shoulder-length hair, he had an air of confidence that portrayed a man who had everything.

The file consisted of photographs and text which recorded my life's history as if Eamonn Andrews had presented me with the book after starring in an episode of *This Is Your Life*. However, the book was black, not red, and no guests appeared from behind a screen to celebrate my life's achievements. Although, apart from failing at my business, losing my wife and living on the streets, my achievement list was somewhat lacking.

Those life's achievements, detailed in the folder, were totally accurate in frighteningly good detail. Born on the 30th of March 1949, with a grammar school education, then married Jemma Causton in 1977. I rubbed my hand over the picture of Jemma wearing her fairy-tale, full-length, lace wedding dress – she was stunning. The image taken on our wedding day captured us both as we appeared to have turned and laughed at what one of our guests had said. That moment in time was just as the confetti was thrown, showering the foreground with pink and red petals.

She was truly beautiful, and I'd lost her only two years later. Unfortunately, I'd wasted those years, failing to always show my burning love for her as I should have. We were both busy professionals: Jemma, a junior solicitor and recently elected MP, and me with my own company. We had loved each other, however, our lives were often separated, only making time for each other on Sundays. I never made enough effort to show her how much I loved her. If I had, would she have gone out that evening with Clare? Perhaps we would have spent the evening cuddled up on the sofa, and then my darling wife would never have disappeared.

The folder detailed my working career, my once successful building company, which Paul Wilson and I'd started in 1976, and its ultimate collapse less than ten years later. Stone & Wilson Builders failed for two reasons. Firstly, my drinking and gambling took hold in the early '80s, thus leaving me permanently pissed and incapable of playing my part. Secondly, Paul raped the company's assets, causing the once-thriving company to fall from grace and into bankruptcy. This was the point at which I started my slide from successful businessman to street dweller.

For a few minutes, I studied the photo of my beautiful Jemma as she held up a glass of champagne. The picture showed Jemma as her parents hugged her, with me, Clare, Tobias and a few others huddled close for the shot to be taken. This was when she'd been selected as the parliamentary candidate for the Conservatives in 1979. I successfully mentally attached a name to all the people in the photo apart from one man who stood to the left and, unlike the rest of us, didn't look at all happy as he scowled at Jemma.

A few pages, which included copies of the newspaper reports, were dedicated to when Jemma disappeared and when her body was discovered in a shallow grave in Fairfield Woods ten days later. A picture on the Fairfield Chronicle front page from October 16th 1979, showed me when I attended a press conference flanked by two police officers when appealing for witnesses to Jemma's disappearance. The headline below, although over thirty years ago, still stung—

'Husband, Frank Stone, arrested for our talented MP Jemma Stone's murder — just two weeks after pretending to appeal for her to return.'

Although never convicted, the suspicion hung over me and stuck. I still vividly remember the last interview the police conducted with me before being released after the charges were dropped. DCI Barker, the SIO, had escorted me out of the building, and those words he delivered have stuck in my head forever.

'We know you did it. Someday, somehow, I'll prove it. Keep looking over your shoulder, Frank, because I'll get you.'

But I hadn't done it. I didn't murder my wife, even though the whole world were at the time totally convinced I had. That day was the start of the end of my life. Although it took another twenty years before I ended up a homeless, destitute alcoholic, the day I walked out of the Fairfield police custody suite was the start of the slow descent to living in cardboard city on the streets of London.

8

Iron Maiden

Click.

The sound of the lock turning dragged me out of my daydream as I thumbed through my life history folder. I glanced up as the door handle turned on my palace-like prison cell. An SAS-type chap entered, although I didn't recognise him from this morning's adventures. Closely following in behind him stepped a woman in her thirties, blonde bob-style hair, smartly dressed in a tweed trouser suit and red patent stiletto shoes. Her stunning good looks were destroyed by a perfectly symmetrical downturned mouth that could have modelled for the Frown Emoji.

SAS man closed the door and stood guard. If I was ever unsure that my palatial hotel suite was a prison cell, SAS man confirmed it was as he stood with his back to the door and hands clasped in front of him. He didn't utter a word as he stared straight ahead, like a Grenadier Guard without the red tunic and bearskin hat.

"Mr Stone, I'm Ms Walters." Although her sweet, sugar-sexy voice wafted around me, her cold demeanour was enough to indicate this wasn't going to be a friendly chat.

"Are you the doctor that this Mr Hartland bloke stated would visit?" I asked, pointing to my welcome letter whilst still studying her frowned expression. I could only assume she didn't particularly enjoy her job; either that or she'd just finished sucking a lemon.

"Yes, Mr Stone. I will be assessing your health and dietary needs so we can place you on a programme that will support your recovery. I'm glad to see you've washed and cleaned up." She turned her nose up and sneered at the black collection bag I'd placed by the door as the welcome letter had instructed. Perhaps my sense of smell had left me some years ago. However, it appeared Ms Walters could clearly smell something unpleasant.

She turned to the SAS guy. "Agent Mathews, please arrange for a barber to visit. Mr Stone clearly needs a proper haircut."

Although I'd washed my hair, it hadn't had the attention of a pair of professional barber scissors in over ten years. So, I guess there were some styling issues to address if my head was going to fit with my newly acquired designer clothes.

Ms Walters placed her leather doctor bag on the coffee table. It appeared to be a classic doctor bag you see in an old '50s movie and, as she yanked apart the opening, I wondered if this was the time to become concerned. I was half expecting glistening tools of torture to emerge clasped in her hand. Then Agent Mathews would spring into action, pinning me down whilst this Ms Iron Maiden wielded her instruments of torture. Fortunately, only a stethoscope emerged, and she requested I remove my shirt – it had been many years since I'd had an instruction from a stunning woman to remove my clothing, even from one with a Frown-emoji mouth.

Dr Iron Maiden performed various tests after listening to my crackly chest, which even I could hear, and I wasn't the one wearing the stethoscope. However, I then had to perform a full striptease whilst she inspected the rest of my unkempt, dry, pock-marked frame. My penis retreated into my grey pubic hair in pure embarrassment. I'd hesitated before complying with the strip request, but a raised eyebrow from Agent Mathews was enough to convince me that I complied or I was to be forcibly stripped. Even if I wanted to, with a locked door and a beefy-looking agent on guard, there was no opportunity to *Run to the Hills*. Finally, I was allowed to dress before she pulled my eyelids and tongue in every direction.

"Three times a day, before meals. Complete the course for twenty-one days. Do *not* forget to take your medication," stated the Iron Maiden, as she slapped the packet of pills on the coffee table.

"What are they?"

Dismissing my question with a slight flaring of her nostrils, she continued relating her assessment from her examination. "Your tombstone teeth are a perfect example of chronic gum disease and decay. However, we don't need to concern ourselves with those. I assume you're not in any immediate pain?"

"No."

"Good. Although your breath is vulgar, we'll leave those be then, as they'll regenerate when you travel."

I shot her a questioning look but also noticed Agent Mathews give a slight shake of his head towards her. Presumably, she wasn't supposed to offer the last line of information.

"What d'you mean, regenerate? And travel where?"

Her nostrils flared again before plucking up her leather bag and nodding to Mathews to be let out.

"And what are these pills you've given me? What will they do? Will they cause pain? I've got a high pain threshold, but I want to know what they are?"

Mathews opened the door to let the Iron Maiden out. She turned to face me; her mouth, for the first time, started to climb out of its frown. "Amoxicillin. You have a chest infection, Mr Stone."

"Right." Not pills to cause hallucinating episodes or a pill form of the green liquid serum which would transfer me from Mr Stone to my very own version of Mr Hyde – that said, my appearance over the last few years was more akin to my Mr Hyde side.

"Goodbye, Mr Stone, and good luck." She smiled.

Good luck with what, though?

The Iron Maiden really was stunning when she changed her Emoji face. Also, I thought there was room to improve her bedside manner, but this probably wasn't an appropriate time to suggest that.

Agent Mathews held the door and spoke for the first time. "Mr Stone, an agent will return for you in about an hour or so. It just depends on Mr Hartland's afternoon meetings schedule. So, rest, and one of us shall return soon.

The door closed.

The lock engaged.

Click.

9

Colonel Mustard

Outside of the palatial concrete box which had become my home for a few hours, the corridors and what appeared to be office suites confirmed this was no hotel. I hadn't had to wait long to be collected after Ms Iron Maiden had left and now expected I would be meeting Mr Hartland. What the hell this seemingly well-drilled, clandestine organisation wanted with me, God only knows. However, I hoped it would be better than my street life existence, and surely that wouldn't be difficult.

After exiting what appeared to be a goods lift into a dimly lit corridor in the building's lower levels, the SAS-type chap frogmarched me to a nameless heavy oak-panelled door. My escort had seemed to know which of the thirty-odd numberless chrome lift buttons to push, and I presumed we were on a lower level because of the lift's downward motion. For sure, I wasn't in an average office block or hotel.

When a buzzer sounded and the lock disengaged, my escort left me standing in the corridor. The nameless door opened, revealing a large office which reminded me of my prestigious grammar school headmaster's study.

"Frank, step in, step in," offered a gent who appeared to be of a similar age to myself, although his grooming routine had prevented premature ageing. He displayed an air of aristocracy, accentuated by his sharp double-breasted suit and a deep, formal voice.

Seated behind a modern glass-topped desk that didn't fit into the décor of the oak-panelled walls sat a similar-looking gent dressed in an almost identical suit to the doorman. He sported an aura of seniority, with hooded eyelids which cloaked his piercing grey eyes. He smiled broadly, his teeth slowly revealing like a vampire ready to swoop into action.

"Frank," said the vampire, as he dropped his cigarette in the glass ashtray, jumped up, and offered his right hand. "Douglas Hartland, good to meet you. This is my associate, Keith Morehouse." He gestured to the doorman, who in turn offered his hand.

Pleasantries over, Hartland offered the vacant seat in front of the desk, then retook his whilst Morehouse stood by the obscured glass window – the first window I'd seen in the building.

Hartland studied me with those half-cloaked eyes. "Accommodation, clothes and refreshments have been to your liking?"

"Err ... yes. But who are you? What am I doing here? And where is here?"

"All in good time, all in good time." He flipped over a leather-bound file, plucked up a sheet of paper whilst retrieving his cigarette, then rested back in his chair. "Doctor Walters states you have a chest infection. Also, your muscle tone is below what is required, but all other health issues aren't of an urgent concern. Rather remarkable, considering your lifestyle." He turned to Morehouse. "That's a stroke of luck … and should reduce preparation time."

"Err … excuse me, but are you going to tell me what's going on?"

"Of course, Frank, of course." Hartland leant across the desk and lit another cigarette before offering one to me, which I enthusiastically grabbed hold of. It had been a long time since I'd had a whole cigarette and not a half-smoked crushed one I'd foraged from the pavement.

"Well?" I asked, after coughing loudly and clearing my chest – an action I'd performed for years. Unfortunately, I'd probably had a chest infection for that length of time.

"Last cigarette for you, Frank, I'm afraid," he responded, as he took back the heavy paperweight desk lighter.

I glanced at my cigarette and then back into his grey eyes. So, this was it; a condemned man. My last cigarette, and then I suspected I'd be offered a last meal before my hideous end.

Did it matter?

"Frank, don't look so worried. Last cigarette because we need to clear your chest infection. We have to get your health in tip-top condition."

"For what?" I asked, as I worriedly glanced at Morehouse and then back at Hartland. "For God's sake, is someone going to tell me what's going on?"

"Frank, I'm the Senior Committee Director of an organisation which seeks to correct certain situations which need correcting."

"What, government agency stuff, like MI6?"

"No. We don't work for the Government. In the next hour, you're going to make an important, potentially life-changing decision. If you decide our offer is not for you, we'll deposit you back where you came from. Although, old chap, it will be without the roll of notes which are secured in your pocket that you seem to keep tapping. We have your old clothes, so you'll have them back if you choose not to take us up on our wonderful offer. If you tried to tell anyone where you've been, no one would believe you. We're a secret organisation. No one knows we exist or who we are."

"I was told if I came here, I could keep the cash."

Hartland grinned, allowing the smoke to drift from his mouth as he spoke. "You can, Frank, as long as you stay."

"Bastards! You cheating bastards."

"Frank, listen to my offer before you cast your views." He leant forward again. "We need your wife, Jemma Stone, to continue her career and attain the position in Government which she was supposed to ascend to." He pointed at me. "You, Frank, are going to help us achieve that."

"Well, you're thirty-odd years too late because she's dead. And judging by the information you have on me, you already know that!"

Hartland took one last drag of his cigarette and stubbed it out in the glass ashtray. "We do, Frank. However, in the summer of 1979, she was very much alive."

"Yes, but, as I said, that was bloody years ago. Nothing I can do about that now!" I retorted, shaking my head.

"But there is in 1979, my good man. We want you to return and stop her death. That's assuming you didn't kill her in the first place, which our research suggests you didn't. You didn't kill her, did you?"

"What the bollocks are you talking about? Go where? And no, I didn't kill my wife!"

"Good! So, you have an opportunity to ensure whoever did … doesn't."

"Err … is this some joke? Look, let me keep the cash, please. I'll say nothing. Please, can I go?"

I'd clearly dropped into some super-rich nut-club for bored aristocrats who were playing some kind of real-life who-done-it game of Cluedo. Was this Hartland bloke Colonel Mustard? Although Morehouse didn't look like Reverend Green, too much hair and no dog collar. Certainly, when the Iron Maiden smiled, she was good looking enough to play Miss Scarlet. Did they think my wife was the murder victim instead of Dr Black? Strangled with the rope in the study and not in Fairfield Woods.

"Frank, we'd like to send you back to 1979. You'll have the chance to relive your life; correct every mistake. You get to have another go and, most importantly, stop the murder of your wife."

Yep, nut jobs. Oh well, I'd had a great sleep in a proper bed, two good meals, a lovely hot shower and a packet of pills to stop me hacking up green lumps every day. Now, I'd need to secure some new bedding, as I suspect some bastard would have nicked my tartan trolley by now. I huffed and leant back in my seat, once again tapping the roll of notes in my pocket.

"Okay, so you bunch of nutters all holed up in this secret club, reckon you're going to ping me off back to 1979 through some rabbit hole or a time machine that you all knocked together with a few bits of scrap you found in your garden sheds. For God's sake, why does it always happen to me? I lose everything; I end up homeless and destitute for the best part of ten years, and now I'm 'rescued' by Professor Frink!" I performed the bunny ears motion on the word rescued whilst rolling my eyes. Hartland and Morehouse nodded and smiled at each other but offered no reply.

Leaning forward, I pointed at Colonel Mustard or whatever this nutter's name was. "Anyway, I might be a bit of a down-and-out, but I think there are laws against kidnapping. You turf me out without this cash ... I'll work out where this place is, you know. We were in that van for only a few minutes from Queen's Walk. This might surprise you as you sit in this palatial concrete box, but living on the streets does provide a fair bit of free time. It's not as if I have appointments to attend or lunch dates at the country club. So yes, loads of time to hunt you nutters down!" I ranted, then pointed at Morehouse and back to Hartland, who both hadn't moved a muscle as they continued to smirk at me.

"Oh, bollocks to this!" I snatched up the cigarettes and lighter off the glass table.

Hartland waved his hand. "Fair enough, Frank ... but that *is* your last cigarette until your chest is better."

"So, can I go ... with my cash you promised?" I questioned through a few chesty coughs.

Hartland steepled his hands and continued with his bullshit. "Frank, let me tell you about our organisation and what we actually do here. Let's give you a sense of proportion and the opportunities we have on offer for you."

"Bollocks to your opportunities. I don't want any of your Frankenstein experiments on me, thank you!"

Hartland moved around the table and perched on its edge, now peering down at me. "Well, Frank, at this point in time, apart from sticking your fingers in your ears, you're going to have to listen. No choice, old chap." He turned and smiled at Morehouse.

"It's the usual reaction, sir ... almost look forward to the day a candidate can't wait to leap back in time."

"Yes, that will be quite refreshing," chuckled Hartland.

Clearly, I was going nowhere. Even if I could escape from the Chuckle Brothers, I'm sure there were a few of those SAS types milling about, ready to pounce. Perhaps Hartland was Baron Bomburst, and this was Vulgaria. If I escaped, would the sinister Child Catcher snatch me up? I guess there would be no Caractacus Potts and Truly Scrumptious swooping down in their flying car to save me.

"Go on then, have your fun ... I'm all ears. I'm ready to hear your fantasies," I replied, shaking my head whilst enjoying my second full-length cigarette which wasn't pre-smoked.

"Good man," replied Hartland.

"Frank, I'm a senior member of the Correction Years Association, and Morehouse here is our Data and Technical Services Director." Keith offered a wave as I glanced over towards him. CYA, that explained the monogrammed fluffy towels. Not The Crooked Yuppie Association, as I'd assumed.

Hartland moved around his desk and re-took his seat, swiftly lighting up another cigarette before continuing. Clearly, the smoking ban in buildings didn't apply here. "Frank, our organisation has operated for over half a century. I can quite confidently advise you, without us, the human race would probably be wiped out by now."

Oh, for God's sake! How long was I going to have to listen to this shite for?

"Without going into technical details, we're able to accurately predict future events which will not be favourable for our country or the human race. What we also have the ability to calculate is at which points time can be successfully altered to avoid the said event. That also provides us with the data on *who* can change that event."

"Yeah, right!"

For Christ's sake, they really were off their heads. I glanced at the door, momentarily wondering if I could make a dash for it. Although instantly realising that was pointless.

"Understandably, Frank, this will seem all fantasy stuff, but hear me out. We've learned over the years that changing a relatively small event which doesn't change too much else has delivered a higher success rate in averting or altering the catastrophic event that we predict will happen." He held my stare and paused for effect. "What we can predict, and as I said with some accuracy, is *when* and *who* will cause that change without significant disruption."

Christ almighty, he was as bat-shit nuts as old Marge, who camped down by Waterloo Station. I didn't actually know her name, but she was known as Marge as she repeatedly spouted out to the world that she was Marge Simpson, as she sat and rocked back and forth on an old piece of carpet calling out to her imaginary husband, Homer. To be fair, like Marge Simpson, she did have that honeyed gravel voice and yellow skin. Although I think those conditions were caused by smoking and a touch of jaundice, judging by the copious amounts of cheap sherry she swallowed each day.

Hartland bashed on with his ridiculous story. "So, Frank, as I said, we intend to pop you back into your former self in the summer of 1979. Lovely opportunity for you. India tour that year, and you could nip along to Lords and watch the cricket."

"Bob Willis, Ian Botham, and David Gower, what a treat that would be … I'd love that opportunity," threw in Morehouse from where he stood in the slips.

Hartland glanced over to Morehouse, pointing his cigarette at him as he leaned back in his chair. "Bob Willis; now they don't make bowlers like him anymore," he chuckled.

"Err … for Christ's sake! You're sending me back to watch a bloody cricket match? What the bollocks are you two talking about?"

Hartland's smile evaporated as he turned back to glare at me. In an instant, the atmosphere had changed. A shiver sprinted up my body, causing my hair follicles to tingle. This Hartland bloke either suffered from bipolar or was some kind of psychopath who could instantly change his demeanour.

"Frank, I'm not pissing about. You're going back to 1979." His finger seemed to pin me to my seat as he jabbed the air in my direction. "This isn't some ruddy joke, and you *are* going to have to change your attitude. This is an extremely serious situation, and we are running out of time! If you don't make the journey successfully, we've lost valuable months of preparation. So, start listening, and realise this is real … very real!"

"What d'you mean, don't make the journey?" I thought I'd play along with him as he seemed to have become quite unpleasant, and feigning Stockholm Syndrome might afford me an escape route. Otherwise, chest infection aside, I had a feeling I'd had my last cigarette.

Hartland sat back and nodded to Morehouse, who took up the story. "I'm afraid we do have a small percentage of casualties on these journeys. We have improved significantly over the last fifteen years, but alas, some of our older, less healthy travellers struggle to get through."

"What? So, if I don't get through, I just stay here, and you let me go?"

"Frank, we like to be straight with our travellers. The sad fact of the matter is, if you fail to get through, I'm afraid you just disappear … we haven't worked out where to yet, but we've never discovered a lost traveller so far."

"I … I'll just disappear? What, like evaporate?" I now felt a mixture of concern and trepidation about what they had planned – obviously, I wasn't going to travel in time – but this was the first indication that after they'd had their upper-class-toffee-nosed-sick fun with me, I wasn't going to see the outside world again.

10

Swingers' Party

Morehouse moved from his position as third man in the slips, taking up wicket-keeper position behind me, where he pulled down a projector screen. As I swivelled around, he clicked on the projector which displayed a very familiar image on the screen. However, as they still used projectors and slides, I very much doubted they had the technology to perform time-travel.

"Frank, a familiar landmark, I suggest?"

"Yep, it's the last thing I see before closing my eyes and usually the first thing I see in the morning." Now, with my back to the vampire, I could feel his hooded eyes burning into the back of my head.

"Quite." Morehouse picked up a long wooden pointer and tapped the screen. "The Cantilever Ferris Wheel, more commonly known as the London Eye, or if you prefer, the Millennium Eye. It sits in a specific area which holds a wormhole that provides opportunity to move through time."

"Ha, yeah. Course it does."

Morehouse shot me a disapproving look as I dismissively shook my head, then returned to look at the projected picture.

"The wormhole moves around this area in the space of about one acre. However, the centrifugal force of the wheel holds it in place. This provides us with a marked improvement in our performance from when we had to use the Skylon, which was positioned where Jubilee Park now stands. Prior to the wheel's construction, locating the wormhole was extremely hit-and-miss. Thus, the survival rate was … well, at best, poor. Now, with the Wheel in place, our organisation is able to ramp up our missions." Still holding the pointer to the screen, he turned to check my attentiveness. I nodded, not knowing what else to do, as I clearly had no option but to play along with these nut-jobs for the moment.

"You'll travel in pod thirteen at 1:00 a.m., approximately six weeks from today. The wheel rotates at nought point six miles per hour. However, for your journey, we'll increase that to one mile per hour as we find that is the optimum speed to hold the wormhole in place, thus ensuring you safely make it through." He turned and smiled. "Any questions, Frank, or is it all reasonably straightforward?"

"Oh yeah, clear as day! So, I hop on the ride and disappear back to my old life. What's not to understand?" I raised my hands, leaned back in my chair and looked at the ceiling. "Beam me up, Scotty!"

"I know, Frank, it's a lot to take in. However, you'll see when your time comes what we propose is actually doable. Not everything in this world is always as it seems, and we require you to have an open mind, my friend."

"Yeah, okay … but what happens to all those selfie-obsessed millions who ride on the Wheel every day? I don't see them disappearing and landing back in time. Come on; this joke has gone far enough."

"Those tourists don't travel in pod thirteen. If they did, we would have a problem!" he chuckled.

"Well, there's never an empty pod. So how do you ensure that one doesn't get used?" Why I was still playing along with this stupid game, God knows. But I guess I didn't really have any choice. I glanced at the door, thinking about an escape plan.

Hartland moved from his desk and stood next to Morehouse whilst pointing at the door. "Frank, you can keep glancing at the door, but I can assure you, old chap, it's not going to open for you. As I said, when we've finished our discussion, you make your decision. At that point, you either stay with us and have the opportunity of a lifetime or, if you wish, we deposit you back to where you came from."

"Minus the cash?"

"Correct. Minus the cash. See Frank; you catch on quick!" He grinned.

"If you want me to listen to this shit, I'm going to have to have your cigarettes."

"Help yourself, but if you stay with us ... no more after we leave this room because we need to get your health in tip-top condition."

Lighting up and savouring my third full-length cigarette, I slumped back in my seat and waited for the lecture to continue. Morehouse moved away to stand in his favoured position in the slips next to the window. The low autumn sun streamed through the frosted glass, highlighting the haze of cigarette smoke that Colonel Mustard and I added to with every puff.

Colonel Mustard took up the lecture. "Pod thirteen doesn't actually exist, well, not to the rest of the world. There are thirty-two pods, numbered one to thirty-three. London has a long history of triskaidekaphobia, and at the time of construction, we enhanced that concern to ensure pod thirteen was available for our use only. Incidentally, the thirty-two pods represent the thirty-two boroughs of London. Anyway, that aside, you'll travel in our pod and arrive back on the 17th of August 1979."

"So, you reckon I land back then ... but where exactly? Because that wheel doesn't exist then," I questioned, now deciding to play along because clearly, there was no escape at this point. I was enjoying his cigarettes and, for as long as I could, I wanted to keep hold of the roll of notes secured in my pocket.

"No, no, Frank. You'll arrive back as yourself on that day, wherever you were at that point in time. As we send you back at 1:00 a.m., most travellers arrive back when asleep in their beds." He pointed at Morehouse and clicked his fingers, clearly trying to remember something. "Morehouse, what was the name of that woman we sent back about ten years ago? You know, the swingers' party incident?"

Now, this was getting more interesting.

"Gloria," Morehouse replied, eyes wide with a smirk.

"Oh yes, ha, young Gloria. That was a funny one, Frank, I can tell you. Gloria returned to 1959 and found herself in bed with two other young women and two men servicing her from every angle, if you know what I mean ... nudge nudge, wink wink!" he grinned after taking a long drag on his cigarette.

"Hell of a shock. Although she said it was the best orgasm she'd ever had!" chuckled Morehouse.

Hartland continued grinning as if he was hiding behind the school bike sheds thumbing through a copy of Playboy magazine, something I remember doing with my mates back in my school days.

"So, yes, you arrive at that precise time, doing whatever you were doing on that day. You'll only know you've travelled when someone says your name. What I mean by this; you'll arrive back, and you'll have no knowledge of your future until you hear someone say your name. At the point that you hear your name, your future memories will be instantly remembered. Think of it like plugging in a hard drive, with all the data from that timeline to when you travelled reformulating in your brain. Fortunately for young Gloria, one of the excited men on top of her reached a climax and blurted out her name. The lucky girl had the experience of time travel and a rip-roaring orgasm at the same time."

"Well, disappointingly for me, I can only recall being in bed with one woman at any one time. So, I guess the chances of landing back in some sex party I've forgotten are slim to zero. Though I do seem to remember a particularly raunchy party in a girl's dorm at Uni in '69 … now that's an experience I wouldn't mind reliving."

"Never mind. The really wonderful thing is you'll have your thirty-year-old body back. I suggest that will be enough excitement." He gestured to my rather run-down, dishevelled frame, which hadn't fared well on the streets over the last decade.

"Now, Frank, there are some clear rules of engagement that we need to take you through." Morehouse moved over to the projector and pushed the button, which flipped along the carousel to the next slide. Two images of elderly gents, somewhere, I guess, in their seventies, appeared on the screen. "These two gentlemen, whose names will remain undisclosed, are gagging to return to 1979. They work for us but will only travel if required."

"Oh, what's that requirement?" I wondered who the two ancient-looking guys were, who both appeared to be in a sorrier state than I did.

"If you step out of line and start altering history in a way that will cause attention to be brought upon you, one of these gents will travel back. Their mission will be to terminate you."

"Them old gits? Even I could handle myself against them!"

"Highly unlikely, old chap. Both men in 1979 were ex-special forces and trained mercenaries. They have both killed hundreds of times and will make you disappear with ease. As I said, both are gagging that you cock-up so they can grab a chance to travel, even though they know being in their seventies travel comes with its risks."

"When you say cock-up. What exactly d'you mean?"

"Well, there's lots of examples ... but let's say if you brought unnecessary attention to yourself. Anything from saying you're a time-traveller, although that will probably result with you ending up in the funny farm—"

"I'm already there, I think!"

Hartland's demeanour once again became dark at my outburst, causing his boyish grin he'd sported earlier to vanish, revealing that dark, menacing vampirical look once again. I thought this was a good time to grab another cigarette and shut up.

"As I was saying, Frank, anything that alerts attention. Another example is betting. Let's say you start placing bets on sporting events and amass a fortune which could place you in the public eye." He turned and pointed to the two gents on the projected screen. "At that point, one of these will get his chance to travel, and the consequences for you are dire."

"Well, you're safe on that front, as my memory ain't so good. I can't remember any events back then."

"Frank, as you are discovering, we know everything about you. We know your dislike of tinned tomatoes, and we also know back in your younger years you were quite an authority on boxing. So, Sugar Ray Leonard had his first title fight when?"

"Alright, you got me. Yes, I know."

"Well, when?"

"November 1979. He flattened Benítez with only seconds to go in the fifteenth round."

Hartland nodded. "Your memory is not so slack as you suggest. So, start making ridiculous bets that only a time-traveller or psychic could know, and one of our friends here will get his opportunity."

"Yes, well, this is all immaterial because we both know this conversation is pointless. Whatever nut-job, crazy game you're playing, it's not time-travel planning. So, whether I know the ins and outs of boxing history through the latter half of the last century, it really doesn't matter, does it?"

I'd had enough now. Perhaps it was time to go, even if I would lose that lovely roll of cash. Michael-Kors-pink-trainer lady would deposit two pounds in my paper cup in the morning. Although not a fraction of the content of my pocket, at least it was real.

Morehouse stepped over to the projector and clicked the button. The whirring carousel flipped around, which commenced an automated sequence that displayed a new image every few seconds. I stared at the screen and pictures I hadn't seen for many a year. Jemma Stone beamed that gorgeous smile back at me in every shot. Some from our wedding day, beach holidays, and the odd one at Christmas with both of us wearing paper hats and kissing under the mistletoe that hung from multicoloured paper chains.

The room became hush quiet. Hartland and I smoked whilst watching the picture show, and Morehouse moved back to his favoured position of third-slip. Tears poured – something that hadn't happened for as long as my memory was prepared to go back to. Jemma Stone was the most wonderful person ever to be born. Intelligent, sexy, fun, caring, loving, and most importantly – she was mine. I'd taken her for granted and then lost her along with everything else.

It wasn't fair that they were playing with my emotions. Of course, I'd give anything to go back and be with her, but I had nothing to give. Also, unfortunately for me, it wasn't going to happen.

Hartland broke the silence. "You'd give anything to be back with her?"

I nodded and stared down into my lap as I thought about what could have been if I had just made more effort. Would Jemma have been with me that night? Could I have picked her up instead of leaving her to get a taxi? Those thoughts had terrorised my mind – every day – for over thirty painful years.

"You're thinking you have nothing to give, and it's not going to happen, aren't you?"

I shot him a look through watery eyes. Christ, they could read my mind as well.

"Frank, you have nothing to lose ... nothing. Stay with us, and you might have everything to gain. The worst that can happen is you're right, and we're nutters. If that were to be the case, and it's not ... then it's back to the streets. Nothing lost."

"Well, he could be vaporised when he travels. That could be classed as worse," stated Morehouse, with a chuckle from third-slip.

"Ha, yes, he could! Good point, Morehouse. Although, even that's got to be better than back to cardboard city!"

11

Darth Vader

Morehouse left the room, replaced by a woman in her forties, who I only afforded a cursory glance as she entered. My mind had drifted and now was consumed by my thoughts, memories and plethora of regrets. Life on the streets had, over the years, sanitised my mind. Although every day the memory of Jemma and my previous life came back to me, I was strong-willed enough to push it back into my mind's do-not-open memory-box and sit on the lid – preventing it from escaping again – until the next day.

The reasons rough sleepers have for ending up on the streets are as varied as the people themselves. However, the one thing we have in common is we are lost, having come last in the game of life. There is a fact which most fortunate people don't consider – no one was born to sleep rough. Whatever start in life we have, a series of events can very quickly lead to life in cardboard city, as Hartland called it.

What was certain, whoever these crazy mad people were, and whatever their real motivation was for delivering this elaborate charade, they had no idea how tough it was to be homeless without hope and not really caring when you fell asleep if you ever woke again. I knew it so well, and after making a few wrong turns in life, that's where I ended up.

"Frank, let me introduce you to Penelope Blatchford. She heads up our Preparation and Travel Team. They're going to be looking after you for the next few weeks to get you back into tip-top condition," said Hartland from somewhere behind me.

I peered up from my lap, where I had been staring for a few minutes, no longer able to look at the projected pictures. The tears had stopped, but my cheeks were still damp. Penelope stood in front of the projector, which had ended its sequence on a photo of Jemma that I believe was her official House of Commons portrait. Penelope's standing position replaced Jemma's head, and the attractive lady in front of me could be my Jemma in her forties if she'd had the chance to achieve that age.

"Hello, Frank. As Douglas said, I'm Penelope. My team are going to take right good care of you," she said, as she struck out her hand, offering her greeting with a friendly, albeit efficient smile.

I didn't offer my hand to shake. I know that was rude, but come on, this was ridiculous. "You another one of these nutters who think you're characters from an H.G. Wells novel?" I offered, as I glanced past her to take another look at my beautiful lost wife, who continued to smile back at me.

Penelope raised an eyebrow as she glanced behind me, presumably at Hartland.

"Penelope, don't worry. Frank's having a tough time getting to grips with this. But he'll be fine. Isn't that so, Frank?"

I swivelled around and stared at Hartland, who had lit another cigarette. The man was nailed on for every cancer that was known to man. "Not sure I have much choice, really. Unless you let me go with this cash."

Hartland smirked and slowly took another long drag on his cigarette. "No, Frank, that's not going to happen."

"Wanker," I muttered. "Anyway, you reckon you've been sending people back in time for decades to sort out history when things haven't quite gone to plan. Well, you and your cronies are doing a pretty shite job. I can think of quite a few issues that needed stopping since the Second World War, and you ain't done that ... have you?"

Hartland swivelled from side to side in his chair, finishing his cigarette with one last drag. "It's not an exact science, I'm afraid. However, you're quite right, and I take your point. We've had many failures in the past, but many, many more successes." He leant forward and pointed, his demeanour changing in that instant. *'Psychopathic nutter.'*

"1979, on the day of the Trooping the Colour, a terrorist organisation assassinated the Queen and Duke of Edinburgh."

"Bollocks, did they!"

"I'm afraid they did. It took us twelve years back in the '50s, through to the early '60s to find a *Correction Target* who could successfully change that history. Fortunately, Connor Hanrahan was successful and, in 1939, he changed an event that altered history. That minor change was enough to stop our Monarch and her Consort from losing their life and, ultimately, the break-up of the Union which led to the forming of a republic state. Unfortunately, that change did cause a shift in time, and the terrorist who would have killed our Queen went on to murder Lord Mountbatten.

However, here at the CYA, on many occasions, we have to accept the lesser of two evils."

"Huh," I responded to his fantastic story whilst shaking my head in disbelief that this seemingly intelligent man was capable of trotting out such bollocks.

Well, I'll give them something – they had one hell of an imagination, if nothing else. This CYA should be writing Sci-fi books; that's one thing they might be good at.

"Bollocks! Total bollocks."

Hartland leant back in his chair again and smiled, his more amenable side returning. "Not bollocks, Frank ... fact."

"Okay, so what pile of shite do you reckon stopping my wife from dying will achieve? Can't *wait* to hear this ... what, World War Three? Or some intergalactic Star Wars, where Darth Vader becomes President of the United States? No, hang on, I know ... she's going to stop man-eating aliens who eat us all up and turn Earth into a wasteland desert ... that's it, isn't it?"

What started as a low chuckle from Hartland formed into a roaring laugh, which started Penelope off and, in turn, me. For at least a minute, the three of us all laughed as if the comic of the day entertained us at the London Palladium. Then, as Hartland abruptly stopped, so did Penelope and I.

Still grinning, he once again leant forward. "Thankfully, Frank, none of our intelligence suggests Darth Vader will become President of the United States. However, with some certainty, we can suggest that Cameron and his rabble will announce a UK referendum on the UK's continued membership of the European Union. It will be a straight stay or leave vote. In June next year, the UK will narrowly vote to leave the European Union."

"Bloody good job! Sounds like a plan to me. I can't see the downside to that!"

"To be honest with you, neither can I." He shifted forward in his seat as if preparing to divulge a piece of secret information, thus feeling the need to hush his voice. "Trouble is, leaving the good old EU leads to what we call the *European Fault*."

"Oh?" He really was deluded and, concerningly for me, probably quite dangerous.

"Yes. Oh, indeed!"

"What has this got to do with Jemma? I can't see anything that could link her to a referendum nearly forty years after her death. And just to remind you that my wife is very dead!"

"Well, our data strongly suggests that Jemma rose up the greasy pole of politics, and her pro-European views had a profound effect on the Conservative Party. This change resulted in the ERG – European Research Group – having a much smaller impact on right-wing politics."

"Yeah, okay, whatever, and?"

"And, my dear fellow, because of her influence, Cameron and his rabble never feel the need to call a referendum. Thus, my friend, avoiding the *European Fault* in the '20s."

"Oh, right. All James Bond secret agent stuff, then?"

"Well, not quite, Frank, but good that you see the issue."

Christ, he was a fucking fruit-loop. And he actually thought I was being sucked into his stupid game. Somehow, I needed to find a way out of here. Otherwise, I would end up in a padded cell when this delusional-bat-shit-crazy organisation fried my brain.

Perhaps they were some kind of cult? Had I fallen into some wacko organisation similar to Wako, and Hartland was their version of David Koresh? Why couldn't some sex-mad swingers' organisation have kidnapped me instead of this bunch of nutters? Well, come on, I'd not seen any action for years, and unlikely to now. Come to think of it, the Iron Maiden and sexy Penelope weren't half bad.

Oh, Christ, that's it! I was already falling into a delusional state. I'd only been here a few hours, and already they'd probably drugged my food, now causing me to suffer from wild hallucinations. Was this all in my mind? Was I on some drug-induced trip?

"What issue? Sorry, Hartland, or whatever your real name is. I don't see the issue. And quite frankly, I think you're all barking mad. Anyway, what's this *European Fault* thingy you keep on about?"

"Frank, my friend. There is nothing mad about us. The *European Fault,* which must be avoided at all costs, is the direct result of the UK leaving the European Union. That will be the catalyst which leads to—"

"Douglas!" called out sexy Penelope from behind me.

Hartland abruptly closed his mouth, glanced up and nodded at her. "Frank, that's probably too sensitive information to divulge at this time. Right, Frank, it's decision time." He raised his eyebrows, taking another cigarette out of the packet and offering them to me.

"Do I have a choice? I mean, I'm locked in here." I nodded to the door as I retrieved his lighter from the glass-topped desk.

"Yes, Frank, you have a choice. We are a serious organisation who take our ethical code of conduct extremely seriously. As I've stated all along, you can go back to your old life and that will be that. However, as I said, what have you got to lose, man?"

I pulled out the roll of notes and stood them on their end on the table. "There's ten grand here. If I was never going to keep this cash, why offer me such a large amount in the first place? I'd have probably come with your goons for a tenner."

Hartland glanced at the cash, probably concerned my answer was going to be no. "To do what we do, it takes a serious investment. We're funded primarily by the Board, and money is no object. That cash is just slush fund … you see, some travellers require a little more persuading to come with our agents when we extract them."

I nodded and looked at the cash I had unrolled and carefully counted earlier. Although they were all clearly deluded, there was serious money in this place and I hoped some integrity. At sixty-six, the wrong turns I'd made had probably sent my life too far down the wrong alley to be able to reverse back up and start again. However, that cash could be put to good use.

"Hartland, I will stay with you and see how this pans out. Although, don't for one minute think I have started to believe you."

A broad smile erupted across his face, and his hooked eyelid softened. "You will, Frank … you will."

"There are two conditions if I'm going to stay. You've talked about integrity, so this is your opportunity to put your money where your mouth is." I stubbed out my cigarette, picked up the roll of cash and pointed it at him.

"Go on."

"Firstly, a homeless old girl who you'll find near Waterloo Station has some serious health issues, and I don't think she's going to make it through this winter. So, your lot help her off the streets and put her in a private clinic where she can recover. You can't miss her, as she thinks she's Marge Simpson and, apart from not having a blue hair-do, she looks and sounds like her."

Hartland nodded.

"Secondly." I banged the cash on the glass top. "Denzel Warlow. Black guy in his late thirties, although he looks older. Wears a green beanie hat and blue Parker with a fur collar. He spends every night on Queen's Walk, near where you found me. During the day he tends to hang around the station area or further round near the Aquarium. He's not been on the streets for long, and life has really shit on him. Denzel Warlow just needs a helping hand." I waved the money in front of him. "This roll of cash ... one of your agents drops it in his hand and tells him it's a gift from grumpy old Frank."

Hartland nodded and smiled at sexy Penelope, who must still have been standing behind me. "Yes, Frank. You have my word those two actions will take place. I will personally guarantee it."

"I can trust you?"

"Yes, Frank, you can."

"What's the stupid grin for, then?"

"My stupid grin, as you put it, is what you've said is proof you're the right man. You're prepared to take a leap of faith, but your immediate concern is for others. That proves to me that our intelligence-gathering teams have got it right. Frank Stone, you're a good, honourable man ... and for that, we're going to give you your old life back."

12

The Thirty-Nine Steps

After the meeting, I left Penelope Pitstop and Hartland, The Hooded Claw, and was escorted by the usual detail in a black jumpsuit back to my room. Although I'd been upgraded from the Reception Suite to an apartment of similar opulence – apparently, I was now in the Preparation Suite. Key differences were windows, a rooftop terrace adorned with a spa, and various shaped box hedges in flashy looking pots strategically placed to soften the edges of the rattan furniture.

The main lounge area had an offensively large TV, which I spent the evening gorging on the millions of channels on offer. Years had passed since I was able to sit and watch TV, something millions of Britons took for granted. But for me, this was a real treat.

Over the years I'd often peaked through some office windows at the TV screens in their receptions, reading the news feed and lip reading the newsreaders as the news programmes played continuously on a loop. Usually, I would have a few minutes before some burly looking guard would encourage me to move on. Mostly, their encouragement was verbal, but some didn't bother opening their mouths as they physically threw me down the street. I guess an elderly tramp-like character with his face squashed against the glass of some corporate reception window didn't fit into their global image.

Although cold, the rooftop terrace afforded me my only escape to fresh air and stunning views across the capital. Straight ahead was the giant London Eye, with the low autumn sun glistening off the glass pods as the wheel, slowly, ever so slowly, turned. Could they really put me in a pod that didn't exist and send me back to 1979?

~

The weeks passed, and I fell into a routine involving a couple of Penelope Pitstop's employees visiting me every day. I formed a friendship with Shaidun, my personal trainer. However, I was careful not to fall on the wrong side of him because he could have probably flicked me off the roof with his little finger. My assigned nurse, Precious, a robust lady with a tray-of-beer chest, didn't suffer fools or stand for any messing about but checked me over once daily. Along with Shaidun, they ensured my health steadily improved.

By far, the best part was the food. Never in my life had I enjoyed such wonderful culinary delights. Also, every other day, I was provided with a couple of bottles of beer to enjoy whilst watching TV.

Every three or four days, I would have an hour-long meeting with Penelope Pitstop to assess my progress. These were the only three humans I interacted with for just short of six weeks. However, I wasn't as lonely as you might imagine.

For the last ten years, I'd been in close company with millions of Londoners. Every day, they bustled past me, rushing to get somewhere. No one ever spoke to me – no one ever acknowledged me – *that* was real loneliness.

Having Shaidun and Precious to chat to was a cherished gift of conversation, which I desperately didn't want to lose. However, the conversations always dried up when I questioned where the hell I was or what would happen to me. After a couple of weeks, in fear of being dumped back on the streets with millions of faceless commuters, I stopped asking.

I guess it's not surprising, but living on the streets undoubtedly changed my personality. Back in my twenties, I was a popular bloke with lots of mates and never struggled to chat up girls which many blokes do. I remember spotting Jemma in the Bell Pub in the town centre of Fairfield, where we'd both lived. It was the summer of 1976, a boiling hot evening, and I was out with my new business partner, Paul. We were on the *pull,* as most people were who visited the Bell on a Saturday night.

Paul had nudged me and nodded to two women standing about twenty feet away. Most of the blokes at that end of the bar were doing the same thing, ogling these two women who were nothing short of stunning. Both had long Farrah Fawcett style hair. Jemma caught my eye, and I recall thinking she looked like Lindsay Wagner from the Six Million Dollar Man – she was definitely my bionic woman.

I'd recognised her from the Cricket Club where her father was the Chairman, but I'd never asked her on a date because I thought she had a boyfriend. So, with no apparent boyfriend around and a few pints of Dutch courage inside me, I made my move. Embarrassingly, whilst humming the synthesised music, I impersonated the Bionic Man by exaggerating my steps as if in slow motion.

I expect every bloke in the bar thought I looked like a right dick. Fair enough, I probably did. On the other hand, I guess they fully expected the two untouchable-out-of-our-league-girls to give me short-sharp shrift and rebuke my silly advance.

However, as I performed my silly moves, Jemma burst out laughing, and I knew I had to get her to go out with me – totally stunning.

"Hi, you must be Jaime Sommers. I'm Steve Austin." My cheesy opening line delivered, I kissed her cheek whilst every guy in the bar burned green with envy. Somehow, this wonderful girl thought I was funny and not a total tosser.

Paul tried to chat up her friend, Clare. However, as she was Champions League status, the Barcelona of gorgeous women, and Paul was non-league Hartlepool, he stood no chance. No offence to that northeast town where my grandfather was born, and where as a child I spent many a happy summer, but the football team were shite. Clare dealt with Paul's advances efficiently and swiftly.

See, here's the thing, and ladies, I ask your forgiveness as this sixty-six-year-old man, whose life ain't been too great, reminisces about his lost love. Most genuinely gorgeous women don't know they're gorgeous – that's what makes them gorgeous. I know Jemma and Clare used to wonder why blokes wouldn't ask them out, but as I pointed out to her, blokes' minds work differently – it's just nature. Most blokes who see a Jemma or a Clare think, 'out of my league,' which is a very sexist attitude. Jemma just wanted what most people desired – to be loved, feel secure, and happiness – not some suntanned Greek Adonis. I was definitely not that, nor was I Steve Austin, but my awful chat-up line worked.

~

By late November, as the days grew colder and the nights pulled in, I'd made significant progress. I actually enjoyed using the exercise equipment in my personal gym. Shaidun stated he was impressed with my improved muscle tone and general fitness level. Although he disapproved, he did sneak in some contraband cigarettes for me. However, as I started to feel better and no longer coughed for hours in the morning, I did enjoy a cheeky fag in the evenings with a nice cold beer whilst sitting on my roof terrace. Precious softened around the edges, was happy with my general health, and Pitstop stated I was nearly ready for travel.

'Can we rebuild him? We have the technology.' Well, yes, I could be considered *Bionic* compared to my rather shabby physique of six weeks ago.

Pitstop's assessment concerned me because I'd become comfortable in my new life. However, I'd always known it wasn't real and would end somehow – whether I would be used for some medical experiment or some other Dick Dastardly deed they had planned. Still, for sure, I wasn't going to whiz around a giant Ferris wheel and see my Jemma again. No, as much as I daydreamed about seeing her, I knew in reality when I left this new home, it would be for the worse, not better.

The first time I left the Preparation Suite was for another meeting with Hartland – The Hooded Claw.

"Well, Frank, what a transformation! You look fantastic, almost as fit and healthy as me." Although Hartland was, I guess, in his early sixties and did look in reasonable condition,

I'm not sure smoking at least sixty cigarettes a day kept him healthy. But hey, that was his problem.

"So, I wanted to give you an update on two things. You'll be delighted to hear that Mary Hurst is doing well. She's had a blood transfusion and, with a team of clever psychiatrists, she's now on the road to recovery. We have secured accommodation for her over in Kempston Flats in Hackney, and it will be ready to move into when she's well enough to look after herself. I must say it was really quite lovely to see her progress when I nipped in last week to say hello. She's quite a character, isn't she?" He grinned as he looked up from the file in front of him.

"Sorry, I have no idea what you're talking about." Hartland was off on one of his bat-shit fruit loop rants again. Jesus, this really was a nut house.

"Frank, I'm talking about Marge Simpson, one of the conditions you gave us regarding staying with the programme. Surely you remember?"

"Oh my God, Old Marge, really? You helped her?"

"Of course! I gave you my word. She's not that old. In fact, she had her fiftieth last week, and the team at the clinic threw her a little party. Quite an affair, apparently."

"I don't believe you," I threw back at him as I sunk back into my seat. Of course, he said he would help them, but he could just say anything. I wouldn't know and probably never would because I suspected I'd never make it out of here alive. They could've made up whatever they wanted to and, based on their bat-shit time-travel ideas, they probably did.

Hartland opened the file and placed an array of photos on the desk. There she was, Old Marge, and she did appear to be a lot healthier. I thumbed through the pictures after plucking them up from the table. Marge was actually laughing in one shot when she was cutting her birthday cake. If this was true, it was up there with some of the best news I'd ever heard. I sensed my eyes welling up, and then the first tear slid out and rolled down my cheek.

"You could have Photostopped these," I muttered, as I lobbed the photos back on his desk. "I bet they're not real."

"Frank, they are real. I assume you mean Photoshopped, and anyway, they're not. They're genuine."

"Is it Photoshopped, not stopped?"

"Yes, Frank, it's called Photoshop. But I can assure you these aren't."

"Oh right. And Denzel? Denzel Warlow?"

"Yes, likewise. We set him up in a small house in Finchley we had going spare after a previous traveller vacated it. He's enrolled in the Open University and doing rather well. Gives you a good feeling, doesn't it?" He grinned. Although he still looked evil, and I was sure he was preparing some hideous deed. I guess there was no Ant Hill Mob about to trundle over the horizon to save me.

I couldn't hold back as the tears poured whilst I stared at him in disbelief. But his eyes were honest and, unless he was an accomplished actor or some sick psychopath, he really had helped them. Whatever happened to me now, I couldn't care less. Hearing this news, at last, meant something good had happened.

The Hooded Claw plucked up a leather-bound folder from the desk, lit another cigarette, of course, and flipped through the sheets of paper whilst I sat and dried my eyes with the back of my hand.

"Hmmm ... looking good, looking good," he muttered to himself, then lobbed the folder on the desk and smiled. "You're ready, Frank. Tonight is D-Day!"

"Ready for what? You're not still going down the route of the Ferris wheel time-travel shite, are you?"

Over the last few weeks, Shaidun had me working on my running stats, stating that he wanted to focus on improving my speed and distance performance. Knowing I wasn't being trained for the Olympics, I'd come to the conclusion that I was to be the 'fox' in a human hunt. They needed my health to improve to ensure the hunt had a competitive edge and the kill wasn't too easy. I felt it was a reasonable assumption to make.

If this was D-Day, I anticipated tonight I'd be let out to run across the remote Scottish Moors, Richard Hannay style, whilst trying to escape my pursuers. Although, I anticipated they'd be sick aristocratic British toffs, not Prussian spies as in Hannay's case. Then, this group would saddle up, blow their horns and chase me down. The end would be at the teeth of a large pack of bloodthirsty hounds. After that, I expect they'd arrange for my head to be stuffed by some sicko taxidermist and mounted on a wooden plaque with a brass plate positioned somewhere below my chin, which once a week, one of the domestic staff would polish.

'Frank Stone. 2015. Ran four miles before capture and death.'

Hartland brought me back from my day-nightmare. "We are, Frank. I must say we're delighted with your progress, although I'm disappointed with your lack of belief. That said, we've had a fair few who've travelled not believing. Well, not until they arrive, that is."

"Right." I huffed.

"You'll be our two hundredth traveller! There's a landmark for you."

"Oh, great. Do I get to cut a ribbon, receive a bunch of flowers and a bottle of Champagne?"

"I like you, Frank, I really do. But you really must deal with that cynical attitude; it doesn't become you."

"Right." I sunk further into the seat, disappointed that the last six weeks had now finally come to an end. But hey, I knew it was coming. However, what that actually was, I guess I was about to find out. As I sat slumped, allowing a cloak of depression to flood over me, the electronic click of the door engaged before Pitstop and Reverend Green entered.

"Frank, you know Penelope, and you'll remember Keith Morehouse, our Data-Tech director."

I glanced sideways at them without offering a greeting. Both pulled up a chair on either side of me. Then Morehouse started the conversation as he handed me a file.

"Right, Frank. Penelope has signed you off as fit to travel, and the Board has ratified the committee's recommendation. So, you'll travel at 1:00 a.m. tomorrow morning."

I glanced at his expressionless face. Then, turning to look at Pitstop, she just smiled.

The Hooded Claw leant forward and pointed at me. "Frank, we need to take you through the set-up for tonight and landing conditions in 1979. Now, as many have before, you think this is all nuts. However, when you land, you'll be grateful that you listened to this briefing. So, all I ask is that as a thank you for helping Mary and Denzel, you listen and play along."

I nodded, mainly because I wanted to ensure Mary and Denzel were able to continue their new lives. Whatever this fuck-nutty organisation had given them, clearly, they could also take it away. If pretending I was about to time-travel would keep them both safe, I would play along.

Morehouse flipped open his file and nodded to me, indicating I should follow suit. "Okay, so firstly, let's go through travel arrangements for your mission."

I held the cover before opening the file. "Will this self-destruct in five seconds after opening?" I asked whilst sporting a wry grin.

"Frank!" boomed Hartland.

I held up my palm and found a serious face, just to convince him I was playing along.

We pored over my itinerary for the next half hour, which was similar to sitting in a branch of Thomas Cook as the young lady took you through a brochure of an apartment on some Greek island and completed the booking forms. However, according to Morehouse, there was no Greek island destination, golden beaches, and an all-inclusive bar, but a midnight trip to the London Eye that was surely closed at that time of night. What was clear to me, I had no idea what they were on about. However, at just before 1:00 a.m., two agents would escort me to the Wheel and the Travel Department team would ensure my safe journey.

"Err ... what about vaporisation? I seemed to remember weeks ago you said some travellers don't make it and are vaporised."

Pitstop gently laid her hand on my arm. "Frank, that's my responsibility. Since I've headed the department, we've only lost one traveller and that was because I made it quite clear she wasn't fit to travel. However, I was overruled." She scowled at The Hooded Claw, who dismissed her glare with a wave of his cigarette. "Every candidate who I've recommended is ready has made it safely through. Now, I can't, of course, guarantee it, but I would bet my sizeable mortgage on my Grosvenor Square townhouse that you'll be fine."

"Never been much of a betting man myself." I swallowed hard at the thought of being vaporised. "How big is your mortgage?"

"Four million."

"Yep, you're right; that's sizeable."

"Okay, good. So, Frank, let's move to landing." Morehouse nodded at my file, indicating I should turn to the next brief, not surprisingly headed up 'Landing'.

"You may recall we are placing you back in 1979 on the 17th of August. I'm led to believe it's a lovely sunny day, and first light is at 5:12 a.m." he grinned.

I nodded.

"The date has been specifically chosen as it provides you with enough time to change Jemma's fate, but not too early where you could cause historical damage which might jeopardise the whole operation."

"It's not an exact science, so check the date when you arrive. It should be the 17th of August, but it might be out by a day or two at the worst," added The Hooded Claw, as he reclined in his chair, savouring his cigarette whilst gently pushing the smoke to the ceiling.

I just nodded again and tried not to roll my eyes.

Morehouse continued. "When you land, we expect you will be asleep, but that's not guaranteed. Data suggests you were never much of a night owl and, as long as you're not at some debauched swingers' party like Gloria, you should be fine."

The Hooded Claw chuckled. Pitstop shot a disapproving scowl at the two men's schoolboy smut.

"You'll remember us telling you that when you land, you'll remember nothing about the life you've lived—"

"Thank God for that! As it ain't been too terrific."

"Quite. As I was saying, you won't remember your future life until someone else states your name. Now, of course, that could be almost immediately, like Gloria." Both men once again exchanged a lewd, smutty grin, and Pitstop rolled her eyes. "But it could well be days until you hear your name. But that doesn't matter. When it does happen, it will be quite a moment for you. You'll have to deal with it in your own way. However, this is the crucial and important bit … when it happens, you'll feel compelled to tell someone … but you can't. You never can. That's the tough bit about time-travel; it's your secret, and that's how it stays. If you do break this golden rule, two things will happen. Firstly, you'll be treated like a nut case. Secondly, do you remember the two retired mercenaries we've secured on a retainer?"

I nodded.

"Well, one of those lucky chaps will get their opportunity to live their life again after we've sent one of them back to liquidate you."

"Right." Liquidation and vaporisation. This lot were keen on those two disposal methods, although I wasn't quite sure what the difference was. Perhaps one was being placed in a bath of acid, and the other was a final moment inside a blender.

Deciding to continue to play along with their silly game, I thought of another concerning question. "So, the Millennium Wheel wasn't there in 1979. Will I just drop out of the sky and land in the Thames?"

"No. Frank, as we've already stated, you land in your own body wherever you were at that precise moment in history," chuckled Morehouse.

"Right, of course." How silly of me. Jesus, surely this lot needed committing to a secure unit. In fact, if they liquidated people, an extended stay in Broadmoor might be appropriate.

I thought of another crucial question.

"So, do I need to stick an advertisement in the personals section of The Times to say I've arrived safely? I could use the code words *The Eagle Has Landed.*"

I thought it was a good codeword as I'd always saw myself as a Michael Caine type character. In my youth, I would always imitate Charlie Croker after repeatedly seeing The Italian Job at the old ABC cinema in Fairfield. *On Days Like These*, the theme tune, rolled around my head as I imagined driving an orange Lamborghini Miura along the hairpin bends of the Great St. Bernard's Pass, high up in the Italian Alps. I still knew the lyrics, but like everyone else, I struggled with the opening line sweetly sung by Matt Monro. My Italian had always been somewhat limited to *Grazie* and *Per favore,* so I guess I was never going to master those lyrics.

Whilst I daydreamed, all three of them burst out laughing. "Err, sorry, but what's funny? If I don't leave a message, how will you know I made it through?"

Both men were in fits of hysterical laughter, but Pitstop managed to calm herself. Grabbing my arm again, she explained, "Frank, my dear. The second you travel, we'll instantly know you've landed because history will have changed. What we're expecting and hoping is, a few seconds after 1:00 a.m. tomorrow morning, your lovely wife, Jemma, will be a very popular, well-respected politician enjoying her fourth successful decade as the MP for Fairfield. She'll be the longest-serving Cabinet Minister, holding the position as Foreign Secretary in a Coalition Government led by Sir Vince Cable, who we believe will be Prime Minister and not David Cameron."

Once again, the reality hit home.

They were all bat-shit nuts.

13

To Boldly Go …

After The Hooded Claw and Reverend Green had shaken my hand and wished me good fortune, Pitstop hugged and kissed me on the cheek.

The Hooded Claw stepped forward and gripped my elbow. "Frank, you have six weeks to change history. Here at the CYA, we very much hope in a few minutes the catastrophe that the world faces in a few years will have been averted. Although no one will ever know what you did, you will have a greater impact on the human race than anyone who ever lived!"

"Yeah, right!"

"Attitude, Frank!" His grip on my arm tightened.

I grinned and nodded, just to appease him. Although what I was heading to, as I left them in the lobby of the CYA, hell knows. With the goodbyes completed, a couple of SAS-types escorted me out of a side door into The A-Team bus, which had been my mode of transport six weeks ago.

Six weeks – it seemed like a lifetime.

The Frank Stone who journeyed back to Queen's Walk was a different man to the one who'd left it. I was considerably healthier, a stone heavier, and I didn't have a cloth bag over my head – oh yeah, and I didn't smell like a polecat which had slept in a sewer drain.

We arrived at the London Eye which appeared fully closed up for the night, well of course it was – it was closed. So, would they just let me go? And where would I go? Although I was a new man, I had no possessions, no money, and no home. Would I just have to curl up under a heap of cardboard by the toilet door? I peered down to where I expected some of my old acquaintances should be sleeping, but the whole area seemed to be empty. Had the SAS-types cleared the area? Come to think of it – I could remember some blokes forcibly moving me on about a year ago.

One of the Travel team grabbed my arm and led me down to the white steel gates, leading to a stairwell that descended underneath the cantilevered wheel. Producing a set of keys, he unlocked the gate and led me down the dark steps towards the river. I considered the possibility I was about to receive a bullet in the back of my head and then be pushed out into the Thames. Would I then be fished out a few days later as I washed up to the Thames Barrier? But why?

At the bottom, he led me through under the giant wheel and through another white steel gate leading up to the base of the Eye where the capsules rotate around to allow passengers to board. There stood two more agents next to an open door of a still pod – the white lettering suggesting it was number thirteen.

My escort released his grip from my forearm and disappeared the way we'd come. Two more agents offered their arms to the open pod doors as if gesturing the way forward to be presented to a feudal lord holding court. I half expected The London Philharmonic Orchestra to be bashing out Händel's *'The Arrival of the Queen of Sheba.'*

Then I imagined I'd step through a cloud of smoke to the other side, where I will announce to Matthew Kelly and the audience, *'Tonight, Matthew, I'm going to be Frank Stone the Younger.'*

It appeared neither the Queen of Sheba nor Matthew Kelly would be waiting on the other side, where the lack of light afforded the pod a cavernous appearance. As I stepped forward, I felt I was entering the Temple in The Canyon of the Crescent Moon. Was I going to find the Holy Grail, drink from the cup of youth and live an eternal life?

Bollocks was I! This was more Monty Python than Indiana Jones.

"Do I need to wear a seatbelt?" I asked, as I gingerly stepped inside. Yeah, I know, a stupid question which didn't receive an answer.

As I turned, the door closed. The pod jolted, then slowly moved backwards. Hang on – the eye was rotating the wrong way. From this side of the river, the Eye rotated anti-clockwise, but I was clearly moving clockwise. I knew this happened every October during the last hour of British summertime but, other than that, it never rotated backwards.

With my hands slapped to the glass, I watched as the London skyline crept into view. So, they *had* put me on the London Eye. It was clear from my time at the CYA that they were powerful and wealthy, and it appeared they had the connections to dish out free rides on London attractions in the middle of the night. Had they saved a few quid with a three-attraction saver ticket? Was it an open-air bus tour next? I hoped it wasn't the London Dungeons because I was easily spooked and didn't like that sort of thing.

Squinting at the ever-shrinking Queen's Walk, it appeared The A-Team bus had left, nor could I spot any of the Transportation team milling about. Surely someone down there could see the Eye rotating? I mean, it's not small and can be seen from quite a distance.

As the Eye slowly rotated and my pod gracefully glided to the top of the ride, the deserted streets of London slowly came into view. Okay, so it was just after 1:00 a.m., but shit, this was London – the city that never sleeps – where was everyone? The whole of Queen's Walk, Jubilee Park, Waterloo tube station, and every street on the South Bank appeared deserted. Spinning around, I peered up the river – not a moving boat in sight. Across on the north bank, all the way along the Victoria Embankment, appeared empty, with no cars and no people.

"What the bollocks!" Where was everyone? How could there be no one down there? Christ, nine-odd million people lived in this bloody place; where the hell were they all? Since entering the pod, had those man-eating aliens arrived from Mars? Was I the only survivor?

"Get a bloody grip, man!" I exclaimed to no one but myself.

This wasn't some re-run of The War of the Worlds. Although, I had accused The Hooded Claw and his mad crew of operating inside some nutty H. G. Wells-inspired movie. No, this had to be a fake cityscape they projected onto the pod – nine million people just don't disappear. Come to think of it, nor do old tramps time-travel.

Or do they?

Feeling giddy, I gripped the steel handrail whilst inhaling some deep breaths. The motion wasn't a problem, even though they'd said they'd increase the speed to one mile per hour so the centrifugal force could hold the wormhole in place. The climb to the top of the wheel wasn't exactly speedy – Captain Kirk hadn't just asked Mr Chekov for warp factor ten.

"To boldly go where no man had gone before," I chuckled. Then, resting my bum against the rail, I glanced around the pod. It was much larger inside than I'd imagined. When squinting up at them from the ground, they'd always looked so tiny – as if you could hold it in the palm of your hand.

"Christ, Frank! You've lost it, my old son."

What was I thinking – who gave a shit how big the sodding thing was? What the fucking hell was I doing at the top of the London Eye in the middle of the night?

"Captain's log, Stardate November 2015. It is now official. After ten years of trying to survive street living and six weeks in a palatial funny farm, I, Frank Stirling Stone, have officially lost my marbles."

14

1979

Luftwaffe

"Oh, come on, get out of bed. You've got that doctor's appointment at ten this morning. Christ, I hope they give you something because your snoring is driving me mad!"

Jemma stood by their bedroom door wrapped in a thick, white, fluffy towel as she tried to comb her wet hair with her fingers. If Frank carried on snoring like a castrated pig, she might feel the need to perform such an operation on him.

She thought she heard him grunt as he turned over to face the wall, but nothing else. Plonking herself down at her dressing table, Jemma fired up the hairdryer, determined to make as much noise as humanly possible.

If Frank could snore all night, she would ensure her new Supermax Hairdryer destroyed his morning slumber. Unfortunately, her long blonde hair took ages to dry. However, on the positive side, the hairdryer sounded like Concorde was firing up its Rolls Royce turbojet engines in the back garden, so no way could he sleep through that!

The House was in recess, so no need to rush into London this morning. However, she had surgery duties to attend to. Then, she was the guest of honour at the opening of a new out-of-town supermarket near the Broxworth Estate – an event she was dreading for two reasons. Firstly, she detested performing the civic duties her role demanded. However, the previous town's MP had excelled at 'kissing babies', so there was no way she would be criticised for not being active in the community. Secondly, why had anyone thought it was a good idea to put a new supermarket near that awful estate? It would be ravaged by thieves and end up as another no-go area for which the estate was well known.

The last six months had taken her on a journey which she could never have imagined. Jemma felt as if she'd stepped through the back of the wardrobe and into Narnia. Certainly, Mrs T's demeanour could be akin to the White Witch. Thank God for Willie Whitelaw, who was the Aslan character, a kind, gentle, moderate man who kept the witch at bay and away from ravaging her new MPs. Many of whom felt out of their depth – she was certainly in that group.

It wasn't supposed to happen like this. A year ago, she was settled and happy in her job as a junior solicitor in Greenland's and Co Solicitors. However, her father, Cecil, had persuaded her to stand for the candidacy representing the Conservative party in the May General Elections.

The Committee, led by her father, sanctioned her candidacy at a last desperate minute when the already agreed candidate, Brian Grey, had to step aside due to a scandal. In April, Brian had been discovered in a seedy hotel bedroom with a large West-Indian man, who smoked a joint whilst Brian savoured the delights of the said West-Indian's reportedly enormous, stiff lollypop – enough said. Of course, Brian had to step down, and his wife unsurprisingly left him.

At the time, the campaign had been fun. She'd never concerned herself about the possibility of actually winning because Malcolm Haig, the long-standing Labour MP, was extremely popular. Also, as Labour had held the Fairfield seat since 1945, she thought it would be unlikely that she would win. So, it came as a bit of a shock when standing on that stage in the early hours of the 4th of May as the returning officer announced Jemma Helen Stone was duly elected to represent the constituency of Fairfield, narrowly beating Malcolm Haig by turning around his sixteen-thousand majority. Her speech that night was pathetic, totally unprepared, and she winced at the memory.

"Frank! Frank, are you getting up?"

Presumably, he hadn't heard her as the Concorde-hairdryer now had all engines at full throttle, causing her long hair to fly behind her at supersonic speed at right angles to her head.

The other worry she'd not expected to concern herself with was the Tobias issue. And then there was the other more significant problem which would resurface when the House returned for the autumn session. With her inability to rebuff the flirtatious advances of a male colleague, coupled with her insatiable appetite for sex, Jemma knew she was playing dangerous games. She'd bet her lovely new VW GTI Golf, with its recently fitted leaking sunroof, that he didn't snore! Christ, how had that happened? She'd have to end it before it reached the point that it really shouldn't. Otherwise, within less than a year, the Fairfield Conservative Association would have their second scandal to deal with. However, it wouldn't be of the same magnitude as the ten-inch-throbbing-black-lollipop scandal as was the last one.

Also, although he snored like a castrated pig, Frank didn't deserve this. He's a genuine, loyal and loving man, and Jemma knew she shouldn't treat him so poorly. No, that's it; she would end it next week before it got out of hand. And as for Tobias, well, he would have to accept what she'd said, or she'd act upon the ultimatum she'd threatened him with.

Clicking off Concorde, Jemma turned and studied her husband as her dried hair floated down to land. He was quiet now. Well, it's a pity he couldn't have been like that during the early hours when his snoring reverberated off the walls.

Jemma was so proud of him. Frank had been brought up on the Broxworth Estate after the council moved his parents there when they knocked down their old prefab house, which his parents had moved into at the end of the war. Along with sixty others, their Victorian terraced house had been destroyed by the Luftwaffe in 1941 when a German Heinkel Bomber crew had mistaken the north end of Fairfield Town for the London dockyards. As the bomber was thirty-five miles adrift from its target, one could only assume the night before the raid the German navigator had enjoyed a heavy night on the schnapps.

Frank had attended the Eaton Grammar school, which was unusual for any lad from that estate. Then, after university, he'd started his own business that now had begun to show the green shoots of success.

She detested his business partner, Paul. A lecherous tosser, who undressed her with his eyes every time she saw him. He'd tried it on with Clare the first time she'd met Frank in the Bell Pub in '76, but Clare had soon batted him away.

Frank had embarrassingly tried to perform an impression of Steve Austin, but he'd said she looked like Jaime Sommers, which she'd liked. Anyway, no lad had dared to ask her out for months, so she'd said yes. Looking at Frank whilst the heat from Concorde burnt her leg through the towel, Jemma realised she was glad she'd said yes back in that awful meat-market of a pub. A good job some dissident Irish terrorist group had stuck a bomb in it a couple of years ago, as the newly built pub was much nicer. However, Jemma now felt guilty for those thoughts, thinking about the sixteen people who lost their lives that day.

After putting her face on, Jemma rummaged through her wardrobe, searching for her blue suit. She called it her Maggie suit, as it was exactly like the one Mrs T wore on the steps of Downing Street when she delivered her St Francis of Assisi speech. However, Jemma's skirt was definitely above the knee.

Hanging her suit on the doorframe, now dressed in her underwear, Jemma sat on the edge of the bed and lifted Frank's golden-blond hair away from his eyes. He needed a haircut, but she knew he liked it at shoulder length, and Jemma thought it afforded him a sexy surfer look.

Why had she landed herself in this mess? Jesus, what was the matter with her? She had Frank, wasn't that enough?

She gently kissed his ear, then whispered. "Frank, I've gotta go. I'm due to hold surgery at nine." Jemma kissed his lips and ran her tongue suggestively across them, letting her hand drift under the bed sheet to his lower regions.

Frank slowly opened his eyes.

15

The Nutty Professor

The sunlight ravaged my dilated pupils as I peeked open my eyes, so I quickly closed them.

My lips felt wet.

Rarely these days did I have erotic dreams.

No, they were a thing of the past, from a very long time ago – and if I ever did, it was never enough to stir my long redundant friend down below. I had to admit I'd had manly thoughts about Michael-Kors-pink-trainer lady, but of course, as a smelly sixty-six-year-old, grey-haired street dweller, they were just fantasies.

This dream was new. I'd not had one like this for a very long time and, if I wasn't mistaken, my old mate down below was proving he still had the ability to perform.

"Now you get an erection! I wouldn't have minded a bit of that last night, but you were too drunk!"

Did someone say something? Who cares! I wasn't interested because this dream was reaching new heights. An erotic young woman with long blonde hair, dressed in sexy bra and knickers, was stroking my best mate through the sheets – God, this dream was the best!

"Frank, I'm off; I'll see you tonight. Please make sure you attend your appointment at ten and get Doctor Mayhew to prescribe you something for your snoring. I've got to get some sleep tonight ... well, after you've given me some of that lovely stiff friend of yours. Don't go messing up the sheets; I want you to save it for later."

My eyes sprung open.

Dream or no dream, or a hallucination. Had I been sniffing nitrous oxide like that group always did down by the river? I'd vowed never to do that. Life on the streets was bad enough without going down that route. But the sexy girl in my dream was there in front of me, zipping up her skirt.

The Hooded Claw!

Instantly my best mate shrunk back even though the sexy young blonde in front of me had removed her bra to adjust the straps, allowing a perfect set of boobs that I'd not had the pleasure of seeing for over thirty years to fill my field of vision.

"Ah, the sexy surfer awakes! Oh, but I see your mate's gone to sleep even though you're copping an eyeful," the blonde chuckled.

Blouse buttoned over the re-applied bra with her jacket folded neatly over her arm, she blew me a kiss and left the bedroom. I spotted her bend and grasp hold of her heels from the landing carpet before bounding down the stairs as I croaked out, "Jemma?"

Stunned, I just listened as the front door closed and the sound of a throaty car engine fired in to life.

"Bloody hell!"

I peeled back the quilt and inspected my body. Sure enough, my mate had shrunk back as Jemma had pointed out. But he looked a lot younger, not that I'd had much reason to look at him over recent times. Usually, it was just fumbling around down there as I quickly pointed him into a hedge to empty my bladder, which seemed to be an operation I had to perform more often as the years rolled on.

Jumping out of bed, I traversed my way to the bathroom. I knew the house well, and my memory of the layout was accurate. Although, why we'd papered the landing with orange and brown psychedelic square-patterned wallpaper, God only knows. I now remembered Cecil helped me put it up when we moved in a couple of years ago – or was it thirty-six years ago?

Standing naked on the landing, I fought with my brain which seemed to have two sets of memories. Firstly, last night I went on the piss with Paul. We ended up at the Murderers Tavern, and I'd downed six pints of Hoffmeister, or Hoffy as we called it. How could I remember that? Secondly, last night, I was sitting in a briefing room with The Hooded Claw, Reverend Green and Penelope Pitstop. I can't have been in both places.

Pushing open the bathroom door, there on the glass shelf below the mirror was Jemma's favourite perfume – Opium, and next to it was my bottle of Aramis cologne. Above the shelf hung the smoked-glass bathroom cabinet with mirrored doors. Staring back at me – was me – a young, fit, healthy me.

Transfixed by the sight of myself, I stayed in position whilst gawping at the handsome bloke. I'd never thought I was good looking, but now I thought I was that Greek Adonis. I rubbed my hand over my stomach – is that a six-pack?

"Bugger me. I've got a six-pack," I muttered.

The last six weeks were clear and real. Yup, no doubt I'd spent all that time in that wacko house full of crazy deranged nutters. The cast of Cluedo and the Wacky Races were definitely real and not some dream. So, had they drugged me to make my brain think I'd time-travelled? But why?

With this newly acquired fit, suntanned physique, I felt the urgent need to run around looking for Spandex. I grabbed my muscley pecks and started shouting Eddie Murphy style about the instantaneous disappearance of my once rather ugly moobs as I wiggled around in front of the mirror.

Like a narcissist, I'd fallen in love with my reflection and now stood rubbing my youthful hands over my body. As I thought about Jemma, my old friend below re-awoke and joined me in my self-appreciation.

As I grinned at the mirror, I spotted a complete set of reasonably decent teeth that had miraculously regenerated, which now filled my mouth and displayed a half-decent collection of pearly whites. I pulled my cheek apart like a rough-handed dentist as I counted twenty-eight teeth out loud, still with my hand rammed in my mouth and touching each one in turn. "Wan, ooo, fee, ooor, ive …"

This was nuts. Yesterday, I was missing half of them, and what was left were at best a dark brown colour.

Desperately trying to keep the vision of myself in eyeshot, I backed out of the bathroom, frightened if I looked away, a saggy grey old Frank would return. I stopped at the door again and ogled at myself.

Had The Hooded Claw and his nuthouse of clowns been telling the truth all along? Did that journey on the Millennium Wheel really take me back to 1979? Well, if I had started snorting nitrous oxide from soda syphon capsules, and this was all a hallucination – bring it on! If I'd known they could have had this effect on your brain, I'd have started years ago.

Laying on the bedroom floor were a heap of Jemma's clothes. On the top was my '78 Midsummer Night Dream Festival Genesis t-shirt. Jemma wore this in bed as she hated nightdresses, preferring to wear my t-shirts and often picking one of my favourites – which this was.

Jemma and I had attended the festival with her best friend, Clare, and her husband, Tobias. However, I now remembered they didn't enjoy it much. Tobias was a bit of a hooray-henry type, and I knew he looked down on me. God knows why, but I quite liked him.

Tobias was more of a Northern Soul man, also having a thing about The Three Degrees, so Prince Charles was in good company. He would often put me down by making snide remarks about my upbringing and saying I was punching above my weight with Jemma. He'd pointed out that no one from the rough Broxworth Estate ever managed to achieve anything. Well, apart from a stay at Her Majesty's pleasure, and to be fair, he was right concerning most of its residents.

What I can't fault him for was his support when I managed to get myself arrested for Jemma's murder. He was the only one fighting to clear my name. As for Clare, well, unless it involved horses, standing in a field and listening to a rock band was too rustic for her. Those memories were crystal clear. But yesterday, I doubt I could even remember who Genesis were.

Scrunching up the t-shirt, I lifted it to my face and sucked in her now long-forgotten scent. Half an eye caught sight of a pair of her knickers. Thankfully, even though this surely was a dream, I didn't pick them up because that would be way too pervy.

Washed and dressed in clothes I vaguely could remember owning, I took in a quick tour of the house. Yep, everything looked like it came from the '70s. The lounge housed the orange leather Queensway sofa Jemma's parents bought us as a wedding present when Jemma and I had married a couple of years back. On top of the hefty small screen TV sat a framed wedding photo. The exact picture the CYA had placed in my *This is Your Life* folder, which was left for me to read the day of my extraction – the day I fell into The Hooded Claw's lair.

In the hallway, a push-button address book lay next to the retro red-coloured dial telephone. I slid the dial to M and hit the open button. The cover flew up and displayed at least ten numbers, the top one being – *Mum and Dad 22714*. Helen Causton, Jemma's mother, died in 1989. Whilst dialling the number, I wondered if this would confirm my new addiction to nitrous oxide or, ridiculously, that the Correction Years Association had actually transported me through time.

"Fairfield 714. Hello." A voice came back down the line. A voice I hadn't heard for many years but knew so well.

"Helen?" I questioned, although I knew it was her. I wondered if I should ask her if she was dead. No, maybe not, as that would be a strange question. However, at the very least, I should tell her to make sure she has regular mammograms over the next ten years.

"Oh, morning, Frank. I'm afraid you've missed Cecil as he's already left for the office. I presume you're calling about the match tomorrow? Cecil mentioned it this morning and was hoping you could still play."

"Err ... the match?"

"Yes, the match. Frank, you okay? You sound a little odd."

"No, no, I'm fine ... fine."

"Oh, okay then. Oh, is Jemma alright? Nothing's happened, has it?"

"No, Helen, she's fine. She has surgery this morning and left half an hour ago."

"Well, enjoy your day off. We'll see you tomorrow at one."

"Err, tomorrow?"

"The match, Frank! You will be there, I take it? Cecil has picked you to open the batting."

"Yes, yes. I'll be there. Err ... bye, Helen."

Still holding the receiver, the line cut out. Was I in Nitrous-Oxide land? The only other possibility was I'd just had a phone conversation with my dead mother-in-law.

The last conversation we'd had was when I was released from police custody when they failed to charge me for Jemma's murder. Cecil believed me, but Helen wasn't sure, and the seeds of doubt about my innocence had grown in her mind. The last time I saw Helen was at Jemma's funeral.

Cecil had phoned me to tell me Helen had passed away when I lived in a small rental flat up at the Broxworth Estate. After losing everything, I'd managed to go full circle and ended up living back on that no-go estate after escaping it in my teenage years. Cecil had said he thought I should know about Helen. However, out of respect for the other mourners, he requested that I didn't attend the funeral after the tricky scenes that transpired at Jemma's ten years earlier.

Jemma's funeral was a memory that I didn't struggle to recall. Unsurprisingly, the turnout at the All Saints Church was enormous. Crowds filled the Church, spilling out into the graveyard and along the narrow lane. The police presence was massive, plus TV camera crews, news reporters and national newspaper photographers swamped the small lane which leads from the main road down to the church.

Not that I knew this at the time, but a few years later I could empathise with Lady Diana Spencer. As she was to later repeatedly suffer, like her, on that particular day, I endured the attentions of the paparazzi as they hounded me with their camera lenses inches from my face and microphones stuffed up my hooter. Paul and my close friend, Dave, tried to push them away as they led me to Paul's car. The media had latched onto the fact that although released from custody without charge, the police firmly believed I was responsible for my wife's – the local MP's – murder.

'Frank, we'd like to send you back to 1979 and prevent the murder of your wife.'

The voice of The Hooded Claw reverberated around my head as I gripped the telephone receiver.

"Jeeeesus." If I was here, back in good old 1979, that was it – stopping her murder.

Life would start again. I could save my business, and perhaps we would have a family. Could I be this lucky?

16

The Rockford Files

The journey from a young, successful business owner to a rough sleeper was gradual. However, after Jemma's death, I did monumentally slide off the rails. Paul held the business together in those proceeding years, and we certainly could be classed by the mid '80s as being part of the 'loadsamoney' generation – Harry Enfield style. Although the lame-duck of the business, we were at the time coining it in – business was booming.

However, as I slipped further into a gambling addiction, Paul lost his patience with me and, by the time Helen Causton passed, he'd syphoned off all the cash. I was declared bankrupt and living Wayne-and-Waynetta style on the Broxworth Estate. The Waynetta character was a short fling I endured with some dreadful older woman who needed somewhere to live, but I didn't care by that point. From that particularly depressing moment in my life, it was only a few further poor decisions to put me in cardboard city as The Hooded Claw had described it.

Still holding the phone receiver, I pushed the dial on the address-book gadget to 'S', but the number I wanted didn't show. Selecting 'F' provided it, as Jemma had listed the required number under *Frank-Work*. Stone & Wilson Builders – I dialled the number.

"Stone and Wilson's." It was Alison. Alison Hay, our receptionist. In the early '80s, she'd emigrated to Australia after marrying some rugby player. I remember she had a huge crush on me in the late '70s, something that Jemma was not happy about, and Paul often said I should just shag the girl and make her happy. Although, at this stage, I'm struggling to work out how I was there, but last night, after a few beers, Paul had rattled on about Alison and how he'd like to poke her as he couldn't take his eyes off her super-tits as he put it.

Paul, although my business partner, was a lecherous git. Jemma had always detested the man because she said his eyes had a way of removing her clothes. I knew he would also love to poke her because he'd often commented that, as his business partner, we should share everything. He was one of those blokes that made women's skin crawl. On reflection, apart from working with him, I have no idea why I associated with the man.

"Hello, can I help you?"

"Alison. Alison, is that you?"

"Oooo morning, Frank," she purred with her wafting, smoky, sexy voice. "Not the same here without you. Hope you're enjoying your day off."

"Is Paul in?"

"Yeah, d'you wanna speak to him? He's in, but I think he said he was out this afternoon." The purr in her voice had evaporated at the sound of his name.

Now I wasn't sure if I wanted to speak to my business partner after not seeing him for over twenty years. Back then, he'd stiffed me, taking everything and leaving me bankrupt.

"Err … no. No, it's okay. I'll ring him later." I stuck my finger on the receiver button to disconnect the line.

I thought for a moment.

'Frank, we'd like to send you back to 1979 and prevent the murder of your wife.'

Stop her murder – where was Paul on the 28th of September 1979?

After spending too long looking at the red soda syphon on the drinks trolley and wondering if I had sniffed the nitrous oxide from the capsule inside, I ventured out of the house heading for the doctor's appointment that Jemma had insisted I must attend this morning. I was reasonably confident that laughing gas provided a short, calm, euphoric state of mild hallucination. As I'd now been on this 'trip' for nearly an hour, I perhaps wasn't in a gas-induced stupor by inhaling hundreds of capsules. The only other possibility, as ridiculous as it might seem, I was in 1979.

Before venturing out into yesteryear, I'd turned on the big box TV I know we rented from the Radio Rentals Shop in the High Street. This further confirmed that I was in the pre-digital age because BBC2 showed the Test Card with the little girl and the green clown playing noughts and crosses. BBC1 displayed a Ceefax weather map, with the blocks of square-shaped colours producing an angular version of the UK. It reminded me of the Tetris game, with the green blocks denoting Scotland filling the screen. I half expected 'Game Over' to appear on the display.

Although I knew I owned the black Pontiac Firebird, I was still super-shocked to see it standing there on the drive. I'd spend months thumbing through Auto-Trader and knew the prices inside out in that year's Parker's Car Price Guide as I hunted down my desired car. I'd wanted a right-hand drive gold Firebird Esprit, so I had the identical car that Jim Rockford had. Unfortunately, as it was not a popular car in the UK, I'd finally settled for a black Pontiac Firebird. Although not an Esprit or Trans-am, it was close enough.

Although Jemma had joked that she thought I loved Jim Rockford more than her, we'd always settle down on the sofa together and watch the show. We'd had an ongoing lighthearted debate about the opening credits, where there was a brief shot of a topless woman.

Jemma said there wasn't, and we used to laugh as the title tune played, and we both stared at the TV. Every episode, I would exclaim, "There!" as I pointed at the TV after the scene had moved on. However, she never saw it and always maintained I was wrong. A few years after her death, I finally joined the technological revolution and purchased a VHS recorder. I remember taping an episode and playing the opening sequence frame by frame. There was the one frame of the topless woman. I'd cried, not because I was right, but because I wanted Jemma beside me to watch the show together as we always had. Tiny insignificant events could always send me further down my swirling hole of depression.

'Frank, we'd like to send you back to 1979 and prevent the murder of your wife.'

Now was the time to be like Jim Rockford. Could I be a PI and track down the murderer?

Yes. No choice – I had to.

"Morning, Frank. Lovely day again. Saw your missus this morning. I gotta say, although she's a Tory, she's a lot easier on the eye than the previous MP. Ha, yes, easy on the eye, I'd say."

"Oh, morning, Dennis. Sorry I didn't see you there." Why was everyone commenting on my wife's appearance or what they wanted to do to her? Now, Dennis, my bachelor neighbour, reckoned she was easy on the eye after Paul last night had repeated his long-held mantra that he wished to knob her. I don't remember this feeling the first time around. But hey, then, I didn't know someone was going to murder her in six weeks. The police had always maintained their belief that the perpetrator was someone she knew, which was probably why they seemed fixated on me.

I narrowed my eyes as I stared at my neighbour, watching him dump a black sack at the end of the drive ready for the bin collection.

'Frank, we'd like to send you back to 1979 and prevent the murder of your wife.'

Where was Dennis on the 28th of September 1979?

"You're a lucky bloke, Frank, having a woman looking like her, I can tell you. Although come the revolution, with her right-wing views, she'll be one of the first to hang."

"Err, sorry, Dennis, but that's my wife you're talking about."

"Hey, no offence, Frank. Just friendly banter," he replied as he sunk into the seat of his Blue Ford Granada after straightening the metal RAC badge attached to the front grill. He waved and pulled out of the drive. Dennis Tranil, now I recall, was a communist and never missed an opportunity to share his vision of the future.

Deciding a walk in the morning sunshine would give me time to think, I headed off to attend my doctor's appointment. Snoring aside, it certainly would be a good idea to have a quick health check. If, and that was a very big if, I *had* travelled back thirty-six years, it might be a good idea to get a health professional to give me the once over.

However, I remembered Doc Mayhew was ancient, and the Coke-bottle-bottomed glasses he wore suggested he wouldn't be able to assess whether I was thirty or sixty-six years old. Moreover, I very much doubted Doc-Magoo-Mayhew could ascertain if all my internal organs had landed in the correct positions following my apparent time leap.

My excursion to the doctors had provided three further reasons, which provided great sway to the theory I was actually now living in yesteryear. Firstly, the walk was pleasant, and I wasn't out of breath from my mile jaunt into town. Usually, just shuffling up to the Mission with my tartan trolley for support was enough to leave me whacked out.

Secondly, if I was in nitrous-oxide-land, this hallucination was good. Cars, shops and people looked very different. The McDonald's looked somewhat retro, with the shop sign stating McDonald's Hamburgers. The window poster taped to the front glass stated *Now Open* with the Slogan *'Nobody can do it like McDonald's.'* There was no *'I'm loving it'* anywhere to be seen. The picture of a Big Mac appeared very similar to how I remember, but it was significantly cheaper at fifty-one pence.

I'd often used McDonald's to provide my evening meal when street living. It was relatively cheap, and I could purchase a Big Mac for only a little more than what Michael-

Kors-pink-trainer lady gifted me each day. The tricky part was getting served and not booted out by some overzealous young manager who thought I was lowering the tone. I think they had an over-inflated idea of their fast-food operation. Although my appearance wasn't great and unlikely to make it onto the front cover of Men's Health magazine, many of the other more acceptable clientele weren't much better. Come on; it wasn't exactly The Ivy!

And thirdly, I stopped and gawped for some time at the large billboard poster high up on the sidewall of the Fine Fare supermarket. The poster, now tatty and faded, was some months overdue to be changed. However, I recognised it instantly, and the exact year it was produced. It was perhaps one of the most iconic billboard posters of the twentieth century. *'Labour Isn't Working'* in giant letters above a picture of a snaking line of people heading to the Unemployment Office. What this lot around me didn't know, and I did, was that unemployment continued to rise over the next few years.

After advising the receptionist that I had arrived for my appointment, she informed me that there was quite a wait as Doctor Mayhew was running late after his morning home visits, a service I was surprised to hear doctors provided.

Nestled between two elderly ladies, I settled into an empty seat and flicked through a well-thumbed Custom Car magazine from 1978. The front cover displayed a TR7 with a very scantily clad young lady splayed seductively across the bonnet – easy to see why it was well-thumbed. However, the old-dear beside me, whose appearance wasn't too dissimilar to Nora Batty, loudly tutted at the front cover.

Minding my own business while enjoying the magazine, I witnessed a commotion that, even for me, I was seriously shocked by. A familiar-looking middle-aged gent wearing a flat cap was not happy with the receptionist, and I had to intervene.

"I'm sorry, Mr Hackett, but Doctor Mayhew has a backlog of patients to see. So, if you're insistent on an appointment, we have a locum doctor this week who can see you."

"I'm not letting one of those touch me!"

"Sir, I understand. But Dr Patel is fully qualified and comes highly recommended."

"He might well do! But I can tell you I'm having no darky touch me. I don't want to see some punkah wallah!"

Amazingly, no one in the packed waiting room batted an eyelid. I jumped up and grabbed the gent's arm, aghast at the out-and-out racist remark. "Err ... hang on mate, hang on. You can't say things like that! Firstly; it's against the law, and secondly; it's totally immoral. What on earth is the matter with you?"

"Get off me! It's got nothing to do with you!"

"Yes, mate, it has. Offensive language like that is unacceptable. I suggest you apologise to the receptionist. Perhaps it would be a good idea to apologise to Doctor Patel as well!" I glanced towards the receptionist, who just shrugged and didn't seem too bothered by his racist outburst.

Mr Hackett brushed aside my hand. Then, with fury burning in his eyes, he glared at me. "Oh, it's you! That bloody bimbo girl's husband. Well, sunshine, this has nothing to do with you, so bugger off."

I now recognised him as the miserable bastard who lived a couple of doors down from us. Although we'd never really got to know the couple, they always scowled at us.

He pointed at me with his scrunched-up tweed cap in his hand. "And another thing. No good will come to this town having some blonde dolly-bird parading about in short skirts pretending to be an MP. Let's hope someone does her in so we can get a proper man doing the job. And another thing, my Joan says her skirts are so short you can see what she's had for lunch. That, my friend, is what *I* call immoral!"

'Frank, we'd like to send you back to 1979 and prevent the murder of your wife.'

Where was Mr Hackett on the 28th of September 1979?

The Rockford Files PI idea I had conjured up wasn't going to be easy. I now had three suspects for her murder in the space of a couple of hours of being here. By this rate, come early September, I could have a potential suspect list longer than the unemployed queue on that billboard poster.

17

Legs and Co.

A relatively large crowd had gathered outside the supermarket, so mingling without being noticed was reasonably easy. Most of them were here either waiting to do their shopping in the new fancy supermarket or wanted to get close and personal with the new Member of Parliament who seemed to have already started to enjoy celebrity status.

Some had said she looked like the sexy-leggy blonde in Legs and Co dance group, who performed each week on Top of the Pops. If the truth be known, it was probably the only reason half the male population of the UK watched the Thursday night programme.

With his dark shades and old fishing hat pulled tight on his head, he knew he was unrecognisable. Anyway, no one was looking at him; everyone was looking at her.

After some shuffling around, directed by the photographer from the Fairfield Chronicle, the dignitaries were all in position. Jemma Stone stood holding a large pair of scissors, flanked by Howard Brooks, the Mayor, to her right and presumably the supermarket store manager to her left. The photographer suggested they called out 'Great deals' instead of

'Cheese' as he snapped away to get his shots. He expected one of those pictures would fill the front page of the Chronicle in the morning.

Ribbon cut and handshakes completed, Jemma stepped up to the microphone to deliver a short speech. She composed herself and took a deep breath after an initial round of booing followed by a couple of wolf-whistles.

Then, a young man standing near the front called out, "Get your tits out for the boys."

This had clearly unsettled her, but the comment wasn't a total surprise based on the location near the rough Broxworth Estate.

"Well, err ... umm err ... good afternoon, everyone, and what a lovely turnout."

Huh! She's never going to make an impression at the despatch box if this is her standard of speech making. She needs a speechwriter, he thought.

"As I was saying, thank you for coming today."

"Get on with it, love, or we'll all starve to death if you take much longer!" shouted a bloke near the front of the crowd, causing a ripple of laughter.

Jemma pushed on. "In my role as your MP and servicing ... err ... serving the community at large—"

"You can give me a good servicing if you want, love!" called out some beer-gut-bellied middle-aged man in the centre of the crowd. More laughter ensued, and the young MP blushed a deep shade of scarlet.

"Yeah, I wouldn't mind checking over your bodywork. And you can check out my dip-stick any day," the beer-bellied man's mate called out, who received a smack around his head from some scraggy-looking woman who presumably was his wife.

Clearly now very self-conscious, she fiddled with her collar and tried to flatten the front of her skirt. "Yes, as I was saying, thank you all for coming today. I'm delighted that we have a new supermarket which will create jobs and opportunities for the town, and specifically for the residents of the Broxworth Estate nearby."

"Only opportunity we need love is to buy some food!" shouted a woman from the back of the crowd.

"You won't be buying; you'll be nicking it! You lot on that estate are all thieves!" called out an elderly lady who looked well capable of taking care of herself. Her heavy-looking clasp handbag, which she gripped tightly to her chest, appeared ready to double up as her weapon of choice.

A young woman, trying to control her grubby, snotty-nosed child, took umbrage to that slur. "Who you calling a thief, you cow? You're likely to get your face smashed in saying stuff like that, you old bat!"

He took a step back, suspecting this was going to regress into an unpleasant scene. He needed to remain incognito and could ill afford to be caught up in some fracas.

A young man who claimed to be the handbag-weapon lady's son stepped across and shoved the young woman after giving her a mouthful for suggesting his mother could have her face smashed in. After that, it was all-out war as the vast majority of the crowd, who probably lived on the Broxworth, piled in with fists and handbags flying everywhere – it seemed everyone was game for a whack with whatever came to hand.

Jemma Stone was clearly flustered and shocked, and he spotted the supermarket manager corral the frightened young MP into the shop and out of harm's way.

He stepped further away from the crowd to avoid being drawn into the brawl. Why he'd come to watch her open the supermarket, he didn't know. However, he just had to keep tabs on her. For some unknown reason, she drew him in. He knew he was becoming obsessed with her and, as that obsession grew, he knew there was nothing he could do about it.

∼

Bruce 'Pinkie' Sinclair smiled to himself as he sat in his car watching the events. He wound down the driver's window of his red Mk2 Jaguar and flicked out his cigarette, blowing a plume of smoke to follow it. He chuckled at the scene in front of him as blokes threw random punches, young women grabbed hold of hair, kicking and slapping, and a few older ladies randomly whacked anyone near them with their handbags.

There was nothing Pinkie liked better than a good fight. However, he would stay out of this one. His name, Pinkie, had been acquired after a particularly raucous fight in a bar a few years back when some bastard had bitten off his little finger during a mass brawl. However, Pinkie had the last laugh as he held the man's mouth shut and forced him to choke to death on his severed digit.

The bloke in the fishing hat and dark glasses had presumably come in disguise to avoid being recognised. Clearly, he wasn't skilled at surveillance because he stood out like a vicar in a brothel. Although, at this stage, he was unaware of who the fishing-hat man was – but he'd become a person of interest.

Whilst Pinkie completed his surveillance, he was oblivious to the man in the brown Ford Consul watching him.

It would transpire to be Pinkie's biggest mistake.

18

Bob-a-Job

Following the scene in the waiting room, I endured a fairly pointless assessment with Doctor Mayhew. He suggested that the best way to solve the snoring issue, which was keeping my wife awake at night, was to sleep in the spare room. As I sauntered home, I took in the town's sights, which was once my home for over fifty years.

Although mesmerised by the town's appearance, I felt I didn't belong. Now, I acted like a tourist as I wandered around. However, that didn't take long because Fairfield didn't attract tourists. The average Hertfordshire town offered little apart from the ruined Abbey, which I'd remembered was the go-to place on field trips when attending primary school.

Whilst serving my time as a disinterested member of the Sea Scouts, I would cut the grass for the Abbey curator during Bob-a-job week. Why Fairfield scouts were affiliated to the sea, well, hell knows, as the coast is over a hundred miles away? Also, I don't recall our division owning a boat. Certainly, I never knew it when I was an impressionable eleven-year-old, but I think the middle-aged Abbey curator held unhealthy fantasies about the little blond Frank.

With a glint in his eye, he'd often invite me into his lodge with the offer of cool lemonade and a promise to see his puppies. Of course, I doubted he owned puppies, and I never went for the lemonade – a wise decision I reflected upon.

I purchased a fifty-one-pence Big Mac just because I could. Now home, I needed time to plan and think carefully about my next move. So far, back in 1979, I couldn't describe my activities as particularly successful. I'd already caused a scene at the doctors, nearly started an argument with our neighbour, Dennis, had a surreal conversation with my dead mother-in-law, and chickened out of speaking to my business partner – not a terrific start to my mission. However, there was one highlight of the day so far – the first minute after waking.

I almost trembled with excitement at the prospect of welcoming my wife into my arms and the anticipation of what she'd said earlier about saving my manhood for her to enjoy. However, these thoughts also petrified me. Part of me felt our relationship was normal, and part felt like it was a distant memory or someone else's life. I now seemed consumed with worry about the potential awkwardness when she arrived home and feared this could overwhelm me.

The doormat offered a heap of letters, mostly addressed to Jemma in manila envelopes, providing that official look. Just the one for me – Britannia Music Club. The brightly covered envelope offered six LPs or tapes for just ninety-nine pence each, as long as I signed up to the club's rules, which appeared extensive and written in extremely fine print.

The phone rang, startling me as I tossed my post aside. Now I was nervous about answering it. However, as I stood mesmerised, the ringing persisted, so I tentatively plucked up the receiver.

"Err ... hello. This is the Stone residence."

"Ha ... very formal, Frankie! Has Jem got you going posh in case it's a government call?"

"Um, no, err ..." Now I was stumped. Who was this? Yep, I recognised the voice but just couldn't quite place it.

"Is she home?"

"No, sorry. Jemma said she had surgery this morning. I can't remember where she is this afternoon."

"Oh, no worries. I was just between clients and thought I'd catch up for a chat. You okay, Frankie? You sound a little off."

"No, no. Just ... a little weary. It's been a long day."

"It's only midday! Keep your strength up because you need to be ready for tomorrow. Tobias is opening the bat with you, and you know how competitive he can be!"

Clare Heaton. Right, at least now I knew who I was bloody well talking to.

The last time I'd seen her and Tobias, they'd stood outside the Hippodrome Theatre before taking in a play in 2008. I was settled down on the pavement with my begging cup about twenty yards from them. They both looked straight at me but didn't see me because, by that time, I'd become invisible to most people. I couldn't recall the last conversation we'd had. However, I was grateful to Tobias for his support after I'd suffered lengthy, persistent questioning regarding Jemma's murder.

"Yes, of course. Shall I ask Jemma to call you?" Now I was tongue-tied and really couldn't think what to say or pretend to have a conversation.

"Yes, please. I'll get Tobias to call you tonight so you can talk batting strategy. I'm not sure where he is this afternoon because he's out of the office. Anyway, I'd better go because this call is peak rate."

The call ended with Clare once again asking if I was alright. Although both parts of my life were fused together, older Frank was dominant. I had to be mindful that I was probably acting differently from how the younger Frank was yesterday.

Beside the telephone was our answering machine, a hefty lump of equipment with a fetching faux walnut front. I remember we bought it when Jemma was elected. She said she would be in high demand and couldn't afford to miss any calls. The little red light in the top corner flashed.

After studying its controls for a couple of moments, I pressed rewind. The tape whizzed back, and then I pressed play. I listened to young Frank and the message I'd recorded to play to callers, which was odd being able to hear my voice that no longer had those gravelly tones. Jemma had stated my message was totally unprofessional and had insisted that I change it. We never did, and rarely did anyone leave a message. Also, I recall her mother saying she was not speaking to a machine. I listened in wonder with nostalgia—

This is Frank Stone. At the tone, leave your name and message. I'll get back to you.

Christ, I'd even recorded it with an American accent in my attempt to sound like Jim Rockford. The tape rolled to the one message which had presumably been left whilst I attended my pointless assessment with Doctor-Magoo-Mayhew.

'Call me.'

I stared at the recorder, expecting it to continue, but that was it. I rewound and played it again. The message was about two seconds long. I had no idea who'd left it or whether it was for Jemma or me. The voice was male and, although the message was very short, I detected a huff as the caller replaced the receiver. Those two short words were said with frustration. Although I replayed the message several times, the caller's identity remained a mystery.

Giving up on the message, I wondered if I should attempt driving and take the Pontiac for a spin – my *baby,* as I recall calling it. I hadn't driven for years and now seemed to have lost my confidence about leaving the house again. Anyway, where would I go? Did I go out on this day the first time around? Had history already changed? I couldn't recall arguing with a bigoted, racist fascist at the doctor's surgery, but would I remember that? It was thirty-six years ago and, to be fair, I really couldn't remember much of the late '70s or the whole of the '80s. Therefore, it could have happened. But the first time around, would I have thought the racist git was using offensive language?

Racism was rife at this time. Although aberrant, perhaps that argument did occur, and I wouldn't have batted an eyelid at Mr Hackett's conversation. The receptionist wasn't offended, nor did anyone else in the waiting room appear to be, so maybe I wasn't either. However, I remembered the clashes over the last few years between the Anti-Nazis-League and the National Front, and how it all came to a head when Blair Peach lost his life earlier this year.

Hang on – why am I worrying about detecting who murdered Jemma? All I have to do is make sure she doesn't go out that night, or if she does, just sit outside the restaurant so I can pick her up and take her home to safety. Surely then, problem solved, and there won't be a murderer to catch as no murder occurred.

Sitting in the driver's seat, I wound down the window. Then, plucking up a packet of Dunhill cigarettes and a box of matches that lay on the passenger seat, I lit up and blew a plume of smoke out of the car window.

If I had time-travelled back thirty-six years, why wasn't I more excited? Instead, I seemed as melancholy as I was when street living. Maybe I should stop smoking now, because it really had ravaged my lungs in later life. Yes, perhaps I could save my younger lungs from the black-tar onslaught I knew I would give them – maybe smoke this packet first and then see.

"Bollocks," I huffed.

"Bollocks, bollocks, bollocks."

Jemma was murdered, and no one was convicted. There were no other murders in the local area that fitted the same modus operandi. The police were probably right – Jemma was murdered by someone she knew. She wasn't sexually assaulted, and there was little evidence of a struggle. I couldn't solve this by protecting her that night – that wouldn't work. If the police were correct and she knew her attacker, they would surely strike another night. The question was why and who.

The police back then, no hang on, now, failed to get anywhere with the investigation. There was a whole task force deployed, with investigators drafted in from the Met. I remember they installed some temporary storage units in the police compound because the millions of typed reports and statements caused the CID offices to be cluttered, and there was concern the sheer weight would cause the floor to collapse. So, considering a whole task force of detectives had failed, and even though I re-owned my beloved PI's replica car, what chance did I have of catching the murderer?

"One day at a time, Frank. One day at a time," I muttered, as I dismissed my previous idea of quitting and lit another cigarette. What I had to do now was get into younger Frank mode. Otherwise, this second life was going to be tricky. I had this Jekyll and Hyde thing going on. Young Frank, the Dr Jekyll character, now haunted by Old Frank, the Mr Hyde character. I had to try and bury Mr Hyde before anyone noticed a dramatic change in my personality.

Not that I knew this then, but looking back, younger Frank was a cool dude – carefree, laid-back and likeable. However, that all changed on the 28th of September 1979.

19

Wile E. Coyote

"Frank, I'm home ... Frank?"

After deciding against the idea of inflicting my forgotten driving skills on other road users, the rest of that afternoon had been super unproductive. Apart from pacing around the house and deducing I was not in nitrous-oxide-land and actually reliving my life, I achieved very little. The realisation of this should have delivered a euphoric feeling of epic proportions – well, it surely would to anyone – and even more so to me after the last crappy thirty years. However, as I paced the house, I became more anxious and concerned about how to act like young Frank. I now felt terrified of re-meeting my wife after thirty-six years, discounting the one minute of pleasure I'd experienced earlier this morning.

"Oh, there you are. I've had one hell of a shit afternoon, I can tell you!"

Jemma kicked off her high heels and let them skid across the kitchen Marley-tiled floor. The stiletto heel of one shoe caught a chipped tile by the back door, causing a piece of flooring to ping off. I seem to remember years ago that it was discovered these tiles contained asbestos – should I be worried? It could affect our health.

'Jeeeeesus, Frank. Your wife is a few weeks away from being strangled and dumped in the woods. Now you're thinking about Asbestosis! Get a bloody grip – and fast, I might suggest!'

Self-bollocking over, I gawped at Jemma as she slumped into a kitchen chair, tipping her head back and releasing a huge sigh.

"Make me a cuppa, my love. I'm pooped!"

I just continued to gawp at her. I deduced that the connections from my brain to my vocal cords had become severed because my mouth opened, but no words were released. Unable to move as my feet seemed welded to those floor tiles and, along with my seemingly now redundant tongue, I'd morphed into one of those weird street artists who painted themself gold whilst pretending to be a statue on the South Bank. No, actually, as all I was capable of doing was blinking, I think I'd morphed into Wile E. Coyote and now considered my only option was to hold up signs as a way to communicate. I believe in his efforts to catch Road Runner, he was crushed or blown up over two hundred times. So, in my quest to catch my wonderful wife's killer, I had to improve on his woeful performance.

"You're in a trance, love. Oh, what did Doctor Mayhew say?" Jemma asked, as she leaned forward and removed her jacket before lobbing it on the kitchen table.

My God, here she was in the flesh – stunning. A couple of weeks ago, the CYA showered me with pictures of her as the projector carousel performed its automated click-through. For many years before my extraction by the CYA, I'd always held an image of her in my mind. However, those memories and projected pictures had not done Jemma justice – the apparition which sat at our kitchen table had to be the most alluring vision of a drop-dead gorgeous woman I'd ever feasted my eyes upon. Drop-dead – poor choice of mind talk, perhaps?

'Get a grip, Frank! Stop being a lecherous old git! You're not ogling Michael-Kors-pink-trainer lady. This is your wife, and you're a thirty-year-old man!'

"Err … well, he wasn't much help, really. He suggested I sleep in the spare room."

"Oh, is that it? Well, that's no bloody good. You'll just have to tire me out before sleep," she giggled.

"Ha, yes … lovely idea. Quite lovely."

'Lovely idea! Lovely idea. What's the matter with you, man? She didn't just suggest a stroll in the park! She wants you to screw her brains out every night! Come on, Frank, come on!'

"Well, let me tell you about today, and what a hell of a day it's been! I had some idiot this morning at the surgery who wanted me to withhold licences on two new taxi firms that have started up in town. He said, can you believe, that as the MP, I should be managing this sort of thing and ensuring that Lawson's business wasn't compromised. I mean bloody hell, we're trying to pull the country from the sewers which that idiot Callaghan and his government dropped us into, and all he can worry about is taxi licences!"

She'd become animated with her hands flying in all directions, a trait of hers that I'd forgotten. I started to grin at the wonder of this returned memory.

"Then would you believe I had to open that ruddy supermarket up at that bloody Broxworth Estate? When I was giving my speech, a fight broke out, and I had to be whisked away to safety. It was horrible, really horrible," Jemma took a breath, stopped her tirade and frowned. "What you grinning at?"

"You're gorgeous."

"Frank Stirling Stone, don't start getting all amorous with me. I'm telling you what happened today! And where's my cuppa?"

I turned and filled the kettle, grabbing the necessary to make tea whilst this amazing woman continued to relay her story.

"I don't think I'm cut out to be an MP. There are too many idiots I have to deal with, and I really hate public speaking. Why the hell did I agree to stand? I should have told Dad I wasn't going to do it."

"Step down. You could get your old job back at Greenland's. I know they'd have you back."

"Oh, I can't. How would that look? And Mum and Dad would be furious!"

"If you're not happy, you should chuck it in. We all only get one chance in life, so there's no point doing something you hate." One chance? Well, in my case, that appeared not to be true.

"No. I'll stick it out. I do seem to make so many enemies, though, and I'm not used to people not liking me."

"Enemies. Who?" Now I thought of Mr Hackett, the racist – that's one.

"Well, there's Lawson's Taxis for a start. You should have heard him when I said taxi licences were not my concern. He practically threatened to kill me!"

That's two.

"Then that mob this afternoon. They all jeered me, and one bloke actually suggested I should get my tits out for the boys!"

Oh, this list is growing. That's possibly three hundred now.

And then what about Lawson's Taxis? They were the ones who let her down *that* night. Had they failed to collect her on purpose after she'd refused to get involved with licences? Did people get murdered for such a thing? Then this Broxworth mob – surely they couldn't be dangerous, could they? Well, hell, I should know, as I came from there. Half the inmates of Wandsworth Prison were murderers, drug gang members, and general low-life from that estate.

I mentally totted up the list of potential candidates to investigate – the list was exponentially growing – now already up into triple figures. Unfortunately, The Hooded Claw and his crew had failed to provide me with detective skills coaching, which it seems I was going to need and lacked.

"Ohhh hell! I'd forgotten. I'm supposed to be going out with Plain-Jayne tonight. Christ, she'll spend all night boring me with her tales of school antics, which I really have no interest in. I could do without that after a day like today."

I plonked her tea down on the table. "Jayne?"

"Yes, Plain-Jayne. You know ... Jayne Hart."

I had to think. I really couldn't remember who she was.

"Oh, schoolteacher Jayne?"

"Yes, silly. Who did you think I was talking about?"

"Yeah, sorry; I know who you mean."

"Well, you should do! She was around here only a couple of weeks ago. You know she fancies you like crazy, don't you? Frank, you're a bit distant today. Are you alright?"

Thinking of Alison Hay, our receptionist-cum-general-dogs-body, it occurred to me that Jemma thought all women fancied me.

"No, I don't think she does. Anyway, whatever you say, I like Jayne." I seem to remember that I did like her. She was, without doubt, the most interesting and intelligent of all of Jemma's friends. I'd never really understood why she had the nickname Plain-Jayne because I remember she was anything but plain and certainly was very easy on the eye, as Dennis would put it.

"Well, she's a bit of a square, that's all. She hasn't got very far in life. I mean, who would want a dead-end job like teaching? Hey, don't get ideas, Mr Stone ... Plain-Jayne might be all gooey-eyed over you, but she can't have you."

Jemma stood and seductively kissed my lips, raising her eyebrows as she rubbed her hands over my chest. With an alluring grin across her face, she lifted my t-shirt and proceeded to rub her hand across my newly acquired six-pack. Pathetically, I froze; this was not a situation I was used to being in.

'Err ... Frank, you there? This is it, mate ... wake up, buddy!'

As she flirtatiously licked her lips, Jemma leaned back whilst unbuttoning her blouse, performing the routine like a pole dancer who teased and tantalised a tongue-wagging, lusting audience. With her partial striptease completed, she placed my hand on her right breast, helping my hand to caress her – she had a wicked glint in her eye. As this gorgeous woman leant forward and seductively licked my lips, I detected an instant stirring below.

"Come up and scrub my back?" She gave a slight growl as her hand drifted from my stomach to the front of my jeans. "Hmmm," she licked my ear and whispered. "Forget the bath. Take me to bed … I want you."

Now, for the best part of thirty years, I'd been forced into celibacy. The last was some older woman who lived with me in that rank flat on the Broxworth, just prior to my move to alfresco living in London. After that, I wasn't much of a catch for anyone. It's difficult to forge loving relationships when living on the streets, and my appearance didn't really lend itself to a Tinder profile. Even old Marge, in no uncertain terms, would have told me to bugger off if I'd have made eyes at her, and I didn't.

However, young Frank was back and ready for action – step aside, old man!

~

Jemma wandered from room to room as she prepared for her evening out. As she strolled about naked, I lay on the bed watching her after a lovemaking session, which was nothing short of out of this world. She'd been in a hurry to savour the delights of my lower regions, as she put it. However, as I'd missed out for thirty-odd years, there was no way I was rushing this adventure, ensuring I savoured every inch of her beautiful body. I was pretty sure I'd never experienced such an erotic hour before. Yes, I had memories, but they fade. This experience brought them back in full technicolour: vibrant, real, and explosive in more ways than one.

"You've got a pervy look in your eye, Frank Stone. You've had your fun for today, so stop ogling me like some lecherous old git," she threw over her shoulder as she wiggled her bum while returning to the bathroom. Well, up until this morning, I was an old git. Not lecherous, but definitely old.

"Where you going tonight?"

"Think we're going to the Maid's Head Hotel. The Courtyard Bar is okay and certainly won't have to face any of that mob from the Broxworth in there!" Jemma called back as she returned from the bathroom.

She'd thrown on a high-necked pink nylon dressing gown, which disappointingly covered her drop-dead gorgeous, luscious, nubile figure but was practical, I guess. Glancing at my shrinking best mate below, he and I both thought it was a real passion killer. If Jemma felt the need to cover up, then the short silk dressing gown hanging on the back of the bedroom door would have been my preferred option. Yes, okay, a typical male attitude, but hey, cut me some slack here. I'd re-acquired a fit new body, and I was keen to give it another run out after I'd successfully taken it for a test drive.

Her passion-killer gown had performed well in its task to distract my thoughts. My mind drifted from my desire for a re-run of the last hour to what someone else had planned for her in a few weeks. What if time has changed, and the murder is tonight and not in a few weeks? Christ, I can't let her out of my sight.

"How you getting there? Are you getting a taxi home?"

"No, Plain-Jayne is picking me up. You getting all protective in your old age?" replied Jemma, as she settled at her dressing table and started rummaging through the plethora of brushes, lipstick, powder and whatever else that covered the top of the dresser and most of the carpet surrounding it.

"And Jayne is bringing you home?"

"Uh-huh," she replied, staring wide-eyed in the mirror, caking her eyelashes with mascara. "You going up the pub with that idiot Dave? Don't drink too much because you have to open the batting tomorrow, and Dad is relying on you and Tobias to put in a good innings." Wide-eyed, waving her mascara brush, she turned and stared at me whilst I lay on the bed as I pondered how I could protect her every minute.

Stopping a repeat of the 28th of September 1979 was not good enough. I had to apply my non-existent detective skills and expose the murderer before it happened – I wondered if that was actually possible. Why had she called Dave an idiot? Better not ask. Otherwise, she really would find that odd after I'd struggled to remember who Jayne was.

"I said Dad is relying on you to have a good game tomorrow."

"Yeah, okay. Jayne *is* definitely bringing you home?"

"Yes! Why the concern all of a sudden?"

"Just you said earlier that you were now making a few enemies. So, I wanted to make sure you weren't walking home alone … as you did … well, you know when."

Lipstick in hand, she spun around again. "What d'you mean, like you know when? What you on about?"

Oh poo. Time-travel! First cock-up.

'How would she remember walking home alone the night she was murdered, you dickhead!'

I jumped up from the bed, still in wonder of my new found agility – getting old really did suck. I seriously liked this young, agile body – especially with my wife's body pinned on top.

"Nothing, Jem, just looking out for you," I replied as I whizzed past her to the bathroom, hoping she would continue with her face paint and forget what I'd said.

I'll have a couple of pints with Dave, then nip into town and keep an eye out for her when she leaves the pub. Then I could follow them home, and that will be day one of my save-my-wife campaign completed. We would be together all day tomorrow, and then I could formulate a strategy for the next few weeks.

I was looking forward to seeing Dave, my old school chum. Although he was supportive when Jemma was murdered, like the rest of my friends, he drifted away as my life fell apart – just at the point I needed my friends to halt my steep decline.

Could I forgive him for that? Well, a couple of beers, and I'll find out.

20

Half Crown

Leaving Jemma to finish off getting ready, I sauntered off down to the pub. She'd shovelled me out of the house, saying I was pacing about and getting in her way.

I couldn't remember the last time I saw Dave. We were best mates at school and stayed close as we moved on with our lives. He hadn't attended university but chose to venture straight in to working at the local supermarket as a trainee manager. Although he was coining it in whilst I was a poor student, I thought his career choice was odd. I mean, who the hell wanted to be a shopkeeper?

His parents would often invite me to stay during my summer breaks from university. Naturally, I was always jealous of his comparative wealth and the red two-door Ford Consul with a retractable white roof he'd purchased. In the late '60s, we would cruise around town, eyeing up the girls whilst naively hoping the car would be the magnet to persuade a couple of lasses to join us at the Saturday night dances up at the Festival House. It cost two-bob entrance fee, and a couple of pints of bitter could be secured for less than a half-crown. Although, as a poor student, I recall Dave having to sub me a few bob.

My parents had produced me at a much older age than usual for most couples in the 1940s, and they'd described me as their little miracle after years of trying. Indeed, my mother giving birth at the age of forty-three was a concern for her doctors at the time. Both weren't blessed with good health, and I lost them when at university studying architecture. In my late teens and early twenties, Dave's parents became my surrogate family.

Dave was now the deputy manager at one of the large out-of-town supermarkets in Watford and fully expected to be appointed to store manager position within a couple of years.

Our drinking hole of choice, if not going into town, was the White Bull. A local, estate-type pub on the outskirts of town near to where both of us could walk to. As I approached, I racked my brain trying to remember his wife's name. I'd been best man at his wedding as he had been mine, but for the life of me I couldn't remember – old Frank's brain was dominant over young Frank's. So, I would just have to wing it and hope it came back to me, along with their young daughter's name that also alluded me which I was reasonably convinced I had no chance of remembering.

"Alright, Dave? How's the missus?" Determined to appear and act as young Frank would, I slapped him on the back and grinned as he stood at the bar.

"You taking the piss?"

Oh, bollocks. It was this summer I remembered they had a short separation after Dave and a young lass, who worked in the cash office in the supermarket, were caught in a compromising position whilst preparing the wage packets on Friday pay-out day. Dave had protested his innocence but admitted he struggled to explain why the young lass's uniform had become unbuttoned and how his hands had found their way inside her bra and cupped around her ample chest.

"Err ... sorry, mate. Just wondered if you and—" Oh, come on, what was her name? "You and her had made up yet?"

He huffed and shook his head. "No, she's got the right hump. Now her father is threatening to punch my lights out!"

"It will blow over. I know it will." And it did. I seem to remember it took a couple of weeks, then Barbara ... yes, that's her name Barbara, forgave him.

However, thinking about it, she should have given him his marching orders. Although they did have a little one to think about. "Babs will come around; you'll see."

"Well, I hope so. I'm not cut out to live on my own, and I'm missing little Sarah like crazy. You wanna pint?"

I nodded, thinking I needed to get on board with my memories quickly, and wished young Frank's brain would come to the forefront as it had managed when bouncing around with Jemma only an hour or so ago.

"You want a Black & Tan or Light & Bitter?" asked Dave, as he waved at a member of bar staff. Although, over the last twenty years, I'd not been a connoisseur of fine beers, I seem to remember both choices were not now my preferred tipple.

"Nah, I'll have a pint of that Worthington E." Not that I could remember the beer, but I certainly could remember Fairfield Bitter which was the sludge the local brewery dubiously called beer. Unless you were over eighty or had your taste buds removed, no one drank it. I seem to remember the company went bust in the '80s and, apart from the redundant workforce, it was a massive relief for everyone.

Now Jemma's comment made sense. Poor old Dave did look down in the dumps. But she was right; he deserved everything he got. I was half tempted to assist his father-in-law with his threat.

The bar appeared exactly how I remembered it, including the blue haze of cigarette smoke that hung at eye level throughout the room. But then I guess it should do, as today was probably one of the last times I'd frequented this rather drab establishment.

I wondered what it was like back in 2015. Probably had a giant plastic dinosaur-shaped slide in the beer garden and rebranded to be called the Hungry Bull, with fake plants and laminated menus offering half-price meals for kids. Glancing at the cracked plastic dome, collecting all sorts of bacteria, which unsuccessfully covered a few curled-up dead-looking cheese rolls on the bar, I considered perhaps the future vision of my old local pub was progress. I accept the family of flies buzzing inside the dome may disagree as they tucked into their evening meal.

"There you go, mate." Dave pointed to my pint, which was deposited on the bar, hauling me out of my daydream. "See your missus had a tough time this afternoon, then."

"Oh?"

"That opening of the supermarket up at the Broxworth."

"Oh yeah. She said it was hell. Apparently, they booed and jeered her. Some bloke even asked her to get her tits out. Can you believe?"

"Yeah, that was funny!"

I raised my eyebrow at him. "Think you're in no position to comment on other women's chests, my old friend."

Dave huffed and waved his hand. "Yeah, sorry, you're right. That was bad taste."

"Anyway, how d'you know about her afternoon?"

Dave continued to slouch as his head slowly sunk towards the bar. As a first night out in my old world, this wasn't exactly how I would have planned it. Not that I believed for one moment it would actually happen. However, propping up the bar in my old local with a depressed Dave while watching the buzzing flies was well down the list of evenings of choice with the opportunities now available to me.

"My store manager sent me up there to check it out. That new supermarket is one of the biggest in the area, so we need to keep abreast of the competition."

"Abreast ... poor choice of words, my old mucker."

"Yeah, you're right," he chuckled. "You don't reckon Jemma could have a chat with Babs, do you? You know, get her to see sense and all that."

"I think it's you who needs to see sense, mate. Anyway, Jemma would probably persuade Babs to leave you permanently."

"Oh, Jemma's got the hump as well, has she? Alright for her with her fancy job, as she swans about town, lording it up. She's getting above 'er station, your missus. If she's not careful, someone might bring her down a peg or two."

"Err ... hang on mate, that's my missus you're talking about! And she's not the one who's going around fondling cash office girl's chests, is she? Think you're out of line, mate."

Dave swung around to face me, red-faced and almost aggressive, as he slammed his beer mug on the bar and poked a finger in my chest. Dave is larger framed than me and at six feet an inch taller, but he was never usually aggressive. This was a new Dave who I didn't particularly warm to.

"Well, if the truth be known, buddy. Babs and I always thought she was a bit stuck up. She's got that air about her, and God knows why. She ain't nothing special, and it's us who got the grammar school education, not 'er. It's women like her and that bloody Thatcher woman that really piss me off. All power-crazed, instead of doing what they should do ... being at home and raising a family."

"Whaaat!" I stepped back from his pointing finger. "What the hell's the matter with you? If you think like that, and Babs is so great, perhaps fondling that girl wasn't such a great idea."

"What's the matter with me, mate, is you thinking your precious bird is better than anyone else's. Sticking her up on some pedestal, worshipping her like she's some Greek goddess. And another thing ... I didn't vote for the silly cow!"

Stunned, I stood open-mouthed as he picked up his beer and slugged down half a pint.

"Gents. Keep it down, please," one of the bar staff called over to us. I didn't see who it was as I stared aghast at my best mate, who I'd not seen for thirty years. No, tonight definitely was not panning out how I'd hoped.

Almost frothing at the mouth and his eyes bulging with anger as he slammed down his empty mug, Dave snatched his car keys from the bar and turned to leave. "Frank, you're besotted with her. You should be a man and make her toe the line. Otherwise, you're going to be the pathetic bloke behind a power-crazed *bitch*. She needs to be taught a lesson." He pointed again at my face as I stood rigid with shock. "Sort her out, or someone will. In fact, I wouldn't mind doing it myself!"

Then, verbal tirade delivered, Dave spun around and stormed off.

An elderly gent positioned in Dave's flight path took off as Dave careered through the bar in his attempt to distance himself from me. The unfortunate gent and his beer landed a few feet from his original position once Dave had barrelled his way past.

After apologising to the gent, who looked longingly at his lost beer now splattered on the floor, and purchasing another half of mild whilst helping him to a seat, I beat a retreat to the end of the bar.

'Frank, we'd like to send you back to 1979, and prevent the murder of your wife.'

Where were you, Dave Bolton, on the 28th of September 1979?

21

Danger Mouse

Whilst supping my pint and mulling over when to go into town to check Jemma was okay, it occurred to me that the argument with Dave absolutely didn't happen the first time around. I never knew he held that view of Jemma, which I felt was totally inaccurate and unfair.

After whizzing around the Millennium Wheel last night, well, alright at one mile per hour, but in Ferris Wheel terms, that's whizzing. It would appear this version of the 17th of August differed from the first – why? What had I done to cause the shift in time? I certainly hadn't done anything which I thought could require one of those killer mercenary types to be despatched on a one-way time-travel excursion with a pocket full of traveller cheques and a Beretta to keep him company.

Twelve hours since landing, assuming this was real, which I guess it must be, and apart from a particularly wonderful hour earlier, it hadn't been a terrific day. I wasn't too fond of Dennis and his banter. Dave was not the bloke I remember and, come to think of it, I was a bit miffed with Jemma with her catty description of Jayne. I remember liking Jayne;

however, would I now consider Jayne an immature twenty-nine-year-old?

Perhaps it was wisdom. I was a man in my mid-sixties, now living in a thirty-year-old body. Although I'd not lived a terrific life, I had wisdom and maturity. My wife and friends lacked the maturity I had – was that the problem? I hoped I still liked Tobias and Clare when I met up with them at the cricket match. Maybe my business partner, Paul, wasn't that bad, and the failed business the first time around was caused by my drinking.

With interest in my evening in the pub waning, I abandoned my pint and decided to move to the check-Jemma-is-safe plan. I was fully aware my planned operation would involve a fair bit of standing about on pavements waiting to check Jemma makes it out of the pub and home safely. Not that I was bothered, because hanging around on street corners is something I'm quite skilled at, with years of experience to pull on. The only difference this time, I didn't have my tartan trolley with me, no empty coffee cup hoping passers-by would deposit some spare change in, and I smelt considerably better.

Successfully driving the Pontiac without major incident, and after whacking on the windscreen wipers instead of the indicators a few times, I parked up on the old cattle market car park in the centre of town. Now, I planned to zip along to the Maid's Head Hotel, sneak a peek through the windows to check Jemma was still with Jayne, then strategically place myself at the top of the hill in Chapel Street Gardens. From that vantage point, I could sit on the park benches which afforded me a clear view down the road and the hotel bar entrance.

I could have easily walked into town but felt I needed the car if, for some reason, Jayne didn't give Jemma a lift home. If that scenario played out, I could pick her up so she wasn't waiting for a taxi. Explaining why I was in town if that happened could be tricky, as I certainly didn't want her thinking I was spying on her, but this was about safety first. If Jemma knew she was only a few weeks away from being strangled, I'm sure she'd understand.

The day the police landed on our doorstep to advise me they'd found Jemma's body is as clear in my mind now as it was thirty-six years ago.

That fateful day was now less than six weeks in the future.

Two police constables, a sergeant and a detective inspector, did seem slightly over the top to convey the news. However, it became clear why they'd employed the heavy-handed approach once they'd quite unsympathetically delivered the information. The Inspector asked me to attend the station for an interview, and it didn't take a degree in architecture to work out something was amiss when the detective read me my rights, whilst a constable applied handcuffs. It became clear later that day they were fixated with one suspect and, although there was zero evidence against me, they persisted.

Casually glancing in the hotel bar window, I couldn't see Jemma or Jayne. As expected, the bar area was pretty busy for a Friday evening, and I couldn't spot any free tables. Although not a bustling town centre pub, it was a popular bar if you were looking to step upmarket for the evening. I recall their beverage prices matched the ambience.

Assuming she would be there, I decided to stick to my plan and wait for them to exit the bar later. Just as I turned to carry on up the hill and head to that park bench, a group standing near the window moved and afforded me a clear view of Jemma and Jayne chatting as they sat at a table to the left-hand side of the bar. Happy that she was there and once again about to go, I spotted a man approach their table. Judging by his aggressive finger-wagging and Jemma's expression, it suggested this wasn't a friendly chat.

Jayne joined in the heated altercation, which now appeared to be developing into a full-blown argument. I was now faced with a dilemma. I considered rushing in, but that would have blown my cover, and then I'd have to explain why I was there. When another man grabbed the finger-wagger, the problem resolved itself as he pulled him away to the exit door. As they exited, the finger-wagger shrugged off his mate's hand from his arm. Clearly, he hadn't calmed down and, whatever the problem was, it was quite clear he seriously didn't like Jemma.

"Stupid bitch!" he muttered, as they walked past me. I didn't know him, although his face seemed vaguely familiar. I glanced back through the window, where I could see the girls. As they appeared none the worse after the altercation with mystery man, I moved up to my planned stakeout position.

Pondering what I'd just witnessed, I lit up a cigarette whilst keeping a beady eye on the bar entrance. Clearly, that bloke's belligerent manner suggested he had an issue with Jemma, as did Mr Hackett at the doctors earlier today. How come, in such a short space of time from being elected, had she amassed so many enemies? I'd witnessed two today so, by the bounds of probability, there must be hundreds. What I was sure of, when I lived this summer the first time, I couldn't recall her having this problem. Although that racist, Mr Hackett, was clearly not one of Jemma's supporters, I didn't know whether the altercation I'd just witnessed had any political bearing – there could be another reason.

The Hooded Claw, or was it Pitstop, had suggested she became one of the longest-serving MPs in Parliament. So, if that were to be true, she must have done something right to be re-elected six or seven times. Although reluctant, she had taken the candidacy to appease her father. Neither of us actually thought she'd get elected, and I don't think Jemma was that bothered about politics. But, if the CYA were correct, she obviously had changed her view.

I remember the celebration at the Conservative Club when her selection was confirmed. Not that I was particularly interested in politics, but to support my wife I threw myself into supporting her campaign. As the weeks ticked past, it became clear she was gaining support. I'd assumed her upsurge in popularity was due to her engaging voters with her policies and commitment to supporting the local area – not because some of the electorate found her rather easy on the eye.

Cecil, her father, was convinced she would win the seat from the outset. However, after her candidacy selection, Jemma said she hoped her father wasn't too disappointed when she failed to win the election campaign – who would have thought she'd actually win?

One of the photos in my *This is Your Life book*, the CYA had left for me to peruse on the day of my extraction, was taken the day she was selected as the prospective candidate. How did they get that photo? I pictured her parents raising a glass of champagne as they hugged her, with me, Tobias, Clare, and a few others all huddled around. Hang on, the bloke at the bar – standing behind us – the one I didn't recognise –

that was him! The finger-pointing man who just walked out of the Maid's Head muttering *Stupid Bitch* was the bloke I hadn't recognised in that photo. Who the hell was he? Why had he just had an altercation with Jemma?

Bored on the park bench and in danger of looking like some pervert who sat and watched people, I decided I wasn't cut out for this surveillance malarkey. Anyway, my cotton-wool-wrapping protection plan I had for Jemma really wasn't going to work. How could I live a normal life whilst keeping close tabs on her to ensure she wasn't murdered? Unless I took the next few weeks off work and trailed her like some MI6 agent, she would be out of my sight for many hours of the day. That wasn't going to work because I didn't think I was cut out for the secret agent role. I suspected I would be more Penfold than Danger Mouse.

I had to presume her timeline hadn't changed and she would be murdered on the 28th of September. The plan would be to determine who the killer was in my real-life game of Cluedo. If I failed as the police had, I would just make sure I follow her that fateful evening and bring her home safely – simple.

Rather than sit on the park bench looking like Billy-no-mates, I decided to walk down to the hotel bar and say Dave wasn't much company and join the girls for a drink. Jemma hadn't wanted to go out with Jayne tonight, so she'd probably be pleased to see me.

I was surprised to see the girls weren't at their table when I entered the Courtyard Bar. As far as I knew there was only one entrance, and I knew they hadn't left as I'd diligently watched from my stake-out position. Turning to go, I glanced through the glass-panelled door which led through to the hotel. There,

I spotted Jemma chatting to some bloke in a corner near the hotel lobby. However, I couldn't identify him because a large cheese plant obscured his face. As I hovered in position, wondering who he was and where Jayne had evaporated to, the man stepped clear of the plant as he grabbed Jemma's arm –Tobias Heaton.

What the hell was he doing here? And why was Jemma huddled in the corner of the lobby with him? The mystery of Jayne's disappearance resolved itself when a slim, petite woman with long chestnut hair exited the ladies' toilets. A quick glance in her direction suggested it could be Jayne, although my brief view suggested she was far prettier than I recall. So, not wanting my secret surveillance operation rumbled, I stepped behind a group of businessmen who stood chatting near the Courtyard Bar entrance. I peered back into the lobby and caught sight of Jemma shrugging off Tobias's hand from her arm before turning and stomping back to the bar. It was time to go.

I now remember that I didn't know where Tobias was *that* night, either.

'Frank, we'd like to send you back to 1979, and prevent the murder of your wife.'

Where were you, Tobias Heaton, on the 28th of September 1979?

22

Pussy Galore

I can certainly remember playing cricket for the Eaton Cricket Club on many occasions. Whether the first time around I played in this particular game, who knows? Was I going to be bowled LBW first ball and be out for a duck? For sure, old Frank was a touch out of practice with wielding a cricket bat. For many years, time spent in the cricket nets hadn't been high on my agenda on how to spend my leisure time, so I hoped young Frank could pull this off.

When Jemma arrived home last night, she was a tad thin with her answers from my casual questioning about her evening. When I asked if she had seen anyone else when out, she said she hadn't. There was no mention of finger-wagging man when I questioned if she had any more horrible encounters after the Broxworth supermarket incident.

I had intended to ask her about the '*Call me*' message on the answerphone, but when I arrived home and played it again someone had erased it. Had I accidentally erased it when fumbling with the controls earlier? Or had Jemma deleted it before going out? For the moment, I decided to keep my powder dry on this one.

Perhaps she should open the wicket today because her skills at batting away my questions and avoiding being dragged into a conversation she clearly didn't want to join in on was impressive. Also, her coolness and ability to lie was a skill I'd been blissfully unaware she possessed. Well, she'd undoubtedly sharpened it up, and it appeared that she'd learnt a lot whilst performing her MP duties over the last six months. As with most MPs, Jemma had mastered the ability to slither her way out of a tricky situation.

Day two of my mission and, without really trying, I'd learnt a lot. Half the town seemed to hate my wife, and the other half wanted to screw her – female population excluded. Well, actually, I didn't know that. Could that be another amazing discovery? Was Jemma having a full-on lesbian affair with Plain-Jayne?

'Ridiculous, get a grip, man! You're now taking it too far. Jemma and Jayne – that's probably the smutty side of your brain and a bit of wishful thinking.'

Anyway, lots of people seemed to dislike her or have an issue of some sort. Also, the fact that I'd learnt that my wife was a skilled and accomplished liar was disappointing. However, on a positive note, last night, I'd rediscovered that Jemma is a ferocious feline sex-mad animal in bed. This particular rediscovery was definitely a positive, which for the moment absolutely outweighed any negatives – well, I was hardly thinking about her lying skills as we tumbled in the sheets, was I?

Saturday morning, my mind floated back to the negative discoveries and why there seemed to be many events occurring, which I must have been oblivious to the first time around.

What I didn't know before, but did this time, was at this stage Jemma was a few days pregnant. Only I, the pathologist who completed the post-mortem, and the police knew that information – that's how it stayed. As far as I know, Jemma was blissfully unaware that she was pregnant. The evil bastard who killed my wife, unbeknown to them, also murdered my unborn child. So, the information she was pregnant went to her grave, and fortunately for her parents' sake, that's where it stayed.

Not only was it vital to save my wife, but I must also save my child. Presumably, if successful, The Hooded Claw and his crew would be delighted that I'd avoided Darth Vader becoming President of the United States, or man-eating aliens invading the planet, or whatever the *European Fault* was.

"Come on, Frank, stop dawdling, man! We're due to start in a minute." Cecil had stuck his head in the changing rooms as I fumbled with my cricket box to ensure it fully protected my now back-in-play previously redundant tackle.

Although many years have elapsed since donning my cricket attire, one thing you never forget is to ensure your cricket box is correctly fitted. During my school days there had been an incident whilst playing hockey which, even now, fifty-odd years later, made me feel queasy thinking about it. One of the lads had struck the ball sweetly, resulting in a direct hit as the ball flew into the nether regions of poor James Frobisher. Apparently, they had to perform surgery because his right testicle had disappeared back into his groin. Unfortunately for poor James, when the surgeon located the squashed organ, he had no choice but to remove it as it had been damaged beyond repair.

As I recalled that particular nasty event, I started feeling nauseous and spewing my breakfast over the changing room floor was a real possibility, which is what transpired with the rest of the hockey team on that day. After that horrific incident, and when hockey was on the agenda, many of the boys produced notes from their mothers saying they had a sprained ankle and needed to be excused from games lessons.

We'd arrived at the Cricket Club late. The teams were ready, and Tobias was all kitted out, swinging his bat around pretending to be Ian Botham. I wondered if Clare knew where he was last night.

With my cricket box correctly positioned and my pads and gloves on, although a little concerned no helmet was on offer, I made my way out of the changing rooms, striding along, John Wayne style. Jemma had stated after my attentions last night she was a little saddle sore this morning.

"He's here, Cecil. Frank-Boycott-Stone is ready at last!" Tobias called out to Cecil, who came bounding over, appearing a little flustered. Although this was amateur cricket of pretty much no consequences, to Cecil, the Cricket Club was serious stuff. He corralled Tobias and me together to deliver a pep talk before we made our way out to the crease.

"Right, gents. They've got Tomkins on the first over, so he'll be lobbing bouncers at you. Frank, I need your usual game today. Nice and safe and no wild swings, and be ready for a yorker."

"They don't call him Boycott for nothing. He couldn't swing a cat. It's all safety first where Frank's concerned." Tobias winked and jabbed me in the chest with his gloved hand.

I scowled at him, not really bothered by his jibe but desperately wanting to know what that conversation was about in the hotel lobby last night.

"Frank. Remember, this is the last game of the season. Victory will mean we retain the Fairfield Cup for the third year." Cecil bulged his eyes at me as if the next few hours would decide the Ashes. Of course, we weren't playing Australia, but this was almost life and death as far as Cecil was concerned.

"Yeah, I got it, Cecil. No wild swings, and watch out for a yorker."

"Good man. Now Tobias, try and leave Frank at the crease. He's better at safety play than you. If we can settle down and get through their first few overs without loss, we can dig in and notch up a nice run total."

Tobias grinned, slapping Cecil on the back. "Don't worry, Cecil. I'll look after Frank. You just keep that scoreboard up to date because I'm going to smash this lot out of the park. Oh, and get the girls organised with tea, as I'll be gasping once we've wiped the floor with this lot!"

Tobias had played at the Club for many seasons. It's where he met Clare the summer I met Jemma. Before Clare and he started courting we weren't close friends, but after Jemma and I got together we'd become a tight-knit foursome. Now I wondered how close after seeing my wife and Tobias last night.

With his dashing good looks, thick mob of dark hair and chiselled jaw, Tobias had a confident swagger about him. He was probably the only man on the planet brave enough to ask Clare out. I wouldn't have been surprised if he'd become the new James Bond when the film producers eventually worked out that a fifty-plus Roger Moore didn't really depict the character who Ian Fleming had envisaged.

'Heaton. Tobias Heaton' Yes, I could hear him saying it.

After we'd all seen *The Spy Who Loved Me*, he'd bought his Lotus Esprit, although I didn't believe it was equipped with the amphibious features which Bond's enjoyed. But, without doubt, he did have the Bond girl on his arm and often referred to Clare as his Pussy Galore. A comment only he could get away with because Clare was not a girl to be messed with.

"Right, Frank. Come on, last game of the season. Let's make sure we win today and make Cecil happy," announced a grinning Tobias, as he slapped me on the back – he seemed to do a lot of slapping.

We made our way to the crease, although my mind wasn't on the game. Nothing for it, but I decided to dump everything out of my head and enjoy the match. It had been a long time since I'd played cricket, which I'd always enjoyed, and I never expected I'd have an opportunity to play again. The last game of the season, so might as well try and enjoy it and hope young Frank is on form.

'Last game of the season – Cecil said it was last game – Tobias had said last game.'

As I stood frozen still in the middle of the wicket, the gentle applause which had wafted across from the cricket pavilion came to an abrupt halt.

"Frank." I heard someone call, but I didn't know who.

"Frank, you okay, mate?" I think the call came from the wicketkeeper this time. Although clueless as to what his name was, but he looked vaguely familiar.

I glanced back at the plethora of deckchairs filled with spectators wearing their wide-brimmed sun hats and Panamas. I spotted Cecil raise his hands, questioning why I'd stopped and now stood in the middle of the wicket. Jemma had stepped out of the pavilion to see what was going on. Everyone stared at me as I stood rooted to the spot.

Although I'd been out of circulation, I'm reasonably confident that the cricket season *didn't* end in August. Cricket was played through to the middle of September – always.

"The date has been specifically chosen as it gives you enough time to change Jemma's fate, but not too early where you could cause historical damage that could jeopardise the whole operation."

Keith Morehouse, AKA Reverend Green's voice, came spinning into my head.

'It's not an exact science, so check the date when you arrive. It should be the 17th of August, but it might be out by a day or two at the worst.'

The Hooded Claw's voice replayed in my mind.

I'd landed yesterday, the 17th of August – but I hadn't checked.

Swivelling around as I stood rooted to the spot. I spotted Tobias striding towards me with his bat held out wide and his other hand raised in a questioning motion.

"Frank ... Frank, what's going on? What's the matter?" he questioned, appearing concerned as he came close – I guess I appeared odd.

My mind raced.

"What's the date today?"

"Hell, man, I don't bloody know! Who gives a damn? Come on, Frank, you're in a daze. Get a bloody grip!"

"Tobias, what's the date?"

He huffed and shook his head. "Um ... err ... 15th September. Bloody hell, get in the crease. We have a bloody game to win!"

~

Not that I could remember the exact details, but even a few days ago I would have known my batting average was up there with the best for the last fifty years of all batsmen who played for Eaton Cricket Club.

Now, as a red-faced Cecil pointed out on the honours board in the pavilion, this year I would not be crowned top batsman. For the last three years, I'd achieved that status with a more than an impressive average of over seventy. It was clear I was usually the match-winner – not today.

"Christ, man, what the hell happened? You're not going to be the top batsman this year, are you?" Cecil stormed off, leaving me forlorn as I gazed at the gold lettering which stated Frank S Stone Top Batsman 1978, 1977 and 1976.

Cecil's bluster was caused by the embarrassing incident a few minutes ago. When I'd taken up position to receive the first ball, I failed to swing my bat, resulting in the red ball taking out the middle stump and sending it cartwheeling towards the wicket-keeper – I was out for a duck – never before had that happened.

But bollocks to cricket. Somehow, I'd landed a whole month out, and I now had less than two weeks to stop some bastard from killing my wife and child.

23

Onatopp

"Well done, Tobias! Bloody well done!" Cecil enthusiastically shook Tobias's hand whilst the applause continued as the teams headed in for tea. After the regulation fifty-overs, Tobias had achieved one-hundred-and-sixty-five not out. His batting performance placed Eaton in a commanding position to win the match, and clearly Cecil was delighted. He beamed like a child at Christmas who'd just ripped off the paper to discover their forever-desired toy.

I, on the other hand, had sat on the pavilion veranda, chain-smoking, with my mind whirring at what my next move was in my Save-Jemma's-life mission, which had just lost a precious four weeks of planning and detecting time.

Time to think was not a problem. Following my early dismissal, the lower order of batsmen who slumped awaiting their turn at the crease failed to make eye contact leaving a furious Cecil to say his piece, which probably covered all their thoughts at my woeful performance. Helen Causton had shaken her head and then headed back into the kitchenette to carry on preparing the cucumber sandwiches after calming her husband, who looked like he was heading for a cardiac arrest following his verbal tirade.

What had really pissed me off was Jemma's reaction. After her father's verbal mauling, she delivered hers and informed me in no uncertain terms how I'd let the side down. She then proceeded to stomp off to jump around with Clare as they applauded Tobias whilst he sprayed the ball from one boundary to the other as he amassed his sizeable run total.

What I would have expected from my wife was some modicum of support. Maybe she could have been the one to tell me I was just unlucky and perhaps remind her father of the matches I'd won this year. But no, it was the cold shoulder and swooning over super-duper-Tobias.

Apart from bedroom antics, and yes, they were amazing, the last twenty-four hours with my wife were not as I would have hoped they would be. For so many years, I'd pined over her loss, remembering what a wonderful wife she was and the devastation of losing her. Now, bedroom aside, I wasn't sure I actually liked her that much.

Grabbing my cup of tea and standing alone as all the players and women huddled in a melee of chatter, I stood and people-watched – that skill I'd perfected over many years.

Jemma and Tobias appeared in deep conversation as they huddled near the kitchenette doorway. Clare and Helen chatted on the veranda, whilst a gaggle of men in whites ogled Pussy Galore as she flicked her hair back and the gentle breeze pinned her light cotton dress to her ever so perfectly proportioned curves.

The conversation with Super-batsman and my Judas-wife appeared heated, although in hushed tones. Tobias gesticulated with his hands whilst Jemma shook her head – this was odd; something was going on here. Was this a continuation of their conversation last night? A conversation which yesterday evening Jemma seemed not to remember or keen to ensure I didn't know had taken place.

With the play about to restart and Tobias-Botham-Heaton tossing the ball in the air, ready to bowl, I ensured I had Jemma to myself. Clare had disappeared to assist Helen and a few other ladies clear away tea. Presumably, my wife thought she was now too important to assist with kitchen duties.

I sidled up to where Jemma was standing whilst she watched the field of play. "What were you and Tobias chatting about at tea?" I questioned without looking at her but swivelled my eye to see her reaction.

"What?" she answered, without looking at me.

"I just wondered what you and Tobias were talking about. You looked ... well, annoyed."

"Don't be silly. I wasn't annoyed."

"Oh, okay. Well, what were you talking about then?"

"Nothing. Nothing in particular."

"Jem. Jemma?" As she turned and looked at me, I detected a coldness in her eyes. Not a look I had remembered, and certainly not a look that she'd given me yesterday.

"What, Frank?"

"You, okay? You seem a bit miffed or put out. Did Tobias say something?"

"Like what?" Her lips twitched as they had last evening – a tell-tale sign she was agitated.

"Well, I don't know. That's why I'm asking you!" I exclaimed. Now a bit pissed off with the cold-shoulder treatment.

"Frank, what's the matter with you? You're getting all silly. Questioning me last night and now today like Dixon of Dock Green trying to unearth some tales of the unexpected," Jemma aggressively answered before turning on her heels and marching off to the kitchen.

"Tales of the Unexpected," I muttered. There was something unexpected going on for sure, I thought, as I pictured Clare and Jemma as the naked silhouetted girls dancing around a spinning roulette wheel and Tobias-Botham-Heaton as the villain in the story of some Roald Dahl twisted mystery.

"Howzat?" came a cry from Tobias as he held his arms aloft.

The umpire's arm rose, and a huge cheer erupted as Tobias had bowled out their second batsman – the shouts jolting me from my daydream. I stood and gawped at the fielders who'd all huddled around Tobias, slapping his back as they congratulated him for dismissing the opposition's best player.

As the group dispersed back to their fielding positions, and the disgruntled batsman trudged his way back to the pavilion whilst lobbing his gloves on the boundary line, I had a clear view of the opposite boundary. A man stood smoking a cigarette as his dog obediently sat beside him.

Just a man and his dog watching a Saturday afternoon cricket match – nothing unusual in that. However, this was the finger-wagging man from the Maid's Head Hotel. The same man who stood at the bar scowling in the picture as we all held up our champagne glasses.

Helen had appeared from the kitchenette and was settling into her deckchair.

"Helen ... Helen?" I called out.

My mother-in-law scowled in my direction, presumably like the rest of the club members still annoyed regarding my pathetic batting performance even though it was clear our team were now well on the way to victory.

"What, Frank?"

"I won't point because that's rude. But d'you know who the man is with a dog standing near deep extra cover?"

Helen glanced to the exact point, clearly knowing her fielding positions well, and held her hand to her brow to block out the glare from the slowly sinking sun. "Oh, I think that's Miles. Miles Rusher. I must say I'm surprised to see him here. I never thought he was a cricket man."

Miles Rusher! Now I remembered. He won the by-election in December 1979, which ran because Jemma's death had left the vacant seat. He'd been a prominent councillor and was expected to take the parliamentary candidacy when Brian Grey was forced to step down following his West-Indian-lollypop sucking incident. However, as the local Conservative Association leader, Cecil had vetoed his selection, favouring his daughter. The committee voted for Jemma after Cecil had brow-beaten them into submission – Cecil could be very persuasive.

I seem to recall Miles stepped down from politics in 1996 to spend more time with his family. However, the truth be known, he was forced out just after he survived an exposé by the News of the World when, as a junior Defence Minister he'd involved himself with a Russian prostitute who turned out to be a highly trained undercover FSB agent. Now I remembered the headlines:

Onatopp, the Thigh Crusher – From Rusher with Love

So why, if Miles Rusher wasn't a cricket man, was he standing watching a cricket match in Fairfield, which just happened to be run by the local MP's father? And why had he been in the Maid's Head Hotel last night having a finger-wagging session with my wife?

'Frank, we'd like to send you back to 1979, and prevent the murder of your wife.'

Where were you, Miles Rusher, on the 28th of September 1979?

Part 2

24

28th September 1979 ... the first time.

Norman Bates

As Jemma reached the top of St. Stephens Hill, she'd calmed down and was no longer stomping in those sensible shoes. However, when she eventually arrived home, she'd be subjecting Frank to a bloody mouthful for not answering the phone. Jemma now regretted not taking the lift when Clare offered it, but she really didn't expect to be let down by Lawson's Taxis.

She now remembered the heated exchange a few weeks ago when Ted Lawson sat in her offices complaining about the issuing of taxi licences and the potential damage he believed that would inflict upon his business. Well, clearly, after tonight's debacle, the sooner there was a bit of healthy competition in the town, the better.

Jemma stepped into Queen's Road, one of the main roads out of the town centre, which led back to her house. Although still faced with a long walk, her initial frustration had abated and her pace now slowed from a stomping march to almost a stroll.

Had that pillock at the taxi office purposely let her down? Had their driver really suffered a flat tyre? Or was it payback because she didn't listen to Old-man Lawson when he came to her for help? One thing for sure, in the morning, she fully intended to make some calls to a few acquaintances in the local council and ensure those licences were granted. Lawson's stranglehold on Fairfield was going to come to an end – she would make sure of that.

Although only just past eleven, the road was reasonably quiet. A few cars passed Jemma, but Fairfield was a sleepy town and didn't offer much in the way of nightlife. As Jemma stepped off the kerb to cross a side road, a car pulled up close, and the driver wound down the window – initially making her jump in surprise.

"Oh, it's you! You made me jump. What you doing here?"

"Well, I could ask you the same thing. Why are you walking at this time of night?" the driver replied.

"Well, I had a taxi booked but, apparently, the driver had a flat tyre. They said they didn't have another car available, would you believe? I called Frank, but he didn't answer."

"Well, I'm your knight in shining armour. Hop in. I'll drop you home."

"Err ... okay, thanks." Although she thought this could be a little awkward because the last time they'd spoken, it resulted in a heated argument. However, now relieved that she didn't have to walk the rest of the way home, Jemma nipped around to the passenger side and hopped in the car.

Jemma had always been a talker, and Frank had often said he didn't know how her brain could formulate the words so quickly to enable her to babble on at such high speed. As she shot her mouth off, delighted that the hour walk was now reduced to a five-minute drive, her knight in shining armour didn't reply. It was only when she asked a question, and he'd remained silent, that she noticed a few moments ago that they'd passed the end of her road and were now hurtling through the middle of Fairfield Woods.

"Oh, you idiot, you've missed the turning. Pull into the picnic area. You can turn around in there."

As instructed, he pulled in and swung the car around in a full circle.

He killed the engine.

"What you doing?" Jemma called out, but he'd already opened his door. Still utterly confused as her jaw dropped, she watched him jump out and scoot his way around the front of the car. Before Jemma could compute what was happening, he'd yanked open her door and grabbed her coat collar.

"Stop! What the bloody hell? Stop!" Before Jemma could scream out anything else, he clamped his hand tightly over her mouth and dragged her from the car. The back of her sensible shoes caught on the doorsill, causing them to flip off and lay in the passenger seat footwell. Pain whooshed up her legs as her heels thumped down onto the stony ground.

Initially more confused than frightened, Jemma realised what was occurring, causing her surprise to give way to gut-wrenching fear as he clamped his hands around her neck and squeezed. Never had she seen his eyes so wild before and, as he concentrated intently on the task in front of him, Jemma felt her head go light as she desperately grappled at his jacket sleeves.

Jemma detected a tear trickle out of her eye. Then, as her vision fuzzed, the image of the face of her knight in shining armour started to distort, morphing his appearance to that of the death-head smile of Norman Bates.

Psycho was the last word to cross her brain.

25

2015

Cromer Crab

The night of travel always delivered mixed emotions for Hartland. Over the years, he'd seen many travellers leave and always had that same feeling in the pit of his stomach – the anticipation of success and the dread of failure.

He'd grown to like Frank, or Smelly-Frank as the Preparation Team had nicknamed him. Maybe he liked him because they were the same age, and he could sense a good man underneath that gruff exterior. He was sad for Frank that his life had panned out how it had. As Hartland reclined in his leather chair and took a sip of his single malt, he hoped, not only for himself but for Frank, he made it through the wormhole.

These nights, he hunkered down in his office. In a few minutes, he would know if they'd achieved a successful mission. Then he could relax, pour himself another large whisky and enjoy finishing his report, which he would present to the Board in the morning.

Of course, his family were blissfully unaware of how he made a living. Marjory assumed he worked for MI6 or some secret Government agency, so staying away from home was quite normal. In fact, these days, he rarely returned to his estate in Oxfordshire. Marjory didn't mind as she had her own life and, although they would always be married because divorce was so lower class, he found the woman a bit of a bore.

The only requirement Hartland stipulated of his wife was that she toed the line and avoided any scandal which could cause him embarrassment. After the toe-curling episode ten years ago, when one of the house staff had stepped into her bedroom suite only to find Marjory enjoying the delights the young pool man's pole could offer, she had behaved herself.

Hartland, apart from nights like these, always stayed at his club. Whenever he felt the manly need, he would enjoy a pleasant evening up at Frannie's – an exclusive club for like-minded gentlemen. There, he could savour the delights of a variety of young ladies who were significantly more desirable than his tedious wife.

Hartland glanced at his watch – 1:09 a.m. The turn in his stomach was caused by the dreaded fear the mission was unsuccessful. Either Frank had not made it through, and now his dismembered body would be floating through the atmosphere or wherever the failed travellers ended up, or he had made it but failed with his given assignment.

Failed missions were messy and caused a mountain of reports and committee meetings to decide on the appropriate action required. Worst of all, that bloody woman, Lady Maud Huston-Smythe, would be down on him like a ton of bricks. Douglas despised the woman and, although he enjoyed the fieldwork, he bristled that she had been the one who vetoed his Board appointment.

Once again, he glanced at his watch. 1:10 a.m. He would always leave it to the quarter past the hour before checking. Hartland never looked before as he was highly superstitious, and his brain had convinced him that it would result in bad news if he checked before that time. Of course, it didn't work like that, but he stuck with his routine. His team knew never to disturb him, irrespective if it was to be good news or bad. They would all be doing the same as him, lingering in their office and praying for success.

Hartland rechecked his watch. 1:12 a.m. Three minutes. Morehouse and his team would know by now. However, Morehouse knew never to contact him at this point, whether it was celebration time or disappointment. He touched the keypad on his PC, causing the blue screen to awaken and display the CYA crest in the centre.

The cursor blinked in the login box.

"Patience, Douglas ... patience," he muttered to himself. After aggressively stubbing out his cigarette in the already full ashtray, he grabbed another as he blew a plume of smoke at the screen. With his right index finger, he typed his name in the login box.

Hartland rechecked his watch, 1:14 a.m. His fingers hovered over the keyboard as the cursor blinked in the password box.

The page he would load up would be the BBC news feed. At 1:00 a.m., the news headlines reported on Prime Minister David Cameron's comments prior to the Iceland Summit of the Northern European Leaders. As his finger hovered over the keyboard, he now hoped the news feed would have changed to show Prime Minister Vince Cable's comments. The Foreign Secretary would be the RT Hon Jemma Stone, and the news feed would not be reporting the clamour from right-wing MPs to leave the European Union.

Hartland was a strong supporter of right-wing politics and would be delighted to see the UK leave the EU. However, he knew the data, which suggested the *European Fault* was unavoidable if the UK trod that path. His responsibility was to ensure *Faults* of that magnitude were averted and corrected.

The time displayed in the right corner of his screen flipped to 1:15 a.m. He punched in his password, clicked the BBC news feed page, and hit refresh. The curser spun as he took a heavy, deep drag on his cigarette.

The curser still turned.

"Bloody hell. This isn't the time for buffering!" he announced, as his cigarette bounced up and down where it hung from the corner of his mouth. Finally, the page started to load, and the BBC logo formed, then stopped.

The buffering continued.

"Oh, Christ, come on!" he bellowed at his screen. That seemed to do the trick as the page fully loaded in an instant. He immediately hit refresh again. The page reloaded, producing the same image.

Douglas snatched up his phone and dialled the three-digit extension number.

The line instantly answered. "I'm on my way, sir," came the reply.

Morehouse had anticipated the call from his boss as he waited by the phone, his hand hovering, ready to snatch up the receiver. Replacing the handset, Morehouse marched out of the Data room with his leather folder tucked under his arm. "Keep me updated with any developments," he called over his shoulder as his team furiously punched away at their keyboards.

As Morehouse entered Hartland's office, his boss stood by the window with his back to the door. Hartland turned, removed his cigarette from his mouth and downed the large whisky he held in his right hand. Morehouse knew the form and didn't waste time on pleasantries.

"What the bloody hell happened?" boomed Hartland, as he took his seat behind his desk, slamming his cut-glass tumbler down and reaching for the bottle of single malt that was now close to an appointment with a glass recycling bank.

"My team have located Frank."

"So, he made it through?"

"Yes, sir. He made it through."

"But he failed?" questioned Hartland, as he held his glass and pointed it at Morehouse.

"It appears so, sir. As I said, sir, we've located him living on the North Norfolk Coast.

"Bollocks. What went wrong?"

"He's now Sir Frank Stone. Smelly Frank managed to get himself knighted last year for his work with the homeless. The charity Frank set up in 1990 looks to have had a profound effect on supporting rough sleepers. Frank has influenced Government policy, and one of the lesser Royals is the patron. He's taken a back seat now, and his son-in-law, Denzel Warlow, runs the day-to-day operations. He and his wife have a particularly lovely house near Sheringham that overlooks the sea. We ascertained that he has four children and seven grandchildren. His social media posts suggests he and his wife spend an awful lot of time with them.

"Jesus Christ, man. I don't give a shit if Smelly-Frank is crabbing off Cromer Pier with his brattish grandchildren! What the hell happened to Jemma Stone? Why the blue blazes hasn't she changed history?" Hartland fired back, as he bolted out of his chair.

"We're working on that at the moment, sir."

Hartland huffed and raked his hand over his hair. "Any category one changes caused by Frank that I need to be aware of?"

"None. We've identified one category seven and four eights. It appears that Frank's return has changed very little."

"Well, that's lucky. Otherwise, we would have to liquidate him." Relieved, Hartland downed his whisky.

Category one or two changes would require them to immediately despatch one of the mercenary type fellows to eliminate Frank the day he arrived. Category three to five would be a Board discussion and could result in the same outcome. Anything above five was deemed an acceptable change, which the CYA Board believed could be tolerated.

Morehouse bowed his head. He felt sorry for his boss as he knew the shit storm that would erupt later this morning, and Hartland would be in the direct firing line of the Board's wrath.

Hartland sunk into his chair, deflated and defeated. "Out of interest. What was the category seven change?"

"Yes, quite a good one, actually. One of my analysts, Claydon, you know the one? The Norfolk lad who sounds like he should have straw in his ears or could audition for a Bernard Matthews Turkey burgers advert."

Hartland nodded, waiting for Morehouse to get on with it, fearing he could be launching into one of his shaggy dog stories, which he was prone to do.

"Well, he always checks the football stats on the night of travel, as he's desperate for a change in fortune for his beloved Norwich City. He always hopes there is a change and his team have won the Premier League at some point. But, of course, I always point out to him that would be classed as a category one change as it would take a seismic movement for that to happen!" nervously chuckled Morehouse, realising by the stern face of his boss he was rambling.

"Is there any point to this story?" barked Hartland.

"Err ... yes, sir. Sorry, sir. Well, when Claydon was checking, he found that back in 1986, in the World Cup Quarter-Final between England and Argentina, Maradona's famous hand-of-God goal was disallowed. The linesman spotted it, and Maradona was booked and later sent off. Gary Lineker scored a hat-trick and repeated that feat in the final when England thrashed Germany 5-1. England won the World Cup!"

"Is that it?" exclaimed Hartland, as he jumped out of his chair. Hartland wasn't interested in football. As far as he was concerned, it was a sport followed by lager-swilling, foul-mouthed louts. Moreover, football was a working-class game.

"Yes, sir. That's it."

The phone on the desk shrilled. Hartland snatched up the receiver. "What?" he aggressively spat back. Although for a second became concerned it might be Lady Maud Huston-

Smythe, and her Ladyship would not appreciate his demeanour at this time of night. He listened for a few seconds, then handed the receiver to Morehouse. "It's Johnson, your senior analyst. He urgently needs to speak to you."

Morehouse took the receiver and listened, offering the odd 'uh-huh' here and there during the three-minute call. Then, finally, he laid the receiver gently down on its cradle and glanced up at his boss.

"All is not lost. We may have an opportunity."

26

September 1979

Olivia Neutron Bomb

Sunday was an odd day. However, on a positive note, Jemma had thawed after her ice-maiden performance on Saturday. Apparently, we were off to her parents' house, so I hoped winning the Fairfield Cup had also defrosted her father who'd refused to further converse with me following his verbal mauling.

I believe over thirty years had elapsed since I'd enjoyed the delights of roast beef and Yorkshire puddings. Apart from the company, Sunday lunch was a delight.

My father always insisted I displayed impeccable table etiquette. Sit up straight, hold your cutlery correctly, and never chew with your mouth open. However, over the years, my table manners had somewhat drifted. I reapplied my father's teachings following odd looks from Jemma as I'd hunched over my plate shovelling down my food as if my life depended on plate clearance in less than a minute.

Jemma and her parents yacked on about this, that, and everything whilst I remained quiet and gobbled down my food. A point Jemma raised with me on the way home, questioning whether I was still sulking following her father lambasting me at the cricket match.

Maybe I'd viewed my life through rose-tinted glasses. As I'd shuffled around the streets of London, I firmly believed Jemma was the perfect wife – a flawless woman. Well, that's what my mind had imprinted in my head for many years.

However, that's not how I felt now. Perhaps Dave was right, and I did place her high on that imaginary pedestal. Yes, okay, as a figure of a vibrant thirty-year-old woman, she was, to a man, totally stunning. Jemma Stone turned heads. Men would ogle her whilst trying to soak in her beauty without their gawping becoming too obvious. Their wives looked on with envious eyes, feeling inferior as they read their husbands' minds.

She was mine. Now I considered my younger self to have been rather shallow. Because, back then, I'd only concerned myself about her stunning good looks and revelling in other men's jealousy. What about love and friendship? Had I not cared about that?

What I was fast finding out in the three days since reliving my life, she was without a doubt still a stunner and still turned heads – but I didn't like her much. As hard as I tried to love her, I found it slightly annoying every time she opened her mouth.

Now I felt deflated after the euphoria of awakening two days ago and realising The Hooded Claw was capable of providing time-travel excursions, albeit exclusive, and not available to all who purchase a three-venue saver ticket.

Whatever I was feeling, I had to stick to the plan and stop her murder. After that, well, I'd concern myself with that dilemma later. Then, maybe young Frank's mind would take over, and I would start to like her again. We had a child on the way who would need loving parents. Perhaps once the child was born, Jemma would mature. Maybe then, we would fit together better – God, I hoped so.

My memory of Helen was tainted by her non-verbal accusations that I'd murdered her daughter. However, our relationship improved after a tricky start when Jemma had introduced me, and her mother discovered I'd come from that God-awful Broxworth Estate. As Jemma and my relationship blossomed, her mother ignored my upbringing, focusing on the fact that I had a grammar school education, had attended university, and was now a qualified architect. More to the point, I made her daughter happy – something I seemed to be struggling to do now I was back. Although, going by the squeals in bed, it would suggest she enjoyed that part.

Nursing a cup of tea on that Sunday afternoon, I couldn't get the post-murder Helen out of my brain and I struggled to warm to her. But Cecil, despite my bollocking yesterday, was different.

After the murder, he'd not held his wife's belief. I have no idea why, but I knew at the time he just didn't buy it. Instead, he'd publicly supported me on the steps of the police station on the day I was released from questioning when reporters had crowded around constantly screaming my name, trying to secure a quote. Tobias had delivered a statement he'd prepared, and Cecil added his support to a wagging microphone as dozens of reporters frantically captured his words in shorthand on their reporter notebooks.

Before that cup of tea, I endured a tour of Cecil's greenhouse. He provided me with gardening tips, specifically on how to grow and nurture tomato plants. He'd said that although Percy Thrower and Geoff Hamilton presented a good show on Gardener's World, they didn't know the tricks he'd learnt on how to produce a bumper crop.

To be honest with you, if this had happened the first time around, I'd have probably glazed over whilst yawning and constantly glancing at my watch. For sure, I'd be checking the exits as I planned my escape route from his glasshouse. Not that I'd ever had the opportunity to dabble in gardening and, apart from enjoying the flowers in the various London parks where I sometimes slept, I'd never experienced the joy which plants can provide. Now, at sixty-six and living in Frank's young body, I surprised myself with how much I enjoyed Cecil's guided tour.

∼

Jemma's Monday morning would be full of local Party business and a surgery session. Tomorrow, she'd return to London following the end of recess. For me, it was a return to my office at Stone & Wilson Ltd, last venturing there sometime in 1986. As Jemma and I shared the bathroom, readying ourselves for work on Monday morning, I couldn't get Paul's treachery out of my head.

I'm aware my work performance after her death was somewhat lacking, perhaps could be described as disastrous. However, the bastard cheated me out of everything whilst he watched as I slid into the gutter. After the late '90s, I completely lost touch with him. To be honest, I hoped his life had fallen apart, which I'm aware is not a charitable thought.

Just my luck, the bastard became a millionaire and was now living in the Cayman Islands. Probably, he'd be cruising around on his hundred-foot yacht, fishing for barracuda whilst sipping champagne and enjoying the delights of a few scantily clad ladies. If he was, I hoped Jaws would resurface and gorge on his treacherous body. Well, no, not *now*, as Paul wouldn't be flailing in the mouth of a great white, more's the pity, because he'd be in the office this morning. I was still struggling to not think of *now* as being 2015.

"Jem, I'm off now. I'd better get a shifty on as I've had three days off," I said, as I poked my head in the kitchen where she looked to be preparing breakfast in that passion-killer dressing gown.

"No ... you need to eat some breakfast, Frank Stone. No man of mine leaves the house on an empty stomach," replied Jemma, as she tossed a packet on the table and cracked two eggs into a dish. "Make the orange juice, and I'll whiz up some scrambled eggs for us."

Plucking up the packet, I chuckled, causing Jemma to frown. "Rise & Shine! Bloody hell, I didn't know they still made this stuff. Not had it for years."

Jemma frowned as she ferociously beat the eggs. "Err ... Frank, we buy it every week; you drink gallons of the stuff! I must say you've been a bit odd the last few days. What's the matter with you? Is something going on at work that's worrying you? Is that lech, Paul, causing problems?"

"No, Jemma, I'm fine." Well, I could hardly tell her the truth.

Jemma poured the egg mixture into a pan on the stove, providing me a moment to collect my thoughts on the time-travel cock-up that fortunately seemed to have washed over her. Still amazed we bought the stuff, I studied the packet and read the instructions.

"You know I can't stand that man, and I hate that you're in a partnership with him. I just wish you could strike out on your own, so we had nothing more to do with him," she added, as she turned and looked at me whilst prodding the mixture in the pan. "That Alison trollop better not be coming on to you. She's all tits and teeth, flaunting it at anything with a penis. You know she's obsessed with you like some lovesick teenager?" Jemma dropped the spatula, turned and clutched her chest. "Hopelessly devoted to yooooou," she sang, swishing her dressing gown from side to side.

Even I could remember the scene from the film Grease that the girls insisted on seeing, and Tobias and I had to suffer.

"Yes, very funny, Olivia Neutron Bomb! But I think your suggestions about Alison are unfounded. She's just a nice, friendly girl, that's all." Well, I'd not seen her for nearly forty years and, apart from speaking to her on Friday, I could only recall her being a bubbly girl with a silly crush on me.

"Ooo, haha, that's funny, Olivia Neutron Bomb!" replied Jemma, as she plucked up the spatula again, wiggled her bum and restarted her woeful attempt at singing. I carried on reading the ratio of water and powdered orange juice required to make the drink.

Jemma was a fair few places higher ranked in the gorgeous woman charts than Olivia Newton-John. However, Olivia was far superior in the vocal cords department. Jemma banged out the song, which sounded more like a strangled cat as it was forcibly rolled through a mangle. No, Olivia definitely had nothing to fear on that front.

"Clare suggested we go see The Muppet Movie next weekend. Although I think Tobias said he'd rather see Moonraker."

"The Muppets! Oh, per-lease. Christ no. And as for Moonraker, apart from Octopussy, that has to be the worst Bond film ever!"

"You've not seen it. It's only just come out. And I've not heard of Octopussy; I can't say I remember that one."

Glancing up from the packet, now fully educated on the water and powder ratio required, I realised I'd blurted out my second time-travel cock-up.

"Is that what you and Tobias were arguing about on Saturday? He wanted to see Moonraker, and you and Clare preferred the Muppets?" Not that I thought, for one moment, their spat had anything to do with decisions regarding Miss Piggy and Miss Moneypenny – now there's a great idea for a movie.

"Oh, Frank, give it a rest. We weren't arguing. Can't even remember what we were talking about. Grab two plates, please." Well, that was another lie she'd just spun out.

"Err … yeah, whatever. Muppet movie it is, then." Not that I was really into puppet shows. However, I'd loved Spitting Image and chuckled to myself remembering the Maggie and vegetable sketch. I wondered how the programme makers would have depicted Jemma if she were supposed to become a successful politician. Now I couldn't get the image of the Kylie Minogue puppet with all that backcombed '80s hair out of my head.

Jemma dished up, and we sat in silence for a few moments as we munched our food.

"Frank." Her dead-pan face gave nothing away. Although she shifted her bum as if uncomfortable with what she was about to say.

"What?"

"Lech Paul might say something this morning. He phoned here last Friday evening, just before I went out. He said you phoned earlier in the day, and he was returning your call. Well, you know how I can't stand him. One thing led to another, which ended up with us having a bit of a stand-up row. Sorry, Frank, but he just brings the worst out in me."

"Oh. What was the argument about?"

She waved her fork around in the air whilst finishing chewing. "Oh, I can't remember now. But he might make some sarky comment when you catch up with him later."

"Oh, okay." I left it at that, not knowing what else to say. However, I was curious why she seemed to have severe memory loss when recalling arguments with my male acquaintances.

Keen to get on with my day, I shovelled down my eggs. The atmosphere had changed since I mentioned Tobias, and she'd mentioned Paul. I thought it would be good to get going before I blurted out some other time-travel cock-up, which I would struggle to explain.

27

Wildcat Strike Action

"Morning, Frank. Hope you had a lovely weekend." Alison flicked her ponytail hair and smiled as I entered the office, which had a bizarre déjà vu feeling about it. Was Alison fluttering her eyelashes at me? No, surely not – was she?

"I'll get you a coffee and bring it through," she said, before jumping up and brushing past me.

Alison did seem to push her chest at me, and it wasn't difficult to see below her low-cut top that she'd forgotten to pop on her bra when dressing this morning. That surely was unprofessional. What would clients think when they copped an eye full of our very own Page Three Girl sitting in reception? I imagined when Paul arrived, his tongue would be hanging out, salivating, and hardly able to control himself. At some point, I thought I'd better have a word with her.

Momentarily hovering in the small hallway which separated Paul's and my office, I spotted through the frosted glass the distorted outline of my treacherous business partner. It appeared he was already in and on the phone. I wasn't looking forward to our first meeting in twenty-odd years. Although I had to be mindful at this stage, Paul doesn't know what a Dick Dastardly bastard he became.

As I scanned around my office, I thought how strange it was to be back here. The huge elevated draftsman's board, which held several drawings that I presumed I'd been working on last week, captured my attention. The top drawing had the title *Chapel Street Multistorey Car Park Second Draft*, penned across the top. I remember this now, and our delight when we won the contract to build a three-storey car park to provide sufficient parking for a new shopping mall which would be built next year.

Alison bounded into the office, nipples first, holding my coffee, which she deposited on my desk as she leant over and held that position, presumably waiting for me to gawp at her evidently large chest and exposed cleavage which her thin blouse woefully failed to hide.

"I have four telexes for you. Let me know how you want to respond, and I'll get that done straight away. You have Bill Parsons from the Council in at eleven."

I didn't comply with her non-verbal request to gawp at her chest because I was still transfixed by my draftsman's board. Anyway, gawping at her chest would have been pervy.

"Frank?"

"Sorry?" I looked at her whilst desperately trying to avert my eyes from the obvious.

"Frank, did you hear me?"

"Yes, yes. Thanks, Alison. I'll look at them later." Of course, I was referring to the telex, but I think Alison was hoping I meant her nipples.

"Oh, okay. Anything you need?"

"Er ... No. No, that's it, thanks."

"Oh, okay." Frowning, she appeared a little disappointed as she straightened up and turned to leave.

"Oh, Alison, one thing." This was going to be awkward, but that dress sense just wasn't appropriate – time to man up and have that conversation.

Alison stopped at the door, held the frame, and leaned back into the office. "Yes, Frank?"

Did she just bat her eyelashes again?

"Your um. Well, your ... err ..." I rubbed my chest and nodded to hers, struggling to find the right words in this delicate situation. "Your top ... it's ... err—"

"Ooo, you like it! I put it on especially for you." She rubbed her hands over her chest, pouted her lips and disappeared.

"Oh, well done, Frank! Pathetic," I muttered. Now she thought I liked her dress sense and would probably rush home, bin all her bras, and then turn up tomorrow in a bikini top and G-string.

"Morning, partner," called out Paul, as he stuck his head in the office, replacing Alison in the exact same pose as he held the doorframe. Fortunately, unlike Alison, he didn't have nipples straining against his shirt. Grinning and licking his lips, like the lecherous pervert he was, he nodded to where Alison was sitting in reception. "What an eyeful that is! Makes coming to work a pleasure, doesn't it?"

"Morning, Paul. It's not really appropriate, is it? I'm not sure what clients will think. I'm sure Bill Parsons from the Council will be a little shocked when he's in later."

"Oh, come on, don't be such a prude! She's bringing in the business. I reckon half the contracts we win are because they all want further meetings with her serving the coffee."

God knows why, but I was a little shocked at his statement. Still shaking my head in disbelief, I grabbed the coffee our inappropriately dressed receptionist had earlier provided. Jemma was right – he really was a lech.

"Anyway, Bill Parsons isn't due for a couple of hours. Just time for you to take Super-Tits into the back room and give her a good seeing-to! I'd love to, but she seems to only have eyes for you, you lucky bastard."

"Oh, Paul, leave it. She'll hear you if you're not careful."

"Oh well, your loss, mate. Right, I'm off up to the site. Ronny reckons there's some issue with the foundations on that new build. Don't do anything I wouldn't while I'm out." Stepping into the open doorway, he dramatically pumped his hips and moaned in fake pleasure as if auditioning for a porn movie. "I'll be back in an hour, so plenty of time for you to give 'er one." He offered a few more fake moans before winking at me, then disappeared down the corridor.

After studying my drawings for a good half an hour, sipping my coffee and trying to work out if I could remember how to perform my job, the phone on my desk shrilled. Studying the various buttons beside the dial, I pushed the red one that was flashing.

"Frank, I have Jemma on the phone for you," said Alison. There was no sing in her voice, which she usually had, and I detected a hint of disdain, too. I guess she detested saying my wife's name. Jemma was right; Alison wanted me. Paul was wrong; regardless of how erect she made her nipples, I wasn't going to give Alison what it was obvious to see she wanted.

"Thanks, Alison."

"Frank?"

"Hi Jemma, what's up?" I could see the reception phone line still connected, indicated by the flashing light – Alison was listening in to my private conversation. I remember she'd often do this when I received personal calls, and I recall having a delicate conversation with her about it. Presumably, that chat had not taken place yet. Now, I faced the prospect of two awkward conversations with our receptionist. Clearly, I would need to improve my management skills based on this morning's woeful performance when highlighting her inappropriate office attire.

"Frank, I'm furious. Absolutely bloody furious! You're going to have to have a word with him later."

"Woah, woah, calm down. Who?"

"Calm down! What d'you mean, calm down? Bloody hell, Frank, don't tell me to bloody well calm down!"

"Alright, Jem. Okay. What's happened?" I imagined her now gesticulating with her free hand as she hollered down the phone at me.

"That bloody man next door! How dare he … how dare he!"

"Jem, d'you wanna tell me what's happened?" Surely Dennis hadn't commented that she was easy on the eye this morning? If he had, was that enough to get Jemma steamed up like this?

"Huh. Yes, okay." She calmed slightly then, in Jemma's usual way, launched into her verbal tirade without stopping to catch her breath.

The red light denoted the reception connection was still on – Alison was still listening in.

"He collared me as I came out of the house this morning. I was polite as he said hello, but he came over and said he needed a word. Then the lefty, socialist, Marxist tosser started ranting that he'd heard the Government were considering intervening in the telecommunication strike. He suggested we're planning to take legal action against the Union. Then he said, can you believe, that the Government had no right to get involved in union business, and what was I going to do about it. Frank, you still there?"

"Yes."

"Then, the tosser said that every Union had the right to call its members out, and the ACTT, Association of Cinematography, Television and Allied Technicians Union, were right to strike. He said he hoped other unions followed suit in a one-out-all-out protest at the woeful fifteen per cent pay offer. He *then* said, as he was the shop steward at Anglia Studios, he would be advising his members that they were to hold out until the bosses all caved in. The lefty bastard said if the Government decided to intervene in Union business there would be civil unrest, and he'd ensure that his counterparts in other unions would organise secondary picketing." She took a breath, although only a tiny one. "And there was a very real possibility that workers would be organising Wildcat strike action!" Her voice had reached a crescendo, and I imagined her arm still flailing as if swatting a swarm of wasps.

Now I remember the ITV strike, which went on through the summer of '79. That's why when I turned on the TV on Friday, Channel Three just displayed an announcement stating their apology for the interruption of service. Jemma's mother was obsessed with Crossroads, and I was surprised she hadn't moaned about not being able to watch her favourite program when we were around there on Sunday.

Jemma hadn't finished. "Dennis Tranil is a lefty socialist git, and I can't wait until we put into legislation the Bill to curb Union powers which we announced in the Queen's speech. You'll have to have a word with him, Frank. Having a row with me on our doorstep is totally inappropriate, and I'll be taking this up with the Employment Secretary. Something has got to be done about him."

"Alright, alright. I'll have a word with him tonight."

"Oh Frank, my secretary is waving at me. There's another call, and it sounds important." The line disconnected.

I wasn't into politics, but was fully aware Dennis did harbour those strong views. He would almost bristle with excitement when strike after strike occurred, probably because the toilet paper was the wrong colour in some staff facility in some factory.

However, unlike Jemma, I believed Unions had their place, ensuring fairness and looking after employees' welfare in less colleague-focused businesses. Although, I recall keeping my views in the shadows to avoid arguments. Clearly, whatever call had come through that caused her to cut the line, they were more important than her husband.

Now I had two people to have a difficult conversation with. Once again, my wife managed to get embroiled in an argument with a male acquaintance. At least she could remember what this one was about, unlike the ones with Tobias and Paul.

Christ, if she carried on with this attitude, I might be inclined to strangle her myself.

Super-Tits, as Paul delicately put it, stuck her head around the door. "Frank, Bill Parsons just called. He said he'll be about half an hour late."

"Oh, okay."

"It was lovely to speak to Jemma this morning. I've not had a chat with her for ages." She smiled and batted those eyelashes again.

Liar.

Why were all the women around me lying?

28

Schindler's List

Deciding to stop worrying about difficult conversations, I devoted an hour to catching up on what my meeting with Bill Parsons would entail. Fortunately, young Frank's brain had kicked in, and I seemed to be fully up to speed with the multistorey car park project. The Bill Parsons meeting was to discuss highway disruption when our contractors started the project, and I felt Paul would probably lead the meeting as that was more his side of the business.

It was time to focus on more urgent matters – my drawings could wait. So, I settled down to plan the save-my-wife mission, which was higher up my list of priorities than some split-level concrete slab.

Rummaging through the desk drawers, I located a well-used reporter's notebook underneath a pack of airmail envelopes, a pad of carbon paper and a fax paper roll. Musing over the pointless content of my desk, I flipped over to a blank page to make some notes on what I knew so far and perhaps some ideas on how I was going to play out the next two weeks.

All the evidence suggested Jemma's murderer was someone who knew her. There was no sexual assault, no evidence of a struggle, and it was believed she was murdered and buried at the same spot. What I can deduce and clearly remember is she failed to get a taxi and walked home. At some point on that walk, she got in a car, which would suggest her own volition. Pity there weren't street cameras or CCTV systems in place then. That surely would have solved everything, as the police would've caught the assailant within days by capturing the licence plate.

Although it was unseasonably mild on that fateful night, a week of heavy rain leading up to the 28th of September had resulted in the pull-in area up at the woods becoming a quagmire. This was further exacerbated as the pull-in area became churned up by lorries when truck drivers would often pull in for rest periods. That's why they failed to detect any recognisable car tyre prints, but surely the car and the murderer were caked in mud.

After my release from questioning and post the funeral I fell apart, and now my memory of that time was letting me down. Weeks morphed into months, and then I slid down to oblivion. Rather than passionately fighting to get the murderer caught, I sunk into a drunken stupor where day and night merged and time drifted. When you're constantly pissed and not allowing any sobriety time, you're not much good to anyone. Also, that perpetual state of inebriation didn't help to support memory capture.

Leaning back in my chair whilst twiddling my pen around, I tried to think of who would have reason to kill her. All the evidence pointed to the fact the perpetrator was someone she knew. Random strangers don't go scooting around strangling one woman and then choose a different vocation after considering their career options when realising murder was not for them. So, with no other strangled women in the area, the perpetrator had to be an acquaintance.

What I'd seen of Jemma in the last four days did suggest she seemed quite capable of pissing people off – including me. Did I kill her?

'No! Get a grip, Frank!'

That night was pretty clear in my mind. Jemma planned a dinner with Clare, just a girly catch-up if I recall. I planned to meet Paul-The-Lech, but that didn't happen as he cancelled just before I left the house. So, I'd nipped up to the White Bull for a pint, hoping to catch up with Dave. However, he wasn't there, so I'd assumed Dave was repairing his marriage with Babs or maybe on a late shift at the supermarket inspecting that cash office girl's chest again.

I'd enjoyed a couple of pints, then wandered home and crashed out on the sofa whilst watching Petrocelli, the detective series. The storyline was spookily apt for the events of that night. A woman who'd hitched a lift was then strangled, and an innocent man arrested. As with every episode, Petrocelli, the lawyer, saved the day – well, for the innocent man, that is. Unfortunately, the strangled girl was still strangled, and although Petrocelli was good, he didn't time-travel.

Then I must have dozed off and only woke up when the TV programmes had finished for the evening. By that time, it's believed that my wife and unborn child were dead.

I made a list on my notepad of potential suspects, wondering if this was how Jim Rockford would approach the issue. Not that I recalled an episode of him sitting in his trailer home making lists.

Jemma Stone List.

I underlined it and stared at the blank page. Only four days into this life re-run, and factoring in Jemma's performance thus far, I considered this list could end up being longer than Schindler's.

Tobias James-Bond Heaton. There was something going on with him and Jemma over the last couple of days. The hotel lobby and the cricket match incidents. What were they about? But why would he have ferociously defended me when I was questioned if he was the culprit?

Clare Pussy-Galore Heaton. Could she have had the strength to strangle Jemma? But why? I could think of no good reason.

Dennis Lefty-Marxist Tranil. Odd bachelor type, pleasant enough, I guess. But just because his political views were at odds with Jemma's, would that be enough to commit murder?

Dave Chest-Fondler Bolton. Best mate. He went off on one last Friday night about how much he despised her. Dave? No, surely not.

Miles Thigh-Crusher Rusher. Well, I guess he had a motive because he'd been overlooked for the party candidacy. He did benefit from her death, well, until the Russian thigh-crusher incident. However, I guess he didn't know at the time he was going to get caught up with Onatopp, the leggy blonde FSB agent. Then there was the finger-wagging incident on Friday night – what was that about?

Paul The-Lech Wilson. Traitor. Has a horrendous attitude toward women. Never had a girlfriend longer than a week, probably because they all quickly worked out what a bigoted male chauvinistic tosser he was. Jemma hated the man.

So would she get in a car with him? She wasn't much of a walker and would never contemplate strapping on a pair of hiking boots – she just wasn't that type of woman. If getting in a car with him meant just a lift home, yes, that was possible. Then, there was this argument on Friday night that Jemma seems to have conveniently forgotten.

<u>Cecil Buster-blood-vessel Causton</u>. I instantly scrubbed my pen across his name. "Stupid thought," I muttered.

<u>Alison Super-Tits Hay</u>. I giggled like a schoolboy as I wrote it. Well, I think Jemma and Paul were right. She was definitely coming on to me, although she might run a mile if I actually acted upon her outrageous flirting. It was bloody obvious she fancied me. I really couldn't remember her being that way with other men – certainly not The Lech – but who could blame her for that. But surely, she wouldn't murder my wife to get to me. And after Jemma's death, I don't recall her rushing around to console me.

<u>Mr Bigoted-Racist-Neighbour Hackett</u>. No. Although he was a horrific human being. Just because some of Jemma's skirts were a little on the short side, and according to him, she was a silly bimbo dolly-bird, that wouldn't be enough motive. Although he had said someone should do her in.

<u>Brian West-Indian-Lollypop-Sucker Grey</u>. His career and marriage were destroyed, but that was caused by his own doing. However, Jemma had trashed him during the whole election campaign. A strategy employed to distance the Party from his antics and ensure the more conservative voter wasn't put off by the scandal. He had nothing to lose, as he'd already lost everything – could be.

<u>Lawson Taxi's employees</u>. Christ no! I crossed that out as well.

<u>The whole population of the Broxworth Estate</u>. Christ, that was a bit tenuous!

<u>Everyone who voted Conservative in May</u>. Because they would have preferred a more conservative with a small-c candidate, and not a 'Bimbo' as Mr Hackett had so eloquently put it.

<u>Everyone who voted Labour in May</u>. "Really, Frank?" I muttered under my breath.

<u>Anyone that she might have pissed off</u>. That could be a long list!

<u>Any woman in Fairfield who had seen her husband ogle her</u>. Oh, come on, Frank!

<u>The male population of the south of England</u>. Yup, that summed it up. It could have been anyone. Oh shit, I was getting nowhere.

Alison stuck her head around the doorframe. "Frank, Bill Parsons is here. Paul is still out, so can you kick the meeting off? I know Paul said he wouldn't be long, so I'm sure he'll be back soon."

I glanced up from my notepad, pulling a folded drawing across my writings. Not that Alison could see it from where she was standing, but I felt a bit silly with what I'd written.

"Yeah, sure. Send him through."

"Okay, will do. I'll bring coffee through in a moment."

"Thanks, Super-t … err Alison." Now I'd flushed bright red. Bloody hell, two minutes with Paul and his personality was rubbing off on me. "Christ's sake, get a grip," I muttered.

I studied Bill, who now sat opposite me after Alison had ushered him in. I didn't believe we'd ever met before.

Well, clearly, we had the first time 17th September happened, but you know what I mean. After we shook hands, he settled down in the chair opposite. We waited for Alison to deposit the coffee mugs and close the door before starting the meeting. Although Paul was supposed to be leading this, the swotting up I'd done an hour ago left me in a comfortable position to be able to guide us through the agenda.

Wearing grey slacks, a blue shirt and tie, and a sensible anorak with a drawstring waist, I thought Bill looked like a councillor. I guessed he was in his forties, and I wondered where he was in my timeline. In all likelihood retired, living in a bungalow and whiling away his days pottering in his garden. He would probably still be involved in some parish council regularly discussing dog fouling and the disturbing number of fast-food wrappers lobbed in local hedgerows. I guess he would become the Victor Meldrew type character and, going by his dour persona, he was already heading that way. He sported a scrunched-up scowl as he peered across at me – not the life and soul of a dinner-party-type character, I mused.

"I'm glad I have got you on your own for a few minutes because we need to discuss another matter," announced Bill as he folded his arms.

"Oh?"

"Yes. We need to discuss what the hell you're going to do about your bloody wife!" I think I detected some steam drifting from his ears. Or was that from the coffee cup he held up to his lips? He raised his eyebrows at me.

Oh, great! Another person my lovely wife seems to have pissed off. As he was a Labour councillor, was he in my fourth-to-last group of potential murderers I'd penned on my notepad? Had Jemma done something specifically to piss him off? Maybe I would need to add Bill Sensible-Clothes Parsons to my list and underline his name.

Whilst time evaporated, the list just kept growing, as we careered full steam ahead towards the 28th of September.

29

Right to Buy

"Bill, sorry you have me at a disadvantage. What's the problem with Jemma?"

"Bloody everything! As the man of the house, I expect you to sort her out and get her to bloody-well toe the line." He still defensively held his arms in a crossed position. However, I'd deduced that the steam emanated from the coffee, not his ears. By the colour of his ruddy complexion, I'd ascertained he was clearly very pissed off.

Plucking up my coffee, I feared I would have to push on and try to understand what she had done now. "Bill, as I said, I don't know what you're talking about?"

He unfolded his arms and leaned forward. Not that I believed this change of body language was a move from a defensive position. "She's above her station and completely out of control. If things don't change, we'll be forced to refer her behaviour to the local Party office and the Leader of the House. Although the idea of having anything to do with that Tory, Norman St John-Stevas, is not a pleasant thought."

"Bill, if this has to do with her role as our MP, I'm sorry, but that has nothing to do with me. I'm her husband, not her boss."

"Oh, you're like that Thatcher bloke, are you? Hiding behind the woman's apron strings." He leant further forward and pointed. "Be a man, for Christ's sake! Take hold of your little woman before she gets herself into trouble."

Jesus, was this era really like this? Christ, we had a female Prime Minister, and unless no one had noticed, the head of state was also a woman – the word Queen gave it away. Bill and Mr Hackett both had the attitude that the woman should be at home wearing a pair of rubber gloves whilst caressing her bottle of Mild Fairy Liquid.

"Bill, sorry, I can see you're worked up. But as I said, her work as an MP has nothing to do with me."

"Well, you should be the man of the house. What we won't tolerate is her throwing her weight around at the Council. She has no jurisdiction there, and she needs to keep her bloody Tory-nose out of our affairs. The Right to Buy legislation might be in that bloody right-wing fascist manifesto, but the legislation isn't in place. We at the Council control housing, not her. I can tell you we'll be fighting it with everything we've got!"

"Alright, Bill. Look, I can't really get involved. But specifically, what has she done to annoy you?"

"It's not just me. It's the whole Council!"

Another extensive list of candidates to underline on my notepad – oh, great.

"What that little girl has done is demand to sit on the Council committee for housing so she can explain the Right to

Buy legislation due in the next Parliament and how that will affect our stock of council houses in Fairfield. When Martin Blair, our Council leader, put her straight this morning, the silly girl lost control of herself and started shouting at him. That bloody wife of yours actually stated she was the MP, and he was just some tin-pot local councillor who needed to understand his position. That girl of yours is power-crazed and out of control!"

"Oh, right," I sighed. "Is this an official meeting we're having?"

"No, man! This is a man-to-man chat. Take control of her before someone sorts her out!"

The door creaked open as Alison squeezed her head through the crack. Although I wanted to distance myself from Super-Tits, I was glad for the breather her interruption provided.

"Err ... Frank, Paul has just pulled up. He'll be in at any moment."

Bill didn't look around but just sat back in his chair and folded his arms.

Alison mouthed, "What's going on?"

I shrugged.

"Are you okay?"

I nodded.

Now we were holding a silent conversation, with Alison exaggeratingly mouthing the questions whilst I provided non-verbal gestures in reply.

"Shall I warn Paul?"

I shook my head.

"Alright, Super-Tits? Don't move. I want to squeeze tightly past you." Paul pinned Alison to the doorframe as he squashed his chest against hers and grinned.

"Oh, you're disgusting!" She extracted herself from where Paul had pinned her, turned and disappeared out of view.

That had to be blatant sexual harassment in the workplace. Surely there were laws against that kind of behaviour in this era? If there weren't, I would be suggesting to my out-of-control-tory-wife that legislation was now overdue.

"Bill, my old mucker, great to see you. Sorry I'm a bit late." Paul shook the upset councillor's hand as Bill stood up, who now seemed to have thawed at the sight of my business partner.

"Everything alright here?" Paul questioned as he continued to shake his old-mucker's hand, as he put it.

I guess Paul had detected the atmosphere which invisibly hung in the air after Bill had provided me with his opinion of my wife. Bill clearly had an issue with Jemma, and I considered telling him to form an orderly queue of those who wanted harm to come her way.

"Yes, Paul. Everything is alright now *you're* here." He nodded in my direction. "Frank and I were just discussing a private matter that he *will* be taking care of."

"Great! Let's get down to business. Oh, you want another coffee? I can get Super-Tits to rustle up another cup."

"No, Paul, I'm fine, thank you. Ha, you're right, though. I'm not sure we have anything that good looking at the Council Office."

"Yes. She's got more than the average BSH," stated the lech, as he mimicked squeezing her chest with his hands.

"BSH?" asked Bill.

"British Standard Handfuls," replied Paul, still mimicking squeezing our young receptionist's chest whilst grinning from ear to ear.

Both men roared with laughter. I offered a slight shake of my head and wondered if I would ever fit back into the '70s.

30

The Beano

Through the passage of time over the last thirty-odd years, I'd completely forgotten the lonely nights at home when Jemma stayed away. When the House was in session, Jemma would be spending most of her time in Westminster. Often, late-night sessions in the House would result in her staying over because the last train out to Fairfield from St Pancras Station would've long since gone. Jemma never drove in because she was terrified of driving in London. With no congestion charge in place, the city was permanently gridlocked.

Jemma and two other MPs shared a three-bedroom house in Westminster near St James's Park. All three MPs regularly made use of these facilities after late-night debates discussing some Bill that would surely piss the country off just a bit more than it already was. Some of those Bills led to rioting, and I vaguely remember the Poll Tax riots in the late '80s. I imagined my neighbour, Dennis, would have been in the thick of the action as I was aware he was heavily involved in the Anti Poll Tax Federation set up to defeat the Government.

Their opulent house in Westminster was all funded by us, the taxpayer. I was sure in my time, following the expense scandal of 2009, that wouldn't have been allowed. I followed that story from discarded newspapers or watching the news feed on office reception TVs as I squashed my face against the glass of some corporate conglomerate building before a Jason Statham-type character booted my arse off down the road.

I hated her staying over, as it was always a last-minute decision when House business had extended into the late evening, plus the other two MPs were male. Not that I didn't trust her. But you know – I just didn't like it.

After our evening meal, Jemma and I washed the dishes. She had her rubber gloves and pinny on, with the bottle of Mild Fairly Liquid positioned on the draining board – Bill Parsons came to mind.

"What was that call you had today? Y'know when you had to cut me off this morning?"

"I didn't cut you off. I just had important business to attend to."

"More important than me?" That was cheap, and I regretted saying it.

Jemma turned and faced me with her hands still stuffed in the soapy water. "No, Frank. But you must understand that I hold a position in the community that requires my attention at the drop of a hat. I'm not some office girl at your beck-and-call. I'm a Member of Parliament. That makes me important!"

I dried the plate I was holding and slotted it into the plate rack next to the loose tea dispenser. Not that I think we still used it, but there it was still on the wall. Look, I know being an MP is important, but her comment had a feel of I'm-better-than-you and I didn't like it. This Jemma was different from how I remember, and I was hard-pressed to warm to her.

"You grumpy now?" Jemma threw over her shoulder as she focused on attacking the caked-on pastry from a glass dish. I didn't answer because I didn't want to fuel the conversation, which was brewing into an argument.

"I'll be staying over after the late sitting tomorrow and maybe on Wednesday as well. You'll have to sort your own meals out. You could go to Mum's if you want or pick up a pie at the pub."

Remembering the fly-infested cheese rolls at the White Bull, I quickly dismissed that idea. As for going to her mother's, no, that was off the cards because my future relationship with my mother-in-law was something I just couldn't shake out of my mind.

"Oh. Do you know tomorrow will be a late session, then?"

"Yes. The first week after recess is always busy. So best plan for it now."

"Will the other two be staying over?"

"Charlie and Roops?"

"Yes."

She turned and looked at me again, giving the glass dish a rest from her scrubbing. "I expect so. Your tone is suggesting something?"

"No." I shook my head but didn't look her in the eye. I was being silly and now annoyed with myself for displaying jealousy. Yes, I was struggling to like her, but I loved her – didn't I? The thought of her wandering around that rented house in her nightie with two hooray-henry types gawping at her after a late-night session in the House bothered me.

Now I remembered their names, Charles Markland-Waller and Rupert Barrington-Scott. Rupert! Who the hell calls their son Rupert? I bet he dressed in yellow checked trousers when back with Mummy and Daddy on the Estate at weekends. Why did these Tory toffs all have double-barrelled names? Both men were newly elected MPs from the local area, so they'd formed a friendship in May.

'How friendly?'

As a lad come good from a working-class background on the Broxworth Estate, I struggled to operate in her posh colleague's circles. My poor old dad would be performing cartwheels of despair in his grave if he knew I was married to a Tory. If he wasn't already dead, knowing my wife was a Tory MP would definitely kill him.

Both men probably stayed over for a bit of upper-class fun. Charles had young children, so presumably, any excuse not to have to get involved in bath time. Roops, as Jemma called him, turned up with some posh girl to Jemma's funeral. Phoebe or Prunella was her name. I can't remember what she looked like, but easily recalled the stuck-up, plummy mouth.

Did I need to add Charlie and Roops to my list of suspects?

How could I remember all this? On Friday, I couldn't remember Jayne Hart or the name of my best mate's wife. Perhaps young Frank was now taking control because I'd been here for four days. Would that mean I might start to like my wife soon?

Not proud of how I was reacting to the questions, I changed the subject. "Had a meeting with Bill Parsons today. He's an odd bloke, isn't he? Do you have to deal with councillors in your role?"

"Oh, he's a right one! Can't stand the bloke ... although I think the feeling is mutual. He's on the Housing Committee, and I can't wait to rub his nose in it when we land the Right to Buy legislation. That will shut the little lefty looney up!" She sniggered whilst applying extra force to the pan scourer. The surface of the glass dish was probably receiving the treatment she'd like to dish out to Bill Parsons and the rest of the Labour Councillors.

It was time to drop this conversation. What was clear, Jemma was out to bully her way through the town. At this point in my life re-run, I felt ill-equipped to slow down her blitzkrieg assault on the unsuspecting council officials. I don't think my opinion mattered, and I doubted I had any chance of getting her to understand she was elected by the people, for the people. Jemma seemed to be more in the mould of Pol Pot or General Pinochet. That said, she was seriously better looking.

"I'll finish these. As you promised this morning, can you go and have a word with *him* next door?"

"What?"

"Dennis the Menace! You said you'd tell him not to berate me on my own doorstep."

"Oh yeah. Okay, I'll go and have a word."

"Thank you, my love. He really did frighten me this morning. Don't listen to any of his lefty lies. Just give him what for!"

"Leave it with me. I'll make sure he understands."

Jemma blew me a kiss as I headed out of the kitchen. Although I'd said I'll deal with it, I wasn't relishing the conversation. From what I'd seen over the past few days, I was surprised anyone could frighten Jemma.

I grabbed my cigarettes and enjoyed a smoke on the driveway before tackling Dennis the Menace.

Dennis was an odd bachelor type who never seemed to invite any friends around, and neither Jemma nor I had got to know him well. To my knowledge, he never had a girlfriend or was interested in courting female company – despite his easy-on-the-eye comment.

I've always been apolitical and never voiced strong opinions in that area. Although I believed in fairness, that view cut across the whole political spectrum. Dennis was, without doubt, a communist. He admired the car manufacturing union boss, Red Robbo, and would get excited when the British Leyland car workers would strike, an event that seemed to be more often than not. To be fair to Red Robbo, he was doing the British car-buying public a great service – the fewer British Leyland cars produced, the better.

When Dennis and I had an occasional chat over the metaphorical garden fence, he would quickly turn it into a political conversation about how excited he was about another strike in a particular industry. As I mused before, many of those strikes were due to some minor issue, like the toilet paper being the wrong colour or the wrong variety of potatoes in the staff canteen. With shop stewards like Dennis, it was a miracle that British industry produced anything.

What was not right, is he felt he could lambast my wife on our doorstep. Whether he thought she was a right-wing fascist, and I'd never thought she was, it didn't make it right. So, as I pushed the doorbell and listened to the chimes from the other side of the door, I felt perfectly within my rights to set him straight.

"Evening, Frank. Your missus run out of sugar and sent you round with a begging bowl?" chuckled Dennis, as he stood there wiping his hands on a pink frilly pinny he wore over his shirt and tie. Odd look, I thought, to say the least. But hey, each to their own. Maybe he was one of those secret cross-dresser fans. Although I didn't see him as a Danny La Rue type, neither did he seem like Dennis the Menace. However, Jemma was undoubtedly turning into a bit of a Gnasher. Perhaps that's why he didn't have a girlfriend because he was Dennis during the day and Denise in the evening, so he was covering all bases on his own.

"Ha, no, no. I just wondered if you've got a moment?"

"Sure. I know, you've had enough of living with a right-wing fascist, and you're ready to convert to communism," he said, without a hint of sarcasm. I think he meant it.

"Err, no, mate. I think you know I'm not really into all that stuff."

"Alright. How can I help?"

We stayed standing on the doorstep; there seemed to be no prospect of him inviting me across the threshold. Either he was a private person, or he had his frilly dress on the ironing board and didn't fancy showing me his planned evening attire.

"Look, Dennis, I don't want us to fall out. Being neighbours, this is a bit delicate. But look, mate, collaring my wife on our doorstep about your frustrations with the Government really is quite unacceptable. I know you and Jemma are poles apart on the political spectrum, but I can't have my wife in tears because you feel it's okay to rant at her."

There, I'd said it. Although he looked a bit miffed as he stood there open-mouthed whilst still clasping the bottom of his pink frilly pinny.

"Frank, I'm sorry, mate, but you've got your facts all wrong. Yes, I agree, I have a real issue with your wife's politics." He dropped the hem of his pinny and, whilst bearing down, pointed a finger at me. Although Dennis stood a few inches shorter than me, his doorstep afforded him the higher ground and he now appeared ready to launch his attack. "However, politics aside, I know how to conduct myself. The truth of the matter is, I politely said good morning as I came out to get in my car, and your wife stomped across and started screaming at me that no good would come from the strike I was organising. She said she would see to it that the Government took control and sorted the unions out once and for all."

Now I was the one looking a bit miffed.

"Now look, Frank, you seem a nice bloke. I'm not one to come between a married couple, but your young lady has got her facts all wrong. I'm bloody furious that she thinks she can spread lies about me." He leant in towards me for the finale of his rant. "She needs to be careful. Otherwise, I will be suing for defamation of character!"

With my mouth gaping open, catching flies, I watched as the door flew shut into the frame. The glass panel rattled whilst the letterbox lid performed a couple of backflips.

You can usually just tell when someone is genuine and telling the truth, can't you? Although spotting a lie can be quite tricky, the truth is a lot easier to see, especially when someone is ranting.

Dennis-The-Menace-Tranil was telling the truth – Jemma-Gnasher-Stone was lying.

My blonde gnasher wife was out of control, power-crazed and building a considerably extensive list of enemies. What had happened to her? Was she like this the first time around? And if she was, why didn't I see it?

31

Sugar Ray

In the interest of maintaining the peace, I didn't challenge Jemma about her version of the chat she'd had with Dennis the Menace. I guess if this happened the first time I would have, but things were different now. I needed to understand what was happening so I could get to the bottom of the mystery and ensure she wasn't murdered. After that, well, I just didn't know. For sure, she needed to change if I was going to fall back in love with her.

On Tuesday morning I dropped Jemma off at the station, then headed off to work. Apart from my list, which wasn't very scientific, all I had achieved so far was struggling to like my wife again and realising she had a propensity to get people's backs up. My concern regarding what games my wife was playing was further enhanced when Alison buzzed through to say I had a visitor, asking if I was free.

Clare Heaton and I had always got on well. Although she was a bit of a posh horsey type, she'd instantly liked me that day I performed my bionic man impression in the Bell Pub. She was the one who had pushed Jemma to go on a second date, saying that I was a real catch and Jemma should grab me – that was nice, I guess.

Alison hadn't previously met Clare and, judging by the catty stares on offer as she ushered her through to my office, Alison evidently didn't like her.

With her long strawberry-blonde hair, shapely legs up to and beyond her armpits, plus more than the required BSH, Clare Heaton is a total stunner. Her vivacious hourglass figure did more than turn heads. Clare Heaton's looks stopped traffic.

Paul was in reception when Clare arrived and, after undressing her out of her pencil skirt suit with his eyes, his tongue scraped along the floor as he followed both ladies to my office. Even though she'd rebuffed his advances in the pub that Saturday night in '76, Paul still thought he'd have another go. I quickly shut the office door on him, narrowly avoiding wedging his wagging tongue in the doorjamb.

Clare's usual radiance wasn't on show today, and appeared sullen as if she carried the world on her shoulders.

"This is a nice surprise, Clare. Can I get you a coffee or tea?"

"No, Frankie, I'm fine, thanks." After carefully smoothing the back of her skirt, Clare perched on the chair opposite. We sat in silence for a brief moment as she stared past me out of the window.

"You okay?" Although I liked Clare, visiting me at work was odd.

"Your reception girl needs to wear a bra. She'll take someone's eye out."

"Don't go there. I was going to have a word, but, I dunno, it's a bit of a delicate conversation to have."

"Get the lech to tell her," suggested Clare, as she nodded to the door, where I suspected Paul was trying to retrieve his tongue.

"You're joking, aren't you? He'd tell Alison she's overdressed and would suggest it would be better if she came in with a little less on!"

"Ha, yes, he would. He really is a bit of a perv, isn't he? I know Jemma can't stand him." Clare fiddled with her fingers, squeezing them tightly, causing her knuckles to turn white.

I assumed she hadn't come to discuss Super-Tits' lack of underwear or muse over Paul's lecherous tendencies. So, rather than speaking, I waited for her to continue. Plucking up my cigarettes, I lit up and offered the packet to her. Clare shook her head, declining the offer. Silence descended as I puffed away on my cigarette, and Clare continued with her hand-wringing routine.

"Hey Clare, are you alright?" I asked again after blowing smoke to the ceiling.

Whilst staring into her lap and picking at her nail varnish, Clare shrugged. "Have you noticed anything different about Tobias recently?"

Well, apart from having clandestine conversations with my wife and knocking ten-bells of shit out of that cricket ball on Saturday, I, old Frank, hadn't seen much of him for thirty-odd years. So, difficult to say, I thought.

"Um, what d'you mean?"

She looked up, a little teary, maybe. "Does he seem different?"

After stubbing out my cigarette, I shimmied around to her side of the desk, perching my backside on its edge. As Clare bowed her head, I detected the snivels.

"Hey, you. Come on. What's up? You said he seems different. What d'you mean?"

"Well, when you went to the pub last week together ... did he say anything?" she huffed whilst continuing to attack that nail varnish.

This was tricky. I could remember about a week ago meeting Tobias in the Murderers Tavern. However, at that time I was presumably in the Preparation Suite at the CYA headquarters. Without a doubt, it was a bloody weird feeling having both memories – although the Preparation Suite memory was far stronger.

"Well, yes, he said lots of things as we were chatting. What are you specifically getting at?"

"Did he say anything about me ... or ... if he was, perhaps ... maybe, unhappy?"

"No, not that I can remember." That was the truth. Well, the *not that I can remember* bit was.

"Oh, okay."

"What's going on?"

She looked up again and stared into my eyes, presumably trying to read my reaction. "I'm worried Tobias is having an affair."

"No! No, no-no. You've got that wrong. Play away from his Pussy Galore ... no way!" I flushed bright red. Pussy Galore was her nickname, but it was an unwritten rule that only Tobias could utter those words.

"It's okay, Frankie. I know you all call me that. Jemma had the same reaction when I asked her on Saturday. I asked her to ask you, but I take it she didn't mention it?"

"No, not a peep." That was odd. Why hadn't Jemma said something to me about this? I mean, this was big news about our closest friends. Pondering that thought, I pushed on, now fitting pieces of a puzzle together that, in reality, didn't actually fit. "But why on earth would you think he's having an affair?"

"He's been acting strangely for a while now. He's often out of the office and, when I ask where he's been, he becomes coy and avoids the question. Harriet, his secretary, is such an airhead she wouldn't know if he was off to the moon. So, as usual, she's no help."

"Okay. But Clare … he could just be visiting clients. Nothing really strange about that, is there?"

"No, it's more than that. He went out Friday afternoon and didn't get back until late evening. When I casually asked him where he'd been, as his dinner was all curled up in the oven, he became really defensive and said he'd been in the pub with a few mates but wouldn't say who. Frankie, there's something going on. I know there is."

"Friday. Last Friday?"

"Yes. Did you see him that night?"

Yes, I did. However, we weren't enjoying a beer together. Although, I did watch him having an argument with my wife in the Maid's Head Hotel lobby. At this stage, I wasn't going to offer that information.

"No. Jemma was out with Jayne, and I had a couple of pints down the local with my mate Dave."

"How is Dave? He's a lovely bloke, isn't he? Babs is lucky to have a genuine, loving man like him. I always think they're the perfect couple, and that little Sarah is adorable."

"Yeah, Dave's a terrific guy." Although maybe not when he's got his hands all over cash office clerks' chests. But with Clare in a bit of a state at the moment, furnishing her with the news of Dave's misdemeanours wouldn't help. Rather than burst that bubble, I thought it best to leave her thinking that the Boltons were a perfect family who could nicely feature on the cover of Woman's Weekly.

"Look, Clare, I think you've got it all wrong. But I can see why you're worried. I tell you what, why don't I take him out for a pint this week and see if I can get him to open up? He's probably stressed about work, and there's actually nothing to worry about."

"We do have a big case on at the moment, which I know is playing on his mind."

"There you go! That'll be it; I'm sure of it. I'll give him a bell and take him out for a couple of beers."

"Oh, thank you, Frankie. Please don't say anything to Tobias about today, will you?"

"No. Mum's the word. You'll see this will all pan out fine, I promise you."

Clare took me by surprise as she stood, flung her arms around my neck, and hugged me. Unfortunately, the launching Clare toppled me backwards, resulting in us lying across my desk. The pen pot cascaded its contents over the side, and my wife's best friend lay suggestively on top of my prone body.

The door burst open. Paul stood there pumping his hips back and forth, sporting a massive grin and giving a decent impression of Lord Flashheart from Blackadder.

"Get in there, my son! Wouldn't mind a bit myself."

Clare instantly pulled back, her face burning with embarrassment as she tugged at her skirt hem that had ridden up above her knickers when falling on top of me.

"Don't stop on my account. This could be better than one of those top-shelf wank-mags!"

"Clare, excuse me a second." I gently touched her arm and smiled. I guess she thought I was going to politely ask Paul to leave the office – she thought wrong.

Two paces forward, I sent my fist straight into the centre of his face. Sugar Ray Leonard couldn't have done it better himself. Paul rocked back straight through the open doorway. The frosted glass panel opposite halted his flight, causing it to crack in a spider web formation as his prone body slithered to the ground and blood poured from his nose. He was now sporting a very shocked expression.

"Wow!" I heard Clare exclaim.

"Wayda go, Frank!" shouted Super-Tits, as she stood grinning in the hallway.

I turned and faced Alison whilst shaking my hand, which hurt like hell. I wouldn't be surprised if I'd broken a few fingers.

"Right, Alison. Take the rest of the day off. Tomorrow, and every day going forward, I expect you to dress appropriately for work. You're a really lovely girl who could have the pick-of-the-bunch of fellas. But, unfortunately, walking around with your nipples stuck out like coat hooks doesn't really attract the man you want. Although it's wrong and unfair, it's the way the world is, I'm afraid. But the simple fact is, your dress sense only serves to give lecherous tossers like *him* licence to think their behaviour is acceptable," I said, as I pointed at Paul on the floor with my painful fingers.

"So, at work, I expect you to wear a bra from now on and, if that's an item of clothing you don't own, you can nip up to Marks and Sparks this afternoon and introduce yourself to the women's underwear department!"

Clare burst out laughing. Alison nodded, then sheepishly turned on her heels as she headed back to reception.

Pointing at the blood-stained Paul, I continued my rant. "I've had enough of your pathetic, chauvinistic schoolboy attitude. We're going to make Stone and Wilson a successful company and not known for one of the partner's wandering hands who can't behave like a proper man! So, if you can't change your ways, I suggest you bugger off!"

"Oh, Frankie, that was wonderful! What a lucky girl Jemma is," said Clare, as she gently took hold of my now throbbing hand. "I think we need to get some ice for that."

Something had clicked in my brain the moment my office door had opened when Paul had performed his hip thrusts. Five days into my restart of my life, in a split second, I'd decided to start taking control. It was time to start putting things right.

Of course, after this conversation with Clare, it had occurred to me that my Jemma could be having an affair with Tobias and I would need to investigate that. Whatever my lacklustre detective skills conjured up, I would deal with that when the time came. But my first task was to deal with Paul

The-Lech Wilson. As he'd stood there pumping his hips and pretending to give himself a hand job, I knew the course of action required.

Perhaps my next task could be to provide some tips to Sugar Ray. I knew his next fight was later this month and, unfortunately for Andy Price, Sugar Ray KO 'ed him in round one – similar to the Stone Wilson fight which took place five minutes ago.

In front of thousands of fans, whilst live pictures were beamed into millions of homes, Sugar Ray fought at Caesar's Palace – my fight was not in such salubrious surroundings, had only two spectators, and wasn't televised. However, it took me about four seconds to KO Paul The-Lech Wilson, two and a half minutes quicker than it will take Sugar Ray to despatch Andy Price next weekend – the very night Jemma was due to be murdered.

32

Ten Pound Pom

I wasn't proud that I'd resorted to using my fists to deal with my business partner. But, that said, he had it coming. In my youth, I'd been more than capable of handling myself; it's a product of being raised in the concrete jungle of the Broxworth Estate. The brand-new grey, monolithic blocks had very quickly, after construction in the early sixties, turned into a police no-go area. Unfortunately, living there required the need to learn to punch first and ask questions later – it was just that kind of place.

Paul left the office on Tuesday immediately after he regained his composure, holding his bloodied nose as he staggered past me to his car. He hadn't benefited from my survival-of-the-fittest upbringing, so he wasn't going to fight back. In the late '80s, some pissed-off husband of a woman he had a fling with did realign his nose. This time around, maybe I beat the jealous husband to it.

Paul failed to turn up for work for the rest of the week. Although that left me to conduct some meetings alone, I was happy he'd put some distance between us. What would happen to our flourishing business now? Well, to be honest, I didn't care. I had one task that The Hooded Claw assigned me, which was my sole focus for the immediate future.

Alison did turn up for work on Wednesday morning. She appeared as bubbly as always, greeting me with her usual dazzling smile – all tits and teeth, as Jemma had called her. She didn't mention yesterday's boxing event in the doorway of my office. After a perfunctory glance, I ascertained she'd obviously visited Marks & Spencer's lingerie department the previous afternoon. Either that, or she'd discovered the appropriate previously missing garment in the nether regions of the back of her knicker drawer. In fact, she may have gone too far as she seemed to have morphed from Stone & Wilson's very own centrefold from a top-shelf men's entertainment magazine to looking like she could grab a starring role in Little Women.

I thought my description was politer than what Paul had called those publications. You know, the ones that are placed high on the top shelf in the newsagents where men pretend to flick through a copy of Caravan Monthly magazine, whilst all the time they're raising their eyeballs to the top shelf deciding which one to buy. Then, when they considered the coast was clear, with lightning agility, they'd drop the Caravan Monthly publication, grab the top shelf mag of their choice and make a dash for the till. With the first part of their manoeuvre accomplished, they'd then be wishing the young girl operating the cash register didn't embarrass them with a knowing smirk. Then, after silently imploring the assistant wouldn't take all day scanning the cover trying to locate the price, he would slot it into the middle of the folded broadsheet newspaper he had no intention of reading. The final part of the process was dashing out of the shop whilst praying one of his neighbours or work colleagues hadn't witnessed the event.

Anyway, Alison was a lovely girl, and it wouldn't be long before the hunk of a rugby player swept her off her feet and whisked her off down-under in her very own version of Thornbirds. If I remember correctly, Alison and her musclebound fella took up the Assisted Migrants' scheme just before it closed, or Ten Pound Poms, as it was popularly known in Australia. I just hoped that my rant about her scantily clothing choices hadn't changed time for her. Would this now mean the rugby hunk wouldn't ask her on a date? Perhaps my intervention would change her life path to become an old spinster looking after ten cats.

Jemma called on Tuesday to say she expected another couple of long days and would be staying in town until Friday. Hmmm, I thought.

Tobias was up for a pint, and we planned to catch up this evening. He said he looked forward to reminding me of the seventeen boundaries he scored on Saturday that helped elevate him to Top Batsman 1979. *Tosser*.

I scooted out of the office just after six, heading into town to catch up with Tobias, and planned to grab a snack in the pub. Tobias had suggested we try out the new Wine Bar next to the Wimpy on Elm Hill. Aghast at his suggestion, he relented and agreed to meet in the Murderers Tavern where they still served beer, and I hoped one could pick up a pickled egg along with some dubious meat pie and chips.

His mention of a wine bar got me thinking of the decade I was heading into. Perhaps I would master the Rubik's Cube this time around. If I save her, would Jemma have big hair, leg warmers, shoulder pads, and, God forbid, a pair of parachute pants? One thing for sure, this time, I wasn't going to purchase a shell suit. Without a doubt, Tobias would become a Yuppie and be the first to get one of those brick-shaped mobile phones.

The music culture was a depressing thought, and perhaps I could give Phil Collins a call and ask him not to sell out to commercialism; *Invisible Touch* was a pile of shite. I'd fancied the lead singer of Culture Club when they performed on Top of the Pops and then felt silly when I found out *she* was a man – it was the era of men and makeup. I never admitted to anyone that I fancied Boy George, although I think many men made a similar assumption. Someone shot JR – I have no idea who, so I could get into Dallas with no spoilers in my memory to ruin the entertainment.

A red Mk2 Jaguar pulled away from the kerb behind me. A distinctive car, and I thought I recognised it. Then I remembered it was like Inspector Morse's car from the detective series, although it would be a few years until that series is created. John Thaw had finished playing Jack Regan in The Sweeney. Presumably, he had to wait for Kevin Whately to be free from filming Auf-Wiedersehen Pet so that he could take up the position as Morse's long-suffering Sergeant Lewis.

I wondered if I could be as successful as either character in solving the case. I deduced I had the two main ingredients of both characters. Firstly, like Regan, I was handy with my fists. Secondly, like Morse, I was good at The Times crossword. Over the years, I liked to complete that publication's daily crossword – usually correcting mistakes the purchaser had made after I'd retrieved said paper from the bin where they had dumped it. I often received odd stares as I slumped against the tube station wall with my begging cup whilst completing yesterday's crossword.

Just before sending my fist through Paul's face, my decision on Tuesday was to take control. So, this evening, Tobias James-Bond Heaton was going to receive a grilling. When I left his company tonight, I needed to be in a position where I could rule him out as a potential perpetrator or underline his name on my list as my prime suspect for murder one. I could have benefited from the services of a highlighter pen, but my office pen pot hadn't acquired one yet.

My Mk2 Jaguar tail stuck with me, noticing it only a few spaces behind when I parked up near the pub. Probably a coincidence, and I thought nothing more of it after I entered the pub and found Tobias perched on a bar stool tucking into the bowl of peanuts, which presumably had seen the attentions of many an unwashed hand. It's a fact, ladies – most men don't wash their hands after pointing peter at the porcelain.

My time on the streets had sanitised my concern for what I could catch from previously owned, half-eaten food. Considering the millions of different bacteria I'd swallowed, I'd probably built up a robust immune system. Now young again, and not benefiting from years of consuming bacteria from food, which river rats and I fought over, I declined the nuts when Tobias offered for fear of what may be deposited on them from the male toilets.

Pint in hand, I launched straight into my interrogation.

"It's jam-packed in here tonight. Shall we have this and then nip into the Maid's Head? We can grab a bite to eat up there. To be honest with you, I don't fancy the pies they serve up in this place."

"Maid's Head?"

"Yeah, you know where I mean. I was in there on Friday night, and it's alright, actually."

Tobias didn't register what I'd said for a split second. Then his eyes narrowed.

"Err ... yeah, alright. Were you in there Friday? Last Friday?"

"Maid's Head? Yeah, I was there. Were you there as well? It's a bit odd we didn't bump into each other?"

The relief on his face was almost palpable. But I had seen him. However, as with my wife, Tobias desperately needed that meeting to be kept a secret.

"Oh, no. Clare and I went over to that new American burger place on Mousehold Heath. You know the one? It's called Zaks or something like that. It cooks up posh burgers and is all done up like a '50s diner."

Liar.

Tobias was thinking on his feet and coming up with whatever bollocks came to mind. Catching him out was going to be easy, even though I had doubted my detective skills.

"Oh really? You sure you've got the right night? I'm talking about last Friday, the 14th."

"Course, I'm bloody sure. Anyway, *mate*, you're the one who doesn't know what bloody day it is, not me!" Now, that *was* a defensive response, and I could see Tobias was becoming annoyed.

"Well, mate, that's bloody odd, as I'm sure I saw your car parked up on Chapel Street on Friday. That's why I asked if you were in town. I mean, it's a pretty distinctive car, and I don't know anyone else in this small town who owns a Lotus."

Of course, I'd not spotted his car. However, as I know he was in town and arguing with my wife in the lobby of the Maid's Head hotel, he must have parked it somewhere. His desire to have the flashy Bond-style car was going to unravel the man. I was now drilling him to the floor as he nervously shifted on his stool. Tobias plucked up his pint to buy some urgently needed thinking time.

"Oh, hang on. Yeah, you may have, actually. I think I popped into the Maid's Head on the way home to have a pint with Hugo. You remember him? He's at Greenland's now; y'know where Jemma used to work. Anyway, I thought you were out with Dave on Friday night up at your usual haunt, the White Bull?"

"Who told you I was there? I certainly didn't."

"Oh, I don't know. You must have mentioned it on Saturday at the cricket match."

There was none of his usual bombastic banter at the mention of the match. Normally, I would have expected him to launch into recounting his heroic performance and how he'd unilaterally won the Fairfield Cup. Very un-Tobias like – he was nervous and squirming.

Tobias seemed relieved that this conversation was moving on as I changed the subject and, for a brief second, the tension between us lifted. "Oh, it doesn't matter, mate. Anyway, I wanted a chat as I'm worried about Jemma."

Tobias's relief was short-lived as concern returned to his paling face. "Oh, what about?"

"Well, I don't know, really. I know she's finding the MP game tough at the moment. But she seems … distant. Yeah, that's it, distant. I saw you two having a long chat on Saturday and wondered if she said anything? Or perhaps you picked up a vibe?"

Tobias frowned, shook his head and grabbed his drink, although necking down the rest of his pint didn't appear to give him time to think of what to say. He placed the mug down carefully on the beer mat without looking up.

"Well?" I probed.

"Well, *what*?"

"Your heated conversation with Jemma on Saturday. What was that all about?"

Tobias waved his hand and turned away. "Oh, hell, I don't know. I can't even remember having a conversation with her. And absolutely not a heated one."

"You're a liar!"

"What? What did you just call me?"

Call Me. Call Me. Hearing him repeat those words, I knew it was his voice on the answerphone – the message I'm now certain Jemma deleted. I think it was reasonable to suspect what Clare was worried about was true. And it didn't take too much of a leap to place Jemma as the scarlet woman.

Leaning forward on my barstool, I pointed at him, "I said, mate. You're a liar."

"Frank, I have no idea what you're on about, *mate*. You're losing your bloody mind. This is what you were like on Saturday when you couldn't even remember what bloody day it was. I suggest you get some professional help 'cos I think you've lost your marbles."

"No, I haven't. Something is going on with you and Jemma, and neither of you are telling me what it is."

"Wh-what you suggesting?"

"I'm not suggesting anything. But tell me what you were talking about. The truth, not some bollocks you've just made up."

"Nothing! I just told you, dickhead. I can't even remember the conversation."

"Friday night then, in the hotel lobby. What was that conversation about?"

"Err ... what?"

"You and Jemma, having a row in the Maid's Head Hotel lobby. You grabbed her arm, and she pulled away, then stomped back to the bar."

"I'm not listening to any more of your wild fantasies. You're off your bloody rocker!" He slipped off his stool, plucked up his suit jacket, and stormed out of the bar.

Only a week back in 1979, and already I'd managed to have two arguments in a pub with two mates that resulted in them storming off. I don't think I'd amassed enough evidence to confidently underline his name as the prime suspect, but I did have clear evidence that both Jemma and Tobias were lying and covering up their conversations. Clare was probably right. Tobias and Jemma were having or had an affair. Perhaps Jemma had ended it, and Tobias wasn't happy about that? That would explain their heated exchange and maybe explain why she was strangled. Had Tobias killed her in a jilted lover's rage?

Assessing that I still had half a pint to drink, I decided to order the dodgy pie and chips and then head home. Clare would call tomorrow, and I didn't have good news for her. If this had happened the first time, I would now be devastated. However, I didn't notice any of this back then because I was too wrapped up in work, or it never actually happened. Now, the second time around, although it was sad, I wasn't devastated as I'd already concluded Jemma wasn't the woman I thought she was.

After I stopped her murder, which had to be my top priority, I would have some difficult decisions to ponder regarding the future of our relationship. If we did split up, there was a future baby to consider. Although now I wasn't sure it was even mine.

Whilst I pondered how my second life seemed to be unravelling, I turned around as I thought I heard my name called.

"Frank ... Frank? I thought it was you. Oh, it's so lovely to see you!"

33

Holly Golightly

The woman who'd called out saying how lovely it was to see me lay her hand on my arm as she turned and waved to a striking woman with long auburn hair as she left the pub holding the hand of an older bloke with sticky-out ears. I thought they looked like Noel Edmonds and Jessica Rabbit. Although I don't believe Noel had protruding ears, and the woman wasn't a cartoon.

"Sorry, that was just my boss and his wife. We nipped in for a quick drink before going home. So, as I said, it's lovely to see you. Oh, are you drinking alone, Billy-no-mates?" she giggled.

I believe we can all think of a few times in our lives when we see someone and something odd happens to your brain. It's a feeling that the person in front of you is the missing link, and now everything seems whole – perfect. It had happened once before when I kissed Jemma's cheek in the Bell Pub.

This was the second time.

She lightly held onto my forearm and leaned closer to me, sporting a concerned look on her face. Although her full smile lit up this stunningly beautiful face before me, her eyes held me hostage.

"Frank, you alright?"

The feeling of her skin as her hand lay on my forearm caused my hair to rise and, as she smiled again, I realised she was so jaw-droppingly gorgeous. How come I'd never really noticed before? She lifted her long chestnut hair away from her face and gracefully swept it over her left shoulder whilst her left hand, still gently lying on my arm, continued to cause a tingling sensation. Her hazel eyes appeared dilated, and I thought I could fall right into them.

There was nothing plain about this woman.

"Oh ... ha. Yes, yes. I'm fine, Jayne. I'm fine. Yes, fine." I shut my mouth for fear of saying *fine* again. She lifted her hand from my arm, which was so disappointing.

"I was only talking about you last week when I saw Jemma. Is she with you?"

"Oh no, she's still in London doing her important House business." I gave the old bunny ears gesture when I said 'House', and I think I crossed my eyes. I was acting like a nervous teenager on a first date – but this wasn't a date. For some reason, I'd gone all silly.

"Oh, okay, well, I won't keep you. But anyway, it was really nice to see you. We must all catch up one evening." Her long hair had cascaded back around her face, and once again, she swished it back around her neck – without doubt, the sexiest movement I'd ever seen. Wonderfully, Jayne touched my arm again and smiled, causing my heart to stutter. "Seeya Frank."

Christ! How had I not noticed her this way before? Yes, as I'd said a few days ago, she was easy-on-the-eye to coin a phrase, and I'd remembered that I'd always enjoyed her company more than any of Jemma's friends. Now, as she turned and stepped away from me, I was mesmerised.

I had to focus on saving my wife. I'm married with a child on the way. Lusting over another woman five minutes after contemplating that my wife may be having an affair with one of my best mates and possibly the unborn child was not mine was not the route I should be taking.

'Let her go, and you get back to what you need to concentrate on.'

Ignoring the voice in my head, I allowed myself to watch her leave the pub. As she drifted away from me, her hair lifted in the breeze which flowed through the open door. Although I will confess, I became distracted and found myself gawping at her amazing bum and the suit skirt that was so lucky to be that close.

"Jayne."

She turned at the door and looked back.

"Have a drink with me?"

"Err." Jayne checked her watch. "Go on then, just a quicky," she replied with a beaming smile as she seemed to float back to me. I hopped off the stool, cupped my hand on the small of her back and leaned down to kiss her cheek – I was in real trouble.

Managing to find other words than *fine,* we sat and chatted at the bar. Jayne smoked those long brown More cigarettes, affording her an Audrey Hepburn appearance. Cheeky, free-spirited, sophisticated, confident, blunt, and freely able to say what she thinks – I was having a drink with Holly Golightly. I imagined her finger-whistling to hail a cab, dressed in a little black dress and a wide-brimmed hat.

As time drifted on, and a few drinks later, I was fully aware I was more than in trouble – I wasn't sure if I liked my wife – I was falling in love with Plain-Jayne. I'd have breakfast with this woman anywhere – let alone Tiffany's.

The guilt had silently sneaked into the back of my brain and, although I tried to tell it to bugger off, it now had achieved a firm grip. However, I didn't want this evening to end, and I hadn't acted inappropriately – yet.

I offered to walk Jayne to her car after finishing our drinks to be with her for a few more minutes. Jayne had parked her little red VW Beetle only a hundred yards along from mine. We walked past my car to get to hers, which was odd, but neither she nor I said so. We stood chatting as Jayne held the driver's door open and, although I guess we both knew we'd reached a line that shouldn't be crossed, I could tell neither of us wanted to leave.

She was one of Jemma's best friends. I'm the local MP's husband, who now stood in the middle of her constituency whilst contemplating kissing another woman. This wasn't right.

Jayne made the right decision and said she better go. I nodded, but we both stood still and looked at each other. Once again, those deep hazel eyes riveted me in place. Neither of us spoke for a few seconds as her lips slightly parted – now I was in serious trouble. Gently taking her arm, I guided her to me – this was it; there was no going back.

Jayne swung her arms around my neck, her hands entwining in my blond hair, and we kissed. Eventually, she pulled back and gazed up at me as she stood on tip-toe, both knowing what we had just done was so wrong. We glanced up and down the street, both silently wondering if someone had spotted us whilst we'd snogged each other's faces off.

Glancing back towards my car, I spotted a bloke who seemed to be looking directly at us. Jayne placed her hand on my cheek and gently turned my head back to face her. Then, kissing my lips, she whispered, "I think I'd better go."

After I closed her car door and stood and watched as she drove away, I knew I wanted to see her again. I prayed Jayne felt the same.

∼

Pinkie Sinclair eyeballed Frank as he held on to the sexy little brunette. Frank Stone was just one of those blokes who seemed to be able to pull the birds. His wife was seriously fit, and the little brunette wasn't half bad either. Pinkie had never had much luck with the ladies. Although he'd never married, he had enjoyed his fair share of birds, albeit most of the time he had to pay for their attentions – working girls don't offer free tricks. Pinkie pulled away from the kerb in the Jag, leaving Frank lusting after the bird in the Beetle. As he passed lovesick Frank, he turned and eyeballed him.

∼

Jayne's car turned at the bottom of the hill as the red Jaguar sped past me. There was something not right here. Now I was confident that car had followed me from work, and it wasn't a coincidence the driver had stood and gawped at us when we had wrongly, although wonderfully, kissed.

"Shit!"

Was he a private investigator? Had Jemma or Clare employed someone to follow me? Why had I kissed Jayne? Well, I knew why because I was mad about her – a feeling that thirty-six years of absence from my wife had stolen from me. I'd eyeballed the driver as the Jag whizzed by. Although I didn't know him, there was something vaguely familiar about his face.

"Oh, bollocks. What have I done?" I muttered.

34

Tomb Raider

Friday morning, I struggled to get moving. Already on my second coffee of the day, and the kitchen clock informed me it was only just after six. Unsurprisingly, I hadn't slept much.

One week today, unless I could prevent it, my wife would be murdered. Jayne was flooding my brain, and although I should just forget her and put last night down to a mistake – I couldn't, and I hope she couldn't either.

Today, I planned to visit Paul. That wasn't going to be easy, but one of us had to make the first move. As I was the eldest by some thirty-odd years, well, my brain was, it might as well be me. And as for Tobias, well, he knew I knew, whatever that was, and I fully expected he would be ringing Jemma today. I suspected when they spoke, he'd have a lot more to say than *'Call Me.'*

This evening, I would have to face my wife, knowing she and Tobias had probably chatted. That would be a tricky conversation because I harboured the guilt about snogging one of her best friends. Also, there was Red-Jag-Man, who was clearly following me, but what for – hell knows? After watching Jayne and I play kissy-face like a couple of teenagers,

Red-Jag-Man now had information on me I would have preferred to keep under wraps.

I had a simple task, stop my wife from getting murdered, and life would be wonderful – how hard could it be? But one week into my significantly shortened mission, I'd discovered I didn't like my wife much and now wanted her best friend instead. Her other best friend thought her husband, my mate, was having an affair, and he probably was with my wife, her best friend. Then I punched my business partner, fell out with my best mate Dave, pissed off the neighbours, and probably ruined Alison's chances of netting her rugby super-hunk bloke now she'd morphed from Super-Tits to Miss Prim after my rant. I now have some private investigator on my tail – to boot! *Brilliant!*

'You could still be living on the streets, in poor health, with only the shapely ankles of Michael-Kors-pink-trainer lady to look at!'

"Good point," I replied to my thoughts, as I boiled the kettle for my third cup of coffee. Unfortunately, the first two hadn't performed well in the wake-me-up process.

Whilst completing my ablutions, I mulled through how the conversation with Jemma would pan out. I considered calling her, but that was a crap idea as it had to be a face-to-face conversation – I would need to see the whites of her eyes. Of course, I could call Tobias and continue our discussion, which he saw fit to truncate when storming out last night. However, I still didn't know the facts, and suspected I'd put two and two together and come up with five, so dismissed that idea.

Tobias might be having an affair, as Clare suspected. Maybe Jemma had caught him out, and that was what the argument was about. She might be completely innocent, and there's me thinking the worst about my wife whilst I'm the one playing away with her friend.

Jayne, oh hell. I was smitten. Although the right thing to do was call her, apologise for kissing her and hope we could put it all behind us. I considered nipping up to my old school where she taught and speaking to her face to face. However, her Noel Edmonds Big Ears boss wouldn't be too chuffed if I turned up during school hours.

Then there was the Clare issue. Would she call me today? And if she did, what the hell would I tell her?

I'd kept a beady eye out for Red-Jag-Man, but as I parked up outside the office there was no sign of my tail. So maybe he'd got the information he wanted last night and was now preparing his report for Jemma or someone else – but who?

"Morning, Frank," beamed Alison. She appeared more normal today, not Super-Tits and not Little Women – just normal. Although, since Captain Kirk and his crew had scraped me off the pavement of Queen's Walk two months ago, I wasn't sure what normal was anymore.

"Frank," she whispered and leant forward, beckoning me over. "He's in!" she hissed.

"Paul?"

Alison nodded as she glanced down the corridor to our offices, then back at me. "He's in your office! He didn't want a coffee, just said not to disturb him."

"Oh," I huffed. I was going to see him today, but it looks like I won't need to take that trip out. "How did he seem?"

"Not himself. And his face is a mess, to say the least!" she whispered. Although with my office door shut, he wouldn't be able to hear us. Alison stifled a giggle as she appeared delighted with how I conducted myself when I'd rearranged my business partner's face.

"Right. Christ, I better get on with it."

"Frank?"

I glanced back before entering my office. Alison appeared teary-eyed as she chewed her bottom lip and hovered, almost hopping on the spot.

"Has Paul upset you this morning? What's that bastard done?" I asked, as I stepped back towards her whilst she shook her head, causing her ponytail to wildly swing about behind her.

"If he's done something, I'll stick my other fist in the bastard's face."

"No, Frank, he hasn't. Look, I want to apologise for, well, you know."

"No, I don't. What d'you mean?"

"Oh, this is embarrassing. For my dress sense, thingy. I thought you both liked it that I dressed like, well tarty … Paul said I need to offer something for clients to look at. He said, every man needs a great set of jugs to feast his eyes on, and having a dolly-bird with nice tits on reception was important."

"Christ! When did he say that?"

"Oh, ages ago. But I thought that's what you both wanted."

"Alison, no. Just be who you are. You're a terrific receptionist, and you don't need to do what he suggested. I'm going to change this company for the better, and you'll play a big part in its future … okay?"

Nodding and smiling, Alison turned a bright shade of crimson, then averted my eyes as she studied the floor carpet tiles. "You know, I've had a crush on you for ages. I'm sorry I've acted, well, y'know … all flirty, coming on to you and all that. I know you're happily married, and I feel silly now."

Happily married – was I? Well, if I was, why was I playing kissy-face with Jayne?

"Oh, that doesn't matter. Honestly, forget it. Anyway, after I've had a chat with that tosser, we'll have some decisions to make. If I can't get Paul to change his ways and we're unable to resolve our differences, I'm afraid that will be it for Stone and Wilson's."

"Oh, really, what about—"

I grabbed her elbow, sensing she was concerned about her future employment status. "Hey, don't worry, I'll strike out on my own. Whatever happens, you'll still have a job, either here or in the new company I'll set up."

Alison beamed that lovely smile. "Oh, thank you, Frank. I always want to work for you." She almost skipped back to her reception desk, her ponytail swinging from side to side.

She was a lovely girl and now no longer gave a competent performance of Lara Croft – I refer to her previously chosen tight tops rather than her archaeological skills. She would be the sort of girl that any prospective mother-in-law would think her lad had landed on his feet. Nice of her to say about always wanting to work here, but I suspected rugby-hunk will have different plans for our Alison.

Paul had conducted the interviews for Alison's replacement as I was in no fit state at the time to do anything apart from unscrewing the caps from whisky bottles. Presumably, he wasn't interested in the content of their CV, more their vital statistics. I recall her replacement was a pretty young girl who left soon after starting; now I think I know why.

I turned and faced my office door, took a deep breath, and entered.

Paul sat slumped in the chair with his legs propped up on my desk. He didn't turn around but dropped his legs down as I entered and closed the door. I traversed my way to my desk and plonked down on my chair before studying his swollen face. His nose appeared to be repositioned, now a few degrees off-centre, and his left eye sported some impressive bruising. Appearing utterly pissed off, he glared at me and folded his arms Bill Sensible-Clothes Parsons style.

"Could have you arrested for assault and battery!"

I nodded. "Go for it."

"Well, I just might. You broke my ruddy nose!"

"Look, Paul, how do we move forward from this?"

"Move forward … move forward! You can start by apologising and begging me not to go to the police … that will be a bloody start!"

"I'm not doing that, mate. You had it coming," I said, as I pointed to his mashed-up face. "Anyway, some bloke realigns that nose of yours in a few years. All I've done is bring that event forward a bit."

"What?"

"I mean, you're likely to get beaten up with your attitude."

"What attitude? You're the one with attitude, mate! For fuck sake, what the hell has happened to you? We used to have a laugh. Now you're all strait-laced and boring. I tell you, it's that missus of yours that's changed you. Since she's become an MP, she's all hoity-toity and la-di-da."

"Leave Jemma out of this. It has nothing to do with her."

"It's got everything to do with her! She's changed you, can't you see that? I don't know what you see in the bloody woman. Well, apart from her great set of jugs, and she's super fuckable. But she needs a sock in her mouth, that bitch!"

I balled my fist and contemplated launching across my desk to plant one on him.

"You not giving her enough, mate? Take her in hand and give her a damn good fuck. If you're not man enough for it, I'm happy to oblige!"

My chair shot back as I leapt up and grabbed his collar, dragging the ignominious pile of shit across my desk. My free arm shot back, fist balled and winding up, ready to smash into his despicable face and force his broken nose out the other side of his head.

I hovered for a second.

"Go on then, big man!"

I shoved him back into his seat. Still standing, I leant across the desk whilst he slumped in his chair, grinning at me.

"Lost your bottle? Would La-di-da-tits be disappointed if you manned up?"

"We're finished!"

"Good! Now you've left the silly bitch, perhaps you can get back to being good old Frank again. She kick you out because she's had her bit of rough and now fancies some hooray-henry-toff to lick her tits?"

"Not Jemma! You, you tosser. Our partnership is done ... finished, dickhead." Although I wondered if he was correct, and Jemma and I were finished.

"Wh-what? Don't be a dick! You're going to let that posh cow ruin our business?"

"You've ruined the business! Now get out. Get out before I kill you."

As I scooted around my desk, I guess my demeanour suggested my threat was real because Paul's expression changed as he scrambled out of his chair and backed towards the door.

He stopped at the door, offering a surrender position with his hands in the air. "Alright, alright. Look, I'll give you the weekend to calm down. Then we can sort this out." Grabbing the door handle, he flung the door open and bolted out.

Hearing him crash through the reception door as Alison called out his name, I swivelled around, glanced out of the window and spotted him scrambling into his car.

"I take it that didn't go well?" asked Alison, as she appeared at the doorway, sporting a concerned frown.

"I could kill him!"

"He's not worth it, Frank."

"No, you're right. Okay, so here's what's going to happen. We'll finish the multistorey contract. If he can't toe the line, then I'll subcontract out as much as we can. The revenue from that build will set us up, and we'll split the business. Then, you can work for me ... what d'you say?"

Alison delivered her best receptionist smile. "Better get you a coffee, boss."

35

Jump Jet

"Extra! Extra! Read all about it! Get your Evening Standard here. RAF Jets collide – three dead in Cambridgeshire. Extra! Extra!"

Jemma fished out some coins from her purse and purchased the Evening Standard from the seller, who repeatedly screamed the headlines every ten seconds. She had no idea why he kept shouting, *Extra*. However, as he appeared to be older than her grandfather, he was from that generation that just did. Jemma copped another ear full as he boomed out his chant immediately after he'd handed her the paper, saying *"Cheers love,"* winking and giving her a good look up and down.

Striding towards the platforms, after making a call from one of the payphones, she waited for the 6:22 p.m. train back to Fairfield. Jemma scanned the front page detailing the sad news that three people had died when two Harrier Jump Jets had a mid-air collision, and one had crashed into their house earlier that day. At least the headlines weren't about the failing Tory Government and the ever-rising unemployment figures. As lowering unemployment had been at the heart of their election campaign only a few months ago, it had become increasingly embarrassing to the Government that the unemployment rate continually rose faster than Jump Jets.

This week had been exhausting with the preparation for the Party Conference, which was due to start in a little over two weeks, and the back-to-back committee meetings that had soaked up most of her time. She also had to prepare her maiden speech and worryingly was led to believe Mrs Thatcher would be in the house to hear it. That thought terrified her.

'If you want anything said, ask a man. If you want anything done, ask a woman.'

The Prime Minister had said this to the female MPs only a few weeks ago; those words reverberated around her head. She must ensure she acted with integrity and not just waffled.

All this aside, acting with integrity in her personal life was becoming a concern. Jemma was fully aware it was all coming to a head. However, her confused mind was hurtling down the track to disaster and she didn't know how to apply the brakes, or even if she wanted to.

She'd always had a close relationship with her father, and last Sunday had taken the opportunity to confide in him regarding the rather tricky situation she'd now landed herself in. As always, he'd listened and wasn't judgemental. However, since then, the situation had escalated. She could never tell her mother as that would be a disaster because Helen Causton didn't cope well with difficult issues, often becoming hysterical. Her mother had to have everything in order, unable to cope when life threw curve balls at her. All her father had asked was that she made a decision and was open and honest about it. Then he would support her. What a dilemma.

The split-flap timetable board started its sequence change. All commuters instantly looked up as the board commenced its flap rotation routine. The sound, similar to that of a thousand typewriters in full flow, filled the station concourse as a hush descended. Hundreds of tired, gaping-mouthed commuter faces scrutinised the board, awaiting the sequence to end. Jemma was ready to dash as soon as the board stopped. It would cause a melee, as hordes of passengers would all stampede in different directions, fighting to get to their trains. If you didn't have your wits about you, there was a real chance of being flattened by the tidal wave of commuters forcing you in the wrong direction.

The Fairfield train information sequence ended before the whole board had changed. This afforded Jemma a head start before the onslaught of the inevitable chaos ensued on the Friday night dash out of town. Handbag and briefcase at the ready, she torpedoed herself through the throng of 'suits' all holding their newspapers, umbrellas, and the few City bankers pompously donning their bowler hats.

Collapsing on her first-class seat, Jemma rested her head on the clean white antimacassars as the guards walked along the platform, slamming the doors shut. As the whistle blew, she closed her eyes, pleased the seat beside her was still vacant. She had thirty-five minutes to run through in her mind what she would say to Frank tonight – it wasn't long enough.

Although so challenging and, at times, terrifying, the last five months had been the making of her. She'd never wanted the job and almost weekly had moments when she considered resigning. Roops had been her rock. He'd kept her focused and determined to succeed.

Jemma could only describe her upbringing as sheltered. She'd always lived in Fairfield and never been on a foreign package holiday. In fact, apart from annual summer trips to Devon, she'd rarely left the county. Her young life was cocooned in a little bubble and, most of the time, protected from the real world by her father. Meeting and marrying Frank had opened her eyes because he was so different from previous boyfriends. Frank was wild, adventurous, and that slightly rough edge about him had made Frank seem exciting to an inexperienced Jemma.

Although it was wrong to use your fists, the day Frank punched a bloke who'd pinched her bum was something she'd never forget. Previous boyfriends would at best have said something in a pompous manner to her assailant and then suggested they leave the pub – but not Frank. It was only their second date, so still at the stage of being polite and tiptoeing around each other. They'd just purchased their drinks from the bar when some bloke walked past them, commented on her chest, then rubbed and pinched her bottom. He was significantly larger than Frank and perhaps thought he could get away with it. However, he didn't know Frank, though a second later his nose was acquainted with Frank's fist.

That incident was only three years ago, but she'd changed. If Frank punched someone now, she'd consider it to be thuggish behaviour. Now a Member of Parliament, her widened horizons had given her opportunities to meet and work with so many different and interesting people. This new life had become exciting and different to how she had initially found Frank to be.

The call with Tobias today was worrying, and Jemma mused over whether she'd have to come clean with Frank tonight, even though Tobias had been clear to keep her mouth shut. In fact, he'd threatened her, which was entirely out of character. One thing for certain, she *needed* to know why Frank was at the Maid's Head Hotel on Friday because she thought he was out with Dave. Was Frank already suspicious?

Jemma had undoubtedly witnessed a side of Tobias which she didn't know existed when she delivered her ultimatum to him last week. Although she shouldn't have been surprised – back a rat into a corner, and they would come out fighting. Clare had been her oldest and closest friend, and she simply could not allow this situation with Tobias to continue.

Opening her eyes as the train left Central London, she sighed, which caused the gent in a pinstriped suit opposite her to glance up from his paper. Jemma offered a smile, which he reciprocated whilst stubbing out his cigarette in the armrest ashtray before continuing to read his paper.

Although this had been brewing for months, it was now coming to a head. Confused by her feelings, but now fully aware she was approaching a crossroads the question was, did she carry on straight ahead? Have a suburban life, two-point four children and end up like her mother in twenty years, pandering after her husband and regretting lost opportunities. Or did she turn at those crossroads and dive headlong into the unknown, exciting, possibly exhilarating direction, which was most certainly on offer?

In less than two weeks, she'd be staying away in Blackpool for the Party Conference. Jemma knew in her heart that was the point she would not be able to hold back any longer.

At the start of her relationship with Frank, it was pure lust that had somehow grown into a relationship. However, their relationship was now just about sex. Although exhilarating sex, that's what all was left. The love was fading for Jemma, and she felt they no longer had anything in common. They spent limited time together and rarely went out. If they did, it was always with friends. As much as she tried, Frank no longer interested her like he used to.

Rupert was different. He was intelligent, connected, headstrong, and determined to ascend to high office. With his unyielding self-confidence, he was one of those men who, with no effort, sucked women to him and men feared – she knew she's become infatuated with him. As much as she tried to deny it, with his rapier wit, Roops oozed testosterone in an intelligent way, unlike Frank, who oozed it in a rough lumberjack way.

Frank was amazing in bed; she didn't know if Rupert was. However, after working so closely together and last night, Jemma suspected there was a high probability she'd find out. If not before, it would happen in Blackpool – she wouldn't be able to resist.

Although now thirty, she'd only had three lovers. That sheltered, protective upbringing had hidden her from many experiences, which she was now realising were out there. Certainly, until she had met Frank, sex had been almost mechanical. With Frank it was wild, as he'd quickly blown away any inhibitions as she discovered the joy of a man's body and what it could do to her. He had unleashed the sexual tiger in her. Before she met Frank, an orgasm was something only her friends experienced.

A few months ago, she could never have imagined feeling this way. She was happy, enjoying her job, and that's precisely what it was – a job. Jemma fully expected she would give that up to have Frank's children and then maybe in later years go back to work to use her legal training again. Now, she couldn't run from what was in front of her. Rupert had widened her horizons, and it was abundantly clear to Jemma he wanted her. She knew men like Roops got what they wanted.

Charlie had not stayed over last night and had grumbled as he resigned himself to assisting his wife with the children when he arrived home. Although nothing was said when Charlie left on Thursday evening, both she and Roops were aware now they had the house to themselves what that could lead to. There was no late sitting in the House, and the last committee meeting had ended before five, so she could have returned home last night and probably should have – but Jemma knew why she hadn't.

Closing her eyes again as they trundled through West Hampstead station, she allowed the thoughts of last night to resurface. Forgetting where she was, Jemma unconsciously writhed in her seat.

They'd gone out for dinner, which was not unusual, although it would normally be the three of them. The sexual tension had simmered all evening, with flirtatious innuendoes and the gentle stroking of each other's hands. At one point, Jemma had rubbed her foot against his groin and could feel his growing excitement.

It came to the boil as soon as they jumped in a cab on their way back to the house, starting with hand touching and entwined fingers. Then Roops laid his hand on her thigh and seductively traced his fingers under her skirt hemline. She could hardly breathe, burning to get back to the house and rip his clothes off – she wanted him.

They'd kissed as soon as they closed the front door. Then, after Roops unbuttoned her blouse and his hand roamed under her bra, she held him at bay just before, for her, the point of no return. Shagging a colleague when you're married just wasn't right, although Jemma knew she was already on rocky ground with that thought. Christ, only a week had passed since she'd ferociously spat at Frank about what a prat Dave was with that young girl in the supermarket. And here she was, ten days later, allowing Roops to fondle her and about to hop into bed with him.

Jemma was glad she'd managed to control herself this time, although, once again, the memory of his hands on her skin sent tingles through her body. Gently writhing on the seat, her mouth parted as her breathing became laboured.

Jemma opened her eyes.

The gent facing her raised his eyebrows. "Are you uncomfortable, my dear? Seats in first class aren't what they used to be."

Jemma returned a tight smile but declined to offer a reply. A year ago, she'd have been mortified and died of embarrassment. Not now – she didn't care. Jemma wanted Roops. If he'd been with her on the train, she'd have dragged him to the toilet.

This morning, she'd risen early, shooting out of the house to get to the office before Roops was up. Jemma knew if they'd had breakfast together, she would end up in his bed. Then both would be late for work, and the label of adulterer would be firmly stamped on her – regardless of any previous misdemeanours that could be slung her way.

Jemma knew what Roops wanted, and the offensively large bouquet which arrived at her office at lunchtime had cemented that belief. The bouquet was so large that she had to clear the space on Charlie's desk, with whom she shared an office, because the bouquet wouldn't fit on hers and leave enough space to work. It would've been like trying to deal with correspondence whilst in the glasshouses at Kew Gardens. Of course, this set tongues wagging in her particular area of the corridors of power.

Roops not only wanted to share her bed, he wanted the whole nine yards. Marriage, children, country estate, powerful position, and Jemma on his arm to present to Heads of State when he became Prime Minister, which he firmly believed he would achieve that position. In fact, Roops was that confident he'd even written his acceptance speech in preparation for when he became leader of the Conservative Party when he fully expected Mrs Thatcher to lose the next election. The life he offered was tempting; the lure of his body was ever more so.

If she *was* going to turn at the crossroads, which were fast approaching, she had to tell Frank first – he deserved that at the very least.

36

Wuthering Heights

Jayne and I hadn't spoken by the time I arrived home from work. Earlier that day I'd thumbed through the telephone directory and looked up my old school's telephone number, lifting the receiver, then replacing it in its cradle at least a dozen times between Paul leaving my office and the end of my working day. Every time Alison patched through a call, my heart skipped a beat, wondering if it was Jayne – but it wasn't.

Jayne probably regretted last night and, forever going forward, it would be that awkward encounter whenever she met up with Jemma. It had been a mistake; I knew it, and she would know it. The sensible course of action was ignoring what happened and letting it be an event consigned to history.

The problem was, I didn't want it forgotten. I knew in my first go at 1979 I'd liked Jayne. Now, on round two, my feelings had changed – I wanted her. She was, well, just more me than Jemma was.

Last night in the pub, we'd chatted so freely as we sat at the bar. She was captivating and funny, and when she smiled, it melted me. A bomb could have ripped the place apart, and I wouldn't have noticed. Jayne was supplying a feeling which I never thought I'd experience again. I was falling for her and hoped she harboured similar feelings for me. When we'd kissed, she didn't hold back and, although it was so wrong, I could have stayed there all night with her in my arms.

'Christ man, what mess have you got yourself into!'

The separation from Jemma for thirty-six years had not made the heart grow fonder. Although she was the woman I'd loved for all those years, I don't think I loved her now. Last night, Jayne indicated she felt the same about me. However, maybe that was just the warm evening and two glasses of wine, and was probably horrified at what we'd done and regretted it. As much as it pained me to think it, I considered she would try to avoid me like the plague.

If Tobias had called Jemma today, there surely would be a showdown tonight. However, I was on thin ice accusing her of having an affair with Tobias because I knew full well I'd have taken it further with Jayne if the opportunity had arisen. The slightly tricky bit was Red-Jag-Man. He'd seen us as we'd stood eating each other's face off. If he was some private investigator who Jemma had organised to tail me, then the cat was out of the bag.

I decided to play it cool and see how Jemma reacted when she arrived home. If Jemma didn't mention Tobias, then I wouldn't. So, the best policy was to throw in some innocent questions and watch how she reacted. Her lips would twitch if my casual questions were causing discomfort, and I would know she was lying.

I would be honest if Jemma asked where I'd been last night. Well, honest about Tobias, not Jayne. I was racked with guilt because it wasn't her fault that we were separated for thirty-odd years and, as far as she was concerned, we weren't.

Also, it wasn't her fault that those years had changed me, and I'd now discovered the second time around that I was no longer in love with her.

Jemma had probably done nothing wrong, and this thing with Tobias was not how it seemed. She loved me, and I was letting her down. I felt like a real shit and was so disappointed with myself, now wondering how I'd got myself into this mess. Assuming Jemma was innocent, I would just have to work hard at our marriage and make it work. She deserved that. Not a husband who goes around snogging her friends.

I had to remember I was the luckiest man alive. The Hooded Claw had given me thirty-six years back, and there I was, thinking about another woman.

I flicked on the TV in an attempt to give my overactive, whirring brain a rest. Nationwide current affairs programme, presented by a fresh-faced Sue Lawley, who, incidentally, I'm sure The Police released a song about in 1978, introduced a news item about the Green Cross Code Man and his visit to local schools. Well, clearly, Dave Prowse was still focused on educating kids about road safety, and not as I'd suggested to The Hooded Claw planning to run for Office in his attempt to become the President of the United States.

My mind wouldn't play ball and refused to be distracted. I'd come to a conclusion this afternoon that my list of suspects was too long to be able to pin down her murderer. The simple plan was to follow her next Friday night. Without picking her up from the restaurant, I would allow her to walk but keep close to identify her assailant. If I just picked her up and saved her from what would happen, then I would never know who killed her. Of course, that could leave the murderer free to strike another night.

If I got this right, I could protect her and identify the perpetrator. Then, I would move into phase two of my mission to deal with him. What the precise details of that second phase were at this point were sketchy.

Aware how super risky this idea was, I knew I had to get my plan bulletproof. However, I had a few days to ensure I covered all bases and, if I could manage to pull this off, I'd probably need to enlist some help. However, that could be tricky based on the fact I suspected every breathing male in the country of killing her. But, as Dave was my oldest pal, I thought I could enlist his support as I'd decided there was no way he murdered her, even if he thought she was 'above her station' as he put it. I'd known Dave for over fifty years and, although we had lost contact, I knew he wasn't a murderer – breast fondler, yes. Murderer, no.

The sketchy plan would involve confiding in Dave that I wanted to follow Jemma because I thought she was up to something. This would tick all his boxes and play to his dislike of her because it was obvious he wasn't her number one fan. Yes, Dave would be up for that. I just had to patch up our relationship this weekend. Telling Dave I was sixty-six and a time-traveller here to stop a murder, he really would think I had lost my marbles.

Of course, there was a gaping chasm of a hole in my plan if Dave was the murderer. I would then be placing him where he wanted to be, assuming, at this point, the murderer had already decided to kill her. The risk was giving Dave the opportunity. However, I deduced he wasn't the murderer – what if I was wrong?

The news item came to a close as the reporter signed off, returning to Sue Lawley in the studio after Darth Vader, dressed in his Green Cross Code superhero outfit, had lifted two small children whilst their excited classmates all cheered. I needed him with me next Friday night, not Dave. That would ensure success, as any potential murderer would run a mile if faced with Darth Vader by my side.

The little red light on the answering machine repeatedly flashed. Rewinding and hitting play, now confident about how to operate this ancient machine, I listened to the one message left by Jemma stating she'd be catching the 6:22 p.m. train and expected to arrive at Fairfield station just after 7:00 p.m. Please could I be there on time and not leave her standing around waiting. I replayed the message a few times but couldn't detect anything from her tone that would give me a clue to her demeanour. By the sounds in the background, I assumed she'd called from St Pancras Station as I heard the unintelligible announcer boom out some mumbo-jumbo from the tannoy system.

~

Jayne had conducted her lessons almost robotically but had somehow managed to get through the day without anyone noticing she was, in mind, somewhere else.

Jayne would never forget the first day she met Frank. Not that anything particularly memorable happened, or the date was synonymous with a famous world event. However, it was the first time and the only time she'd fallen in love at first sight.

Jemma had suggested getting together with her new boyfriend as it would be nice for Jayne and her fella to meet up in town so she could introduce Frank to them. At the time,

Jayne was seeing a bloke called Simon, who she'd been dating for a few months. Although he was okay, Simon was nothing to write home about.

Sitting chatting in the pub that evening three years ago, within minutes, she'd fallen in love with Jemma's new bloke. With his wavy, long, blond locks and muscular physique, she could have been sucked into his bright ocean-blue eyes and happily drowned there. Why did blokes like that not ask her out?

Jemma was gorgeous and, with no effort, sucked in the attentions of every man in close proximity. When they were younger, they'd often enjoyed nights out on the town together. But with Jemma's stunning figure and to-die-for blonde hair, Jayne knew all the blokes they met only had eyes for Jemma. As a result, Jayne would become invisible as the young men swarmed around Jemma like bees around a honey pot.

Over the years, she'd played it cool and never revealed her feelings for Frank. However, every time they met up, she couldn't help but wish he was attracted to her and not Jemma. Jayne suspected that Jemma knew how she felt about Frank but guessed Jemma never concerned herself because Plain-Jayne, as Jemma called her, was no threat. Anyway, Frank had Jemma; why would he look at her?

However, last night had turned her world upside down. As she parked up on her mother's driveway, for the millionth time, Jayne replayed in her mind that kiss. She closed her eyes, her mouth parted and wished he would kiss her again.

It was so unfair; Frank had kissed her because he could but undoubtedly forgot about it seconds after it happened. He was married, and he shouldn't have done it, but then, nor should she. Now Jayne would be in total turmoil thinking about him whilst he just got on with his life, not giving her or that kiss a second thought.

She'd been in a trance the whole bloody day as she replayed their conversations after he'd asked her to stay for a drink. Every word he said, she'd analysed what he meant. Although it just couldn't be true, all his actions and everything he said suggested he liked her – but why? Jayne knew him well and didn't have him down as one of those blokes who would be unfaithful just for the fun of it. So, had she got him wrong? Was he regularly playing away and not caring how he was hurting Jemma?

Now Jemma was the local MP, and by association, Frank had become reasonably well known in the local area. So, standing in the middle of Fairfield whilst kissing another woman was surely a dangerous strategy. Anyone could've seen them – why would he risk it?

Over the last three years, Jayne had settled into her teaching career. Eaton City of Fairfield School was a prestigious school and, although the Head was a bit of a pillock, she had a great relationship with her peers. She got on well with Jason, the deputy head, and looked forward to work every day.

Her relationship with Simon, as expected, petered out as quickly as it had started. There had been a few more dates, but they were never right – they weren't Frank.

Jason and his wife Jenny, with whom Jayne had become close friends, had set her up on a few blind dates with nice blokes who were always keen. Although she wasn't a 'traffic stopper' like Jemma and her friend Clare, she knew she was attractive and was never short of male attention – well, as long as she wasn't out with Jemma, that is. But, unfortunately, none of those dates matched up to Frank. And because of this, none of those relationships had lasted. Now, at twenty-nine, she still lived with her mother whilst all her friends were married and many had children.

A while ago, she wasn't sure exactly when, Jayne had decided to move on with her life. Although she'd met the man who she was in love with, she'd finally accepted the depressing fact that Frank could never be hers and pining for him like a lovesick teenager was silly. Now she'd been on a few dates and, although they had just turned out to be nothing more than friends, she would soon meet the right bloke. She *would* get married and ultimately have what she wanted – her own family. Forgetting Frank would clear her mind to find a loving man.

Up until about half six last night, Jayne was doing well in her attempt to forget the man she loved. Then she'd seen Frank, and he'd asked her to stay for a drink. Now she was back to square one; no, it was worse because he'd kissed her.

Frank had a boyish way about him. Not immature, but cheeky, fun, and his golden hair made him seem younger. He certainly was the man with the child in his eyes. She ruefully smiled as she thought about how everyone said she was the spitting image of Kate Bush. However, Frank was not going to be Heathcliff in her very own version of Wuthering Heights.

"No, Jayne Hart, that won't happen … I'm destined to be *All By Myself,*" she huffed, then started humming that tune which always made her cry. Perhaps she was never going to fall in love again. That man Frank, who didn't look too dissimilar to Eric Carmen, had taken her heart.

Jayne had driven halfway across town during her lunch break, intent on seeing Frank at his office. The trouble was if

Jemma found out she'd been there, that would have been impossible to explain. Although Jayne was sure Frank would apologise and act the gentleman, what would she say to him? It was a stupid idea, and she would leave there like a jilted bride – the embarrassment would kill her. So, after ten minutes of driving, she'd performed a U-turn and returned to school.

"Oh, Frank! Why do you keep doing this to me?" she whispered, as a few heavy tears popped out and trickled down her face.

Jayne opened her teary eyes, sniffed and took a few deep breaths to calm herself. She glanced at her home and spotted her mother peering out of the kitchen window, probably wondering why she was sitting in her car on the driveway and hadn't come in. Now she would face a barrage of questions, and her mother would be convinced something awful had happened.

Well, it had! Frank Stone had relit the fire.

A fire she'd worked so hard to extinguish.

37

Concrete Cows

Friday had developed into a really shitty day. Now he wasn't in the mood to meet up with some of his old mates for their annual dinner and general piss-up in London. They'd called themselves *The Likely Lads,* although, in reality, none of them displayed any similarity to the miserable duo – but the name had stuck. However, just lately, he'd morphed into a Bob Ferris type character, and he knew who was the cause of that. Perhaps a night getting bladdered was just the tonic he needed to rid himself of this melancholy state.

After shouting at the old tosser at the station ticket office who needed to invest in a bloody hearing aid, he slumped onto the bench seat on the station platform and waited for the train. He hated trains: dirty, smelly and full of old grannies or annoying kids. He'd contemplated driving in to town. However, as he was planning on having a skinful, he'd dismissed that idea.

The outbound London train chugged in on the opposite platform. After a couple of minutes, it belted out its diesel exhaust fumes and pulled away, leaving him with a clear view again. Most of the alighting passengers had scuttled off the platform and were now squashed into a tight crowd, all jostling for position as they fought to get through the gates. A few commuters remained on the platform as they either adjusted their coat collars or rummaged through pockets, trying to locate their tickets to wave at the guard at the gate.

Straight in his eyeline, there she was. She'd placed her briefcase down and was now pawing through her handbag as the silly cow searched for whatever. She was the cause of his recent problem and, with the fury which now raged inside him, he thought he could kill her. Fortunately, there were the train lines between the two platforms, otherwise, there was a real possibility after the totally shit day he might have scooted across and bashed her one.

It would have been difficult to hold a conversation, as that would involve shouting across the tracks. Anyway, he didn't want her to see him. He scooted to the far end of the platform, always keeping her in his eyeline. As he positioned himself at the corner of the station building, he glanced across to see Jemma stride to the ticket barrier, confident she hadn't seen him. He dismissed taking the free seat on the bench due to the one occupant who sat there, thumbing through the pages of the Fairfield Chronicle, appeared to be someone you should avoid.

He glanced at the thuggish-looking man, who appeared to be engrossed in whatever article he was reading. However, he deduced there was something odd about him. Feeling somewhat uncomfortable with the surrounding company, he decided it was best to move back to the main throng of passengers, who appeared bored and frustrated with yet another late train.

Jemma was a problem, and he knew he'd have to deal with this situation soon. What dealing with actually meant, well, he wasn't sure. But Jemma was messing up his life, and that just couldn't be allowed to continue.

The train chugged into the station eleven minutes late, as all trains were. However, eleven minutes was significantly better than usual; in fact, anything under twenty minutes could be classed as on time as far as British Rail were concerned.

∼

Pinkie Sinclair flicked through to the centre of the paper. He skimmed the headlines of an article regarding the planned grand opening of the Milton Keynes shopping centre and the news about the Prime Minister who'd be attending to formally open one of Europe's premier shopping malls. The article referenced the concrete cow sculptures unveiled last year, which were now considered by many as a joke. Pinkie kept the paper open but didn't continue reading past the headlines.

His target had walked past him and positioned himself in his blind spot to his right. Swivelling his eyes, he could see the man's shoes but not what he was doing or looking at. Of course, he may have just walked this way to get into one of the front carriages when the train arrived. However, something had spooked his target, and Pinkie considered the possibility he'd been sloppy, causing his cover to be blown.

He held the paper open, giving the impression of a man reading the local newspaper. However, ignoring the details of the penned article, Pinkie kept himself alert and his eyes firmly on his target's shoes. Pinkie needed to be ready to act if there was a sudden movement, although he'd rather not reveal himself at this stage. A couple of minutes later, his target moved back down the station platform towards the ticket office. Pinkie watched his target board the train before returning his attention to the paper to avoid eye contact as the train pulled out of the station.

Over the last month, Pinkie had completed extensive surveillance operations and, with the knowledge gained, felt confident of his next moves. The information he'd gathered had put him in a strong position to act, and he now had a clear plan for how to wrap up this case. Once sorted, he could move on with his life.

Pinkie folded the paper and lobbed it on the bench seat beside him. As he exited the platform, he threw the ticket he'd purchased but never intended to use in the bin. Pulling out of the station car park, he headed back to his digs in London, where he'd planned a weekend of drinking with some mates and a trip up to White Hart Lane to see Spurs play on Saturday. However, he was disappointed to see his team were still as hopeless as ever.

38

Radio Luxembourg

"Shall I put your case on the bed?" I called to Jemma, as she padded into the kitchen and kicked off her shoes.

"Please. I'll stick the kettle on. I'm not really in a fit state to cook tonight, so d'you want to nip up the chippy?"

"Yeah, good idea," I called out, as I trapezed up the stairs with her case.

The journey home was full of unspoken tension. We'd had a quick kiss after I'd opened the car door for her and grabbed her case to plonk in the boot.

As we pulled out of the station car park, I'd asked if she'd had a good week. I'd learnt very quickly back in 1979 that allowing Jemma to talk about herself was a banker when wanting to kick off a conversation, which was never usually too tricky to accomplish. However, as she replied she didn't want to talk, I deduced my conversation starter wasn't working tonight. So, I thumbed the radio dial to pick up a station with some music to fill the unusual silence.

Before my time on the streets, even I had enjoyed the pleasure of digital music. Not that I ever had an iPod, but I did own a Discman. Now, as I twizzled the knob, all that came back through the speakers was crackles. Jemma shot me an odd look, presumably wondering what the hell I was fumbling at. She leant forward and hit one of the pre-set buttons, resulting in the red dial shooting across to the pre-set Radio One medium-wave station. She'd shaken her head at me, wondering what I was messing about at, then resumed her position, head back, eye-closing routine, making it clear she wasn't up for talking. Well, it was alright for her, but I was re-learning 1979 technology, and I was a bit out of practice.

I'd joked it was *my* radio show as I heard David Kid Jensen's jingle, but she just kept her eyes closed and ignored me. Hearing that jingle had reminded me she'd said in her late teens she fancied the DJ when he broadcasted on Radio Luxembourg. Not that Jemma knew what he looked like, but loved his voice. However, when she'd later seen him on the cover of Smash Hits magazine, Jemma had said she was drawn to the picture because he was my double.

I shut up and let my look-alike DJ play the music. I might look like him, but clearly Jemma wasn't interested in listening to me tonight.

Jemma sat slumped at the kitchen table, holding her tea, and appeared to be deep in thought. I joined her and sipped my tea as we sat in silence, the heavy, thick atmosphere hanging between us.

She was probably thinking I was going to mention the conversation I'd had with Tobias. There was a possibility that they'd not spoken today, so she may be in the dark. On the other hand, perhaps she was just tired after a long week and there wasn't any atmosphere which I thought I'd detected as soon as I'd picked her up from the station.

There was a possibility that Red-Jag-Man was a private investigator and, for some reason, younger me had given her cause to suspect something. Had Jemma employed a PI to tail me? If that was the case, and she'd received the full report of my misdemeanours with one of her best friends, then that could also explain the relatively thick atmosphere in the room. I would stick to my plan, play it cool, and wait.

"Frank."

"Yes?"

Here we go, either the Tobias conversation or, far worse, the Jayne conversation was about to start.

"I'm exhausted. I think I'm going to have a bath. D'you want to get fish and chips and stick mine in the oven? I'll have mine later." Jemma plonked her cup down and left the kitchen without looking at me – no offer to scrub her back tonight.

Pretty much no conversation had taken place since I'd collected her from the station car park. Did she have nothing to say? Or was her brain full of accusations and building up to launching it? Jemma, as I remember, was never one to hold back. The silent treatment was not how it worked in the Stone household. Not that we would have full-blown screaming matches when either of us was a bit miffed, but usually it would be said and not left to fester. This was different, this was serious, and I didn't know which serious it was.

Was she preparing to come clean about Tobias? I wasn't sure how I felt about that. Or was it worse? Perhaps she *did* know about Jayne, and that was so horrific for her she still needed time to prepare her accusations.

I wriggled my feet back into my old Gola trainers, which appeared to be standard-issue footwear for the time. It made me think of Michael-Kors-pink-trainer lady. She must have wondered what happened to me. Would she have asked some questions to find out how I was? We'd built a non-verbal relationship over some months, and I hoped she cared what happened. Hmmm, maybe not, and someone else would now be benefiting from her daily donations.

I'd forgotten to get to the bank and withdraw some cash, resulting in an empty wallet. Having readily available funds was still a surprising feeling because visits to a local bank were not usually on the daily agenda in my old life. After all, I'd had no account and no money.

Assuming Jemma would have some cash, I plucked up her handbag and rummaged in her cavernous private space. Locating her purse amongst the various tubes of makeup and used tissues, my eye was drawn to a previously opened pink envelope and the card inside. I glanced over my shoulder, guilty for snooping, but I couldn't resist a peek. The sweetly scented card appeared to be one of those florist cards that accompanied a bouquet. The handwritten note was not in my handwriting, and I didn't recognise it.

Jemma – you know I love you.

Please be mine – I will make you so happy.

xxxxxxxxxxxxx

Thirteen kisses. Was that significant? So, it was true. Tobias and my wife were at it, and Clare's suspicions regarding her husband's extramarital antics were confirmed. Time had changed – this event didn't happen the first time around. Well, it may have, but I wasn't aware of it.

Tobias had been a great support to me back then, or was it in the future? Hell, I don't know, perhaps both. Of course, he had to focus on helping his wife, Clare, through the tragedy of losing her best friend in such horrific circumstances, but of all my friends he'd supported me the most.

Strange that I don't recall him being devastated at losing the love of his life, which this card clearly suggested Jemma was. Had they not had an affair the first time? What had happened to change that? Certainly, I hadn't been back long enough to cause that change – had I?

Jemma was pregnant. I knew; she probably didn't, and definitely no one else did. Jemma would know soon as I calculated, at this point, she must be four weeks pregnant. Did that mean the murderer killed my wife and Tobias's child? The way this card had been written would suggest Tobias was not the murderer. Although if she changed her mind and refused to leave me, had that caused him in a fit of anger to kill her – perhaps an argument which had spiralled out of control?

I replaced the card and retrieved some cash from her purse before placing her bag where she'd left it. I nudged it a few inches to the left, stood back and assessed its position, now satisfied it looked undisturbed from where she'd abandoned it earlier. Then, still uncertain what to do with this information, I headed out to purchase our fish supper.

After finishing my meal, I cleared away my plate and set a place for Jemma. I did shout through the bathroom door to check she hadn't drowned, only to receive a curt reply stating she was still enjoying her soak and would be down later. When I said I was going up the pub, she didn't ask me not to. I guess Jemma didn't intend to talk about Tobias tonight, and I stuck to my plan to hold my cards close to my chest.

My concerns regarding Jayne had now eased because Jemma was in no position to accuse me. That card incriminated her and was clear evidence of her own shenanigans. This week back in my old life had shown me I was no longer in love with Jemma, although I won't deny this new information had ripped a hole in me.

Only a week ago, I'd held a rose-tinted view of my wife for over thirty years – now that had been shattered. Of course, the child could be mine, and if so, was she sleeping with both Tobias and me? The sex we had enjoyed last week would never suggest she was with someone else, but maybe that was all it was – just sex.

When we had started courting, it was clear that Jemma allowed me to take the lead in that department. I think that was a product of her inexperience. However, Jemma was a quick learner and soon took control of proceedings as she'd developed a rabbit intensity to our lovemaking – I certainly wasn't complaining.

Had she now decided that one man was not enough for her? And now enjoyed Tobias and me on alternate days to quench her sexual thirst? That bloody florist card suggested that Tobias and Jemma were at the point of deciding about their future – which way would she jump?

This all pointed to the inevitable fact that our marriage was cruising to the end of the road. The Hooded Claw hadn't divulged this information on the predicted future of our lives and, if they had predicted our break-up, I could see why they kept that information confidential. All they wanted was for me to save her and stop Darth Vader from entering The Oval Office or whatever catastrophe was afoot in forty-odd years.

Did I care what that was? No, I couldn't give a shit. All that mattered at this point was saving Jemma and the child from some bastard killing them next Friday night. Also, I couldn't escape from the plain fact that I was smitten by a young schoolteacher, even though I'd only enjoyed an hour or so of Jayne's company last night. Although that schoolteacher probably wasn't smitten with me. However, that was not the problem I had to face right now. Save my wife, and then see what life can give me the second time around.

Living in a cardboard house, with a four-wheeled tartan trolley as my only possession – surely, I could improve on that performance – couldn't I?

Part 3

39

2015

Madame Tussauds

"All is not lost. We may have an opportunity," said Morehouse, as he gently laid the phone handset back onto its cradle.

Whilst Morehouse listened to what his senior analyst said, Hartland's mind had drifted to the impending doom of being summoned by the Board and the consequences of a failed mission. Also, they would be back at square one, having to find another candidate to alter the *European Fault*.

He peered up at his Data Information Director, raising his eyebrows, awaiting him to divulge what his analyst had said. "Well, man, what is it?"

"Johnson has found some significant information. He's trotting up with the file now, sir."

Hartland had known Morehouse for many years, and he'd become his right-hand man. Morehouse had delivered significant improvements to his department, and the data they now had at their disposal was far more accurate. Although many missions failed, there'd been a time when failure was caused by the Association's inability to harvest the data they required. The improvements Morehouse delivered had substantially improved this technology. Although pleased his Data Information Director had stated there was an opportunity, Hartland became concerned as he could deduce from Morehouse's expression there was a problem.

Johnson had anticipated being summoned to Hartland's office when he made the call. He detested the man, who also scared him shitless. However, Johnson knew he'd have to attend to protect his boss. Within less than a minute, he was outside Hartland's office door, bracing himself before knocking.

Morehouse strode over to the door and yanked it open. "Thanks, Johnson." He smiled at his analyst as he grabbed the file.

"Bring Johnson in!" boomed Hartland.

Johnson slowly blinked.

Morehouse suspected his analyst's heart had just sunk. He mouthed, "Sorry."

Johnson nodded. Then, with great trepidation, he entered the lion's den.

Morehouse returned to stand at Hartland's desk, leaving Johnson hovering near the door, then flipped open the file and skimmed through the report his analyst had just produced.

"Well?"

"Just a moment, sir. I'm reading through."

"I haven't got all night! In less than three hours, my balls are going to be ceremoniously hacked off! Johnson, stop hovering by the door and tell me what's in that bloody report," shouted Hartland. His patience had run out, although he knew he was being unreasonable. However, Morehouse and Johnson didn't have to face the board's wrath, as he did.

The nervous analyst tentatively stepped half a pace forward. "Err ... sir?"

Morehouse glanced up from the report and motioned his head, indicating to Johnson that he should step forward and stand next to him. Johnson glanced at his boss, then back to Hartland, detecting the uncomfortable feeling as his Adam's apple bounced as he swallowed. Then, tentatively, he stepped forward. Taking a deep breath, he looked directly into the lion's mouth, desperately trying not to shake.

"Well, man? Spit it out!"

Johnson glanced at his boss, who nodded encouragingly. "Err ... well, sir. It would appear that Frank Stone succeeded in his mission. Jemma Stone is alive and well."

Hartland jumped up from his chair, balled his fists on the table and leant forward, causing Johnson to flinch. *"What?"*

"Sir, there appears to have been a data error with Jemma Stone. The information was triple checked, and her correction percentage *was* sixty-four per cent." He swallowed again while keeping his line of sight just above Hartland's head to avoid eye contact.

"What! What d'you mean, *was?*"

"Err ... the error which one of our analysts missed is when Jemma Stone was murdered ..." he swallowed again, the noise audible to all three men. "She ... err, she, she was pregnant."

"What the hell has that got to do with it? So now Smelly-Frank saves his girl, and they live happily ever after playing happy-bloody-families! What I want to know is, why is she not the bloody Foreign Secretary? Why is Vince Cable not the PM? And why God damn it, if she's alive and breathing, has time not altered?"

Whilst listening to Hartland's tirade, Morehouse had reached the part of the report which caused his blood to run cold. Now feeling nauseous, he considered the real possibility that he might faint.

Johnson took a deep breath as he composed himself, ready to spill the beans. He had hoped to show his boss the information first, but he hadn't bargained on coming into the office and being interrogated. "Sir, the fact she was pregnant at the time of her death actually reduced her correction percentage to below nought point five."

Hartland stared at the analyst. His jaw dropped, stunned by hearing what he'd just said. Failed missions were disappointing but acceptable because none of their work was an exact science. However, failed missions caused by the incompetence of poor data collection were a total disaster.

Heads would roll – literally.

Morehouse closed his eyes, raising his head to the ceiling. He could feel the movement in the air as Johnson, standing next to him, uncontrollably shook. This was his biggest cock-up ever. Providing data that Jemma Stone had a sixty-four per cent correction had driven the whole organisation to focus on her as the solution to the *European Fault*. If discovered at the time, this tiny piece of missing data would have shown that Jemma was not a target worth considering. He led this team, so he would have to take ultimate responsibility for this monumental cock-up.

Morehouse took a deep breath, lowered his head and eyeballed Hartland, who seemed frozen in time and now appeared like a waxwork figure in Madame Tussauds. Although, as they were a secret organisation operating outside the normal boundaries of time, it was unlikely Douglas Hartland would be immortalised in wax with millions of tourists clambering for selfies with him.

Johnson appeared to be trying to control the shakes as he gritted his teeth and repeatedly blinked. Morehouse spotted beads of sweat as they zig-zagged down the side of his senior analyst's face.

"Sir. This is my fault, and I will take full responsibility for this catastrophic error. I will not shy away from the consequences, and I'm fully aware of what that will entail. Johnson will investigate who is responsible for this error, and he'll act appropriately. All I ask is that my entire team are not blamed for this cock-up."

Hartland came to life. Calmly and slowly he returned his bottom to his office chair. Opening a desk drawer, Hartland fished out a fresh bottle of single malt and three glasses. "Sit," he commanded, as he slopped out three offensively large whiskies and sedately placed them on the glass table. Johnson and Morehouse obeyed his one-word command and now sat facing him. Hartland fished out a cigarette and, with an uncharacteristically shaking hand, lit it with the heavy paperweight lighter. He pointed at the whiskies and his cigarettes. "Gentleman, help yourselves; I think we need this."

Johnson didn't hesitate, throwing the whisky down his neck, having to gulp twice to slug it in one go, then gently placed his glass down and grabbed the cigarettes. Hartland leaned forward, placing the bottle next to Johnson's glass and nodded, indicating that he could pour himself another measure. The terrified analyst grabbed the bottle, although his shaking hand caused it to wave wildly and clang against his glass as he attempted to pour. To ensure the desk avoided a malt whisky bath, Morehouse assisted by steadying the bottom of the bottle. The three doomed men sat in silence for a few minutes, all contemplating what the next few hours would bring.

Hartland's eyes shot up from where he'd been staring at his whisky, which he'd been contemplating would be good to drown in. "Hang on. I thought you two said there was an opportunity. Is there a way out of this calamity?"

Johnson had developed the courage to speak after slugging down his second whisky and powering his way through his cigarette.

"Err … yes, sir. Although it's highly irregular … certainly not protocol."

Hartland nodded, affirming to Johnson he should continue.

"There is a chance we can sort this mess out. When I phoned through earlier, I told Keith that I'd completed some preliminary calculations. At first run-through, they look quite promising. Shall I take you through them?"

"Yes. I think you'd better. Otherwise, we're all standing in one whole heap of shite with the wrong shoes on."

"Yes, quite, sir. Well, I have re-run the figures on some scenarios, which has produced some interesting stats.

Of course, they're complicated and would involve on-the-ground intervention, so to speak. But based on the fact that the entire operation is a total disaster, it could work."

Hartland stubbed out his cigarette and lit another, then shifted forward in his seat and held Johnson with a skull-splitting stare. It would seem that Morehouse had trained his team to waffle as much as he did. "Johnson, it may have escaped your notice, but you, your boss, and I are in serious fucking trouble! So, spit it out, man!"

"Yes, sir. So, the figures I have run would suggest Jemma Stone would still have a correction percentage above sixty per cent if she were no longer pregnant. What I mean, sir … she loses the child before giving birth."

"What are the odds of that happening? And don't we have an issue here because it would appear she did have the child along with a few more? And now she and Smelly-Frank are living it up collecting winkles!"

"Crab, sir. Cromer crab," interjected Morehouse.

"What?" Hartland fired at him.

"Frank is living on the North Norfolk coast near Cromer. That's where you get crabs from, sir."

"Oh, bloody hell! I don't care if he's got crabs, winkles or a whole host of sexually transmitted diseases! If Jemma had this baby, how can we stop it?"

Johnson, once again, appeared to have lost his confidence, so Morehouse took over despite Hartland's verbal tirade about crabs.

"Sir, as we said, Jemma Stone is not dead. She wasn't murdered because Frank was successful in preventing her death. However, the pregnancy prevented her from becoming a cabinet minister because she took a long career break to have her children, thus the explanation for the timeline not changing."

Hartland nodded as he sat back, pulling hard on his cigarette, allowing Morehouse to continue.

"Here's the thing. It appears that Frank and Jemma split up about the time she should have been murdered. She married another Tory MP a few years later, going on to have two more children. Her husband was involved in a financial scandal in the mid-nineties and forced to resign. However, they are incredibly wealthy and now retired, enjoying their lives as socialites in Buckinghamshire.

"Okay, so they split, and the other chap takes on Frank's kid. How does this help us?"

"Sir, if we can put a halt to this pregnancy, we calculate Jemma *will* become Foreign Secretary. This is a crucial piece of data which my team, unfortunately, missed on our first assessment."

"Okay, I hear you. But Smelly-Frank is not going to save his wife and then send her toddling off to an abortion clinic. And even if he would, we'd need to send another traveller back to assist. We both bloody well know that sending a second traveller to correct the first mistake is not protocol. We only send eliminators when the traveller has caused a category one or two change."

"Yes, sir, I know. However, if we could sanction a second traveller, and we succeed, we *will* avert the *European Fault*."

"Christ, man, are you suggesting a second reset?"

"Err... yes, sir. I know it's super risky."

Hartland took a deep breath and nodded. "Christ-all-bloody-mighty! Okay, let's say, for argument's sake, we send a follow-on traveller. Why would Smelly-Frank want his own child terminated?"

"Sir, the child is highly unlikely to be Frank's."

"Oh, how do we assess that?"

Morehouse leant forward and plucked Frank's file from Hartland's desk and flicked through to the page he was searching for, running the heel of his palm down the centre of the page. Then, placing the opened report in front of Hartland, Morehouse pointed to paragraph four, subsection three. "Sir, the medical information on Frank, which we conducted over the weeks he was in preparation. Although not conclusive, those test results would suggest that Frank Stone is, and always has been, infertile."

As Hartland read the paragraph, silence once again descended. "Right, so when she was murdered before we returned Frank, Jemma was having an affair? She was pregnant, and Frank presumably didn't know?"

"Well, possibly, but we're not sure of that at the moment. The missing information *was* detailed in the autopsy report. But as Johnson here has said, one of my team missed it because they just focused on the cause of death, which was asphyxiation caused by strangulation. However, the report does say she was approximately four weeks pregnant."

"So, we send a follow-on traveller to persuade Frank that although he's done well, he now needs to ensure Jemma doesn't have the child who isn't his?"

"That's about the size of it."

"Do we know who the father is?" asked Hartland.

Morehouse glanced at Johnson, raising his eyebrows.

Johnson leaned forward. "Er ... not at this stage. That could be difficult to ascertain because there are several candidates."

"Bloody hell, poor old Smelly-Frank. His lovely wife sounds to be a bit of a good-time girl. And if we get this right, she becomes one of the most respected MPs this country has ever had!"

"Sir, I think half the members of the House are at it, so no shock there, really."

"Ha, no, you're right."

"Okay. Who are you suggesting we send? As I recall, the other candidates weren't that suitable. Also, we don't have much time because I will need to update the board in a few hours." He shook his head, almost in resignation of the impending doom. "They're still going to want heads to roll, even if I offer this solution. We all know that getting that ruddy Board to sanction risky second travellers is bloody difficult."

"Ah, sir. This is where I believe we have an opportunity. My thought is we send one of the eliminators. This will negate the need for Board sign off, and he can ensure Frank complies. If not, the eliminator can clear up our mess and liquidate Frank. Then, if the worst comes to the worst, it's just a failed mission. This solution will be a lot less painful to explain than this current mess of poor data, which resulted in a failed mission."

Hartland sprung forward as he clicked his fingers. "Bloody good idea! Which one do you suggest we send?"

"Sir, I think we send Sinclair to engage with Frank. Then, if successful, he can live his life as instructed. I suggest Frank can carry on with his as he hasn't caused any major category changes. Of course, if they're not successful, we will instruct Sinclair to liquidate Frank because failure to change time to the required outcome will be all the justification we need. This way, we either get the change we require, or it's a failed mission with an eliminator sent as per the standard procedure." Morehouse started to relax now he sensed his boss was going to buy the idea. "This will be a lot easier to explain than our current situation, sir. Although the *European Fault* at that point will not be averted, we'll come out of this all smelling of roses."

Hartland took another drag on his cigarette as he mulled over the choices. "It's unusual to send an eliminator in these circumstances, but I'm inclined to agree. What is critical, the data cock-up information cannot become knowledge the board get hold of." He leant further forward and pointed his cigarette at his Data Information Director. "Right, let's not waste any time. Get hold of Penelope and assess if Sinclair is ready."

The analyst tentatively raised his hand as he shook his head.

"Johnson, what's the problem?"

Johnson glanced between both men, concerned with what he was about to say – but knew he had to.

"There is another slight problem that I've discovered. There is a chance that interference at this stage could cause more damage. I've run the numbers, and some of the team are double-checking the data as we speak."

Both senior men glared at the analyst, once again, causing him to feel extremely uncomfortable, and he could also sense fresh beads of sweat as they started their journey down his flushed cheek.

"I have applied a quantum factor to the possibility of a second interference of an eliminator. I've calculated it could multiply the correction percentage by a negative factor. This would produce a double negative applied to the original percentage, thus leading to an increased effect of over thirty per cent on the *European Fault*."

"My God, Johnson, what are you babbling on about, man? Speak English!"

"Yes sir, sorry, sir. Well, in plain speaking, sending a follow-on traveller who has a mission, not just liquidation, could have the effect of causing Frank to fail to save Jemma. And as this would be a second-time change to the original event, this could ultimately lead to causing an escalation to the *European Fault*. So essentially making it worse, not stopping it."

"How the hell could the *European Fault* be any bloody worse?" boomed Hartland.

"Many more deaths."

"How many?"

"A couple of million. Give or take a few hundred thousand."

"Oh, for God's sake!"

"Yes, I know, sir. It's a bit of a blow."

"Bit of a blow. Bit of a blow! It's a bloody shit storm, man!"

Morehouse raised his hand. "Hang on, sir. Sending Sinclair is our second attempt at the same timeline. If this causes a fall back to the original timeline and Jemma is still strangled that night, we're back to square one. We have Frank and Sinclair back in 1979, and we have the possible scenario Johnson has described of the fault worsening. However, if that is the case, we have the option of instructing a double elimination. That would tidy things up from our end and, although the fault is worse, it couldn't be pinned on our actions. So, we still appear clean and can't be accused of any wrongdoings."

"Your point is?"

"My point, sir. We still have seven years to change the *European Fault*. Although a bit of a let-down that Frank and Jemma failed, at least we're out of this bloody mess."

Hartland clapped his hands together, then poured himself another generous measure of single malt. There were good reasons Morehouse was his right-hand man. Once again, he'd saved his arse and avoided the impending doom of facing Lady Maud Huston-Smythe with this ugly situation.

The eliminators were always on standby and, as long as Penelope had kept them ready, Sinclair could travel tonight. With a fair wind and a spot of good luck, this whole shit mess could be resolved within the hour.

Before dawn broke, and assuming Sinclair was successful, he might be in a position to update the Board that they had succeeded. Indeed, a full Board appointment was a formality if this could be achieved, whatever Huston-Smythe's objections were.

Shame for Frank, living his lovely life collecting crabs with his grandchildren. He'd already saved his wife once. However, back in the 1979, where Sinclair was going, Frank didn't know this.

Poor old Smelly-Frank – if he failed to save Jemma this time, there would be no more crabbing off Cromer Pier with his grandchildren.

40

September 1979

Andy Warhol

Parked on a barstool at the end of the bar, Dave slumped in his usual position whilst vacantly staring at his pint. His demeanour would suggest he and Babs hadn't resolved their issue of his wandering hands. Ha, and there was I only a week ago berating him, and yesterday I stood in the centre of town with my hands wandering all over Jayne's bum as we snogged in public. Although at least Jayne's bum was clothed, unlike the young office clerk's breasts that Dave's hands had roamed.

It was a miracle Jayne and I weren't papped by some eager newspaper photographer. Although it was only last night, so we could have been. If that were the case, then there would be an exposé on the front of the Chronicle on Monday.

MP Stone's cheating husband caught snogging pretty, petite brunette!

I shuddered, imagining that headline with a grainy picture of Jayne and I splashed across the front page.

Was it Andy Warhol who said we'll all have fifteen minutes of fame? Well, I've had mine already. Although it was considerably longer than that, and perhaps it could be classed as infamy rather than fame. However, that infamy was a few weeks in the future after Jemma's death. So, technically, I'd not had my fifteen minutes yet, which Mr Warhol had stated we would all have.

Those few days after I'd conducted the appeal on TV, the media circus escalated. The news reporters and photographers shifted their attention from Jemma's disappearance to focusing on our home. Camped up and down the street, TV crews and, for the time, well-known reporters stalked me as they desperately tried to secure a quote. Photographers hid in bushes as they persistently attempted to capture a shot through a crack in the curtains or when I ventured out to collect the milk bottles from the doorstep.

They had pestered the neighbours, and I remember Dennis appearing on the news after they'd interviewed him on his doorstep – although I don't think he wore his pink pinny. Dennis answered their questions and, if I recall correctly, he said he'd always suspected there was something odd about me.

With a microphone shoved in his face whilst the cameras rolled, and potentially millions of viewers watching the six o'clock news, in true Dennis style, he'd taken his opportunity to rant about the Tory Government. He'd held the reporter's hand who tried to drag the microphone away as he raised a clenched fist, proclaiming *'Power to the People'*, Citizen Smith style, whilst affirming the Unions would stay firm and stop the oppression of the British workers.

During those difficult weeks, friends had rallied around to help. Tobias, Clare, Dave, Jayne and even the lech, Paul, had put a shift in to comfort me, running errands so I could hide from the media circus.

The media didn't relent and continued to hound me, only providing some respite when a dog walker discovered Jemma's body. Then the news crews decamped to the woods but soon returned because I'd become the police's number one suspect.

By far the worst intrusion into my life was at her funeral. Camera crews were intent on securing close-up pictures, determined to capture the one shot of my face which would sell their papers. They achieved their goal when I'd held my hand out to shove a photographer out of the way. The shot they captured portrayed an angry man as I scowled menacingly into the camera lens. That photo ended up on every national newspaper, and one of the headlines has stuck with me for the last thirty-six years.

Is this the face of evil?

As the weeks rolled by and they ran out of angles to report on, the media frenzy abated. As soon as the Soviet tanks entered Afghanistan in December, Jemma Stone and her evil husband, Frank, had disappeared from the TV news reports. The story occasionally resurfaced in Sunday papers, ten or twelve pages in, but no longer headlines.

Hopefully, Jayne and I won't make it onto the front page of the Chronicle next week. I was quite happy this time around to relinquish my allotted fifteen minutes of fame.

Dave spotted me when he momentarily shifted his gaze from the top of his pint. Like my front-page newspaper picture, he appeared angry. This meeting could be another disaster like last Friday night. But hopefully, I could repair the friendship because I needed his support next Friday when I would be launching operation Save-Jemma.

"Dave."

"Frank."

Deciding not to look up as he offered his greeting, Dave continued to sulk into his beer, seemingly finding the froth on top of his pint more interesting.

I caught the young barmaid's eye, who on her own was trying to pull the pints whilst remembering who was next in line to be served. She nodded to confirm she had clocked me, and I had mentally booked my place in the queue for drinks. Although the pub was an estate-type pub and not a swanky town-centre establishment, it was always busy. It wasn't the type of place you took your missus or girlfriend to, and the ratio of men to women was ten to one in men's favour. I guess you could describe it as more of a men's drinking hole with limited frills, where G&Ts were served in tumblers and ice and slice were terms of violence.

The young lass behind the bar, who I recognised but had no chance of remembering her name, appeared highly skilled and ambidextrous. She attended to me in the correct pecking order, pulling my pint whilst managing to flip the top of a bottle of brown ale for her next customer, along with skilfully shoving along a bucket with her foot to capture the overflow from a drip-tray. All this and still able to nod to the next in line, indicating they had secured their place.

With our two pints deposited on the bar, I nudged the froth-starer and motioned we should move away from the bar to the back of the pub where I'd spotted a free table. Although appearing not to be the life and soul of the party, Dave nodded to agree, slithered off his stool and trudged his way to the table like a condemned man footslogging his way to the gallows.

Fondling the chest of a young cash office clerk was not a capital offence. Although Dave wouldn't have to face the brief moment when Albert Pierrepoint would bind his hands and blindfold him before releasing the trap door, Babs was not a girl to be messed with. Before taking maternity leave to look after little Sarah, Babs had enjoyed a short career as a prison officer. She'd met some despicable women, including Hindley, who she firmly believed should have been hanged.

Hangings were still a legal method of execution in the UK. However, after 1964, only treason was an offence deemed severe enough for the ultimate sentence. However, since that date, no one had been sentenced to death. Knowing Babs as I did, I was sure her view of Dave's misdemeanour fitted into the treason category – she might hang him herself.

41

The Slaughtered Lamb

We settled into our seats to the left of the dartboard. I just hoped the gents playing were reasonably proficient otherwise we were in danger of losing an eye.

"I take it Babs hasn't forgiven you then?"

Dave shook his head and took a large gulp of his beer.

"Right." I feared the conversation could be slow tonight.

"Frank, look, I'm sorry about the other night. It's all got on top of me, and I went off on one. I'm really sorry for what I said."

"Hey, don't worry, it's no big deal, mate. Apology accepted."

"Okay, well, I was out of order, and I really shouldn't have lashed out at you when this whole shit mess was caused by yours truly here."

The first time this happened Babs did come around, or she accepted his grovelling, so I assumed that would happen this time. However, as this week for me was undoubtedly different this time, would that mean they were different for Dave as well? The last time I was in 1979, I'm reasonably confident I didn't punch my business partner, and absolutely certain I didn't exchange saliva with one of Jemma's closest friends whilst standing in the middle of the street in the centre of town.

The Hooded Claw had talked about acceptable change. Although this time it would be a different life for me, and Christ, I bloody hoped so, were the small changes I made rippling out and affecting others? What if those ripples had already reached the murderer, and he doesn't try to kill her? What if next Friday Jemma stays in, saying she's too tired to go out like she had tonight? This was a head-fuck. Along with my confused feelings for my wife and my ridiculously quick infatuation with her friend, this whole situation was starting to crush me.

"What you said about Jemma, though, you meant that?" I raised my eyebrows, indicating it was a question, not a statement.

Dave sat back and spread his arms out. "Err … look, mate; I said I'm sorry. I shouldn't have said what I did."

"But it's true? You and Babs don't like her?"

"To be honest. No, not much."

"You never said when we got together."

"Well, you were smitten, mate. It was only a few years ago, and I can remember how you instantly changed. You couldn't stop talking about Jemma and wanted to be with her every second of your life. I was hardly going to tell you I thought she was a wrong'un, was I?"

Of course, he was right. Although that was only a few years ago. For me, old Frank, living in young Frank's body, those memories were fuzzy. Since last Friday some of that fuzziness had lifted, but it was still nearly forty years ago.

"But we've always been able to be honest with each other. I've gotta say, I still find it a bit odd you didn't say anything."

"Look, Frank, you were smitten, and it's all in the past now. You found Jemma and, I have to admit, although you never have a problem pulling stunning birds, she was a few notches above any other girls you'd taken out. I wasn't going to be the one to ruin it by saying she had an attitude and I didn't like her. Christ, mate, I never thought you'd end up marrying her as you enjoyed playing the field. So, by the time you two were serious, it was too late to tell you."

"No, okay. But what is it that you and Babs don't like?"

"What's the point? It's in the past. Me telling you what we don't like about your wife is pointless."

"Dave, I want to know."

"Okay, well, you asked for it, mate. She's a stuck-up silly cow who thinks she's something special, but she ain't. She has that way about her and is always looking down on others, although God knows why she thinks she's above everyone else. Babs says the look she gives her, it's as if she's something from the bottom of her shoe. She's full of her own self-importance, and she only has one topic of conversation, and that's about herself." He widened his hands again as he leant back in his chair, indicating he'd finished delivering his fairly accurate character assassination of my wife.

"Sorry mate, you asked."

I took a large slug of beer to grab a moment to think about what he'd said. We'd been close for so long. I believed I trusted him, and from what I can remember, he was a genuine guy. There were no hidden agendas with Dave; what you saw is what you got.

He never judged me – although I was the one with the university education, he was right. I could score when out in town at the weekend, usually leaving him to walk home whilst I whisked my latest conquest off to some love nest – he never felt that I'd let him down.

Those young lasses that I used to swoon; I wonder what they would have made of me in 2015? How low could a man fall?

Placing my beer on the heavily ringed sticky table, I glanced up and could see he appeared uncomfortable about what he'd just said. "Dave, you're right."

"What?"

"I said you're right. I've realised that Jemma isn't the woman that I always thought she was."

"Bloody hell, mate! You saying you've made a mistake in marrying her?"

"Yes, I am. I don't know how I've not seen what she's like, but you're right."

Of course, I did know. I was thirty-odd years older, and now I wanted someone different. The first time around in 1979 I must have liked Jemma's personality, and without a doubt I'd loved the sex. But, now older and wiser, I knew she wasn't the girl for me.

"Jeeesus! What the hell are you going to do? Christ, you actually going to leave her? Hang on, I know you, Frank Stone. You dirty fucker, you've found someone else?"

"No, of course not." Yes, I had. Although, for the first time for young Frank, I thought that someone wasn't going to want me. Jayne was too intelligent, too discerning, and wouldn't let herself get tangled up with 'Surfer Boy', as Jemma called me. So, for the first time, I think young Frank was going to have to handle rejection. However, my later life had prepared me well for the inevitable, as old Frank, over the years, had learned to accept regular knockbacks.

Dave grinned and pointed at me. "You liar! I can tell it in your face, you dirty git ... you're already knobbing some new bird, aren't you?"

"No, Dave. This is serious, mate. I've just realised I don't love Jemma anymore and have probably now reached the point that I know things have got to change ... even if it means ending up on my own."

"Christ, I don't think I've ever seen you like this. Are you having some kind of loony breakdown?"

"Ha, yeah, quite possibly."

I was bursting at the seams to tell him about my life, Jemma's murder and the CYA. But of course, I knew that simply wasn't possible. If I did blurt it all out, and it became common knowledge that the local MP's husband reckoned he was a time-traveller, that would surely trigger the deployment of a mercenary with his Beretta pistol cocked and ready.

"Look, I'll be honest with you. Although I have changed my feelings for Jemma, I think she's changed hers as well."

"Oh?"

"Yes, oh! I'm convinced she's already moved further forward as well, as I'm pretty certain she's having an affair."

"No way! That's ... that's unbelievable."

"Quite."

Dave leaned in close and whispered. "Who's she shagging?" He always had a way with words.

"I don't know for sure, but I'm certain that something is going on with her and Tobias."

"Tobias!" boomed Dave as he rocked back in his chair, his arms splayed out wide. His outburst caused the melee of pub chatter to die down for a brief second.

A large builder-type chap playing darts missed the board, causing the dart to embed in the wall to the right. He looked at Dave and pointed. "You made me miss. I don't ever miss."

There was something vaguely familiar about this moment. What the dart player had said wasn't exactly right, but it did seem familiar. Then I remembered the two American lads in the Slaughtered Lamb. But that film hadn't been released yet – had it? Was this burly builder type another time-traveller, or was it a coincidence he said a similar line from the movie? Maybe one of the film directors was in the pub and was now frantically writing down this scene to put in that film? No, coincidence, surely? Anyway, I didn't think John Landis would be squatting down in a shitty back-street pub in the unremarkable Hertfordshire town of Fairfield, whilst supping a pint of warm ale and searching for material.

The silence held for a brief second. Although I didn't know the dart player, it didn't take much intelligence to work out that he could be handy with his fists. It was time to calm the waters.

"Look, fella, we're sorry. I'll get you a pint as a way of an apology." Dart-Man nodded and returned to prepare for his next throw whilst I scooted to the bar. Fortunately, the young lass had read the situation and was already pulling the pint for me to collect. As if by the flick of a switch, the chatter in the pub resumed.

With my gesture-of-good-will pint deposited for the dart player, I returned to our table.

"Sorry, mate. That was a close one. Jack 'Jaws' Jones is a bloody nutter; I thought my time was up. Well done with the pint, though, as free beer is always the solution with that headcase."

"No worries, anyway, keep your bloody voice down."

I could see why he had the nickname Jaws, as his sheer size and two metal front teeth made him a perfect fit as a stunt double for a certain Bond villain.

"But Frank, why would you think Jemma is playing away with Tobias?"

I relayed the events of the past week: the hotel lobby incident, the cricket match, the answer-machine message, and the visit from Clare. Dave thought the nose realignment job I gave Paul was hilarious and stated he had it coming because the bloke was a total wanker.

I was fast learning that Dave held a diminutive view of most people I associated with because I never knew he didn't like Paul either. However, seeing Paul again after all these years, it wasn't difficult to understand why everyone on the planet would think Paul was a total tosser. Dave mentioned he thought my receptionist was a right good looker with nice tits, and I reminded him that he was in no position to refer to women's chests. An observation which he agreed with.

"But mate, why were you in town following Jemma last Friday? Did you already suspect something?"

This was the tricky part. I'd followed Jemma to keep her safe from the murderer who was wandering around, not to catch her out. However, that was information that I, as a time-traveller, had to keep close to my chest. Being the only time-traveller was tough, and The Hooded Claw had alluded to this fact. Although I did glance at Jack 'Jaws' Jones as he sunk another dart in the dartboard and wondered if he was also one of my kind.

"Well, after our not so enjoyable drink last Friday, I thought I'd nip into town and catch up with the girls. But as I entered the bar, that's when I spotted her with him."

"Have you asked Jayne? She was there, so she might be able to straighten it out?"

"No, I just done a runner."

"I like Jayne, although I've not seen her for ages. Is she still teaching at our old school?"

"Yeah, she's still there, I think." Well, actually, I didn't know that, but Jemma had alluded that she was still teaching when she'd moaned about her last week. At least he liked someone I knew, and most people did seem to like Jayne – especially me. However, Jemma had that catty nickname for her, which annoyed me.

"She's got a nice set of jugs on her as well."

"Dave! Christ, man! You're obsessed with tits! Work it out; it's that obsession that's got you in this bloody mess."

Dave held his hands up and nodded. "Talking of school, d'you remember that school secretary woman? What was her name? She was in her late forties, early fifties."

"No idea, mate."

"Yes, you do. She was that nosy woman who looked all prim with her glasses and a bun-styled hairdo. She always used to lean forward and look left and right before telling you something she shouldn't … a right gossip."

"Oh yeah, vaguely."

"Colman. That was it. Miss Colman. Is she still there? Although I would have thought she's ancient now, at least in her mid-sixties."

"Ha, yeah, ancient … mid-sixties!" If only he knew. "Anyway, mate, I've no idea if she's still there. Look, although I know Jemma and me are on a glide path to finishing, I want to know who she's seeing, and I might need your help."

"Yeah, okay. What you thinking?"

"Well, I know she's going out for a meal with Clare next Friday night. So, I thought we could follow her and see if she meets anyone else."

"Bloody hell, she's got some front! Meeting Clare, and she's bunking up with Tobias."

"Yes, quite!"

"Hang on. If Jemma sees Clare that night, she certainly won't be seeing lover boy, will she?"

He had a good point. But that's the night of the murder, and I could hardly tell him that. "Well, it might be a cover story, so I thought I'd follow her."

"What d'you want me to do?"

"Well, if I follow her, I can't go in my car as she might spot it. So, I thought we could go in yours. Then, if we need to split up, I could follow on foot and you could track us from a distance in the motor."

"You're on, mate. I'm definitely up for that. It's sad you two are splitting up, but I won't deny I'm well happy. That said, if Jemma is cheating on you, we need to catch her out."

"Yeah, it is sad, but I know we're not destined to be together." I was right on that front, as we weren't together the first time because some bastard strangled her. I just hope it wasn't Dave, as that would be placing the fox in the henhouse.

This time in 1979, Jemma and I were no longer compatible. Well, apart from in the bedroom, although it was a week ago since I'd enjoyed those delights.

"So, who's this new bird you're chasing then?"

"I'm not!"

"You're lying, Stoney, my boy. You've got that glint in your eye!"

"I told you, I don't have anyone that I'm chasing or interested in."

Although I did, and I wished the first time around I'd met Jayne, not Jemma, in that pub in that hot summer of '76. Maybe life would have panned out very differently then. Jemma reckoned Jayne had a thing for me, although that was for young Frank. I wondered if Jayne would be interested in old Frank, now with a very different outlook on life. Was I a parasite in young Frank's body?

42

Charlie's Angels

I felt relieved that Dave and I had patched things up. However, he became somewhat melancholy later in the evening as the conversation regressed to his situation with Babs. He was contrite about his misdemeanour. However, I thought it was wasted on me and needed to be directed at Babs. I hoped history repeated itself, and they sort it out and get back together. Babs was a fab girl, and she deserved better from her chest-fondling husband. I just hoped she could give him a second chance – I knew he wouldn't blow it again.

Jemma was already in bed when I staggered home – I'd had a skinful. A pink satin eye mask covered the top of her head, which I now remembered was her non-verbal way of saying she wasn't in the mood for some fun. She ticked all my boxes in that department, but tonight I was relieved.

Although the Hooded Claw had given me my youthful body back and a beautiful woman to lie beside, I didn't love her. Not that it would have bothered young Frank, but I felt frolicking with my wife would be wrong in this situation. I climbed into bed next to her and noticed my new best mate below had other ideas, but he would just have to go without tonight.

Jemma lifted her eyeshade and popped it back, presumably checking it was me who'd slid in beside her. I wondered if she was disappointed with what she'd seen in that brief glimpse. I bet she didn't wear that eye mask with him! She looked like one of those passengers on a long-haul flight as she lay with her arms crossed over her chest. In the dim light, her satin eye shades gave her the look of a blonde-haired, pink-eyed fly.

I had no idea what someone would look like when they slept on a plane because at the age of sixty-six, or was I thirty, I'd never experienced air travel. My parents didn't have that kind of spare cash to splash out on foreign holidays. During the '50s and early '60s, holidays were usually a week in Clacton. If my parents fancied something more exotic, they occasionally pushed the boat out and we enjoyed a week in Southend, where I would get to ride on the donkeys along the beach.

The highlight I remember as a young boy was the summer of '59. We had boarded the train that chugged its way along the pier. However, when we reached the end of the track by the sea, a fire had taken hold at the pavilion and shore end. Stranded with hundreds of other tourists, all we could do was watch in wonder as the fire rapidly destroyed the pier. A flotilla of small boats was duly dispatched from the shore and, just like my very own version of Dunkirk, we were rescued and returned to the safety of the beach. My father had remained calm; my mother held her hand over her mouth in shock whilst I ran around pretending to be a brave soldier of the British Expeditionary Force escaping the advancing Nazi army. I remember thinking it was the most exciting adventure I'd ever had.

I mused about the rather prim boarding house we always stayed at and how the landlady always called my parents Mr and Mrs Stone. Although we were well known there, the casual use of first names was deemed improper in that era. My father would relax in a deckchair with his trouser legs rolled up and his trilby hat on, even though it could have been over twenty-five degrees. Mother would always buy a 'kiss me quick' hat and never wore anything more revealing than her summer dress.

How times had changed as I thought of our honeymoon on the Isle of Wight and Jemma parading about in her tiny, almost see-through, crochet bikini. Everyone gawped at her perfect body, causing all sunbathing red-blooded males' tongues to drag across the sand.

I was a young man by the time foreign travel became commonplace in the early '70s. My focus at that point in my life was chasing girls and later setting up my business. Hence, the opportunity to join the jet-set never arose. After I'd lost Jemma, my depression had curtailed my desire for holidays. Also, I was probably too inebriated to be allowed on a plane. As the new millennium dawned, and now a seasoned street dweller, aircraft excursions weren't high on my agenda of essential purchase items.

Saturday morning continued our tiptoeing on eggshells around each other. Jemma busied herself preparing to go out, a process that could take hours. She'd planned a shopping trip with Clare. However, now she was the local MP, and to avoid being recognised, Jemma preferred to shop in the modern Arndale shopping centre in Luton rather than Fairfield.

Although it had been many years since visiting Luton town centre, I feared it had gone the way of many towns post the

Millennium. I suspected the shopping centre was no longer so salubrious as it had been when it opened in the '70s.

My girlfriend of the time and I had taken a trip up there because I recall there was quite a buzz about the opening of the first American-style mall shopping complex in the UK. As a newly qualified architect, I was fascinated by the building – my girlfriend was fascinated by the shops in the covered mall. At the time, I recall thinking it was impressive. However, years later, I accepted the shopping mall was a brutalist concrete architectural disaster, as were many of this era. And here I was back in the '70s, planning to build another concrete monstrosity in Fairfield, albeit just a car park. Nevertheless, that brutal lump of grey concrete I had designed would become a drug den by the turn of the Millennium.

Today I was at a loss about how to entertain myself. Based on the fact that my workload could become quite sizeable, I considered nipping into the office and start working on plans to break up the company. However, as I lacked the ability to concentrate on anything other than Jemma's murder and my infatuation for Jayne, I quickly dismissed the idea.

I now felt in limbo, wanting Friday to come as quickly as possible, so I could save Jemma and then get on with my new life – whatever that may bring.

Feeling at a loose end, I thumbed through the local paper and noticed an article about the new Football Alliance Premier League, which Fairfield Town had joined the previous year. There was huge excitement about the new league because the league winners would have the right to apply for professional status. However, with the advantage of time-travel, I knew the league winners were not elected to enter the Football League as the article suggested. I also knew Fairfield only just survived relegation to the Southern League for a couple of years before their slide down the non-league football ladder took hold. The fortunes of the local team tracked a similar path to mine, albeit slightly quicker. So, as today they were playing one of the top sides, I thought an afternoon watching the Town get thrashed might have some entertainment value to it.

∼

Weighed down with a plethora of tough decisions, Jemma struggled to clear her mind. Through her own doing, her life had become super complicated because she couldn't decide which man she wanted. Although racked with worry and decisions, rushing to and throwing up in the toilet this morning had surprised her. She was rarely sick and, when she had cause to stick her head in the toilet, that event usually came after a particularly heavy drinking session at a party. Now, as a respectable MP, those days were firmly rooted in the past. Nevertheless, throwing up in the morning was odd, and she wondered if the fish which had stewed in the oven whilst she soaked in the bath could be to blame.

Jemma was so relieved that Frank had ventured up the pub last night. Although, when on the train, she'd psyched herself up and was ready to be brave, later that evening, she just couldn't face that conversation. However, the sleep had layered some perspective on her situation, and now she wondered if her lust and infatuation for Roops was precisely that – lust.

Her parents had occasionally endured tough times during their long marriage. Not that she knew the finer details of those issues, but she knew they'd worked through them because their marriage vows were important. Jemma could remember her mother questioning whether she was sure she wanted to marry Frank. *"Till death do us part, and not to be entered into lightly,"* she could hear her mother say.

If they split because she wanted out and a life with Roops, her father had said he would support her. However, her mother would be devastated that *her* daughter was a divorcee and the pure shame of it.

No longer would her mother be able to lord it up as the mother of the MP when she attended the Women's Institute's coffee mornings. No, her actions would cause her mother to shrink back, knowing the leaders of her local WI would take great delight in revelling in her shame. Moreover, her mother would be unlikely to continue her winning streak at the annual Victoria Sponge Baking Competition with the shame of a divorced daughter hanging over her, even though Jemma was the local MP.

Sick in the morning – morning sickness? Oh, hell, she thought – was she? She calculated her cycle, and yes, there was a potential problem. Although that could be down to the super amount of stress she was under. She accepted that most of that stress was self-inflicted, like Tobias and Roops, but some put upon her like her maiden speech. Frank and Jemma had never discussed family planning, and since getting together they'd pretty much been at it like rabbits. Not that they'd stuck their heads in the sand, but they would have been happy if Jemma had fallen pregnant.

If they had been at it so long, why now? Then, of course, there was the other potential nightmare – maybe it wasn't his. Now infatuated with Roops, still loved sex with her husband, and a one-night stand with Tobias, who'd pestered her for sex – she'd got herself in a mess.

If Tobias was infatuated by her because he wanted to screw an MP, she could see why he chose her and not another. Hot-babe could not be a description attached to any other female MP. Those ladies would've seriously struggled if they were attempting to audition for a part in Charlie's Angels, which seemed to change actresses every season.

Unfortunately, Jemma had succumbed to Tobias's charms, and he had many. Not only was she an adulterer with her best friend's husband, who now wouldn't leave her alone, but she was also thinking of running off with a colleague. To top it all, she might be having a baby and was uncertain of who the father was.

Jemma racked her brain as she tried to remember when she and Frank had got it on around the time she'd enjoyed that fling with Tobias. Concerningly, Jemma believed she and Frank were at it for days before and after that sordid event.

The other huge issue, following the call from Tobias on Friday, Frank knew something was going on. However, for some reason he'd decided to keep schtum. Although she'd been away all week and not seen much of him, Frank seemed different. Jemma couldn't place her finger on what, but he seemed to have changed.

Then, on Tuesday, she would be staying over in London again, and Roops would be pawing at her, desperate to finish what they'd started last week. Jemma just had to hope Charlie needed a break from his kids and also stayed over. Jemma couldn't think about what to do about the Roops situation until she'd worked out how to get out of this mess. The obvious answer was to tell Frank she was pregnant, and hopefully he would assume it was his. As long as she could convince Tobias it was over, a mistake, and never going to happen again, then she could get on with life. All seemed reasonably simple, apart from the fact that she was falling in love with Roops.

Now ready for her day out, hair and makeup perfect but head in a mess, she left Frank reading the paper and shot off to pick up Clare. Jemma knew spending the day with her could further mess with her head. However, she would just have to play it cool and hope Clare didn't suspect her to be the scarlet woman with whom she suspected Tobias was dallying with.

Clare seemed withdrawn and unusually quiet during the short drive into Luton and only started talking in the café where they enjoyed a coffee before hitting the shops. Jemma decided to rip the plaster off and get to the nitty-gritty.

"How's Tobias?" she asked, picking up her coffee and peering over her cup in to her friend's eyes. Jemma held her breath – dreading the reaction and concerned Clare's silence was the result of her suspecting something.

"Well, I thought this week he seemed to be like his usual self. Although he was out of the office on Monday afternoon again, and that silly secretary didn't know where he was," huffed Clare, as she grabbed her coffee.

Jemma knew exactly where Tobias was on Monday afternoon. He'd arrived at her office, and in between her surgery meetings, he'd pestered her again, continuing the argument they'd had at the cricket match. Tobias wanted to continue the thing they had going, but she firmly advised him there was no *thing* and it was just a mistake. Tobias wouldn't listen, refused to take no for an answer, and had tried to molest her right there in her office with her support staff only a few feet away – the walls are paper thin. He was becoming a problem, and at this point Jemma had no idea what to do about it.

Placing her cup down, Jemma took hold of Clare's hand and rubbed it reassuringly. "I'm sure there's nothing to worry about. As I said, no way would Tobias cheat on you ... he loves you, you know that, don't you?" She gave a tight smile and squeezed Clare's hand, impressed with her own lying skills and convinced she had this technique finely tuned.

Clare delved into her handbag, retrieved a tissue, and dabbed the corner of her eyes whilst continuously sniffing. Jemma surprised herself that she didn't feel as much of a shit as she should have done. One thing for sure, if this got out there would be one hell of a shit storm. She'd told her father about Roops, not Tobias. Although she was so close to her father, even he would have a problem with this scenario.

"I've been a bit silly and have probably made it all up in my head. I should have kept it to myself 'cos you'll both now know I thought Tobias is up to no good. It'll put a strain on our friendship."

"Both? What d'you mean?"

"You and Frank."

"Oh, honey, sorry. I didn't ask Frank if he thought there was something odd about Tobias. Sorry, I know you said to ask him, but it's been such a busy week ... it just fell out of my head."

"Frank hasn't said?"

"Said what?"

"I went to see him on Tuesday last week, up at his office. I asked him about Tobias."

"Oh ... err ...no. No." Jemma felt slightly concerned as she'd thought she had control of this situation. Yes, she knew Frank had questioned Tobias on Thursday night because Tobias had relayed that event blow by blow on the phone on Friday morning – but this was concerning news.

"Really? I thought he would have told you what happened."

"Oh, well, I've been away all week, and we've not had a chance to catch up properly." Shit, she thought. Where was this going?

Clare relayed the events in Frank's office. She was slightly economical with the truth about her accidentally ending on top of Frank, sprawled across his desk when Paul had burst in miming a hand job. But, apart from that, Clare gave a full account of proceedings.

"And that was it. Frank actually gave Paul an ultimatum. Change his ways, or he planned to dissolve the company. I know it was quite thuggish of Frank, but I can tell you seeing his fist connect with Paul's face and him flying through the air was pure magic!"

Although this was a revelation, Jemma needed to keep focused. "Did Frank say he thought there was anything odd with Tobias recently?" Praying and hoping that Frank had not told Clare that he'd seen Tobias and her in the hotel lobby that previous Friday evening.

"No, he said that he thought he was perfectly normal. However, he did agree to take him out on Thursday evening for a drink and have a chat with him."

"Oh, right, okay. Well, Frank didn't say."

"Christ, Jemma! I hope you two are alright? It sounds like you're not telling each other anything!"

"No, we're fine, honey. Just fine." If only that were true. She thought Frank had changed, and this news was confirming something had. Giving Paul an ultimatum was definitely un-Frank like.

Frank would typically always stand up for Paul when he acted the tosser, which was often. It had irked her that Frank couldn't see what Paul was like, and now it seemed her husband had had an epiphany. Although, it appeared he'd used his fists and not his mouth to sort the situation out. You could take the boy out of Broxworth, but never take the Broxworth out of the boy. Roops would never resort to thuggish behaviour because his wit and razor tongue could shred his adversaries with a far greater effect than using brute force.

"Tobias just said he had an enjoyable pint with Frank, and they just talked cricket and the usual stuff. I do wonder if I've made this all up in my head, and now I've blurted out to you both that I think he's having an affair. Of course, he could be totally innocent. I think I've been a bit rash."

"I'm sure that's it, honey. Now come on, drink up and let's go blow some cash." She leant across and squeezed Clare's hand again. The relief that Clare was completely in the dark almost made her feel giddy.

Clare was right. Tobias wasn't having an affair, well, not with her. Yes, they had a fling, but not an affair – there was a difference. Although Tobias might be a father early next year. That concerning thought dampened her mood as they left the café, linking arms and heading off to the shops.

43

Stings Like A Bee

Fairfield Town successfully managed to get themselves thrashed five-nil. It was the result I expected, although entertaining to see the goals. Pity I didn't know the score beforehand, then I could have had a side bet. Although remembering The Hooded Claw's threat – perhaps not.

Surely though, I could have some small bets on big sporting events and get away with that? I was reasonably confident Seve Ballesteros would win the Golf Masters next year. Also, I knew Marvelous Marvin Hagler technically knocked out Alan Minter, and the 'floats like a butterfly, stings like a bee' phenomenon of Muhammad Ali loses to Larry Holmes. I could have a small wager on those; no one would notice that. I wasn't going to bet the house, just a few quid, so that would be alright – wouldn't it? Then there was the Miracle on Ice when the USA Ice hockey team beat the Soviets at the Olympics; I could grab a few quid on that one. Now I was becoming excited at the thought of Daley Thompson's decathlon triumph and the Ovett and Coe battle at the Summer Olympics.

However, would that be noticed? Could I risk it? Was their threat real? I decided it probably was, based on the fact that they hilariously thought they could plonk me on the London Eye and send me back in time – and look what happened.

If I started betting, it would escalate. Then, I would end up building my very own Pleasure Paradise Casino, Biff Tannen style. That really would make me the butthead, and it could be the catalyst for the CYA to send the Beretta-wielding mercenary to finish me off.

Jemma seemed in a better mood when I arrived home, probably because of the amount of shopping bags she carted in from the car. Jemma didn't mention any awkward conversations with Clare, so I guess they just focused on bashing their chequebooks.

"What d'you think of this?" said Jemma, pulling out a cream-coloured mac from one of the bags scattered across the kitchen. "I thought I needed a new coat for the autumn, for when I'm down in London."

Taking a break from preparing some supper, I watched as she swished about in her new mac. "Yeah, that looks nice."

"Nice! Is that it? This cost a fortune, you know. I got it in Kendall's. It's not some cheap rubbish from the market."

"Yes, I said it was nice." In fact, it didn't look too dissimilar to something Michael-Kors-pink-trainer lady would wear, so I guess fashion had turned full circle. However, unless I could stop that murderer, her new coat would be buried in a shallow grave within less than a week.

"Well, it should be! Anyway, I suppose you're not used to nice clothes," she replied. She'd finished swishing and stood with her hands on her hips, quizzically looking at me as I prepared some beef mince.

"What? What d'you mean?"

"Well, coming from that estate! I suppose your parents never had any money, so you're used to wearing cheap stuff. To be honest, I can't believe some of the rubbish Clare buys. She's posh like me, so you'd think she would buy nice stuff. What did you do today? Oh, last Friday, you should have seen the awful top Plain-Jayne was wearing. Ha, but then she's only a downtrodden teacher, so what d'you expect?"

"I went to the football." Although I have no idea why she asked, as I knew she wasn't interested in anything that wasn't centred around her. Clearly, I was right as she carried on with the assassination of her friends.

"And she had some awful brown school shoes on. I don't mind Jayne, but God, she's such a square. Ha, she's so bor—ing, as well! Err … Frank, what the hell are you doing?"

I shot the mince into the frying pan. "Making us some supper."

"Oh, don't be stupid! You can't cook."

"Err … well, I'm a bit out of practice, I admit. But I can rustle up a bolognese."

"No, you can't. You're worse than my father. You can't cook anything more technical than a cup of tea! I'm not eating anything you cook; you'll poison us both."

"Jemma, I'm quite capable of cooking food. Where the hell do we keep the saucepans?" I asked, as I randomly opened cupboards.

"My point exactly! You don't even know where anything is, let alone how to use them."

Well, she was right. I didn't know the kitchen cupboard layout. But after thirty-six years, it was difficult to remember. Let's face it, knowing where the cullender was kept doesn't exactly stick in your mind.

"They're in the bottom cupboard next to the cooker. Oh, Clare was such a miserable cow today. God knows what's up with her."

Well, I knew, and I'm pretty sure Jemma did. But hey, this wasn't the time to go down that particular alley.

"You know, I think sometimes Clare just needs to lighten up a bit. She's always so serious. If I'm honest, she put a bit of a dampener on the shopping trip. Look, Frank, stop messing about in here … there's no way we can eat anything you cook. It'll be totally inedible."

"Err … just you wait and see. I'm perfectly capable of cooking, and I might surprise you."

"The only place that food is going is in the bin! Why don't we try that new Indian curry house? I've never had one of those before, and I've often wondered what they're like."

"I like curry, but tonight we're eating this."

"You've never had a curry, so I'm not sure how you could know that. I think I'd have to have a mild one, though, as I heard they can be quite spicy."

"You probably would want to order a Phaal," I chuckled to myself.

"Oh, is that what they call the mild ones?"

"Look, tonight, we'll have this bolognese. You'll enjoy it … I promise you. There's a lot of things you don't know about me, and you will enjoy this meal."

Well, there was a lot she didn't know because she'd missed thirty-six years of my life. Although, of course, that wasn't her fault. I'm aware I was a bit mean with my curry suggestion, but I would love to see her face if she orders a Phaal at some point. Perhaps one mouthful could burn that tongue out of her head. Surely, she couldn't say anything else more derogatory about her friends.

"Oh, alright then. But I warn you … I'm not eating it if it tastes yucky."

"The football was good; quite enjoyed it."

"While you attempt to cook up the inedible sludge, I'll show you the other clothes I bought today. Ooo, look at this bikini I got in the sale," exclaimed Jemma, as she plucked up the tiny item of clothing and proceeded to wave it around like a stripper on stage who was reaching the climax of their erotic dance.

I carried on preparing the sludge, as she described it. After losing Jemma, I'd started the learning process of how to cook. However, street living had taken away that opportunity. To begin with, most of my efforts were inedible and, as often as I could, I remember nipping around to Dave's house to grab one of Bab's gastronomical masterpieces. Time moved on; Dave and my friendship drifted, and I learned to cook to an acceptable standard.

Jemma had now removed her mac, stretched the bikini across her chest, and swished around whilst inspecting herself. Of course, she would look stunning in it. Although right at this point, if she carried on with her self-centred rant, I felt the bikini would be better balled-up and rammed in her mouth.

"Yes, this will look fabulous on me. Ha, but then I've got the figure for it! Can you imagine Plain-Jayne in it? God, that would look awful on her. Anyway, she'd never buy anything like this because she knows she hasn't got the figure to pull it off like I have."

"Yes, it looks nice," I nonchalantly replied.

"Nice! Christ, is that all you can say? It's better than nice! Think yourself lucky you can see me in it. Christ, Frank, if Plain-Jayne were standing here in this, you really would be ill!"

Despite my wife's mean remarks, I imagined Jayne in that little red bikini – she would look amazing. I hoped I would see Jayne wearing a bikini one day as we relaxed around a pool while sunbathing on some exotic island. Jayne would look stunning as she would in a potato sack because her true beauty lay inside, unlike my wife's whose was only skin deep. But more to the point, we could chat and enjoy each other's company, unlike the spiteful woman in front of me who now whizzed out her other purchases. Of course, all her new clothes would look fabulous on her, although most of them appeared outdated and should have been consigned to the charity shop years ago.

"Right, as all you can say is *nice*, I'm taking these upstairs whilst you carry on messing up the kitchen. Luckily, I'm not that hungry, so it won't matter supper will be inedible." Jemma collected her bags, turned and paused at the door. "Frank, did you hear me?"

"Yes!"

"Okay, well, you're going to have to clean everything up because I'm not doing it."

"Yes! I said I would."

"Oh, what did you do today?" Jemma asked, as she dragged her collection of bags through to the hall.

"Nothing."

"Well, you shouldn't sit around all day. You'll become a boring oaf like Plain-Jayne. You could have gone and watched football or something ... that's got to be better than moping around all day. Right, shout me when that sludge is ready."

Leaving the bolognese to simmer, I lit up a cigarette whilst pondering the conversation I'd just had. How the hell had I ever loved that woman? She wasn't interested in anything I had to say. And Christ, if she said anything else derogatory about Jayne, I was likely to strangle her.

Jemma did eat the meal I prepared and managed to say it was *nice!* We ate in silence, presumably because Jemma had run out of bitchy things to say, and I just couldn't be bothered to talk to her.

On Sunday, we returned to tip-toeing around each other as neither of us pushed the conversation to the inevitable. Tobias must have called her Friday, and presumably Clare mentioned to Jemma about her visiting me on Tuesday, but Jemma said nothing. Of course, by now, she would know all about the impending breakdown of my business and would absolutely know I followed her the previous Friday when I spotted her and Tobias.

Jemma continued to rattle on about how boring she thought Jayne was, how dull Clare had been whilst shopping, and what an idiot that man was next door. In fact, whilst we buzzed about completing household chores, I think she verbally assassinated everyone she knew. Jemma also stated that we needed to employ a cleaner as she was now far too important to lower herself to drag the vacuum cleaner around all weekend.

Jeeeesus, just listening to her self-importance made me want to throw up. I wondered if the CYA had implanted some other self-centred, self-important, oh-look-at-me-aren't-I-great personality in my gorgeous wife. Because, by the afternoon, I would have preferred to lick the toilet clean than listen to any more of it. It's no bloody wonder someone strangled her and, if they do fail this time, I considered I just might finish her off myself. Perhaps Paul was right; she needed a ruddy sock in it.

I stuck by my decision to play it cool, keep schtum, and keep my powder dry until we had moved past Friday night. Then, when I know she's safe from one of the millions on my list who wanted to strangle her, assuming I don't perform that very act before then, we could tackle the inevitable.

One thing for sure, she was pregnant. Did she know? I'm no expert, but I thought women just knew these things. Jemma never said when it was that time of the month; I respected her privacy and never asked. However, I could always guess because that was usually when she'd stop ravaging me in bed. Perhaps that was the issue on Friday night? But then, if it was, presumably she was no longer pregnant.

Was that a good thing?

I berated myself again for thinking a miscarriage could be good, although the circumstances weren't a normal situation. I was bursting to ask her, and it took all my self-control to keep my lip buttoned.

Of course, it didn't take long for my thoughts to drift to you-know-who. I wondered what she was doing today. Maybe she was out with friends, or perhaps a boyfriend? No, she kissed me, and surely Jayne wouldn't have snogged my face off if she had a boyfriend. Unlike my wife, I believed Jayne wouldn't cheat if she were already spoken for. However, I was on thin ice taking the moral high ground – happily married men don't go around snogging their wife's friends. Try as I might to forget about Jayne, I couldn't. The knot in my stomach kept turning.

As my life hadn't panned out that well the first time, I told myself I must now take every opportunity that presents itself. Although it was totally the wrong decision for everyone, deciding I would see Jayne whatever the consequences perked my mood.

Of course, there was the frightening possibility we might be splashed across the front page of the Fairfield Chronicle tomorrow. If that transpired, that certainly would be a conversation starter with Jayne, plus Jemma, all our friends, all of Fairfield town, most of the Members of Parliament, the Civil Service, and even Margaret Thatcher might comment.

The only saving grace was smartphones and social media platforms at this point weren't invented. Because if they were, that would move the risk of being seen from slight-to-moderate to severe-potentially-gale-force, although why my mind talk now sounded like a shipping forecast, God only knows.

However, it got me thinking that since the inception of the mobile phone and social media, for those inclined to have affairs like my wife, that new technology must have made life a whole lot trickier. How could you hide with your lover for the afternoon with a mobile tracking your position? It would be like giving your wife or husband the nuclear codes to fire off an intergalactic guided missile at you.

After this week, and if my suspicions were correct, perhaps I would have to give Tobias the heads up – at all costs, avoid smartphones in the future.

44

Bush Tucker Trial

One event which had undoubtedly remained the same this time was the weather. The rain had started, which would cause that picnic area up at the woods to become a quagmire.

I'd made an early start this morning, opening up the office before Alison, and cracked on with my plan to break up Stone & Wilson a good ten years before the last time – although that was due to bankruptcy.

We had several contracts running, so I thought Paul could take the building side of the business, and the new projects where we were still tendering with designs would be my slice of the cake. I would need to have a conversation with Paul today about finishing the car park project together. That lucrative payday would set both of us up in our separate ventures.

"Morning, boss. Coffee?" A chirpy Alison stuck her head around the doorframe.

Glancing up from my notepad, I noticed she was flashing a broad smile. Well, at least she'd stop flashing anything else. "Morning. You look happy for a Monday morning."

My quick glance concluded, suggested by her beaming smile, Alison had some good news. Perhaps Paul had decided to leave and not come back? No, probably not. I *would* have to face the tosser today.

"Well, I've got a new fella! We met a week ago. I think this could be the one!"

"Oh, that's good. Great news." I said, not sure what else to say, so I just grinned at her.

"He's a real hunk. We can't keep our hands off each other," she giggled.

Why I needed to know the ins and outs of Alison's love life, I had no idea. Was this the sort of conversation Alison and I would have? Did young Frank and Alison gossip like a couple of teenagers about their love life and enjoy a *he said – she said*, blow-by-blow type conversation which should be firmly left on the Dear Deidre pages of The Sun newspaper. Oh, well, I'll play along.

"Oh, good. That's nice." Lost for an appropriate response, I just continued to grin. I wasn't going to say, *'Oooo, tell me all, including the naughty bits.'*

Alison stepped into the office, still holding the doorframe – still grinning. "I met his parents this weekend, and I think they like me. I know he does!" she giggled again. "He wants to take me away before the match on Saturday, so I was wondering if I could have Friday off?"

"Yeah, course, you can. No problem. You off to watch football?"

"Ah, thanks, boss. No, he's a professional rugby player, so he'll be playing on Saturday. The team are allowed to take their wives and girlfriends away this week and make a weekend of it."

Now she had my attention. "A rugby player, and you're getting serious together?"

"Yeah. Anyway, I can't have you, so I need to grab a new fella." She blew me a kiss and winked. "I'm joking, boss. I'll get you that coffee."

"You're officially a WAG then," I chuckled, as she turned to go.

"A what?"

"WAG. You're a WAG now."

Alison pulled a face, clearly not having a clue what I was blabbering on about. By the look of her scowl, she appeared offended.

"WAG. Wives and girlfriends?"

"Oh, I see! Well, I've never heard of that. I'll get you your coffee, strange boss." Then, presumably relieved I hadn't called her some rude name, she skipped out of the office with her ponytail swinging from side to side.

I guessed WAG was not a term used in this era, never mind. However, her life appeared to be back on track to how I remembered it. The intervention of old Frank and introducing an acceptable dress code to the workplace hadn't stopped Rugby-Hunk from spotting her and asking her out – this was a good start to my week. Perhaps I should ask her if she liked Vegemite and Bush Tucker Trials – hmmm, maybe not.

My happy state for Alison soon evaporated as Paul strode purposefully into my office, plucked up a chair, dragged it away from my desk and plonked himself down with his arms folded. Presumably, he'd pulled the chair back to create some space for fear I might be inclined to leap across and grab his throat again. The bruising around his eye was starting to disappear, although the nose appeared crooked, and I guess always would be.

"Morning, Paul."

Alison skipped in with my coffee and placed it down on my desk with a couple of biscuits. She must have fished them out as a thank-you for agreeing to her long weekend request.

"I'll have my usual, Super-Tits."

"Piss off. Get your own. And never call me that again, or my boyfriend will smash your head in! And I can tell you he is twice the size of Frank. So, think on, dickhead." With that, she spun on her heels and marched out of the office.

"She can't say that! We'll have to sack her. Bloody hell, what the hell has got into her?"

"We're not sacking her, Paul. In fact, you could say we're sacking each other. This week, we'll have an agreement signed to dissolve the company. It will split nicely; you'll take the building side, and I'll have the design side."

"You can't do that! What the hell's going on?"

"I can't work with you anymore. That's what's going on, mate. In a few weeks, this company will no longer exist. We'll finish the car park, and then that's it."

"Oh, hang on. It's La-di-da-tits that's put you up to this, ain't it? She's all important now, so she stuck her foot down, and you're just going to toe the line like her pathetic little lapdog."

The feeling of wanting to stick my fist through his face returned. Fortunately for him and my still bruised hand, I managed to restrain myself. I just had to remain professional and ride out the next few weeks.

"Paul, it's over. You will sign the paperwork, and we *are* going our separate ways."

"Well, I might refuse! What you going to do then? Set your posh bird on me?"

"No, it will all be completed legally. Although if you cause problems, I might ask my assistant to get her big boyfriend to persuade you otherwise," I spat back at him, as I pointed to where Alison would be sitting.

"Super-Tits, your assistant! Bloody hell, Frank, you've lost it, mate."

"Alison? Yes. She will be with me another year before she emigrates, so plenty of time to help me set up my new company."

"Emigrate? Where's she going then?"

"Err ... nowhere. I meant graduate if she takes some exams." Oh, bollocks, I really must think before opening my mouth.

"That's it then. You're really going to do this?" replied Paul, dismissively shaking his head. "I could still have you arrested, you know."

Shifting forward in my chair, I pointed at him as I leant across my desk. "You could. But if I were you, I'd start thinking about how *you* behave. I think you'll find in the future that your behaviour in the workplace isn't going to be acceptable. So, it would be best if you start to change your ways. Otherwise, you're going to find the next twenty years very tough."

Paul sprung out of his chair, then appeared to change his mind on his intended action – probably remembering how painful his nose was. Then, dismissively still shaking his head, Paul padded his way to the office door.

"That cow has ruined you, and ruined our great company. You'll regret this when she bins you off in favour of some toff. Your bloody wife's a witch!"

Paul disappeared past the spider-webbed cracked glass, which last week the back of his head had cracked, then slammed the door to his office.

I shuffled through a heap of paperwork to locate my notepad, which contained my 'Schindler's list' and circled Paul's name around and around. He'd made it clear his dislike of my wife, and he had a motive – could it be? The night Jemma was strangled, he'd called saying he needed to take a rain check on our planned drinking session – why was that? However, we hadn't had this conversation the first time around, so where was his motive then?

The shrill of the phone hauled me back to the present.

"Frank, I have a Clare Heaton on the line. Shall I put her through?"

"Err ... yes." Oh, great, this was all I needed this morning. Clearly, I was just going to have to lie.

Clare pushed me on the details regarding my conversation with Tobias last week. I lied and said we chatted about cricket, this and that, and said he seemed his usual self. I lied some more, saying Tobias appeared stressed with a heavy workload. Clare seemed to sound a little brighter at the end of the call. I didn't; I felt awful lying to her. However, I needed some time to work out what was going on, and having Clare on the line going off on one wouldn't have helped.

As soon as I'd ended the call with Clare, telling her I had a meeting to attend – another lie – Alison buzzed through from reception.

"Frank, there's a gentleman in reception to see you. I've told him he hasn't got an appointment, but he's quite insistent."

After my spat with Paul, I wasn't in the mood for some salesman trying his luck whilst cold-calling to drum up some business.

"What's his name? What's he want?" Expecting he was from some wholesaler with a great deal on cement that we couldn't afford to miss. Perhaps Paul could see him? In his current mood, I think the salesman would never return.

"Bruce. Bruce Sinclair. He said it's a private matter."

I'd never heard of him. However, I guess I might know him, but over the years, I'd just forgotten the name.

"Oh, Christ, can't Paul see him? I bet it's not really a private matter. You know all these pushy reps try anything to get their foot in the door. When you've got rid of him, I wouldn't mind another coffee and some of those biscuits, please."

I could hear Alison talking to the visitor, although unable to follow the conversation, presuming she must have covered the mouthpiece.

"Frank, he insists on seeing you. He said it's to do with the Millennium Wheel. I told him we don't have a contract with that name, and I think he's got the wrong company. But he said he hasn't, and you would know what he meant by the London Eye."

Stunned, I held the receiver to my ear whilst trying to register what she'd just said. My mouth gaped open, with my tongue feeling like it had just been freeze-dried.

So, The Hooded Claw had sent one of his mercenary types with a pocket full of traveller cheques and a Beretta. Jesus, what had I done to cause this? Was he going to shoot me dead whilst I sat in my office chair? What about Jemma? If in a few seconds I have a neat round hole in my forehead – who would save Jemma when I'm dead?

"Frank. Frank, you there?"

"Oh, err ... no, yeah. Umm ... right. Send him through." This was it; I'd just invited an assassin into my office.

Alison ushered the gentleman into my office, which I assumed very soon would become a crime scene. I prayed once he dispatched me, he didn't hurt Alison. Although if the assassin fancied killing Paul, that was fine — crack on, mate.

I guess my face said it all, and his knowing smile suggested he knew his presence would afford me this reaction.

Red-Jag-Man had just walked in – a younger version of one of the projected pictures on the wall in The Hooded Claw's office. The very day he indicated if I cocked up, one of these two would be sent to liquidate me.

I feared my appointment with the inside of a human-sized blender had arrived.

45

The London Eye

Alison detected my internal trauma, which I suspect was radiating from me. The shock etched on my face, and I guess my gaping mouth, was a bit of a giveaway. She retreated to the door and waved her hand to attract my attention. In usual Alison style, she mouthed, "Are you okay?" She appeared concerned for me.

I managed to nod.

"I'll get that coffee. It was white with one, Mr Sinclair. Is that correct?"

The assassin turned and smiled. "Yes, love, that'll be lovely."

Well, at least he would have a coffee before blowing my brains across the window behind me – very civilised.

We sat in silence for a few moments, him smiling, looking like a vampire that had cornered his prey and preparing for the bloodthirsty act. I continued to gawp, awaiting the inevitable. Alison returned and deposited the coffees while shooting me several concerned looks to grab my attention. She was worried, but no way could she be as concerned as I was.

Alison left, and Red-Jag-Man picked up his coffee, taking a slurp. "Not exactly Starbucks, is it?" he chuckled, placing his cup down. He plucked up a Garibaldi biscuit, turning it around and inspecting it. Maybe he was checking that all the currants were dried fruit, not dead flies.

I managed to swallow, but no words were forming in my brain. Instead, it seemed to be waiting for the nine-millimetre slug to pass through.

"You've been a busy boy, haven't you, Frank? Although I can't say I blame you. That little brunette is very fit, and I wouldn't mind a go at her myself. You hedging your bets, are you? If you can't save your fit blonde, you can fall back on the brunette … you know, she reminds me of Kate Bush. You remember her? I used to have a thing about her when she seductively writhed around on stage in those sexy get-ups on Top of the Pops. Anyway, now I've got my fit body back, I think sex is the best bit. Don't you, Frank? Would you agree?"

He popped in the biscuit and rolled it around his mouth. Before swallowing, he continued whilst I carried on gawping. "I mean, back in 2015, I was seventy-five. Now at thirty-nine again, shagging the birds is such a good feeling. I've had one nearly every night since I've been back. Cost a bit, mind, but bloody worth it."

At last, I found some words. "You going to kill me?"

"Ah, yes, I can see why you're concerned. Well, Frank, my old mucker, hopefully not. But that really is down to you and the decision you make. Wrong choice, and yes, I'm afraid I will have to dispose of you. But hey, don't look so worried. As long as you do the right thing, there will be no need for any unpleasantness."

My primed and ready assassin held the plate of biscuits up to me. "You having one? If not, I'm liable to scoff the lot ... love Garibaldis. They're one of my favourites."

I shook my head.

"You sure? Oh well, all the more for me."

Sinclair reached inside his jacket – I flinched. I now fully expected to face the barrel of his gun that would surely appear.

"Calm down, Frank. You look like you're about to shit yourself!" He pulled out a packet of No.6 and a box of matches, lighting the cigarette whilst he held my gaze.

Transfixed by his stare, I seemed unable to look away. Sinclair shook the match and, as the wisp of smoke dissipated, we continued our who-blinks-first game.

"Pity you can't get those little disposable lighters these days. You know the ones, they cost a quid or so." He threw the matches on my desk and took a long drag on his cigarette. "Although smoking in pubs again is great, don't you think?"

"What d'you want?"

"Yes, straight to business. Quite right."

"So, Frank. It seems you saved your wife this Friday, which is all good. However, and unfortunately for you, we seem to have a slight problem that we're going to have to resolve between us. Basically, my friend, we have got to go again, so to speak."

"What? What d'you mean I've saved her this Friday? Friday hasn't happened yet!"

"Yeah, I know. Bloody complicated, ain't it? I can't get my head around it if I'm honest with you. It seems that we're here again. They sent you back, and you saved her. However, due to a technicality, the future hasn't changed as expected. Now I know you're thinking this can't be true because you don't remember saving her."

He slotted in another Garibaldi and continued. I listened whilst watching the biscuit turn to mush in his mouth.

"However, Franky boy, only if you're in the future would you know that, and you're not, you're still in the past. That lot at the CYA are bloody clever. Somehow, they seem to operate outside of time. Anyway, I'm not going to concern myself with that. I'm back, and it's great!"

"I don't understand. What the hell are you talking about? How could I have already saved her? And what technicality?"

"Yes, I don't know all the facts. Like any good military operation, it's all on a need-to-know basis. But here's the thing, my friend. It seems you *did* save your wife, but unfortunately, she's pregnant. Now, that has caused a slight issue, which basically means the change required hasn't happened."

He took another drag on his cigarette. I plucked mine up, trying to get my mind around this headfuck. So, I've already saved Jemma, but I don't know that. Who did I save her from? And because I'm still in time before that saving, I don't know I've done it. I think my assumption I was snorting nitrous oxide was a reasonable concern – this was nuts.

"So, we have a couple of issues. Firstly, there is a chance you might not save her this time. Unfortunately, if you fail, I'll have to, well, you know. I'm sure I don't need to spell it out for you because you're an intelligent man, and you can work it out for yourself. But that aside, let's say you do repeat the saving, then we need to deal with her pregnancy. So, the second issue is that the CYA require her to lose the baby, thus ensuring time reverts to the path they expected. The way I see it, all you have to do is get her to abort, and we're all good."

"Abort my child! You want me to persuade Jemma to have an abortion? Anyway, who did I save Jemma from?"

"Sorry, I don't have that info, I'm afraid. But I do know that the incident when she was walking home and strangled never took place. Whatever you did stopped that from happening. So, as you can see, there would be no murder in the first place. Regarding your other point, the child is not yours. I expect that should help focus the mind ... she will be aborting someone else's child. I imagine that would make it slightly easier?"

"Hang on, how does anyone know it's not mine?"

"Good question. The extensive medical tests they conducted on you, and me for that matter, were conclusive in discovering you fire blanks, no pun intended." He grinned again before slotting the last biscuit into his already full mouth.

"What?"

"I'm told you're infertile, Frank. Apparently, you are now and always have been. I'm afraid to tell you, but your lovely wife has been playing away. I've been conducting some surveillance over the past few weeks, as you well know, and I have a good idea who may have got your old lady up the duff."

I couldn't take all this in. Thumping my elbows on the table, I buried my head in my hands after sucking down smoke to calm my brain. At least my brain was still in one piece and not splattered across the window.

"Yes, I know. It's so complicated, mate. But your task is fairly simple. First, you get Jemma to abort the child, then you and I get on with living life again, for the second or third time."

"Who's she seeing? Who's the father?"

"Well, not conclusive, but from what I've gathered, your mate Tobias Heaton has had his fun. The good news, in the last month, I think the only one she's shagged is him ... oh, and you, presumably. But as you're seedless, my money's on good old Tobias. I must say, your old lady is very close to that MP bloke with whom she shares a house just off St James's Park. I don't think she's gone there. Well, not yet. You should have seen the bouquet of flowers he sent her last week. An eye-watering cost, I imagine, even for this era. I've never been one for sending flowers, but then I mostly enjoy prossies, so perhaps I've not had the opportunity. You and her have some open marriage arrangement, then?"

Lifting my head from my hands, I shook my head in disbelief. Tobias! I was right. Jesus, how long had they been at it? Then there was Clare, her best mate, who Jemma was quite happy to spend time with whilst behind her back she shagged her husband. And those bloody flowers were from that hooray-henry in the yellow checked trousers – I bloody knew something was going on with him; it was just the way she said his name. Who was Jemma Stone? Certainly not the woman I thought she was.

"Err... what d'you mean, open marriage?"

"You know, that arrangement where you both can shag who you like as long as it's not in the marital bed. Sounds great to me! Never been the marrying type, although I could handle that kind of arrangement."

"Err ... no, mate. Not at all."

"Well, your good lady seems happy to spread her legs and, looking at the way you were all over that little petite brunette on Friday, it looks pretty open to me."

What a dilemma. I had to save Jemma again. Although I didn't know I'd already done it. I'm infertile, which could explain why Jemma hadn't fallen pregnant. As I suspected, it seems my wife was some hussy putting it about. I knew when she said the word *Roops*, there was a tone that I detected she had a relationship with him that was more than professional. Now I had to confront her and somehow persuade her to lose the baby.

"Some other info for you, which might just help ensure Friday night goes smoothly. From my surveillance, there are three men who concern me. And although I don't know for certain, I would hedge my bets that one of these was responsible for Jemma's demise the first time."

"Who?"

"Tobias, for obvious reasons. He seems to follow her everywhere. The sad man is like a love-sick puppy. I caught him watching her last week when she opened that supermarket. Then there's that weasel." He nodded to Paul's office. "He was spying on her at the train station last Friday night. And lastly, and my personal favourite, there's Miles Rusher. Presumably, you know who he is? You pointed him out at the cricket match last Saturday. Of course, it could be some other random nutter because the world is full of them."

"Rusher, the Thigh Crusher?"

"Yeah, that's him. Ha, that was a funny story! When was that d'you reckon? I think it must have been sometime in the mid '90s. I remember the picture in the papers of the Russian bird with long blonde hair and legs up to her armpits. Couldn't blame him for being sucked into that honey trap."

"Hang on. The cricket match. You were there?"

"Yeah, all day, mate. Gotta say, you're not much good, are you? Christ knows why *you* open the batting ... you were shit. Although, to be fair, the week before, you did hit an impressive one hundred and four not out."

"The previous Saturday?"

"Yes, the away match you had on ... what was it ... Saturday the 8th."

"You were here then?"

"Yes, like you were. Keep up, Frank. I was sent via the Wheel less than an hour after you. We arrived on the same day ... 17th of August."

So, he had landed on the correct day, but I landed a month later for some reason.

With the Garibaldi biscuits all scoffed, Sinclair stubbed his cigarette out and gulped down his coffee before standing and offering his hand.

"Right, Frank. Now we're acquainted, I'll let you crack on. I'll be around Friday night in case you require me for a bit of support but, as you saved her before, I'm confident you can do it again. Then it's the baby situation. Of course, you understand, fail, and I'll have to act. I'm not a stupid man. I know if I decide not to act when I have to, the CYA will despatch someone to deal with me. But chin up, mate, don't look so glum. I'm sure we can sort this out between us, and we can then enjoy our new lives."

I stood and shook his hand as if we had just concluded a deal at the end of a productive business meeting. I'd noticed he seemed to have mislaid his little finger. However, and more importantly, I have no idea why I was shaking the hand of my potential killer. I guess it was an involuntary action as my mind raced away with a plethora of ridiculous thoughts.

46

Bewitched

I guess it's a tough conversation accusing your significant other of having an affair. I hadn't had to do this before, simply because some bastard murdered my one significant other. As for the woman I shacked up with when living Wayne and Waynetta style on the Broxworth Estate, she couldn't be described as significant. I can't even remember her name, although I do remember her having some fling with one of the Gower or Colney sons. The Gowers and Colneys were the evil families who ran the crime business in Fairfield. At the time, I was reasonably nonplussed about her leaving me; also, I wasn't going to fight the Fairfield Mafia for her attentions.

After my newly acquainted assassin friend's visit, what he had said had severely hampered my ability to focus on any work. So, no longer able to concentrate on the building of a concrete slab, I left work early and arrived home before Jemma. Although I'd run through in my mind how the conversation with Jemma would pan out, I had no idea where to start.

I presume, of the millions of couples who go through this each year, not many would have a planned speech prepared. I imagine it starts with an accusation, followed by a screaming match, and ends in objects being lobbed at high speed that lack precision or any accuracy. Then, a couple of days later, a family law firm would be rubbing their hands at the thought of another colossal paycheque whilst skilfully acting sympathetically to the plaintiff as they worked out how much they could squeeze from them.

I decided to scrap my earlier plan of holding off on this conversation until Friday had passed. As long as I saved her, and with Dave's help I figured that would be relatively straightforward, this conversation needed to be had – waiting served no purpose. Of course, I was aware that I wasn't innocent after the kissy-face incident with Jayne, but I hadn't slept with her – more's the pity. But Jemma was evidently seeing other men, so it was time to end the charade of our marriage.

When Jemma arrived home, she said she was super tired and disappeared off to have a long soak in the bath before packing her suitcase ready for her stay-over tomorrow night. Well, with the plethora of extramarital affairs she was juggling, I guess that explained her constant tiredness that seemed to be the case every night she arrived home from work or whatever she was up to.

Only ten days ago, Jemma had ravaged me in bed – now she was distant. If Tobias was the father, she was having that affair when we gave the bed springs a good workout last Friday. This distancing, I figured, was for either of two reasons or perhaps both. Firstly, she suspected or knew she was pregnant. Secondly, by the sound of the bouquet of flowers which my assassin friend mentioned, Rupert and Jemma had moved to the next stage in their relationship and she was considering which way to jump.

After we'd eaten and washed up, ensuring I'd stowed away the dangerous-looking cutlery, I would help my wife make that leap. Sadly, in less than two weeks, I'd assessed that Jemma was not someone I could continue to love. I was old Frank, and I just couldn't relate to her as young Frank must have thirty-six years ago. Although it appears that Jemma had strayed well before old Frank arrived. I guess she had other plans for her life, and I needed to help her on her way.

Wrapped in her bathrobe, Jemma disappeared into the lounge and nestled into the sofa with a cup of tea to watch TV, presumably to avoid a conversation. She knew something was up when I turned the TV off. But with no remote control, she couldn't turn it back on.

"Can we talk?"

"I was watching that!"

"It's only Tomorrow's World." I certainly didn't need to watch it, as I already knew what the future would bring.

"Turn it on, Frank. They were talking about digital telephones and that some company has invented a wireless one."

Before I'd turned off the TV, the presenter, Michael Rodd, was running through the fantastic new technology that would allow phone calls to be made that weren't connected to a phone line. He'd stood in the middle of a park with a dial phone and a large pack in a holdall containing the new equipment that made this new technology possible. Although impressed with the system, he stated that both the Home Office and the Post Office didn't see a commercial reason to grant a licence for its use. Furthermore, there was a belief that there was no requirement for a phone which was mobile and wasn't connected to the Exchange.

See my point? There was no need to watch Tomorrow's World as they didn't have the knowledge which time-travel had provided me.

"We need to talk."

Jemma shifted her gaze to me from where she'd been staring at the white dot in the centre of the TV screen. I could tell that she knew what was coming. Her lips twitched, that telltale sign she was agitated. It gave the impression that her nose had wiggled, affording her that Samantha from Bewitched look. Had she just cast a spell? Well, Paul had said my wife was a witch. Although *she* was the ordinary mortal woman, and *I* was the one with the special powers.

"What about? I'm tired, so I'm not in the mood for a deep and meaningful conversation."

"Jemma, I don't think you're happy."

"What d'you mean? With the job? I told you I'm not giving in."

"No, not the job. I mean with me."

Her lips twitched again. "I don't know what you mean."

These conversations weren't easy. Of course, I wanted to get to the truth without a bout of histrionics from Jemma. However, I could see that wasn't going to happen. Jemma glowered as she tugged her dressing gown around her, aggressively tightening the cord.

"Okay, look, I'll just say it. I think you would rather be with someone else."

"Like who? Frank, what are you blabbering on about?"

"Like Tobias or Rupert."

Stunned into silence, wide-eyed, she glared at me. My beautiful cheating wife was clearly desperately playing for time, wondering what I knew. Would she just come out with it? For sure, it would make this conversation a whole lot easier.

"Oh, Frank, what are you talking about? You have this obsession that I'm having some wild affair with Rupert. So, I take it you don't trust me then? Well, thanks a lot!"

"Jemma, it's not about trusting you. But you *have* had an affair with Tobias. Also, I think *you are* considering having an affair with Rupert. Of course, you can deny it, but I know you have."

My cheating wife shook her head but said nothing as she searched my face for signs. Did I know, or was I guessing? Presumably, her silence was a tactic whilst she weighed up her options. Did she bluff it out, or did I hold all the aces?

"I know Jemma. And look, I don't want to get into a massive fight. If you want out, that's okay. If we've made a mistake and we shouldn't have got married, then so be it. But let's be honest ... please?"

Jemma held my stare for a brief moment before bowing her head. "How ... how d'you know?" she whispered.

"It's true then?"

Jemma nodded but didn't look up as her tears flowed. If this had happened the first time, I would surely have been devastated. Perhaps we would have had that screaming match and would now be in the process of lobbing objects at each other. However, things were very different this time because I no longer loved her, although I wanted her to stay alive.

I resisted the urge to lob an object, although I thought the glass vase her mother had bought her that sat on the windowsill looked favourite for flight. Instead, I hugged my cheating wife. I guess Jemma was somewhat surprised by my reaction. However, she clung to me as if her life depended on it and proceeded to sob.

After a few minutes, when the weeping had abated, Jemma pulled back and peeked at me with red eyes. "Why aren't you upset?"

"I am upset ... but we both know we've come to an end, don't we? We had a great time, but I think you want something different now. I guess we both need to move on."

"Have you met someone else?" Ah, now this was a problem after I had implored her to be honest.

"No."

Well, technically, that was correct. I had feelings for Jayne but feared that would most likely not be reciprocated, and I would just have to bury my feelings for her so not to put her friendship with Jemma in jeopardy.

"Oh God, I'm so sorry, Frank. I do still love you, I think. But I'm in love with someone else as well."

"Rupert?"

Jemma managed a slight nod of her head.

"Well, I don't think you *are* in love with me. If I'm honest, I think it's just the sex you love."

Jemma managed a tight smile, which afforded her a clown-like face caused by the mascara which had streaked down during her sobbing session. "The sex was good, wasn't it?"

"Oh, Jem, the best. The best ever. No one in my life will come close." Well, after sixty-six years, that was true. Now I had another thirty years or more to improve on that.

"I'm so sorry, Frank. I've treated you so badly, and I now feel awful."

"Jemma, it's done. But I have to ask ... Tobias?"

Jemma sighed, but as she'd now admitted loving another man, I guess she was ready to spill the beans about her other adventures under the sheets. "Oh, this is embarrassing. Yes, we had a one-night fling about four weeks ago. I don't know how it happened, but he's been hounding me for sex since I became an MP. You remember that fundraiser event at the Arlington Hotel we all attended?"

I nodded. No, scrub that. It was more of a scowl.

"Well, we'd all had so much to drink, and somehow, Tobias and I disappeared upstairs. You must think I'm a shameless hussy. I've let you down."

After she'd sobbed, for some reason, we held hands whilst we discussed her affairs. Now hearing the news about her and Tobias, I dropped her hand as if it had instantly become white hot. The marriage had obviously meant nothing to her. It hurt to think after a few glasses of champagne, she thought it was okay to nip upstairs for a quick bunk-up whilst her husband and best friend were downstairs oblivious to what they were up to. The sooner I distance myself from my wife, the better.

"Frank?"

"Which suite? Ours or theirs?"

"What?"

"I said, which suite? Where did you two get it on? Our bed or theirs?"

"Theirs." As her nose didn't wiggle, I guess, for once, she was telling the truth. At least they'd done it in Tobias and Clare's room and not ours; I guess that was something.

The memory of that fundraising event resurfaced as young Frank's mind pulled in a memory that old Frank had long forgotten. "That night, we bounced around on our bed for hours, and I think we carried on in the morning. You shagged Tobias, then had me straight afterwards. Nice!"

"Sorry."

Was Jemma the girl for me? Oh no, I don't think so – Roops was welcome to her. I just needed to save his girl from being strangled. After that, she could embark on a countrywide shagathon as far as I was concerned. The rose tint around my metaphorical glasses had withered and died.

"I won't deny I'm hurt, but I guess what is done is done. I'm not going to waste my life wondering why or what could have been. Although I'm tempted to smash Tobias's toffee-nosed face in."

"Don't!"

"Clare?"

She nodded.

"You're playing dangerous games, my girl."

"Christ, you sound like my dad."

"You've told him?"

Well, I probably did sound like her father because I was older than him. Due to time travel, Cecil and I were from the same generation, although he was born twenty-one years before me. Jemma chose not to answer, and now I didn't give a shit either way.

For the moment, I thought I'd save the baby conversation for another night. Christ, that would be something to look forward to. There was absolutely no way she could know who the father was based on the fact that within a couple of hours mine and Tobias's sperm had been jockeying for position.

I had to assume my assassin friend was telling the truth, so Tobias's seed would have had very little competition from mine – this thought made me feel somewhat crappy.

"What do we do now?" Jemma's short, tearful session appeared to be over as she regained her composure.

"Jesus, I don't know. I guess we carry on as usual until we tell everyone we're splitting up. I can't see any point in delaying it. Obviously, we'll need to sell the house and sort everything out. Jemma, we're finished. Whether you and Rupert get it together or not, I think you'll agree you and I both need to move on."

"Well, I must say you're being very civilised about this – thank you. We need to make sure it doesn't come out about my affairs. That could damage my career, so can we keep it quiet for now?"

"Yep, that's fine. However, it's time for honesty. Have you slept with Rupert?"

"No. I promise, no. Although I won't deny I've been tempted."

"You're going to now, I presume?"

She nodded.

Well, I asked for honesty. Your wife confirming that tomorrow night she's going to shag the brains out of her work colleague was tough to take.

"Will you be back on Thursday, as you said?"

"Yes. Yes, I will."

"Okay. Let's have a couple of days to think about when and how we split. We can catch up when you get home on Thursday. What you going to do about Clare?"

"She must never know. Please, Frank. Please … she must never know."

Tobias was one of my three and, if he was pestering Jemma as she suggested, I suspected he could become unpredictable, especially if she wasn't reciprocating. As Rupert had trumped Tobias with the top card in their game of Jemma-Shags-Top-Trumps, this undoubtedly put Tobias high up on my list of potential killers.

For now, I wouldn't push Jemma to come clean with Clare for fear of causing Tobias to become unstable and then acting before Friday.

I left Jemma on the sofa, escaping the house for some fresh air and a cigarette. I'm not sure those two things constitute the same thing, but whatever. Despite the sad situation, I felt relieved it was all out in the open.

If someone hadn't murdered her the first time, would young Frank and Jemma have carried on and been happy? Well, who knows, that was in the past, or was it the future? Bloody hell, this was complicated.

Based on what my assassin friend had said, there appeared to be several different pasts in play, so it was bloody difficult to tell which past I was actually living in.

Perhaps I was in many? Jesus, this time-travel malarkey was confusing. However, now I had to think of the future.

My mind drifted to Jayne.

47

The Odd Couple

On Tuesday morning, Jemma left for work earlier than usual when catching a train into London. She drove herself to the station rather than asking me to drop her off – she didn't ask for a lift, and I didn't offer. Apart from my Save-Jemma operation planned for Friday and the baby issue, we had to start our separate lives.

I guess she wasn't worrying about overnight parking charges. So, driving herself to the station and on to her day's work, then shagging Roops double-barrelled-name-tosser-toff whoever, was probably uppermost in her mind.

Unsurprisingly, I didn't sleep particularly well Tuesday night, as I tossed and turned whilst trying to get out of my head what Jemma was doing at that precise point. As we'd been together for three years and had enjoyed regular bedroom fun, I could easily guess.

Although splitting up was the right course of action, I thought perhaps she could have said she would wait to screw Roop's brains out until we'd both left the marital home. However, I was discovering who she really was. As she had no qualms about taking Tobias whilst Clare and I were in the main ballroom downstairs, I guess it was no surprise – the woman had no morals. As the local MP, she was there to represent the community, not shag them all. Unfortunately, it seemed Jemma didn't receive that particular memo.

For the next couple of days, I ploughed on with my plans to break up the company. Paul and I only spoke when absolutely necessary, and that suited me. I presumed he'd resigned himself to what was happening. That said, Paul was still high on my list of suspects. Let's face it, he firmly blamed Jemma for my decision. So, if he didn't kill her the first time, this time he had a clear motive.

When Jemma returned tonight, we would have to discuss the baby. As many different events were happening from my first life in 1979, was there a chance she wasn't pregnant in this version? After the conversation with Red-Jag-Man, my new assassin friend, this was now my third time in 1979, not the second. The problem was I could only remember one other version. That was too difficult to comprehend, so I decided not to disappear down that particular rabbit hole and try to prevent myself from ending up in a secure unit for the mentally disturbed.

I would just have to ask Jemma tonight – straight out – was she pregnant? If she didn't know, she'd have to do a test. Were home pregnancy tests available at this time? I could nip into town and ask at the chemist and, if they did, pick one up for her – it seemed like a plan.

The issue of what to do if she was pregnant – I had no idea. If I did fire rubber bullets, that meant whatever happened in this new life it would be as childless as the first – a huge disappointment.

'Well, based on your first time and love of off-licences. It's probably a good move that you'll never be a dad!'

"Good point," I muttered, as I glanced up and spotted Paul leaving the office just before lunch.

I buzzed through to reception. "Alison, where's Paul going?"

"Sorry, I don't know."

"Oh. Didn't he say?"

"No."

"Has he confirmed the sub-contractors to complete the ground-works for the car park?"

"I don't know."

"Can you ask him when he comes back?"

"Frank, I can. But this is getting ridiculous. It might have escaped your attention, but I don't want to speak to him either! Can you two talk? Otherwise, the next few weeks are going to be hell. I feel like the mediator in a marriage break-up. You're like the bloody Odd Couple."

"Yes, you're right. Sorry, I'll sort it out."

Alison was right, as Paul and I had become Felix and Oscar. Me, the Jack Lemmon guy heading for disaster after divorce, and him, the Walter Matthau guy – the slob. The difference was, we weren't going to become best buddies again and play poker as we had used to. Instead, we were dissolving this partnership, and I would stop him from killing my soon to be ex-wife, assuming Tobias and Miles were innocent.

Deciding to take an early lunch, I nipped up to one of the nearest chemists on the Eaton Estate. This would avoid the busy town centre, and I'd be able to return to work before more planned meetings about the concrete slab I'd designed to blight the look of what was essentially a half-decent looking town. Of course, the pregnancy test might not be required if Jemma already knew she was pregnant. However, it would be prudent to have a backup plan because if she didn't, somehow, I had to persuade her to do the test as my life depended on it – literally.

Pleased home test kits were around in this era, and the chemist stocked them, I purchased the offensively expensive piece of equipment that resembled a full-blown home chemistry set. I had enquired if cheaper ones were available. Unfortunately, the assistant stated they weren't but suggested waiting nine months, and hey presto, we'd have our answer for free. She laughed; I didn't. I guess the assistant thought she was funny – fair enough, she probably was.

After realising I wasn't in the mood to exchange jokes, the assistant advised that she'd have preferred my wife to purchase the test so she could take her through the instructions. But she sold it to me anyway and wished us good luck. She probably assumed the test was for my wife and we were hoping for a positive result. For all she knew, I could have a mistress and would be hoping for the exact opposite.

However, I didn't have a mistress – my wife had a lover or lovers. I prayed for a negative result because persuading Jemma she couldn't have the baby could be tricky. Telling her to abort because otherwise I would end up in a human-sized blender, ready to be liquidised by the hand of a seventy-five-year-old ex-special forces soldier who'd time-travelled from the future, one hour after me, could be touch-and-go on the believable story stakes.

Okay, I know not all MPs are super clever, and I'm no expert on the workings of the minds of those who govern us, but I don't think Jemma would buy that story. So, I was going to have to conjure up some plausible reason why she had to abort.

I hopped in the motor, clutching my offensively expensive chemistry kit, and cut through Eaton Road towards the main drag through Fairfield that led back to work. Although near my office, this wasn't a part of town I regularly visited. Of course, back in the early '60s, it would have been when attending Eaton City of Fairfield School – the only prestigious Grammar school in the town.

Now, as I parked up looking through the open school gate, it was just another large comprehensive with a few thousand kids and presumably a bunch of well-trodden teachers – one of which was Jayne.

Before I realised what I was doing, I'd parked outside the school and had trotted up the stone steps towards the main office. As I peered through the glass-panelled door, I spotted the school secretary, Miss Colman, who Dave had mentioned on Friday. She appeared to be in hushed conversations with that Noel Edmonds lookalike bloke with the big ears, who I think Jayne mentioned was her boss.

Dave had mentioned something about her constant gossiping, and I think I'd just caught her in the act because both appeared embarrassed as I barrelled through the swing doors.

"Anyway. Thank you, Mr Apsley. I must get on as Mr Clark needs these letters ready for this afternoon's post collection."

"Yes, of course. It'll be a lot easier when we can send letters electronically. That day will come, Mrs Trosh, that day will come," replied big ears, as he smiled, acknowledging me before leaving the office.

Very perceptive of him, I thought. Predicting emails as a form of communication in the future. Almost like he was a time-traveller like me – now I really was being stupid.

"Good afternoon, sir. How can I help?" said Miss Colman.

Although big ears had called her Mrs Trosh, so I guess she must now be married. It wasn't difficult to miss the size and sparkle of the diamond in her engagement ring. If it were boxed, it would state on the cardboard outer packaging that a two-man lift was required for safety reasons – it was that big. She peered over her spectacles and gently tapped her bun hairdo, presumably checking for stray hairs that might have escaped.

"Oh, hello. I wonder, if she's free, could I have a word with Miss Hart?"

"Oh, hang on, I remember you! You're Frank Stone, aren't you?" She held her hands up, closed her eyes and turned her face away as if trying to recall some vital piece of information. "Now, don't tell me. You left here in … '66?"

"Yes, I am. What an incredible memory you have. It was '65, actually, but close enough." For sure, she wouldn't have recognised me in 2015 with my grey beard when sleeping under a heap of damp cardboard. But presumably, she was dead by then because the gossiping school secretary must have been in her sixties now.

"Oh, well, you see, I do try to remember all the old boys, especially from the Grammar days." She took a quick glance left and right, then leant over the desk between us and whispered. "It's not the same now it's a Comprehensive. Of course, it's lovely having the girls here. Although it just seems less exclusive now, unlike when you attended."

"Oh, right," I replied. Although now not sure what else to say or why she'd divulged this information.

Mrs Trosh pulled back after delivering her opinions regarding the changes to state education and continued. "I will admit I recognised you because your lovely wife is our new MP. She's such a lovely girl ... lovely girl. Well, I must say you've done very well for yourself, Mr Stone."

"Err ... yes, she's lovely." She might be lovely looking, but that was about it. And for the last two nights, my lovely wife had probably been bouncing up and down with Rupert The Bear, and I don't mean skipping into Nutwood.

"Now, was it Miss Hart you were enquiring about?"

"Yes, please."

"Before I call the staffroom, can I ask the nature of your visit today?"

"Umm. Personal, I think."

"Personal?"

"Yes, that's right."

"Okay. Let me see if Miss Hart is free. Although classes start in fifteen minutes, so I'm afraid she may be busy."

Miss Colman, or whatever her married name was, clearly didn't like the word *personal*. The way she'd repeated my response was as if it had caused a bad taste in her mouth. Either because a married man was calling on a Miss, which was inappropriate, or because she wanted to know what the content of the conversation would be. Well, that made two of us because, at this point, I had no idea what I was doing here either. However, something had drawn me in, almost sucked me in from the road, and now I awkwardly stood in my old school waiting to see the lady who I'd played kissy-face with last week. Apart from apologising, I had no idea what to say to Jayne.

Mrs Trosh made the requested call. However, I'm convinced by her constant glances over her shoulder, she thought this was all highly irregular. I guess she may consider my visit inappropriate, which it probably was. I contemplated making a dash for it, although I was here now and considered running out could be worse than facing Jayne.

'You're here because you can't stop thinking about her, mate. You're on thin ice, Frank Stone.'

"Mr Stone, Miss Hart is just about to set up her afternoon classes. However, she will see you for a few minutes. Now, we don't ordinarily allow the general public into the school. But as you're one of our old grammar boys, I will allow it this time. She'll be in classroom seven at any moment. Can you remember where that is?"

"Ha, no, sorry, it's been a long time. I left here over fifty years ago! I'm afraid I can't remember that kind of detail."

"Fifty! Surely you mean fifteen?"

"Err ... oh, yes, of course. Sorry, slip of the tongue."

She leant across the desk and pointed left, directing me through the labyrinth of corridors like a traffic policeman. "Through the double door, left and left again, then straight in front of you. Have you got that?"

"Yes, thank you," I replied, as I swivelled around to escape the inquisitive secretary, although still utterly clueless of what I planned to say to Jayne.

"Mr Stone, you will need to swiftly conduct your business and have left the school before classes are due to start. Mr Apsley, our Deputy Head, is a stickler for timekeeping," she called out, as I barrelled out of the office.

Hot-footing my way to classroom seven, I weaved my way through the melee of pupils, hoping Jayne wasn't too embarrassed after I apologised for Thursday night's events. As for what else I would say, well, I'd just wing it.

I was sure Jayne was regretting the whole evening and relieved we hadn't been caught out by now. Although, as a couple of thousand kids attended the school, it would be a minor miracle if none of them had spotted us.

On a positive note, it seemed we hadn't hit the front page of the Chronicle – yet.

~

In disbelief, Jayne replaced the receiver in its cradle and vacantly gawped at the staffroom phone.

Frank was here!

Just about every waking moment since Thursday evening she'd thought about him, although she knew that wonderful snogging session was so wrong. But presumably, he'd turned up to apologise and to ensure she didn't blab off to Jemma or blackmail him.

Of course, she wouldn't because she was as much to blame about the kissing incident as he was. Anyway, telling Jemma would put an end to their friendship and, as much as she'd always had a thing about Frank, she wasn't going to try to split them up out of spite – that just wasn't who she was. Of course, she'd always envied Jemma, but just because she had the power to hurt her didn't mean she could use it. Anyway, what good would it do her? Even if that did put their marriage on rocky ground, Jayne knew Frank wouldn't want her, kiss or no kiss.

Jayne shrugged off her old blue cardigan, grabbed her suit jacket, and then smoothed the front of her skirt. With a quick dash to the ladies, she would ensure her appearance was as good as it could be in her schoolteacher attire. Her suit, although functional, wasn't super flattering – did it matter? Frank hadn't turned up to kiss her – he'd turned up to tell her to keep quiet. So, he wasn't going to give two shits if she showed up in her frumpy old cardigan or a short cocktail dress.

"Get a grip, Jayne," she muttered, throwing her jacket and plucking up her cardigan from where she'd flung it a moment ago before scooting towards the staff room exit. Then, catching sight of herself in the small square mirror, which a few years ago a temporary caretaker had wonkily fixed to the back of the door, she screwed her face up at what reflected at her.

School attire, especially her cardigan, wasn't how she liked to portray herself to anyone but the students. Christ, why couldn't she have worn a cocktail dress to school today?

Dashing back into the staff room, Jayne tugged at the cardigan buttons. But, of course, now short of time and trying to hurry, those pesky buttons refused to undo. Eventually winning the button war, Jayne ripped off her cardigan and lobbed the unwanted garment. Jayne scooted off to the ladies after reapplying her jacket, although still miffed by her flustered appearance.

With a quick brush of her hair and applying a second coat of makeup, Jayne straightened up to inspect herself in front of the mirror.

"Lippy?" she muttered.

Deciding some lipstick was required, Jayne rummaged through her bag, only locating the errant tube after throwing the contents in the sink with frustration. Then, checking the lippy hadn't spread to her teeth, she straightened up in front of the mirror to conduct her second inspection.

"Tarty!"

Studying the tube confirmed this really wasn't appropriate lipstick to be worn during school hours.

'Cherries in the Snow' by Revlon.

Disappointed the only lipstick she could find was a shocking bright red colour, Jayne wiped away the inappropriate makeup with a well-used scrunched-up tissue. Anyway, she never wore lippy at school – she'd just have to go without.

Pleased she'd done her best to improve her appearance in the short amount of time available, Jayne barrelled out of the ladies and narrowly avoided flattening two students who were passing by in the corridor. With her composure restored, Jayne reminded herself that Frank was not here to swoon over her, more's the pity. He'd presumably turned up to tell her to keep *that kiss* a buried secret.

As she whizzed past the assembly hall and school office, heading towards the classroom, Jayne spotted him. Her heart leapt, and *that kiss* came flooding back to her.

Why was he married? It wasn't fair. Now she was going to hear him tell her to keep quiet, which would surely bury any fantasy she harboured about *her* Frank.

Her Frank – God, she wished he was.

She would just be professional and hope he wasn't too horrible to her. Although Jayne had never seen him act that way and doubted Frank was capable of being nasty. However, she was acutely aware these weren't normal circumstances.

~

Jayne and I simultaneously arrived at classroom seven. She smiled and flushed crimson – my heart skipped a beat.

"Hello, Frank. Well, this is a nice surprise!"

"Is it?"

"Isn't it?" she questioned. Probably thinking that I didn't think it was nice – how wrong could she be?

"Oh … yeah. Err … yes, it's nice to see you," I stupidly babbled. Now annoyed with myself because, once again, I seemed incapable of coherently stringing two words together whilst in her company.

'Get a grip, dickhead.'

Two students cruised by whilst we awkwardly remained silent as they disappeared down the corridor, neither giving either of us a second glance.

"Come in, although I've only got a few minutes before class."

The classroom's appearance was how I remembered them. A raised platform at the front, which upon it sat a desk for the teacher. Tall Georgian windows flooded the room with light across the rows of desks. Although time had progressed, and now the old wooden desks with redundant ink wells and sit-up-and-beg style chairs were replaced with laminated-topped wooden benches and plastic moulded chairs. In my day, failure to sit up ram-rod-straight would result in a rap across the knuckles for any boy whose posture was deemed not to be at a ninety-degree angle. A grammar school education was as much about teaching attitude as algebra.

Jayne halted at the first desk just inside the classroom, swivelling around to face me. Because I hadn't expected her to stop suddenly, rather embarrassingly, our bodies collided. There was a similarity to the incident with Clare in my office last week, although we weren't laying on top of each other – more's the pity. During that awkward moment, both of us tried to regain our composure.

"Oh, Christ, sorry," I blurted, as I stepped back, trying to retain the acceptable distance between us. Neither of us spoke for a few seconds as we looked at each other. What was she thinking about? What was I doing here?

"Jayne ... I ..."

Silence again.

"Frank, are you alright?"

"Yeah, I'm fine. I'm fine."

"Oh, okay. Are you going to do that *'I'm fine'* routine again?" she giggled.

"Err ... oh, yes, that. Sorry," I winced.

'Frank, sorry to butt in here, but what the fuck is the matter with you! Can you get a bloody grip and say something slightly more engaging than fine!'

"Jayne, look, I need to apologise for Thursday night."

"Oh, that's okay. I shouldn't have ... well, you know."

"No ... I shouldn't have ... you know."

"Frank, I won't say anything. Of course, I won't. So you don't need to worry. If you like, we can just forget all about it."

"Oh. Yes, of course."

Oh shit, she wanted to forget it. Why I thought this wonderful, intelligent, gorgeous woman would like to do anything but forget we kissed, I have no idea.

I was utterly deluded and now seriously regretted coming to the school. Also, I was already late for a meeting regarding the suitability of reinforced concrete for use in stairwells.

As both of us now seemed to have lost the thread of this stilted conversation, silence once again descended as we just stared at each other. Her lips parted – all I wanted to do was hold her – kiss her.

"How's Jemma? I must give her a call."

"A call. Why?"

"Just to catch up. I won't say anything, I promise. Stop worrying, Frank. We both said it was a mistake, and I assume you don't go around kissing all her friends. It was just a spur-of-the-moment thing, which I'm sure we both now regret."

"Oh, no. I've never kissed anyone else ... I'm not like that. I kissed you because ... because I—"

"Because what?"

Shaking my head in disbelief at what a total tosser I seemed to be and mortified about my competent performance of a complete prat, I considered the best course of action was to make a run for it. I shouldn't have come here. This was embarrassing, and Jayne must think I'm a right tosser.

"Jemma is in London, although she's back tonight. You could give her a call over the weekend if you like." Hopefully, she would still be alive then.

"Okay, I will. But please don't worry, Frank. As they say, it's water under the bridge now."

"Good. As I said, I'm sorry for what I did, and I don't want you to think bad of me."

Jayne gently laid her hand on my arm, causing a tingling sensation to sprint up my body. "Oh, Frank, I could never think bad of you. Never."

"Oh really? That's good."

"Is it?" she questioned.

"Is it what?"

"Good that I could never think bad things about you."

"Christ, yes! That would be awful if you thought that."

"Well, I don't. I never could."

"Look, I'd better go. I presume your class will be starting soon. That school secretary made it quite clear I have to be off school grounds before classes start."

"Okay, I'll give Jemma a call at the weekend."

"Yes, okay, she might be glad of a friend to talk to."

"Oh, why? Is everything alright?"

"Err ... um."

"Frank?"

"I shouldn't say this, but Jemma and I have decided to go our separate ways."

"Oh my God! Why? What's happened?"

"Well, we've just grown apart. No one's fault, really. I think we've both changed." I nonchalantly shrugged. "She just wants to move on."

"Oh, Frank. I'm so sorry." Jayne touched my arm again – more tingles.

"No, don't be. It's for the best, I think. Jemma wants a different life, and I don't think it's the life I want."

"What d'you want, then?"

"You," I blurted it out.

'Oh, well done, dickhead. Just blurt it out, why don't you. Fuck sake, Frank, get a bloody grip!'

The heat on my cheeks suggested I was burning up, or it could have been from the obvious heat radiating off Jayne's face. If mine were as red as hers, it would cause the global warming effect in classroom seven.

Our eyes danced this way and that, as we both searched each other's minds, I guess both of us trying to work out what next.

Why I'd said that, hell, I don't know. Now wishing a large hole would swallow me up, I urgently needed to get the hell out of here. As I spun around, preparing to make a dash for it, Jayne grabbed my arm and pulled me back.

We awkwardly closed the distance between us, neither knowing quite what to do. Jayne tilted her head as she looked up at me, those hazel eyes clearly asking a non-verbal question. Then, a micro-second later, we started round two of sucky-face – we were all over each other.

The heavy oak door burst open, and a tsunami of kids barrelled through the door just as we were about to swallow each other. We instantly pulled away as two lads nearly flattened us in their wake. By the time we'd managed to put an acceptable distance between us, we had at least twenty teenagers gawping and grinning.

"Miss has got a boyfriend! Miss has got a boyfriend," chanted one lad. The remaining students didn't need coaxing to join in, and now there was a full chorus. "Miss has got a boyfriend."

Realising this was a somewhat disastrous situation, I backed up towards the door. Jayne and I locked eyes, neither blinking. What was in her head? Did Jayne have the same feelings? Or had I just misinterpreted it?

'She just snogged your face off, you dickhead! What's to misinterpret about that!'

Before I turned to leave Jayne to sort out her new choir, who were not relenting on their single chorus line, she mouthed, "Call me." I nodded and left.

As the door swung closed, Jayne bellowed at her new choir. "Alright. That's enough! Now, to your desks ... immediately!" The chanting stopped, replaced by the sound of chair legs scraping as the class complied with the given directive. I had no idea such a perfect petite woman could shout that loud.

"What, Marsden?" I heard her call out. I presumed a student had stuck their hand up.

"Are you two bonking?"

By the general commotion and the shrieks that ensued, I assumed Marsden's question had caused the whole class to fall about laughing.

48

The Stepford Wives

For the last fifteen years, I had no job, no career and pretty much no hope. Now, The Hooded Claw and his mad-cap crew had given me my old career back, and I should be focusing hard on making a success of it. Instead, here I was once again, as I was on Monday, utterly incapable of concentrating. Yes, I had the rather unusual knowledge that some nutter intended to kill my wife tomorrow night and, of course, that would be distracting for even the most focused workaholic among us.

However, Jemma's impending strangulation and my task to stop it weren't the distraction. Jayne Hart had sent my brain off running at a tangent to where it should be focused. She had pawed at me and grabbed my arm, hauling me back when I attempted to escape. The gorgeous Jayne Hart had gone on her tiptoes to kiss me. Could I dare to think she felt the same?

'She's always had a thing about you, Frank Stone. Don't get any ideas because she can't have you.'

That's what Jemma had said about Jayne nearly two weeks ago, just before inviting me to scrub her back in the bath, just prior to, well, you know, I don't need to spell it out. Was, or is, Jemma, right? Does Jayne have a thing about me? Jemma is one hundred per cent wrong regarding the last part of that statement because, as far as I was concerned, Jayne could have me whenever and wherever she wanted. I just had to pray and hope she did.

Working with Alison, it was a requirement to be able to lip-read, as that seemed to be her preferred way of communicating when in a tight spot. That acquired skill had left me in no doubt that Jayne had mouthed "Call me," and I wouldn't need asking twice. The only tricky bit was when. Jemma was back tonight, and we had a lot to discuss. Friday, well, that day was kinda full of planned activities, so I would just have to squeeze Jayne in somewhere.

Jemma had arrived home before me, so I assumed House business had finished early for the week. As usual, she would be conducting surgery on Friday in Fairfield. Jemma had prepared supper, and we ate in silence. I didn't ask how her week had been, not wishing to hear the details, and fortunately, she didn't offer any up. I could imagine it for myself, and quite frankly that was enough. As we cleared away the table, Jemma suggested we talk through what we were going to do – this was my moment to approach the baby subject.

"Frank, I've decided to stay in London all week from now. I think it's best we have space. We'll just have to get through the weekends until we've sold the house. D'you want to get an estate agent sorted? Or if not, I can organise it tomorrow."

"No, I'll do it. When are we going to go public with this?"

"I'm going to see Mum and Dad on Saturday. Then I will inform the Local Association because I think I'd better be open and honest with them."

"Right. So, you and Rupert will be official then?"

"Oh, hell no. I don't mean that honest!"

"I thought there was only one type of honest? Or is that the politician in you? Honesty to a point!"

"Don't get silly, Frank. These are sensitive situations. I have my maiden speech to worry about, and Roops and I want to manage our announcement carefully. We can't just blurt it out. This could damage reputations. It's important we get this right."

"Oh, yes, of course. I wouldn't want to damage your reputation! Although I think you're doing a cracking job of that yourself."

"Don't rile me, Frank. I'm not in the mood. I have too many important things to think about, and you chucking in lewd remarks isn't helpful!" Jemma blasted back at me as she turned and stomped out of the kitchen.

"Important things like the fact you're pregnant?"

That stopped her in her tracks. Jemma slowly turned, her mouth gaping open in shock. "What?"

"You're pregnant, aren't you?"

Her silence as she glanced at the floor, losing eye contact, suggested I was right. *Bollocks.*

Now I had a super tough challenge ahead of me. After what seemed an age, Jemma sank into a kitchen chair and peered up at me as I leaned against the kitchen sink.

"Why did you say that?"

"Just a hunch," I shrugged.

"I'm not sure. But yes, I think I might be. No, that's not true. I am definitely."

"Oh, how can you be so sure?"

"I did one of those new home tests. They're very accurate." Well, that negated the need to crack out the small chemistry lab I bought today. Disappointingly, I thought securing a refund was unlikely.

"Whose is it?"

"I don't know." For the first time since we had had that conversation on Monday evening, she appeared to show some modicum of contrition. At last, Jemma had recognised that her casual attitude to our marriage was embarrassing.

"Me? Tobias? Rupert? Or could it be someone else?"

"I'm not some slut! How *dare* you suggest that!" she fired back, the momentary flicker of her embarrassment had evaporated. Well, that was okay then, only the three of us could be the father, nothing slutty in that.

"It could be yours, or it could be Tobias's."

"Not Rupert?"

"No." At least that had narrowed the field.

"What are we going to do about it, then?"

"At the moment, I don't know. It doesn't change us, though. If it is yours, I can't stay with you, Frank. You know that?"

"Yes, I do. Look, Jemma, we have reached the end … we both know that. But hell, this does somewhat complicate things, don't you think? I mean, what if Tobias *is* the father … what then? Are you going to tell Clare? Jesus, Jemma, this is one wholly shit storm of a mess."

404

Jemma bowed her head. She was half my age, and if I had children, I imagined this would be how it played out when scolding my daughter for the calamitous situation she'd got herself into.

I could never have imagined this situation that day I awoke two weeks ago. This new Jemma had shattered my long-held memory of my lost wife. The knowledge of what my wife was actually like had ruined thirty-six years of sweet memories. However, I now had this fantastic opportunity to live my life again.

The super tricky bit now was what to do next. My assassin friend hadn't stipulated a timescale to deal with this issue. However, if Jemma did decide to terminate the pregnancy, there was a time limit on that. Past that point, the timeline would not follow the path the CYA required, and I would have a date with a blender.

"We never really discussed it, did we? I'd just buried my head in the sand and didn't expect to get pregnant. We haven't been using protection since we got married ... that's two years, Frank. Over those two years, we have been at it quite a lot. It would suggest that there's a problem—"

"Quite normal for newlyweds, don't you think?" I interrupted.

"Yes, I know. But hasn't it crossed your mind? Why haven't I fallen before?"

"No idea." I shrugged. Although my assassin friend had furnished me with information that suggested I knew the reason.

"I assumed maybe there was some issue with me, but now I think it might be you. Two years and nothing ... one night with Tobias, and I'm pregnant. So I think the timing is correct."

"Oh, well, super Tobias. Batsman of the year, and now he can claim the top sperm-shooter prize as well. Perhaps we could engrave that in gold letters up at the Cricket Club." I held my hands aloft as if imagining the honours board. "Tobias Heaton Top Batsman, and Sperm Shooter 1979."

"Oh, Frank!"

"We need to get Tobias to wank in a few test tubes so he can re-inseminate the human race when we get taken over by man-eating Martians! Bloody hell, Jemma, when you two bunked up, didn't it occur to you both what the end result could be? You both did biology at school, didn't you?"

"We weren't thinking about that at the time."

"No, I bet you weren't! While you were playing hide-the-sausage with your best friend's husband, I guess that slipped your mind."

"Don't be so crude."

"Alright, let's just say whilst you were *fucking him* ... is that better?"

"Frank!"

Grabbing my cigarettes, I lit up and blew a plume of smoke towards the ceiling. "Look, I think you're right. Sad as it is, I think the problem could be me. So, you're pregnant, and we can reasonably assume you're carrying Tobias's child. So, what the hell are you going to do? Does Rupert The Bear know? That could make your love nest a little crowded?"

"No, he doesn't know. And don't call him that. Only you and I know and, for the moment, that's how it stays."

"What does super-sperm-boy want?"

Jemma tutted at my description of Tobias, but I imagined she realised she was in no position to take the high ground.

"He wants sex. Tobias said Clare lifts her nightie once a week on Saturday night just to fulfil her contract of being a wife. He said it's like having sex with one of the Stepford Wives ... almost mechanical."

"Oh, too much detail."

"It's a mess. You're right."

"Termination?" Although this was required for my future to continue, I felt awful saying it. Who was I to suggest taking another life so that I could go on living? For the first time in two weeks, I wished Captain Kirk had left me in my sleeping bag snuggled down under my cardboard duvet. Although life was pretty awful then, it was a lot less complicated.

Tears had filled her eyes. I know most men in this situation would probably have stormed out, as knowing your wife is carrying another man's child and leaving you for a different man altogether would be far too much to handle. However, this was different. I was old Frank as well as young Frank, and seeing Jemma crying in front of me suggested I should comfort her. So, for the second time this week, I knelt and held her whilst she sobbed.

I pulled away when she'd calmed down. "You're such a good man, Frank. I'm so sorry," she blurted out between her tears.

Was I? I'd kissed her friend, so not that good. However, that information was absolutely on a need-to-know basis.

"I've thought about termination, but I just don't know if I have it in me to do it. Although it's my body, I don't know if that would be the right ... or even a moral thing to do."

Well, I'll give Jemma her due. She had no morals, but at least she was putting the child before herself. That, I guessed, was quite unusual.

I seemed to be living in some strange alternate universe as I initially craved everything I'd lost the first time and was now desperately wanting something different. However, if she kept the baby, I would just have to accept the consequences. I'd had my life and, although losing Jemma was the catalyst to it turning to shite, I'd had my go. This baby deserved their chance, and I would just have to accept that. If Red-Jag-Man stuck a nine-millimetre slug in my brain – so be it.

49

The Enigma Code

The 28th of September had arrived. When I landed two weeks ago, I didn't expect to be where I am now. A marriage break-up, my soon to be ex-wife pregnant, now fallen for one of her best friends, and an assassin hot on my tail and ready to despatch me if I failed to comply with the CYA demands.

For sure, the focus today was to save two lives, my wife and her baby. I say hers because although the CYA could be lying about my less than potent sperm count, it added up that I was most likely not the father.

I perused my list whilst sitting at my desk after Paul and I had engaged in a less than civil conversation about the car park groundworks. I'd taken on Alison's point regarding Paul and me conversing. Otherwise, I'd be leaving our dependable receptionist to keep Paul and me from killing each other. If successful, that could afford her the Nobel Peace Prize. Although she was good at her job, that responsibility was probably a step too far.

Rather than using her as a go-between and trying to mediate two warring factions, Paul and I dropped the wall of silence and communicated by phone, which was ridiculous as we sat less than twenty feet away. Pity texting wasn't available because then we could have conversed without speaking at all.

My list didn't help the plans for tonight. Assassin Sinclair had conducted some surveillance and had Tobias, Paul, and Miles at the top of his list; fair enough, he was probably right. However, Dave and I would have to have our wits about us.

Jemma had a planned evening with Clare in town, the exact same plan the first time around. Although circumstances had changed, she said she wasn't going to cancel and would have dinner as planned. I felt sorry for Clare – she had no idea who her best friend really was.

Obviously, this time around, Paul and I weren't planning an evening drinking session. That would be like Mrs Thatcher and the Argentine Junta enjoying afternoon tea at Chequers – it wasn't going to happen.

I didn't mention to Jemma that I planned to meet up with Dave; she didn't ask where I was going and probably didn't care. Tonight, we weren't meeting at the White Bull or Slaughtered Lamb that I would now always call it. No, tonight's operation would start in the Whitehouse Tavern, conveniently situated on the corner of the street near the restaurant where Jemma was meeting Clare. After that, we planned to wing it.

As soon as lunchtime arrived, I called Eaton City of Fairfield School. Miss Colman, or whatever her name is, answered in an extremely curt manner, giving me the third degree about my visit yesterday. There were apparently some shamefully unsavoury rumours, as she put it, circulating about Miss Hart and a visitor she'd received that day. Miss Colman informed me that she wasn't inclined to place my call to the staff room and I'd better think carefully about how I was conducting myself.

Although bluffing, I advised her I had it on good authority that she was known to be spreading the rumours and, if she refused my request, I would complain to the school's headmaster.

My bluff worked, and she begrudgingly patched the call through, although I seemed to have been placed on hold forever. Eventually, Miss Colman, in a continued unfriendly manner, stated my call had been connected and advised me to go ahead.

"Jayne?"

"Frank?"

"Jayne, is this line secure?" Now convinced the school secretary would be listening in. If Alison could do it, I was damn sure she could.

"What d'you mean?"

"Could someone at the school switchboard hear this conversation?"

"Oh, I see. Yes, I think they could."

"Right. Jayne …"

'Shit, what do I say now?'

'Tell her you've fallen in love with her, and you're desperate to be with her; that will cover it!'

"Oh, great idea!"

"Frank?"

"Sorry, I was talking to myself." I had to get a grip. I was sure Miss Colman would be furiously making notes like a decoder in Bletchley Park, ready to rip off the decoded message and announce to the world that she'd cracked the Enigma Code – now fully armed to spread some juicy gossip.

"Oh, that's the first sign of madness, they say," she giggled.

"Jayne, I hope I've not misread this. But—"

"You haven't misread me, Frank." My heart stuttered, causing me to take a deep breath to avoid light-headedness.

"Frank?"

"I'm here. I'm here. It's difficult to talk and say what I really want to."

"Call me at home later. I will be back by half five. You will call, won't you?"

"Yes, I will."

"I'd better go ... talk later. Bye, Frank."

"Oh, Jayne, what's your number?"

The line disconnected.

Did the school secretary cut the line? Hmmm. Now to find her number, presumably listed under her mother's name, in that hefty blue book.

Hart had thirty-eight listings in Fairfield – oh, just great!

The other predicament was I had no idea where she lived or her mother's initial. How could it be so difficult?

I tried dialling Directory Enquiries. Although the young lady was very polite, I guess asking for a phone number without the address and initial was a bit dumb. However, as luck would have it, the operator said she knew a Mrs E Hart who had a daughter called Jayne. She said her mother regularly went to bingo with Mrs Hart on a Tuesday evening, and the number was duly supplied. I did chuckle to myself as I believe any attempt at that kind of conversation in 2015 would have been long dead and buried along with the number 192.

Chucking in the towel early, I scooted off home. This very evening, the first time around, was crystal clear in my mind. Jemma had plated up my evening meal and left it on a low heat in the oven. As expected, when I arrived home this time, the oven was cold.

Jemma and I hardly exchanged words apart from "Excuse me" as we crossed on the stairs, which I believe is supposed to be unlucky. Whether that was for me, her, or both, the next few hours would decide.

This time, Jemma didn't ask for a lift to the restaurant, and I watched her leave the house as a taxi pulled up and beeped his horn. That taxi didn't arrive the first time, as I'd dropped her into town. Presumably, Jemma would this time, as she had last time, later this evening ask the restaurant manager to call for a taxi. Once again, would they fail to keep that booking? Well, in a few hours, I would find out. When Clare and Jemma leave the restaurant, Dave and I would be in full private investigator mode whilst strategically positioned in the pub opposite.

Fortunately, the operator at 192 had the right house. The E Hart her mother played bingo with on a Tuesday evening was Jayne's mother. So, at last, Jayne and I were able to talk, although I did hear her ask her mother to close the lounge door for some privacy.

Jayne had lots of questions, and although I couldn't tell her I had time-travelled on a giant Ferris wheel built in the latter part of the century, I was honest about my feelings, which, rather wonderfully, Jayne reciprocated. All I required was time and, as long as the CYA assassins left me alone, I had plenty of that ahead of me.

Younger, impetuous Frank couldn't have waited a nanosecond to see her, but older Frank had learnt the art of patience. Street living teaches you many skills – one is the ability to wait. Don't get me wrong, I was desperate to see her. However, tonight I was kinda busy and, once I'd completed my mission, I hoped I had at least another thirty-six years to love her. Of course, I hadn't solved the baby issue. But hey, one thing at a time – patience!

50

Mad Max

Dave picked me up at the agreed time. His mood could only be described as dour, which worsened as he relayed the conversation he'd had with Babs earlier – clearly the cause of his extremely pissed off state.

Apparently, Babs had decided enough was enough and was now considering divorce. However, that wasn't all of it. She'd stated that due to his unacceptable behaviour, she would be seeking a court order that removed his rights to have any contact with his daughter. This was a monumental shift in Dave's timeline because previously, after copious amounts of grovelling and promises he would never grope any more cash office clerks, Babs had relented and they did get back together. Something this time had steeled Babs's resolve, and I wondered if that was a small change caused by old Frank's arrival. I felt a bit shitty. But in the end, Dave would have to face the consequences of his actions.

Dennis the Menace was out when we pulled away from my house, and I wondered where he was. Probably organising support for a picket line at some factory or a planning meeting for the up-and-coming revolution he kept banging on about.

Although Red-Jag-Man had provided his top three, I had to keep an open mind. I asked Dave to take a detour past Tobias's house. As we slowly cruised down his street, I spotted his Lotus on the drive. Tobias-Super-Sperm-Heaton was home – for the moment. As for Miles-Thigh-Crusher-Rusher, well, I didn't know where he lived. However, as he was top of Sinclair's list, I hoped he had tabs on him.

Settled into a window seat of the Whitehouse Tavern, I sent Dave on a reconnaissance mission to casually walk past the restaurant and check the girls were there. Then, safe in the knowledge that Jemma was where she should be, we settled down with our orange juices to wait.

Dave was a bit miffed that I wouldn't allow him to have a pint as he said he fancied getting wasted, but I needed him coherent as my designated driver. He also suspected Jemma wouldn't be seeing her lover tonight as she was out with Clare, but I just asked him to humour me.

We lacked conversation as he sulked, presumably thinking about his soon-to-be lost family. Considering what he was going through, I was grateful for his support. As he pointed out, that was what friends were for, unlike my other close friend, Tobias, who obviously thought adding my wife to his harem was acceptable.

Keeping Dave in the dark about recent events was key to tonight's operation. I had to have him firmly believing I suspected Tobias to be having a fling with Jemma. Judging by his suggestion on what we should do to him, he would be ready to castrate the man if he knew the truth.

After an hour or so, Dave returned to the bar to purchase another round of orange juices whilst I continued to gawp out of the window across to the restaurant. As Dave fought his way to the bar, out of the corner of my eye, I spotted a man slip into Dave's now vacant seat.

My newly acquired assassin friend grinned.

"Evening, Frank."

Shocked to see him, I just gawped.

"I'm not going to get in your way. However, sitting alone at the end of the bar, next to the cigarette machine, is your man."

I shifted to turn and look.

"Don't turn around. Blimey, you're not very good at this, are you?"

"Who is it?"

"Fairfield's most wanted. Well, he will be in about an hour or so if you fail. Miles Rusher." After tapping the side of his nose, Sinclair pointed at me. "I've been doing this kind of work most of my life, Frank. Usually in combat gear crawling through some shit, but mark my words, my friend, that's your man. He's had a few drinks, and the landlord has already told him he'll have to leave if he won't stop spouting his political views. He's agitated and looking for a fight. I'll be honest with you, I'm half tempted to stick my fist down his throat. He's a right tosser who needs a good pasting."

"Right, err … what now, then?"

"That's down to you, Frank. I'm just laying out the path for you." He slammed the palms of his hands on the table, then rose out of Dave's seat and disappeared into the crowd.

"Bloody barmaid is so slow. How long can it take to get two drinks?" announced Dave, as he slid into his seat, unaware the pad had been kept warm by Sinclair.

"What's that?"

"Just a half. I can't drink orange juice all night. Anyway, I think this is all a bloody waste of time. By the time she leaves that restaurant, she won't have long with lover-boy before getting home. At best, she'll only have a quick kiss and fumble in his car."

"Look, Dave, I just have a hunch she's going to meet someone tonight. She said she might be late and said not to wait up," I lied, trying to paint a picture that Dave could interpret.

"Alright, mate. There's nothing I'd like better than to catch her out, but I'm having a pint in a minute. Hey, look, as Babs is going to give me my marching orders and Jemma is about to be caught with her knickers down, we could start going on the pull together. Be just like the old days." He grinned and slugged down his half a pint in one go, wiping his mouth and hopping up to get to the bar again. I didn't move, keeping my eyes firmly riveted on that restaurant door.

Five pints later for Dave and two more orange juices for me, I was faced with one hell of a dilemma. The barmaid called last orders, and across the road the restaurant staff were ushering out guests. Clare stepped out alone, rummaged through her handbag, and then lit a cigarette.

Five-pint Dave was now fully loosened up. How the hell he was going to drive, I had no idea. However, the immediate problem I faced was Fairfield's most wanted. Miles Rusher had shifted from the top of his barstool and appeared ready to leave. He had to be my prime suspect – didn't he? Miles had a motive the first time, and now that motive still existed. I presumed my treacherous friend, Tobias, had stayed in for the evening. Well, his car was so distinctive and we hadn't spotted him driving around town, certainly nowhere near the restaurant. Paul, well yes, he had motive this time, although Jemma was quite open about her dislike of the man, he didn't have sufficient reason to kill the first time. So, Miles Rusher had to be my man.

Jemma still hadn't left the restaurant, leaving Clare to lean up against the window whilst enjoying her cigarette. Considering that all the facts pointed to Miles as the perpetrator, I had to keep track of him and somehow simultaneously not let Jemma out of my sight. So, faced with the dilemma of which one to follow and fully aware my PI skills were somewhat lacking, I decided that five-pint Dave could keep an eye on Jemma for the moment. I needed to see where the Thigh-Crusher was off to.

After providing clear instructions to five-pint Dave, I nipped out of the pub and followed Miles whilst trying to think how Jim Rockford would tail his man without being spotted.

Although not staggering, but with a couple of misplaced steps off and up kerbs, I could see Miles had had a few. Evidently, he would be unable to walk in a straight line if the police were to use that test to determine how inebriated one might be. Although, based on the fact that not once did Miles glance at any road signs, he appeared to know where he was heading. I detected that Miles was muttering to himself as he weaved his way through the streets, and I believed he was far too pissed to notice I was tailing him.

Six street junctions away from the Whitehouse Tavern, I became concerned. Miles was walking due south. In a few minutes, Jemma would be walking due north. Was Miles about to find his car and then drive back north? Why would he park his car so far away from the pub? A couple of hours ago,

Sinclair had stated Miles had had a few drinks and, now assessing his ability to walk in a straight line, I deduced he'd consumed considerably more than a few. Even if he found his car, he was surely too pissed to drive.

A minute later, I sprinted back to the pub – I'd fucked up. Miles had approached the door of one of the posh townhouses on the southern end of town. After fumbling for his keys and a few misplaced stabs at the lock to his front door, Miles hit the bullseye.

He'd successfully inserted the key into the lock after playing his own game of *The Golden Shot*. "Left a bit, right a bit," I heard him mutter before giving himself a little cheer as he fell in over the threshold of his home – Miles was not my man.

As I sprinted back onto Whitehouse Street, the last few punters were leaving the pub. Leaning against the window and cupping my hands, I scanned the bar. A couple of blokes were chatting to the landlord as he placed bar towels over the pumps. However, there was no sign of Dave, so I assumed he must have left and followed Jemma as instructed. The restaurant lights were off; no one was standing outside. Had Jemma left with Clare? Had a taxi pulled up and collected her? Had she walked?

Sprinting to the end of the street and glancing around the corner, Dave's car was not where we'd parked. Well, at least he was tracking her; that was something. Hurtling up to the High Street, I prayed I'd make it in time to see Jemma in that telephone box. Christ, if she walked, I hoped she was now making that call to the taxi company and, in her self-important way, was telling them exactly what she thought. Although that was a side of her since returning to 1979 I didn't like, I just hoped she was having a good long rant which would keep her in that phone box as long as possible.

By the time I reached the High Street, Dave would hopefully be tailing her as long as he hadn't had a crash or got himself nicked for drunk driving. Then, with a bit of luck, we'd be back on track with our loosely planned operation.

As I scooted around the corner and turned onto the High Street, I placed my hands on my knees to catch my breath. Two months ago, I couldn't have run one yard. Now, although gasping for air, I'd managed to sprint half a mile – okay, not in the Usain Bolt category – but pretty impressive, I thought.

However, what I saw wasn't good. The phone box, which was well documented to be the one Jemma had made that call, stood empty. Dave's car wasn't on the High Street or anywhere to be seen.

"Bloody hell, Dave. You'd better have your bloody wits about you and have her in your sights," I muttered.

Believing Jemma couldn't have got far, I started sprinting up the hill. Whilst panting my way up the incline, I silently prayed, to a God I didn't believe in, that either I would catch up with her or she'd actually managed to get that taxi this time. Perhaps Clare had given her a lift home – therefore, I had nothing to worry about.

As I reached the top of the hill near the main fork in the road, that familiar red Jag pulled up with a screech of tyres.

"Frank! Frank, get in," my soon to be killer screamed out, as he leant across and flung open the passenger door.

Without hesitation, I leapt into the seat and into the car of the man who I felt certain very soon was planning to kill me. I was fully aware that if I failed to save Jemma this time, I would be dead within the hour and probably in a shallow grave beside her in Fairfield Woods.

As we shot around the corner into Queens Road, his driving was more akin to Mad Max than Inspector Morse. The tyres screeched, and for a brief moment I was sure two of the four wheels left contact with the road surface.

I wondered what the local police would make of finding two bodies buried in the woods. Jemma strangled and me with a single professional gunshot wound to the head. Would they then go down the route of investigating a professional hit on an MP and her husband – the only positive this time, I wouldn't be the prime suspect for her murder.

51

2015

Penelope Pitstop

2:14 a.m.

Hartland entered his login details.

A fully prepared Sinclair travelled at 2:00 a.m. after Penelope and her well-drilled team expertly choreographed his departure. Although Sinclair was now a man in his seventies, Hartland believed Sinclair's military training and Penelope's attentions had kept him fit. Of course, there were always potential complications with a man of his senior years, but Hartland reckoned he would make the journey with the first-class preparation his team always delivered.

In one minute from now, he would discover success or failure.

The decision to send Sinclair, or someone like him, was not unusual on nights like these. However, that was always to tidy up an operation that had gone south, not to add another layer of change. Those clean-up operations, although always disappointing, were sometimes necessary. The Organisation knew and accepted a certain percentage of operations would fail, and it was essential to clean away any mess caused.

Reporting to the Board in the morning that a clean-up representative had travelled would always be accepted. As long as his report was comprehensive, he wouldn't feel any heat. At that point, it would be just a matter of identifying another *Correction Agent,* and the process would start again.

Tonight, if Sinclair failed or Frank failed, it would be one hell of a mess. Moreover, the consequences of reporting to the Board that a second traveller was dispatched and subsequently failed would put him under significant pressure.

Penelope had delivered impressive improvements to the Travel and Preparation Team's performance. Hartland felt nothing but pride and deemed himself fully vindicated that he'd supported her appointment, which had involved sticking his neck out to vouch for her. However, as he glared at the time clock on his monitor, he was acutely aware if this second reset failed, his protégé, Penelope-Pitstop-Blatchford, would make her move and attempt to oust him from his position.

She was ambitious, and Lady Maud Huston-Smythe would like nothing better than to grab an opportunity to replace him.

During the last hour, his team had pulled out all the stops to prepare Sinclair to be ready to travel. Now they were back in their offices, as they always were, waiting for the news. He took another sip of his whisky, lit up a cigarette, and waited.

2:15 a.m.

Hartland punched in his password. The BBC news feed loaded.

He hit refresh.

Snatching up his phone, Hartland thumped out the three-digit extension number.

Morehouse answered immediately. "I'm on my way, sir."

52

1979

Red Mist

Although only just past eleven, the road was reasonably quiet. A few cars passed Jemma, but Fairfield was a sleepy town and didn't offer much in the way of nightlife. As she stepped to cross a side road, a car pulled up. The driver wound down the window, causing Jemma to hop back in surprise.

"Oh, it's you! You made me jump. What you doing here?"

"Well, I could ask you the same thing. Why are you walking at this time of night?" asked Dave.

"Well, I had a taxi booked, but apparently, the driver had a flat tyre. They said they didn't have another car available; would you believe? I called Frank, but he didn't answer."

"Well, I'm your knight in shining armour. Hop in; I'll drop you home."

"Err … okay, thanks." Although she thought it would be a bit awkward because the last time they'd spoken, the conversation had developed into a heated argument. However, now relieved that she didn't have to walk the rest of the way home, Jemma nipped around to the passenger side and hopped in the car.

"How's Babs?"

"Don't ask."

"Well, you should have thought about that before you grabbed that girl's chest! You really are a bit of a loser, Dave, and you're not going to get anyone as good as Babs. You know that, don't you?"

Dave didn't answer. He would just get this cow home and then try to find Frank. As he'd told Frank, she obviously wasn't meeting anyone else tonight. After he tracked her as she marched up the High Street, he thought it best to offer her a lift and then call it a night. And now the bloody bitch, instead of thanking him for a lift, was telling him what a bloody loser he was! Jesus, thank God Frank had come to his senses about this woman.

"I spoke to Babs a week ago and told her to dump you. She could do better than you, and why she wanted to be with some loser shopkeeper, God knows! If I were you, I'd try to better yourself. Look at me and what I've achieved. You're not going to get anywhere stacking tins of beans. When Babs finally gives you the boot, you should take stock ... perhaps get a degree like Frank. Of course, you'll have to support Babs with maintenance pay, but you're not going to get anywhere in life as you are."

Dave could feel his blood boiling. Who the hell did she think she was? Just because she was the ruddy MP, she thought she was *it*! Dave gripped the steering wheel and stuck his foot to the floor, now concerned that he'd probably kill her if he didn't get her out of the car soon.

"Oh, you idiot, you missed my turning. Come on, Dave, concentrate. I'd have been better off walking. You really are hopeless. Look, turn around in the picnic area up ahead. I tell you what, don't become a taxi driver as you'll be shit at that as well!" she laughed.

"Christ, shut up, you bitch!"

Dave's anger had hit boiling point. Whilst running her bloody mouth off, she'd caused him to miss the bloody turning, and now he'd be stuck with her in the car for even longer. As he swung the car into the picnic area, he considered throwing the bitch out of the car and making her walk from there. That would teach her.

"How dare you! Don't you talk to me like that. I'm not one of your till girls you can talk down to, you stupid man. Come on, hurry up; I want to get home."

Dave negotiated the muddy roadway, now even more pissed off because his car would be splattered with mud.

"Of course, little Sarah will miss her dad. But in the end, there's no point having a father who's as useless as you. Look at my dad and the success he's made of his life. You could learn a thing or two from him."

Dave slammed on the brakes, no longer prepared to listen to her for a moment longer. Even though she was the local MP, and Frank had asked for his help, he intended to throw her out of the car. Flinging open his door, he stomped through the muddy ground around to the passenger side. As he yanked open the passenger door, he was half tempted to punch the stuck-up bitch. Although he'd never hit a woman and wasn't going to start now.

"Get out!"

"Don't be ridiculous. Drive me home, you idiot!"

"Get out!" screamed Dave.

Dave rarely lost his temper; the last time the red mist had descended was when one of the bakers at work received his verbal mauling because said baker burnt all the hot cross buns. Dave had yelled across the shop floor whilst the terrified baker shook, and a gaggle of frightened shoppers looked on. Now his rage had peaked at a few levels above burnt buns.

"Shut the bloody door and drive me home, you idiot!"

As Jemma dramatically folded her arms and refused to get out, once again, that red mist descended over Dave. He leaned into the car, grabbed her coat lapels, and hauled her out. The shock on Jemma's face was priceless, and he couldn't wait to throw the cow onto the muddy ground – that would teach her to run her mouth off.

The doorsill caught the back of her shoes, causing them to flip off. Jemma gasped more in shock than pain as her bare heels thumped onto the ground.

Although Dave had never liked Jemma, he'd tolerated her. Often, when he and Babs had met up with Frank and Jemma, they would both end up moaning about her on the journey home. Frank was his best mate, so under normal circumstances, he would never have said anything to Frank about their dislike of his wife.

He certainly wouldn't have considered strangling her. However, his hands released her coat lapels and, for some reason, ended up tightly wrapped around her throat.

Torrents of endorphins were released as Dave experienced the euphoric excitement at his ability to stop this bloody woman's verbal assault.

He couldn't stop grinning as she was clearly struggling to breathe.

53

General Lee

For a brief moment, as we sped into Fairfield Woods, I thought Sinclair would miss the turning to the picnic area. If we passed it and had to double back, those few vital lost seconds could cause us to be late, resulting in failure for my Save-Jemma-and-child operation. But of course, that's assuming time hadn't altered, and whoever had taken her to the woods to strangle her was still on course to complete the murderous deed.

As I opened my mouth to inform my soon-to-be killer we'd missed our turning, Sinclair performed a hand-brake turn and spun the car around into the picnic area. The front wheels thumped into a protruding rut of earth, momentarily causing the front wheels to leave the ground – Dukes of Hazzard style. Fortunately, his car wasn't the General Lee, so that negated the requirement to squirm through the open window to get out. Yanking the door lever, I flung it open before the Jag came to a halt.

Dave's car appeared abandoned, with both doors open. Sinclair and I simultaneously jumped out of the Jag. Instantly I spotted my best mate, who I'd trusted to help on the operation to save Jemma, as he bent over my wife whilst she lay on the ground. His hands appeared to be tightly around her neck as he shook her like a rag doll.

For some bizarre reason, five-pint-Dave appeared to be strangling my wife. But why?

When I'd lived my life before the introduction of The Hooded Claw and the large Ferris wheel that spun me back in time, it appeared my best mate *had* murdered and buried my wife.

Talk about a monumental misjudgement on my part. I never suspected anything when the following day he'd clearly feigned shock at the news of her disappearance. In fact, for months he acted as a close friend should, by consoling me and being there to help after such a tragic event. Dave was the one who had held me at the church as I struggled to compose myself at Jemma's funeral. He was the friend who'd given the reporters and camera crew a mouthful outside my house. In those early days and months after Jemma was taken away from me, he and Babs had been the ones to comfort and support me. All that time he played the supporting friend, even though he'd callously murdered her.

However, this time, on the re-run of that fateful evening, events were changing. As Sinclair and I dashed towards him, Dave let go of Jemma's neck and rolled on his back. Jemma scrambled away, clutching her throat, as I reached out and grabbed her. Our presence this time must have been the catalyst for Dave to come to his senses and stop strangling her. When this was over, Dave would go to prison for attempted murder – now, that *was* a significant change.

Jemma grappled at my jacket, holding onto me but unable to speak as she continued to gasp for air. Sinclair seemed to have disappeared.

"Jemma ... Jemma! You okay?" Bit of a stupid question, I know. However, it wasn't every day you arrive just in time to stop your wife from being strangled by your best mate, even if I had known for over thirty years that someone had strangled her this very night. Jemma violently coughed, then, still gripping my coat, glanced up with tears in her eyes. She nodded but said nothing.

I had achieved my mission, which The Hooded Claw had set me all those months ago. At the time, I never imagined this would be possible. However, I had time-travelled and Jemma, my once-dead, now-cheating wife, was alive.

I'd spend most of my adult life replaying this day over and over in my mind. What evil bastard had killed her? How would our lives have played out if she wasn't strangled? Why did someone want my wife dead? Now I knew there was no calculated reason, no conspiracy, just the drunken rage of my closest friend.

Miles-Thigh-Crusher-Rusher, Paul-The-Lech-Wilson, Brian-Lolly-Pop-Sucker-Grey and Tobias-Super-Sperm-Heaton were all innocent. Bill Parsons hadn't killed her for infiltrating the Council Housing Committee, and Lawson's Taxis hadn't set about a plan to kill the local MP for failing to take any interest in taxi licences. So, along with the rest of my extensive list of suspects, they were all innocent.

The perpetrator was Dave, who lay on his back on the muddy ground, presumably now wondering what the hell he'd done. Well, best mate or not, he was going to have to face the consequences. I just needed Sinclair to grab hold of Dave, and then we could call the police.

Unsurprisingly, Jemma still clung to me as she stared at her attacker. Now standing barefoot, with her toes squidged into the mud, she turned away from Dave, buried her head in my chest and sobbed. I glanced around to see where the hell Sinclair had disappeared to whilst Dave remained motionless as he lay on the muddy verge.

Apart from a couple of passing cars, the gentle breeze through the trees, and Jemma's rasping breaths, there were no other audible sounds. As they cruised past, those car drivers wouldn't be able to see the events as they unfolded in the picnic area because the thick bushes shielded us from their view. Sinclair was nowhere to be seen. Had he run off? Had he decided he shouldn't be here at this time? Perhaps he'd seen Jemma was alive and skedaddled?

"Sinclair?" I bellowed as I scanned around the unlit area. The headlights from the Jag illuminated Dave's car, projecting long shadows across the picnic area. As if about to be laid out for some satanic ritual, our shadows cast what appeared to be a black tablecloth that now cloaked two wooden picnic benches. A silhouetted man emerged from the tree line, stepped around the benches and casually sauntered towards us.

I'm no expert, but the silhouette appeared to be holding a handgun with a long barrel, which I presumed to be a silencer. Had Sinclair nipped into the trees for a quick pee and was now sauntering his way back? Hell of a moment to decide to relieve yourself, just as my wife was in the throes of being strangled. But I guess if you've gotta go, you've gotta go. Perhaps he had a prostate problem?

"Sinclair, what the hell are you doing?"

The headlights lit up his body, but his face remained blacked out, affording the advancing silhouette the appearance of a headless man. Was this the mythical Headless Horseman character? Or perhaps some evil headless monster from an episode of Scooby-Doo? Was this the time to utter *"Zoinks,"* Shaggy style?

The headless man stepped into view. He did actually have a head, which I think was a relief. However, although no longer headless, this did little to palliate the situation as he held a gun with a long-barrelled silencer. To further complicate matters, unless Sinclair had just undergone plastic surgery whilst having a quick slash in the woods, this was someone new.

"Evening Frank," casually stated the Headless Horseman, as if chatting to an old mate in the pub.

Jemma's grip on my jacket tightened, with her head still nestled on my chest. I'd never known her to be this quiet. But to be fair, this was not an everyday event. When your husband's best friend has just attempted to strangle you, it's probably a bit of a conversation stopper.

I glanced at Dave, who appeared not to have moved a muscle since letting go of Jemma. He lay motionless, as if sunbathing, stretched out on some sandy Spanish beach topping up his tan before hitting the clubs and bars to down copious amounts of beer and flaming sambucas.

The Headless Horseman raised his gun.

54

Boxing Day Hunt

With the car headlights illuminating his face, I thought he looked vaguely familiar – I had a good memory for faces. However, this thirty-something man holding a handgun with a silencer screwed into the barrel wasn't someone I could place.

Apart from Sinclair, I didn't know anyone else who owned a gun. Well, yes, I'd met Rupert-double-barrelled-name-toffee-nosed-wife-stealing-tosser, and he and his father owned a large cabinet full of shotguns, which they'd use when wandering around their estate blowing birds' and squirrels' brains out.

Rupert and his family still conducted fox hunting activities, and I recall how his father belligerently moaned that the ban on using packs of dogs had now spoilt their traditional Boxing Day hunt. Perhaps those packs of dogs could now be used to rip Rupert and his family apart? I'm sure the League Against Cruel Sports would approve. Anyway, apart from them, men with guns were not the usual company with whom I mingled.

The Headless Horseman, who actually had a head, but lacked a horse, held the gun at arm's length, pointing the barrel at my head. I presume, aiming for a clean shot symmetrically between my eyes. Although Jemma had treated me poorly, I felt she deserved to have a go at life, and certainly the child inside her did. I'd lived my life and royally fucked it up. So, fair enough, this was it – I accept death.

Before I hit the ground as the bullet travelled out the back of my head, would he then send the next slug into Jemma's brain? This time, September 28th 1979, seemed to be once again heading for a sad ending. Although with a significantly increased death toll as the bodies piled up.

The Headless Horseman lowered his gun and proceeded to unscrew the silencer.

"Frank, you look a little shocked," he chuckled, as he glanced up and grinned, then pocketed the silencer and holstered his gun under his jacket.

Now I recognised him. He appeared a lot younger, but his smile was distinctive. There were two pictures projected on the wall that day The Hooded Claw informed me that one of these lucky chaps would get the opportunity to relive their life if I cocked up. Sinclair's picture was projected on the left, and this guy was on the right.

My brain raced as I considered the possibilities. Sinclair travelled to affirm an action, namely to ensure Jemma terminated the baby. Was this guy here to clean up the whole mess? However, he hadn't killed me. Instead, he'd put his gun away and now stood smirking like I was the butt of some practical joke.

"Richard Collinson. We've never met, but you know who I am, I presume?"

Jemma's grip on my jacket hadn't released with the lowering of the gun, and we were now into three or four minutes of her silence. Apart from when she was dishing out the silent treatment post an argument or panting whilst she took control of bedroom antics, I don't think she'd ever stayed silent for this long.

"Where's Sinclair?"

Collinson nodded to the front of Dave's car. Peering over the open driver's door, I spotted Sinclair who appeared to be sunbathing like my mate, five-pint-Dave. Collinson seemed to have already started his mission – he was cleaning up. Presumably, Sinclair and Dave were now the owners of a nine-millimetre slug lodged in their brains, not sunbathing in the dead of night – but dead. Assassin Collinson, with his silenced pistol, had dispatched them. Dave hadn't let go of Jemma voluntarily – a bullet had travelled through his brain, thus stopping the instruction to his hands to squeeze the life out of her.

Gently raising Jemma's tear-stained face, I wiped my hand across her cheek, like a father wiping a child's face after they'd devoured an ice cream. Jemma didn't speak but just stared wide-eyed as she presumably tried to work out what had transpired as we stood on a chilly night in a picnic area in late September. I held my hand up to the light produced by the Jag's headlights. What I'd presumed was mud smeared across her face was, in fact, blood. Unless her vocal cords were shot out, blood must have splattered on her when Dave's brains were blown apart.

More change. Now I would need to console Babs and little Sarah when this all came to light and Dave was discovered dead – the tables had turned. However, I guess the issue of Jemma's pregnancy hadn't eased.

Maybe Sinclair cocked up and went on to reveal himself as a time-traveller? Perhaps Collinson had been sent to dispatch him? Had Sinclair gone on a ridiculous betting spree, laying down thousands of pounds on unexpected sporting events like Boris Becker winning Wimbledon in '85, Buster Douglas taking down Mike Tyson in 1990, or even Greece winning the European Championship in 2004?

Jemma had started to shake, although I assumed it wasn't caused by standing barefoot in cold mud and the rapidly dropping temperature. I was reasonably confident the shaking resulted from shock, which abated after the adrenalin rush of fighting for her life.

"I need to get her to the hospital. She needs checking out. Will you let us go?"

Collinson stepped towards us, reaching out to my arm. I flinched and tried to step backwards, but my feet seemed welded to the mud.

"Sorry, Frank, that's not going to happen."

55

2015

Shah of Persia

Hartland slammed the receiver down without answering Morehouse. Then, taking one last puff, he aggressively stubbed out the cigarette in the near-full ashtray causing spent butts to fling out across his desk. He took a deep breath in an attempt to calm himself whilst sweeping away the dislodged butts and ash off his desk with the back of his hand. The next few hours would be critical to stave off any attempts to remove him – he needed a clear mind.

He nudged his mouse. The screen came to life, displaying the picture and headline he'd dreaded would still be there when he logged in only a few minutes ago. As before, David Cameron's face filled the screen – he was still the UK's Prime Minister.

Sinclair had failed.

In a few hours, Hartland would be facing the Board. After they agreed to send Collinson for a clean-up operation, which would be ratified without question, he would face the biggest challenge to his leadership in his long, successful reign as Head of Operations at the CYA.

The next couple of hours would be about getting his ducks-in-a-row, ready to counter the inevitable fallout of the botched operation. Of course, there would need to be a fall guy – there always was. Although he felt slightly guilty, Morehouse was the obvious choice. He would have to offer up a big player for slaughter to get out of this mess. As he attempted to scramble out of this particular shell-hole, he knew blaming a few minions wouldn't cut it with the Board.

So, Hartland had a clear plan set in his mind. First, glean the required information from Morehouse, then set his old friend up for the fall.

Hartland caught sight of the digital clock on his screen before the screen saver kicked in when the CYA crest on the bright blue background would slowly start its floating motion from one side of the screen to the other.

2:25 a.m.

"Where the hell is he?" he hissed.

About to snatch up the phone receiver and bark down the phone to anyone who answered in Morehouse's office, his hand hovered across his desk as Morehouse's distinctive rap of knuckles tapped on the door. Hartland clicked the button under his desk to electronically release the catch.

Morehouse entered, followed by Pitstop and two guards.

"Just Morehouse!" he bellowed and dismissively waved at the guards. "You two are not required, so bugger off." Then, pointing at Pitstop, he narrowed his eyes, now concerned why his protégé was here. "I don't need you here, Penelope. You need to get Collinson ready to travel asap. I want this fuck-up resolved tonight."

Penelope stepped in front of Morehouse, who refused to make eye contact with Hartland, and the two guards stood by her side. Hartland knew the dynamics in the room had changed.

"Douglas, I'm sorry it's come to this. I want you to know it's not personal, and I will always be grateful for the support and mentoring you've given me." Her eyes bore into his; the strength and confidence battles had started. But unfortunately, Hartland sensed she had the upper hand, and he was losing. He slumped in his chair, the momentum causing the wheels to glide backwards and float away from his desk, just like his career that was floating away in front of him.

"I have authorisation from Lady Huston-Smythe to remove you from office. These two gentlemen will escort you. You know where you're going, presumably?"

Hartland managed a slight nod before glancing towards his old friend, who still didn't make eye contact. "Morehouse?"

Morehouse stared straight ahead with no reply forthcoming.

A few seconds ago, he'd planned to throw Morehouse under the bus to save his own skin. However, it appeared he'd been too slow to act. Penelope had outmanoeuvred him by playing her hand early, securing Keith's and probably many others' support.

Morehouse was an intelligent man and could have guessed he would be offered up as the sacrificial lamb if the operation went south. He'd taken steps to protect himself and rallied behind Penelope in the planned coup d'état.

Hartland was long enough in the tooth to know you always covered your back. Unfortunately, he was too slow to react and would now face the ultimate penalty for failure.

A previous mission to stop the Iranian revolution had failed. Now, just like the Shah of Persia, he faced his own revolution. However, Hartland was fully aware, unlike the ousted Shah, there would be no offer of the luxury of living in exile for him.

56

1979

The Mirror Cracked

Collinson's grip on my arm tightened as he sensed my effort to free myself. But in reality, I knew I couldn't escape. He had a gun, and I had a tearful, barefooted Jemma clinging to me. Even if, by some miracle, I could get us out of here and away from this man who had no qualms about dispatching people, the CYA would just keep on sending his type until the job was complete – I guess time-travel cock-ups had to be cleaned up.

The CYA would just file away the Frank Stone story in their vault, probably in the failed mission's section under S.

As the years rolled on, that file would occasionally be dusted off and reviewed for training sessions for new recruits on how to clear up failed operations, thus leaving no trace that the Association had messed with time. Unfortunately, Frank and Jemma Stone were expendable, and I had to accept there was pretty much bugger all I could do about it. I just hoped, for both our sakes, he would despatch us quickly and painlessly.

"Steady, Frank. Don't want you falling over in the mud as well," he chuckled, as he gripped my elbow and pulled me upright from where I was about to slip over, which would've resulted in Jemma and I diving for a mud bath.

I'll be honest – a roll around in the mud with my wife had always been a bit of a sexual fantasy of mine. Yes, I know, a bit weird, but we all have them, don't we? Whether it's mud, melted chocolate, or some slippery oil, those fantasies are there in the best of us. However, tonight, it had kinda lost its appeal.

"I'm afraid Jemma can't go to a hospital, as both of you need to be unconnected to this scene." He smiled almost lovingly, moving his demeanour from a menacing assassin to auditioning for the position of my new best pal. Well, my previous best mate was lying dead in the mud less than ten feet away. Also, I needed a new friend because Tobias had slipped from his perch after knobbing my wife. However, I didn't have Collinson in the running for that position, even if he was flashing a friendly smile.

"By the bins at the end of the layby is my grey Bedford van. The back doors are unlocked, so get yourselves inside. There's some water flasks and blankets, so make yourselves comfortable whilst I clear up this mess. We can then have a chat."

I gawped at him. The shaking Jemma, her eyes wide like a rabbit about to have its throat torn out by a fox, didn't move and just continued to grip my jacket as she held on for dear life.

"Frank, nothing bad is going to happen. The new Operations Director, Penelope Blatchford, has given me clear instructions to keep you both safe." He turned and pointed to

Dave and Sinclair, who obviously hadn't moved and continued their sunbathing pose. "That's why I'm here. Remove Sinclair because the instructions have changed. And as for him, Dave-the-chest-fondler," he chuckled. "Did you meet the young cash office girl? Right good looker ... could see how he got himself in that mess. Anyway, as for him, bloody good job I was here because you and Sinclair were bloody late! So, my friend, take the lass and get warmed up whilst I perform a quick clean-up operation."

~

Twenty minutes had passed whilst Jemma and I huddled in the back of the old grey Bedford van. Jemma had only broken her silence to say *"Yes, please"* when I'd offered her one of the water flasks. Apart from that, she kept her mute-like impression going whilst lying on a heap of blankets. As she occasionally glanced up at me, I could see her eyes were still wide with terror – at least the shaking had stopped.

The driver's door swung open, causing us both to jump in surprise. Collinson slung Jemma's shoes onto the passenger seat and climbed in. When shooting a look over the driver's seat, he took in the scene as I leaned against the van's side, and a blanket-covered Jemma lay with her head in my lap as I stroked her muddy hair.

"I'm renting a house out in one of the villages. It's fairly secluded with no neighbours. We'll go there, and we can have a chat about what happens next. But Frank ... lose the frightened look. Please don't worry. All your problems have gone away. You and me, my old friend, have our whole lives to re-live." He delivered that friendly grin, turned around and fired up the engine of the van.

As we passed the two cars, I spotted their doors were closed and headlights turned off. The bodies had disappeared.

Collinson's rented house had a white pebble-dashed exterior with a climbing rose around a wooden porch – not somewhere that fitted as an assassin's lair – but then I'd only met two assassins, so my knowledge of their potential domestic living arrangements was, at best, limited. The quaint cottage seemed more of a fit for Miss Marple than Collinson-the-Killer. A large ornate mirror hung above the fireplace with a plethora of cracks, presumably caused by the impact with a heavy object at some point. The cracked mirror delivered an odd-shaped reflection of us both as we stood in the parlour awaiting our fate.

It appeared Collinson-the-Killer had no intention of using his skills to dispose of us, instead offering the use of his bathroom so Jemma and I could freshen up. As I had two weeks ago, I scrubbed Jemma's back whilst she soaked in the bath. However, this time, there was no rolling around under the bed covers afterwards. Jemma relocated her vocal cords, although only to ask, *"Pass the soap,"* and *"Help me up."* At no point did she mention the events of the last few hours.

The marks on her throat where Dave's hands had squeezed were clearly visible. However, she confirmed she was okay and her voice, although shaky, was as normal as could be expected. While I helped Jemma bathe, Collinson sponged clean her clothes, ready for her to dress.

Just after 4:00 a.m., whilst nestled into the three ancient-looking armchairs in the quaint parlour, we sipped sweet tea in front of a roaring fire. Collinson had played mother and, once he'd refilled the teapot, we started our chat as promised.

"The night before I travelled in 2015, there was a coup d'état at the Association. Penelope Blatchford made her move and ousted Hartland. After Sinclair was sent and failed on his mission, I travelled the next night to sort this mess out. Pitstop accompanied me to pod thirteen, and we sat and chatted for some time before she left me to carry on with my journey back."

Jemma continued to sip her tea, allowing Collinson and me to conduct our chat. Of course, she must have thought we were both bat-shit nuts. I could almost see behind her now dried eyes her mind as it whirled around, probably wondering what the hell this strange man who'd saved her life was babbling on about.

"Probably like you, my friend, I was sceptical that I would actually time travel. I've gotta say when I awoke the next day, I knew nothing about what had happened until I met with some mates up at the pub later that evening. It was one hell of a shock, I can tell you. Did you have a similar experience?"

I glanced at Jemma, remembering when Jemma had licked my lips and stroked my best mate under the covers. I guess my *awakening* stole a march on his. "Yeah, mine was a hell of an experience."

He clocked my glance at Jemma. Although he didn't comment, he smirked and probably guessed how I re-awoke in 1979.

"Yeah, I can imagine," he paused and raised an eyebrow. "Hmmm. Right, Frank. It seems Penelope had a thing about you and wanted you to be safe. She provided clear instructions to ensure Jemma was saved again and to remove Sinclair from the picture. After I'd successfully completed my mission, she said I could live my life however I pleased as long as I followed the rules. So, here we are. Mission accomplished, and time to have another go," he chuckled, once again flashing his friendly smile.

"Sinclair said he travelled because, although I saved Jemma, the baby was an issue."

Jemma's head shot up. "What?"

Collinson held up the palm of his hand. "This is the complicated bit. Apparently, you did save her—"

"From who? Was it Dave who strangled her the first time? And this second time that I can't remember, was it Dave I saved her from then?"

"What the hell are you talking about? First time, second time? What the blue blazes are you both yacking on about? What Association? What are you rattling on about time-travel for?" Jemma aggressively pointed at Collinson, "And who the hell are you!" Jemma seemed to have rediscovered herself as she delivered her verbal tirade and swung her arm about animatedly, causing tea to slop from her cup onto the hearth rug.

"Hang on, Mrs Stone. Hang on." He turned to face me. "Frank, I don't pretend to know how this works. Whether we're in an alternate time or a parallel universe, or that the Association can operate outside the normal parameters that everyday folk understand, I just don't know. What I do know, wherever this version of 1979 is, we both have a chance to live the next thirty-five years again."

Jemma thumped her cup down on the ring-marked coffee table. "Can someone tell me what the *hell* is going on?"

"Mrs Stone. My name is Richard Collinson. In 2013, I was recruited by an Association that require certain skills.

The exact skills I've mastered throughout my army career and later running paid mercenary operations all over the world. At the age of seventy-three, I didn't really believe what they were offering. However, as I'd had my life and made many mistakes, I thought, well, hell, I'd go along with them as they paid well for keeping me on a retainer. What had I got to lose?"

"What the hell do you mean 2013?" exclaimed Jemma, although she'd calmed down a little. She shot me a quizzical look – I guess trying to understand where my head was with all this.

Ignoring her raised eyebrow, I pushed on questioning Collinson. However, it would've been easier if we'd had this conversation out of Jemma's earshot. Understandably, she kept pulling the conversation away on tangents.

"But the baby? And what happens now?"

"Frank, what's happening?"

I leant across and grabbed her hand, squeezing it but never taking my eyes off Collinson.

"What happens, or has to happen to the baby?"

"Seems Penelope has a soft spot for you, Frank. Her instruction is clear for you both to carry on with your lives. The operation seems to be a complete cock-up. As far as she was concerned, there would be no repercussions coming your way as long as you live by the rules. The time fault they were hoping you two would correct will be reviewed, and other operations put in place to solve that issue. This was Hartland's operation, and she wanted it buried as a failure along with him. Frank, you're both in the clear."

"Did she say anything else?"

"Yes, my friend, she did. I have a message to give to you both."

I held out my hand, expecting an envelope to be thrust upon it.

Collinson shook his head. "Nothing written. I had to memorise it and, at seventy-three, that wasn't as easy as it used to be!"

"Can you remember it?"

"Of course, I can, man. I'm a trained member of the Special Air Services!"

"And?" The anticipation was killing me.

Collinson stood and retrieved a notepad from behind a fifties-style clock on the mantlepiece. "I did note it down when I arrived though, as I thought I might forget," he chuckled.

"Frank?" enquired Jemma. I turned and shook my head, encouraging her to keep quiet.

"Right, let's see," he muttered, as he flipped over the pages. "Ah, yes, here we are. So, Frank, her message to you, my friend." He glanced up to ensure he had my attention before reading his notes. "Go with your gut and believe that your new business will be successful. Trust the love that Jayne will give you. She will make you so very happy and support you in the ventures you start in the next decade."

"Jayne! What about Jayne?" exclaimed Jemma, releasing her hand from my tight grip.

"I presume that's the little brunette you've been seeing?"

"What? Frank! What's this about Jayne?"

"Mrs Stone, I have a message for you as well." He glanced down at the notepad and flicked over another page. "Don't follow your career. Leave and go back to practising the law because you'll be far happier. Your husband, Rupert, will make a disastrous investment which will lead to a scandal in 1996. Whatever you do, make sure he doesn't make that investment."

Jemma's mouth gaped open, probably stunned at Rupert's name being uttered by this very odd stranger. The very man who seemed capable of killing two men, knew how to clean down the aftermath, and somehow knew about her future. Jemma had experienced one hell of an evening, and I fully expected this latest revelation about her future would have hit her like a dead weight. I took hold of her hand again – she didn't resist.

"I have a message for you both. Your son, Andrew, although brought up by Jemma and Rupert, will need the love of you both. Resist the temptation to fight about him. Both of you are to give him the love he craves, and you'll be pleasantly surprised how successful in life he becomes."

"Our son?"

Collinson glanced at his notepad again.

"Yep, that's what she said. Your son."

57

Sometime in the new Millennium

The Lady's Not For Turning

Jemma never quite believed my story, not that I was surprised – who the hell would? And come to think of it, as the years passed, I started to wonder if I'd ever lived in my cardboard tent along The Queen's Walk. But those doubts were short-lived because memories of rough sleeping never leave you.

Although she thought I'd lost my mind and felt it would be sensible for me to voluntarily commit myself to a secure unit, she did accept that Richard Collinson was an unexplained enigma. Any other explanation for the content of his notepad and how he came to be standing in the trees when Dave had attempted to strangle her just wasn't viable. However, I did manage to get her to keep her mouth shut about the events, and I can tell you, as far as Jemma Stone is concerned, that was no mean feat.

Andrew Charles Barrington-Scott, a heavy baby, was born in May 1980. Was he mine? Was he Tobias's? Well, I guess I'll never know. Red-Jag-Man had stated I was infertile. However, unless Jayne was having multiple affairs, he was wrong because we'd produced four children before Ronald Reagan had delivered his famous *Tear down this wall* speech in front of the Brandenburg Gate in 1989. All four of our daughters were blessed with golden-blonde hair, and it was abundantly clear to see who their father was.

In one sense, the latter stages of 1979 were difficult. But, notwithstanding those tricky times, those last few months were the best time of my second life – well, and first life, for that matter. Jemma and I split as we'd decided to before Dave donned his strangling hands. I have to give Rupert his due because Roops-double-barrelled-toffee-nose-man wanted Jemma and committed to bringing up another man's child.

Whether Jemma believed her message from Penelope Pitstop, I have no idea. However, she resigned her seat at the General Election in 1983 and took a few more years off to raise Andy and her two daughters, whom she and Rupert had produced. During the latter few years of the Millennium, Jemma returned to practising law. She started her own company and specialised in family law, which she was fully qualified to practise in, in more ways than one.

As suggested on that notepad, and whether he was mine or not, we stayed reasonably close for Andrew's sake. Rupert, who over the years didn't seem such an upper-class twit as I had him pegged for, was convinced Andy was mine. "Look at him, man, he's the spitting image!" he'd exclaimed one summer evening when the four of us sat on their offensively large lawn sipping Pimm's. I couldn't stand the stuff myself; a good pint of continental lager was more my thing, but hey, when in Rome, as they say.

By some miracle, Rupert had calmed Jemma as she seemed to have lost some, not all, of that rather nasty streak which I had discovered when travelling back for my second life. As expected, Jayne and Jemma's friendship cooled. However, the four of us remained close for Andy, who became part of our lives with weekend and holiday visits. He always said he was the luckiest boy alive because he had two Mums and two Dads, which was nice, I guess.

Miles Rusher was duly elected as an MP in 1983. Although there were many occasions when I predicted the future, in 1996 there was a moment when Jemma, at last, started to believe – if only a bit.

Just after she'd persuaded her husband not to invest in some dodgy Russian company, we met for lunch in London to discuss Andy's planned education after leaving his public school. See, there's another thing that would have caused my dear old dad to spin in his grave. A grandson of his at a public school – never! *"Over my dead body,"* I could hear him now. Well, sorry, Dad, you died too early for me to be able to listen to your protests. Anyway, at that lunch, Jemma had the copy of that week's News of the World. On many occasions, I'd relayed the story of what happens to Miles with a certain leggy blonde Russian and precisely what the headlines would be – but of course, she never believed it.

As I entered the restaurant, I spotted her as she waved the paper, appearing more excited than I could remember for years. We air-kissed each cheek, which would be another thing my poor old dad would have been aghast about.

"Have you seen it? Look, I can't believe it … it's brilliant! It couldn't have happened to a nicer bloke. I love it!"

The newspaper headline was, of course, as I said it would be—

Onatopp, the Thigh Crusher – From Rusher with Love

"I think you need to start believing the events of 1979."

Jemma's face darkened, clearly remembering Dave's hands. I had unintentionally dragged up those memories, and that was unfair – I apologised. You see, unlike Jemma, I cared about other people's feelings.

I could never inform Miles what would happen if he continued to get wrapped up in Onotopp's legs because I had to play by the rules the CYA had set out. However, as we sat and perused the headlines and the picture of a scantily clad Russian FSB agent, I felt sorry for Miles. Jemma literally revelled in his misery, proving, as she so often did, how lucky I was to have met and married Jayne.

So, what about those months from September 1979 to 1980? Those I described as the best time of my two lives. Well, fear not, they are not forgotten, and I'm coming to that in a minute – read on!

Jemma did heed my warning regarding her mother's health and actively pushed her mother to get tested. It had some success in prolonging her life, but the cancer was too strong and she sadly passed only six months after she had the first time.

I hung up my cricket bat that year. My out-for-a-duck score panned out to be my last innings. As Jemma and I'd split, time with her parents and Tobias as top batsman wasn't how I wanted to spend my Saturdays. Anyway, I'd had some tremendous cricketing experiences in my first life, so that was enough.

Cricket was like rolling around in the mud with Jemma in Fairfield Woods – it had kinda lost its appeal.

Tobias and Clare seemed to survive their mini-crisis and stayed together, producing their own brood of children. Tobias retreated from Jemma when she announced that she and Rupert were an item. Tobias, as predicted, was one of the first Britons to get his new brick-shaped mobile phone in the late '80s. He could often be spotted as he walked around Fairfield talking in a loud voice, Dom Joly style. *Tosser.*

The scandal in the Tory party about two MPs getting it together, with one pregnant by her ex-husband, hit the headlines. However, as with all these things, it soon became fish and chip paper. As far as the local Fairfield Association was concerned, it was no big deal because they had previous experience managing scandals. This one was significantly less embarrassing than the West-Indian-lolly-pop incident – I think they were grateful for that.

Anyway, unlike Miles, Jemma and Roops were saved by the Russians. The headlines soon focused on the Russian tank invasion of Afghanistan rather than who was shagging who in the House.

Stone Architects grew to become a successful international business. By the time Gazza cried in the World Cup semi-final against Germany, I employed eleven architects and over fifty support staff. I felt sorry for Gazza as he was too young to play in the World Cup Final of 1986 when England thrashed Germany, twenty years after winning at Wembley in my first life.

My first employee, Alison, left a year later to follow her dream with rugby-hunk, skipping off to eat Vegemite and throw boomerangs.

Jayne continued at what she loved, teaching at my old school. For Jayne, it was a vocation rather than a job.

We became close with her boss, big ears Jason, and his Jessica Rabbit look-a-like wife, Jenny. I had more in common with Jenny than Jason; I guess that was because she was more mine and Jayne's age group, whereas Jason was quite a bit older. However, I found him intriguing and, I have to say, I'd never met anyone with such perception and understanding of how the future would pan out. I guess he was just a well-informed and educated man. Well, there couldn't be any other reason, could there?

Paul Wilson started his own building company and, for a few years, became quite successful. However, we never stayed in touch, and I later learned he was forced into bankruptcy before the Millennium. There were rumours of a police investigation regarding a sexual assault, which was of no surprise.

Jemma and I had left Richard Collinson's cottage just after dawn. I never saw him again, and I can only imagine he went to fight wars in foreign parts – it seemed to be his thing.

The news story literally exploded on Sunday morning when two bodies were discovered in the boots of two cars parked up in the picnic area of Fairfield Woods. The pleasing thing was that retired bus driver, Harold Clarke, didn't discover the bodies, thus avoiding a heart attack, and Pip the dog enjoyed his company for many more years.

The investigation into the murder of an ex-soldier and a local man who worked as a local supermarket manager drifted on for years but was never solved. The initial reports suggested it was some love tryst that went wrong. Fairfield Woods picnic area was apparently well known for 'dogging', a term I'd heard of but never entirely understood. These reports cemented Babs's belief that her husband had been some sexual predator weirdo type and had progressed from fondling the chests of his staff to sordid sex in the woods. Babs remarried a few years later and, although we lost contact in later life, I was led to believe she was contented.

A week after the date Jemma should have died, she moved out and in with Rupert. As that news story broke, Jemma acquired the label of the scarlet woman. However, she survived an attempt to discredit her.

Jayne and I started slowly as we met for meals and drinks over the first few weeks. However, we both knew what we wanted. The school half-term provided my first experience of aircraft travel as we jetted off to Spain. The finer details of that holiday, well, let's just say that's private – use your imagination. We didn't see much of the beaches and, although holed up in a crowded resort, I don't think either of us noticed anyone else was there.

By the time Britain had reached record unemployment of two million, and Lech Wałęsa had organised his strikes in the Gdańsk shipyards, Jayne and I were married. Our eldest daughter entered this world before Mrs Thatcher delivered her *'The lady's not for turning'* speech, and British Leyland had produced that dreadful Mini Metro, which, incidentally, Jayne bought one despite my protest.

Sharon Stone, our eldest, married Denzel Warlow in 2005 after they met when he started working for me at the homeless charity I'd set up in 1990. I did try to protest about Sharon's name, not that I had any problem with it per se, but I didn't want our daughter to have those quip comments about her name when the American actress, come sex symbol, hit superstar status. I was wrong because our beautiful daughter loved her name and, although a lot younger than the actress, many said that she looked just like her – and I guess she did. Let's put it this way – young Denzel fell in love with her the first time they met. He'd sported that very same expression I had the day Jayne had laid her hand on my arm in the Murderer's Tavern after Tobias had stormed out.

Dennis Tranil, I believe, still lives in the same house. For as long as I can remember, he continued his lifelong fight for the communist ideology. As for Mr Hackett, our other neighbour, I have no idea what happened to him and his wife Joan, and quite frankly, who cares. Incidentally, I didn't know this for many years, but the head of the NHS who often appeared on TV was the same Dr Patel who had a short locum stint at Fairfield Surgery. So, Mr Hackett, if you're reading, I believe that's poetic justice at its best.

As you would imagine, I took great interest in the building of the London Eye. Jayne had said I was obsessed with it and couldn't understand my fascination. Jayne booked a pod for the whole family as a treat for my sixtieth birthday. With my obsession regarding the Wheel, the newspapers articles and books I'd read, it was reasonable for her to assume I would be delighted with my birthday surprise. I guess you wouldn't be surprised to hear she was a bit miffed and super shocked when I refused to ride. Instead, I elected to stand on Queen's Walk whilst my family enjoyed the thirty-minute excursion.

I had my reasons.

58

Sylvester Sneekly

The warm breeze which blew in off the sometimes-wicked North Sea gently cooled my face as the sun had reached its peak on the lazy Sunday afternoon. Eyes closed and relaxing on Cromer Pier whilst nestled into my old-fashioned finger-snapping deckchair, I soaked up the glorious weather and listened to the surrounding sounds.

As they played on the crowded beaches, the joyful shouts of many young children mingled with the sound of the dark water crashing and thumping the pier stanchions below me. We'd just finished lunch and wandered down to soak up the atmosphere and purchase ice creams.

Andrew Barrington-Scott, my eldest, followed his mother's and stepfather's footsteps. He became an MP at the 2010 general election. Over the years, I'd neglected my parents' graves. So, one Sunday morning, when revisiting, I cleaned the headstones and laid some fresh flowers. Facing the now presentable headstones, I apologised to my poor old dad because he had a grandson who was a Tory MP. I assumed he wasn't listening to me, but hey, after time-travelling, anything was possible. Anyway, I told him not to be too upset because

Andrew was a credit to him and would have made him immensely proud if he'd lived to meet him.

Denzel took control of the charity's day-to-day operations. Rachel, my daughter-in-law, married to my second eldest daughter, held the reins at Stone Architects, now a successful Limited Company with contracts worldwide. Jayne and I had retired to North Norfolk, and life couldn't have been much better. What was it that Harold Macmillan had said ... ah yes, *'You've never had it so good.'*

Our charity had successfully changed some Government policy, although it was a never-ending uphill struggle. A few years ago, a junior Government minister, after receiving advice from the PM, delivered a public apology to me personally on TV and in the newspapers. Although it was a difficult day for him, it did support in helping raise the charity's profile. When being interviewed regarding the charity and the Government support provided, he had referred to homelessness as a lifestyle choice. *Tosser.*

I was very public in my response, although I refrained from publicly calling him a tosser. His statement was the middle-class attitude that prevented Government policy from actually tackling the epidemic, which had now reached epic proportions as it also had in my first life. I did receive some criticism on how could I possibly know what it was like to be homeless, considering my successful business and posh houses. Well, that was a tough one because I knew better than most, but that information just had to stay buried in my mind.

My focus was to provide for my family and support Andy and the girls for the future. However, I anonymously donated half my wealth to small organisations that tirelessly supported the homeless. In contrast, my charity focused on changing policy and educating the general public.

Homelessness is like Climate Change. Until the masses wake up and smell the coffee, so to speak, nothing will change. I ensured Father Collins' mission received regular donations as he and his support staff were invaluable to me in my previous life. Although he didn't know who the anonymous donor was, I think he had a good idea and indicated as such when I'd met him a couple of years back.

Whilst dozing in my deckchair, I detected the presence of someone hovering close by.

"Afternoon, Frank. Mind if I join you?"

Now, that was a voice I will never forget. Thirty-six years had passed since I'd heard it, but my memories of his tone were very clear. With my lunch I'd enjoyed a couple of glasses of lightly chilled Pinot Grigio. So, as I slowly opened my eyes I was confident that my mind had misheard the voice.

"I must say you look in much better health than the last time I saw you. Don't think I can refer to you as Smelly Frank anymore," he chuckled. "Perhaps I should address you as Frank." He raised his eyebrows, but his hooded eyelids didn't move.

"You!"

"Yes, me, Sir Frank."

Douglas Hartland settled into the deckchair beside me and gazed out across the beach as he undid the buttons of his double-breasted suit and crossed his legs. "Rather lovely here, isn't it?"

My throat tightened, similar to how I imagined it had that night in Fairfield Woods when my best mate attempted to strangle her. Of course, no one was choking me at this point, but his very presence seemed to be constricting my airways.

"You're probably wondering why and how I'm here?" he chuckled, as he turned and faced me, shifting in his deckchair as his eyes bore into my skull. "The CYA is a complicated organisation and, as I said before, we operate outside the normal boundaries of time that ordinary folk couldn't comprehend. Anyway, thought I'd pop up and say hello."

"Why are you here?" I managed to croak out.

"Yes, very perceptive of you. Well, as it happens, we might need your assistance."

"You're joking? I'm not starting again!" I shot back at him, now extremely concerned at the thought of another trip on that Wheel and then waking up as Jemma caressed my old mate.

"Don't panic. But we might need your consulting skills to assist future travellers. Anyway, we've discovered a particularly difficult issue which needs changing. We're calling this one the China Fault."

"The China Fault?"

"Yes, that's right. A particular nasty event happens in late 2019, which originates in China, hence the name. For sure, we're going to have to correct this one because it affects the entire world."

"I'd heard you were no longer at the CYA. There was a coup d'état, and Pitstop took your job?"

"There was a slightly unpleasant incident, but that's all in the past now. I lead the Board, I'll have you know. So, I guess you could call me untouchable."

"What happened about the European Fault? Is that still coming our way in a few years?"

"No, that's all resolved. I have to say, Pitstop did rather a good job on that one. Luckily, we still leave the European Union next year, a kind of win-win situation." He grinned.

"Out of curiosity, what was the European Fault?"

"Darth Vader became President of the United States!" he roared with laughter, and for some reason, I joined him.

"D'you remember saying that, Frank? It made me laugh for years."

"Yes, yes, I do. So, I take it wasn't man-eating aliens either?"

"No. The European Fault was … well, let's not worry about that now. It's in the past."

He tapped my knee and with swift agility stood, then buttoned up his suit jacket. "Toodle-pip, Frank. I'll be in touch."

"Grandad, here's your ice cream." Alesha Warlow, my eldest granddaughter, handed me my 99, with a chocolate flake poking out the top.

My four daughters, three sons-in-law and one daughter-in-law, along with our seven grandchildren, all stood chatting and laughing as they scoffed down their iced treats.

Jayne settled into the deckchair Hartland had just alighted. She reached across and kissed my cheek. "Happy, Frank?"

I squeezed her hand tightly. "Very."

"Good." She beamed her beautiful smile and swished her long, still vibrant chestnut hair around the back of her head.

As I'd thought that day in the Murderer's Tavern, it was the sexiest move I'd ever seen.

"Who's that man in a suit wandering down the pier? I saw him talking to you."

I glanced across to see Hartland sauntering along, occasionally doffing his Panama as he passed groups of ladies whilst they relaxed enjoying the sunshine.

"That, my love, is Sylvester Sneekly."

"Who?"

"The Hooded Claw."

~

What's next?

Thank you for reading. I have good news … you can grab the second book in this series. That villain of villains, The Hooded Claw, has yet more dastardly plans for Frank and Jayne in *Blink of her Eye*.

Can you help?

I hope you enjoyed this book. Could I ask for a small favour? Can I invite you to leave a rating or review on Amazon? Just a few words will help other readers discover my books. Probably the best way to help authors you like, and I'll hugely appreciate it

Free eBook for you

For more information and to sign-up for updates about new releases, please drop onto my website, where you'll get instant access to your FREE eBook – Beyond his Time.

When you sign up, you get a no-spam promise from Adrian, and you can unsubscribe at any time. You can also find my Facebook page and follow me on Amazon – or, hey, why not all three.

Adriancousins.co.uk

Facebook.com/Adrian Cousins Author

Author's note

Regarding Mr Hackett's comments in the doctor's surgery, although we haven't eradicated racism, thankfully, society has improved over the last forty years – let's hope education does finally rid the world of this abomination. As for Paul-the-lech, well, unfortunately, there are still bigoted men like him around, but again, education will prevail. I hope these references did not offend you, as that was not my intention.

British politics … hmmm, tricky subject! So, this era was when we could say the political landscape was at its most polarised. My intention was to poke a little light-hearted fun at the left and right wings of the political spectrum. I certainly did not want to portray a leaning either way. I hope I've achieved that.

Books by Adrian Cousins

<u>The Jason Apsley Series</u>
Jason Apsley's Second Chance
Ahead of his Time
Force of Time
Beyond his Time
Calling Time
Borrowed Time

<u>Deana – Demon or Diva Series</u>

It's Payback Time

Death Becomes Them

Dead Goode

Deana – Demon or Diva Series Boxset

<u>The Frank Stone Series</u>

Eye of Time

Blink of her Eye

Acknowledgements

Thank you to my Beta readers – your input and feedback is invaluable.

Adele Walpole

Brenda Bennett

Lisa Osborne

Patrick Walpole

Andy Wise

And, of course, Sian Phillips, who makes everything come together – I'm so grateful.

Printed in Dunstable, United Kingdom